# A SIGN
## OF THE
# EIGHTIES

# A SIGN
## OF THE
# EIGHTIES

Gail Parent

G. P. Putnam's Sons
*New York*

G. P. Putnam's Sons
*Publishers Since 1838*
200 Madison Avenue
New York, NY 10016

*Designed by Rhea Braunstein*

Library of Congress Cataloging-in-Publication Data
Parent, Gail.
  A sign of the eighties.

  I. Title.
PS3566.A64S5   1987      813'.54       86–25518
ISBN 0–399–13262–7

Printed in the United States of America
1   2   3   4   5   6   7   8   9   10

*For Peter*

# 1

# Astra Rainbow

## Seattle, the Early Seventies

W HEN Astra Rainbow was five, two years younger than what is considered to be the age of reason, she pushed an eight-year-old boy off a cliff to his death.

The Seattle day was meant to be peaceful. The sky was so simple that even the most amateur painter could have captured its cloudless, bright blue. Although newscasters were telling the citizens of that city that there was a ten-percent chance of rain, the people knew there was no chance at all. The pure, mild day begged to be taken advantage of, and since it was a Sunday, there was time to play. Many were drawn to the water. They put their boats and bodies in and found unpolluted territory to make them happy. The experience was a perfect melding of flesh and nature. The city was at leisure on that fresh September day and, although there was a war going on in a strange place called Vietnam, there wasn't meant to be tragedy at home.

Seattle had changed over the years. Once you had to be hardy enough to migrate there. Then, if you lived there, you'd been born there. Eventually you had to be transferred or stationed there. By the 1970s you could wander in. Unwashed, blue-jeaned youth, in their quest for a little piece of unspoiled America, slowly trickled into the state of Washington. There they made their organic zucchini bread, had their love children and smoked their dope until they didn't know they were in the Northwest. Mostly they wandered around.

Helen Blakely, at the age of twenty-two, hitchhiked to Seattle with Astra Rainbow on one hip and all she cared to possess on the other. The torn canvas pouch she carried contained some underwear for her and for her child. Since Helen was so tiny, there was not much difference in the size of her daughter's underpants and her own. Clanking against each other were a muffin tin and an aluminum container filled with beads for working at what she considered her craft. Helen made beaded flowers and sold them in the streets, mostly to people who didn't want them. Sometimes a gift shop took what she had. The pay was all in change, but between the accumulated quarters, the food stamps, the low price of granola bars and the kindness of stoned strangers, there was enough so that food for her and her baby daughter didn't seem to be a problem.

The pouch also contained sweaters, extra jeans for the child, some of which she had outgrown, a security blanket that wasn't needed for security anymore, and a few of Astra Rainbow's toys. Helen was always trying to get her daughter interested in floppy rag dolls that some of her friends had made, but the baby always chose those bright, plastic, commercial things. Rainbow loved all the *Sesame Street* dolls that Granny had given her last Christmas. Often, as they traveled down roads just like this one, Helen stood in the street waving down transportation while the baby sat on her small baby blanket, far enough from the shoulder of the road for safety, clutching Big Bird.

The pouch also had other bits of clothing, papers for rolling joints and a picture of four boys with long hair. They stood in front of a '65 Mustang, their pants down and their arms around each other. Only one cared enough to hold a frying pan in front of him. Any one of them could have been Rainbow's father—Helen had made love (not war) with all of them during the summer she escaped from the suburbs of Cleveland to the East Village—or it could have been Barry. Barry hung out with them that summer, too. He was the one who encouraged the beards and who took the picture. He had taken another with everyone's pants up, but someone else had gotten that one. Maybe someday when Rainbow was grown, Helen would show her the photograph. She figured she'd have to put her hand over the bottom of the picture. She wasn't so far from childhood as to forget that little girls didn't want to face big boys who had no pants on.

They arrived in Seattle on this perfect day. While the child ate cookies that promised to be nourishing, Helen called a friend whom she had met in one of the Carolinas. The friend wasn't there, but the person on the phone thought she might be in one of the Dakotas. Helen sighed at this, her most recent miscalculation, and asked the voice where she could get some good grass. She spent a lot of time explaining that she had gotten some real bad shit in San Francisco that wasn't good for anything; and that wasn't just her opinion. Nobody got high on it, and a forty-year-old man, who claimed to be a marijuana expert, was sure it was laced with oregano.

The stranger said he'd try to locate some stuff and told her he was on his way to Fort Lawton. He told her to meet him behind the snack bar on the southwest side, but he didn't give her any further directions and she didn't ask for any. Directions were not part of her life-style. Many times Helen arrived in a city, made her dope connection and then let the rest fall into place. She had a warm, unthreatening smile and she often became friendly with the people she did drugs with. When they were all high enough or on the same trip, they crashed together, sleeping on couches and floors and mattresses on floors. God bless Astra Rainbow. She could be cranky about a lot of things, but she could sleep anywhere.

It happened in the park. The snack bar was not far from a cliff that hung over Puget Sound. The man Helen had spoken to turned out to be redheaded, shirtless and barefoot. She had known many men like him, fun when they were high, ordinary when they weren't. She bought five joints, already rolled in blue papers, from him. The blue dye came off on her lips. She hoped the dope inside was of higher quality than its container.

The man led them to the others, about a dozen adults from eighteen to fifty and half a dozen children. Most of the adults had dropped out of their responsible lives in order to defy society and feel younger than they were supposed to. They recognized Helen as their own kind and let her and her child in. (She looked and smelled like a wanderer who would do no harm to anyone but herself.) The group formed an irregular circle on the grass. The children played around them, checking in and clinging at intervals. At first Rainbow didn't want to leave Helen and held on to the thin fabric of her mother's gauze blouse. Eventually she found the adults, who were doing nothing but smoking and talking about the great highs they had had, boring. When her mother lay down and went to sleep after allowing her back to be tickled by the redheaded man, Rainbow went off and joined the children, who were throwing a big, uncontrollable beach ball around. At first she didn't reach for the ball. She just stood watching, her hand pulling on the rhinestones that that nice lady in a place called Texas had attached to her jeans. Soon, however, the ball became too tempting. It was big, bright and soft, the kind you could punch instead of catch. When it landed, instead of bouncing, it flattened out on the bottom like a beanbag chair because it needed more air. Rainbow's small arms were outstretched in anticipation of a turn she never got. With the exception of one girl the children were older, and it was their toy and their game, not hers. She couldn't understand why they weren't sharing. Under the trees down the hill, the grown-ups were sharing. The would each slowly suck and then pass on the single cigarette.

The child's frustration grew because the other children seemed to be having such a good time. One of the girls threw her body on the ball when it landed and seemed to have found a comfortable place to rest. The biggest boy laughed very hard each time he gave it a hard sock, but he never socked it in Rainbow's direction. She walked over to the edge of the cliff, expecting to be called back for being too close to danger. But no one called to her. Most of the adults had stopped talking. A radio was on and blaring a familiar song, the one about Lucy in the sky. She was scared to peek over the cliff, so she only did it once before running away. There was no doubt that she understood the danger of falling. She had a choice of watching the children or watching the adults, so she sat and watched as the children continued to beat the hell out of the red, white, yellow and green beach ball.

Then there were cookies and brownies. Astra Rainbow knew all about brownies. Sometimes there were brownies for children and brownies for grown-ups, and you had to be careful not even to taste the ones for the grown-ups because look what happened to that little boy Henry when he ate one. They made him throw up. The grown-ups always got silly when they ate their brownies, so Rainbow used to get silly too, but her mommy asked her why and she didn't know, so she stopped. Most of the time now she didn't laugh and everybody said she was a serious child. Sometimes people would try to get her to smile, but she was very good at not smiling, and the grown-ups could do all the funny things they wanted and bend down and put their faces right into hers and still she wouldn't show them that she thought what they were doing was funny. She was small enough to hide behind her mother's legs. Sometimes she grabbed both of them and popped her head in between. When her head came through, she knew she was supposed to be smiling, but she wasn't.

She wasn't willing to smile, even when they had cameras. Once a man said he was going to take her picture and he said she had to smile. She didn't know why. She knew what a picture was. She even knew it was going to come out of his camera, but she had no idea why you had to look happy just because someone was going to put you in his Polaroid. He asked, "Don't you want to look pretty?" and still she didn't understand. Pretty was the way people looked and had nothing to do with how happy you were. He took the picture of her serious self just to show her how wrong she was to keep her mouth so sad. When the picture popped out of the camera, he handed it to her. What she saw was herself, her blue eyes, her yellow hair, exactly her. Maybe she was pretty. She didn't know. She did know that she didn't feel like smiling.

She wasn't interested in having cookies or brownies. When the children ran to the table for refreshments, she was more interested in the beach ball left behind than in the sweets. Once she was alone, Rainbow ran to the ball and punched it as hard as she could. It didn't quite dance in the air as it had when the others played with it, but at least she could touch its soft sides. She slipped and fell on top of it. It wasn't as accepting or comforting as she had expected. She had imagined a resting place, but what she found was a surface that escaped from under her, leaving her on unfriendly ground. She stood up, rubbed her bottom where it hurt and tried to see if her fall had dirtied her jeans.

Mommy was funny about that. Sometimes she was mad when you got dirty, and sometimes you could stay dirty for days. The little girl brushed off her jeans as well as she could and attacked the ball again, punching it along the ground, letting it determine the direction she would follow. It took her toward the cliff. Fearing she would lose this new toy, Rainbow stood between the sound and the ball, hoping that her small body would act as a wall. It didn't. An insignificant wind pushed the ball over. At first she wasn't scared because sometimes when things seemed out of reach, mothers got them anyway, but when she looked down at the rocks below she saw it was dead. It had been ripped apart and deflated. She was upset that it wasn't round anymore and scared that she would be blamed. Maybe she and her mommy could just go. They did that sometimes, just went for no reason she could figure out, sometimes even after they had gotten into bed.

Rainbow ran back to her mother. Helen was awake now and talking intently to the man who had tickled her back. They sat facing each other, passing a joint between them, stopping in the middle of sentences to suck in the dope. It was Rainbow's tendency to crawl into her mother's lap whenever it was available. Usually Helen let her rest there while she continued doing whatever she was doing. It was as if the child was still a part of her body. The only thing as close to her mother as Rainbow was the pouch that was always by Helen's hip.

Many times, Rainbow joined her mother silently. But today she didn't want to crawl into Helen's lap or lean against her. Instead she took Helen's hand into her own two, and even though she knew she wasn't strong, she felt that with persistence she could pull her mother to her feet.

Helen wasn't budging. While Rainbow pulled, her mother continued to talk about how she was trying to get to Western Canada. She was laughing about the route she was going to take, and the man thought it was pretty funny too. Rainbow continued to tug and pull, urging her to go. "Please, please Mommy. Let's go to Canada now." Astra Rainbow had no idea where Canada was or how it would change her luck, but she did know that it was away from here. Helen neither asked for her arm back nor listened to her daughter's plea. She continued to talk and laugh as if Rainbow weren't there.

The child gave up only when she saw the boy head back to where he had been playing with the ball. She panicked and ran toward the cliff to see if it was still destroyed, hoping that it had been miraculously recovered. It hadn't, and as she turned to go back to her mother, there he was, the big boy. His fists were clenched at his side and his mouth was mean. He was spitting when he shouted. She cried out that she was sorry, but children don't easily accept apologies from each other. She said she would buy a new one with money her granny would give her. An older child would have known not to take the responsibility for the accident. This little girl expected to be forgiven.

When he pushed her she was scared. His hands felt so strong against her shoulders. She had never had a real fight before. Children had tangled with her, but there had always been more tears than terror. She called her mommy, yelling as loud as she could, but her voice was too small to carry all the way to Helen, who anyway was involved in deciding whether or not she was hungry. She was asking a man who had left his law firm, because his astrologer told him to, if he thought she should eat. He didn't know and together they tried to figure out whether it was physical or emotional nourishment that she needed. In the meantime, Helen's child screamed, unnoticed.

After the boy pushed her for the second time, she wondered why he kept hurting her. She knew she had done something bad, but no one had ever kept poking her before. She never actually made a decision to fight back. It just happened. Her fists mimicked his and then, with all the strength she had, without ever knowing his name, she punched him off the cliff. One swift unexpected blow threw him off balance and then, there he was, sliding to his death. Rainbow watched with amazement as he tumbled and screamed. For one brief moment she thought he might stop rolling, but he kept on going and there he was at the bottom, still, not far from the dead beach ball. The bully was gone and Astra Rainbow, aged five, cried for her sin.

Every child knows how to go for help. You go screaming toward the closest adult in your life and drag him into your problem. Too many times when Rainbow had tried that, she had found an immobile mother. Therefore, she ran to the redhaired man and grabbed him from the back by his belt loop. He thought she wanted to play and he reached behind him and flipped her over his head and into his lap. She sat there facing Helen, not knowing whether this time her mother was going to be mad at her or not.

"I pushed that boy," she said, hoping, like all children do, that her mother would understand what she said and fill in the rest of the story.

"Are you hungry, baby? I think I'm hungry." Helen is not to be blamed for her inappropriate question. All she knew was that her young daughter had pushed a boy. She didn't see the small, upset crowd gathering at the cliff.

"The ball got broked." Astra Rainbow sobbed, moving to her mother's lap. She didn't say anything further and neither did Helen. They had been through times like this and had dealt with broken balls. Helen brushed her baby's hair back and hugged her close, rocking her in circles. Rainbow was comforted and didn't explain further about the boy. She put her thumb in her mouth, another thing her mother sometimes got mad at and sometimes didn't.

The circle at the cliff widened as each new horrified person joined it and finally, it disturbed the little girl's peace. Someone was shouting about a boy being dead, and the redheaded man was drawn to the scene of the disaster by a sobbing woman who tripped over her too-long bell-bottom jeans. He ran to the edge of the cliff and Helen and Astra Rainbow ran after him. Rainbow's small steps slowed her mother down. At this point, her five-year-old mind didn't know what it was going to see. Since things had sometimes appeared magically to her—there was that nice man who pulled a quarter out of her ear—she had as much curiosity as any other young child in the crowd.

There were so many people near the cliff that Helen and Rainbow had to get their information thirdhand. It was a child, someone said, a child who had a terrible accident and was probably dead. He was chasing a ball, someone said. Rainbow cried uncontrollably and said, "I hurt the boy," but her mother, as usual, didn't hear.


In those days Helen formed friendships quickly, and since the dead boy was the son of a friend of the redhaired man, she stayed for the funeral. She and Astra Rainbow stayed in the living room of a small apartment that was, appropriately, painted black. Everyone tried to be very spiritual about the death. Artists were painting pictures of the boy, songwriters were writing odes, and one candlemaker was making the poor boy's image in wax.

The funeral was a peaceful affair. The minister wore a lavender T-shirt and jeans that let his knees show through. He spoke softly to the thirty-odd people who were there. His eyes were clear and his light brown hair hung the way we think Jesus' did. He spoke of heaven as if he had been there that morning and assured them that's where little Jeremy Nicholson had gone. He made everyone hold hands and sing "We Shall Overcome," and Rainbow sucked her thumb and asked her mother who was in the box that was going into the ground. She was told it was someone she didn't know. Everyone was thankful that it was a dreary day. It would have been horrible to bury a boy under a sunny sky.

They all went back to the Nicholson home, a small, ordinary house that really wasn't as hip as it pretended to be. There was incense waiting to be burned but a brand-new vacuum cleaner in the closet. Cakes and sandwiches were laid out on elaborate, inherited platters on the dining room table, and marijuana was neatly rolled and available. There were two sets of grandparents. The two grandfathers in suits, ties and gum-soled shoes felt out of place, and the two grandmothers in their print dresses with low hanging breasts tried to act nobly but kept their handkerchiefs nearby. Nana Nicholson couldn't understand why a woman with hair under her arms and who looked and smelled like she hadn't bathed in months was eating sandwiches off poor Aunt Hilly's tray. All four grandparents blamed the tragedy on the hippies.

The children, unable to mourn because of their lack of experience with grief, left through the kitchen and began playing in the backyard. Astra Rainbow watched them from behind the screen door. She had learned what trying to play with children leads to. That night, when no one was near her, she found a pair of scissors and cut off all her hair.

Because Helen had the feeling that her daughter should go to school, five months after the accidental killing Astra Rainbow Blakely was dropped off to live with her granny, who made her go to church on Thursdays and Sundays. She went to confession but never believed she was free of sin. The thought of hell upset her more than it did the other children. The nun she had as a third-grade teacher told the class that every day they lived was one less day they would have to live. Astra Rainbow tended to agree with her.

# 2

# Mickey Burke
## New York, Circa the Eighties

IT was a hot summer day in Manhattan, the kind of day that could turn on you. Millions of people went to their offices under white, sunny skies, and those who had windows saw the sun disappear and the day turn a mean gray. New Yorkers who routinely sweated in the streets wouldn't have chosen this. They knew the gray brought with it the threat of rain. Even if it never rained, the weather would be humid and they would melt on their way home. The day was cursed, even by those who had air conditioning.

Mickey Burke was hostile, but he didn't blame it on the weather. He had been angry since 1977, when it became apparent that he was going to have to write for a living and make other people funny.

When he was nine years old his mother found a discarded television with the tube missing and dragged it home through the streets of Brooklyn for her boy Mickey. The boy was in heaven. He mounted it on four legs and every night, while his mother and Aunt Minn, the two women who raised him, turned raw chicken and carp into something wonderful, he pretended to be on television. He even let his mother change the channels as he jumped from one routine to another. "With you I save electricity," she said to the head in the set, which at the time was singing "Mammy."

He grew up wanting to be an actor, but every time he tried, someone in the business would tell him he was hysterically funny, but too hard for the American public to swallow. (He argued that Woody Allen wasn't exactly Middle America, but he was told that there was room for only one odd-looking, funny sex symbol every quarter of a century.) At age twenty-eight, after ten years of trying to become a comedian, he became a comedy writer. By thirty-eight he had three successful situation comedies on the air and was one of the highest-paid, most successful television writers around. He was also the angriest. He once threw a lamp at a network vice-president because the executive said that Mickey had failed to see the light.

Mickey came out of his office, one hand holding a script, one scratching his scalp where the bald spot was flourishing. "Do you think this is funny?" he asked.

The young woman who stood waiting for him in his outer office was confused. She had been sent there by the Profile Employment Agency and she knew she was going to be interviewed by a writer. No one had told her she would have to say what was funny. "I don't know," she said. Her eyes were clear, and she looked directly at the man whom she hoped would be her boss. She saw a small, skinny man with hair that went in many directions, like Albert Einstein's.

"Naturally. I haven't read it to you yet." Mickey looked up from his pages to see Miss America. She stood stiffly, doubtlessly worried about her future. The heat of the day had not gotten to her. Her beauty came mainly from how new and shiny she looked.

"Even after you read it, I won't know. If that's part of my job, I guess I'll have to go." Mickey didn't want her to go. He wanted her to stay and do wonderful things to his body. He forgot for the moment that blondes got him into trouble. The one he had married for seventeen months had ended up torturing him, many times in the back of limousines by removing his hand from her knee. The blonde he lived with for almost a year still refused to give back his grandmother's pin.

"How about trying?" he asked.

She considered the question seriously, shifting her position as she did. He had already made up his mind to hire her. Even if she had no secretarial skills, she would be worth having around just to look at. Her hair was so long she could sit on it. The other three women the agency had sent seemed efficient but unkind and scary. One had made it clear that she would never give him coffee.

When the young job applicant saw her prospective boss smiling, she decided to take a chance. She was a simple girl who responded to things like the elements and smiles.

"Well, all right. I'll try," she said, putting her briefcase and purse down. She took her trying seriously and her face expressed a trying mode. He couldn't ask for more. It was wonderful that somebody was willing to try for him. His outer office was tiny, but he took stage before he spoke.

"Okay. This husband and wife are divorced but they still see each other, and in this scene they're spending Thanksgiving together." He looked up, not to see if she understood, but because he enjoyed looking at her and he wasn't sure how long she would be in his life. He saw her one imperfection, a tiny birthmark at the base of her ear, and found her more attractive for it.

"You mean they used to be married and they still spend the holiday together?"

"Yes."

"I don't know whether that's funny or not," she said honestly.

"No, look, I'm not finished. I'm not to the funny part yet . . . or I'm not to the part that might be funny yet." Why was he always attracted to women who had no idea what he was talking about? There were plenty of women in New York who kept right up with him. There were too many times that he preferred the beauties who failed to get his humor. He danced for them.

"Oh." This was said very seriously. Mickey would soon learn that he was dealing with the most serious twenty-two-year-old in the country.

"After the funny part, can we do the interview the way we're supposed to?" she asked in her most businesslike voice.

"I've never interviewed a secretary before. I don't exactly know how it's supposed to go." That was a lie. He had had seven secretaries in the last three years. They had all left because he was impossible.

"I do. I'm a graduate of the Ohio Academy of Business. The week before graduation we practiced being interviewed, and Mr. Raphelson gave me an A." She couldn't help showing her pride. Her tiny chest puffed up as best it could, considering its proportions.

"Well then, you can guide us through it. You can tell me what to say and then you can say what you're supposed to, and I'm pretty sure we can do the whole thing without embarrassing each other."

"It'll take about twenty minutes." Feeling he might be too busy a man, she rushed to add, "That's the minimum it can take for a thorough interview. Really." She searched her briefcase for proof and easily found a Xerox copy of instructions entitled "The Business Interview: What to Expect." She handed it over as quickly as she could. Mickey pretended that he was delighted to receive such valuable information. He pretended a lot when he was around women with long legs.

"Twenty minutes is fine. It might even take a half an hour for a really thorough interview. We might even have to have lunch."

"No, look, see. Luncheon interviews are under the category of executive secretaries. I'm applying for the position of secretary in a one-person office." She pointed out the section she was referring to. Mickey Burke, at five-seven, was used to women being taller than he was.

This young woman would tower over him in bare feet. He hoped he would get to see her feet bare.

"Ah, yes. Approximately twenty minutes, and it says here that you're supposed to introduce yourself. That's number one."

She brushed off a skirt that didn't need brushing, straightened a jacket that didn't need straightening, and put on a smile. The smile was upsetting. It wasn't only false, it was unnatural. Mickey had never seen a smile distort a face before. She reminded him of all those young women on television who were thrilled with their deodorant soap. He didn't buy their smiles either.

They were standing too close to shake hands so she took a giant step back and extended her arm. Remembering exactly what she was supposed to do, she made sure her handshake was firm. It lasted between two and three seconds, as prescribed by the Ohio Academy of Business. "Hello," she said, as if she had just entered the office. It was obvious that she was well-rehearsed. "I'm Astra Rainbow Blakely, Mr. Burke, and I'm very happy to know you." Astra Rainbow? What world had she come from?

"I'm happy to know you too." Mickey was as formal as she was. He was a writer of dialogue and usually knew the appropriate thing to say whether he said it or not. His thoughts came quickly. The people in the neighborhood he grew up in didn't name their children Astra or Rainbow. He knew that she had been born into a world that he knew nothing about. Now both the man and the writer wanted to keep her around.

"The Profile Agency sent me over. I'm applying for the position as secretary." Without looking, she opened her briefcase and pulled out the form that the agency had sent to her. She located it so easily because she was new to the work force and had no real need for a briefcase yet. There was only one piece of paper remaining inside.

Mickey accepted the form. "I'm supposed to ask you if you'd care to sit down, right?" He made a grand gesture toward the only chair in the little outer office. It was a fake Early American that had come from his boyhood bedroom. The curve of a boy's bottom had made its impression. Rainbow was narrow enough to slide into the space that Mickey had carved in his youth. She pulled down her skirt and remembered to sit tall.

"Now I'll try to tell you if that's funny." She pointed to the pages that Mickey held, reminding him that he had asked her opinion.

"Nah. It's not important." He felt he was playing the part of perspective boss very well.

"No. I said the funny part could come first. Then we could do the interview." She said this with so much authority that Mickey lifted his pages into reading position. He usually obeyed women he was infatuated with.

"You ready?"

"Yes." She started listening even before he spoke. Her head tilted, she leaned slightly forward. He expected her next move would be to cup her ear.

"Okay. So, this guy and his ex-wife are spending Thanksgiving dinner together. They're sitting there at a friend's house. Did I tell you that he still loves her?"

"No."

"He still loves her."

"And they're divorced?"

"Yes."

"Why?"

"Because she wanted it. She just couldn't live with him anymore. He was too suffocating." The young woman looked sad. She was unsophisticated enough to become unhappy upon hearing that people's lives had fallen apart.

"Anyway, they're sitting there eating dinner when he taps on his glass for attention because he has an announcement to make." She sat up very straight, waiting for the announcement. How could Mickey not love her? She was a very attentive audience. Her name was Astra Rainbow. "So, everyone stops eating and they look at Phil—that's the guy's name—to see what he's going to say. They already know that it's going to be something weird because the guy's an asshole." He heard a swallow and wondered if there could be somebody left in the world who was embarrassed by the word "asshole." She wasn't blushing, but she did look uncomfortable. Wow, he thought. I can make her uneasy and we're not even in bed.

"So, he stands up, this Phil, and he says . . ." Mickey dropped his glasses where they rested on top of his head onto his face, in order to read from the pages and get the words exactly right. To him writing comedy was like writing a symphony. If one word was out of place, he could hear the discord. "So, he says, 'I have an announcement to make,' and then he takes his ex-wife's fork away from her so she can't eat."

The girl chuckled and for a moment Mickey thought that she was going to get it all. " 'I want you all to know that Sharon'—that's his ex-wife's name—'and I are going to get married again.' "

"Was Sharon happy?"

"No. And the funny part or the maybe-funny part is coming up." He couldn't have given her a bigger warning.

She understood that this was it and listened even harder than before. "So the second he announces that they're going to get re-married, she says"—Mickey read very carefully here, making sure that each word rang out clearly—" 'I'd rather be pissed on by a hundred great danes.' And Phil says, 'You can have both.' " Mickey couldn't help it. He laughed without inhibition at his own words. She couldn't miss the fact that that was the funny part, but she couldn't find the humor. To Astra Rainbow, the wife *could* have both.

"Is it a big part of the job, having to know what's funny?" she asked. He wondered if she knew how blue her eyes were.

"No. It's not part of the job. It's really not important. The word 'pissed' wouldn't get by censorship anyway." His arm relaxed and, as a result, the page went limp. "That's one of the reasons why I have to get out of television and into movies. I'm thirty-eight years old and they won't let me say 'pissed.' " He said this with great passion. When he talked about having to get out of television his body became rigid and his voice got louder.

"I type very well. Here's a sample of my work." She took a letter out of the briefcase, leaving it empty, and handed it to her prospective boss. It was a piece of perfectly typed correspondence to a Mr. Jones. Obviously, it was from a business school that had not kept up with the rest of the world. It referred to a loan that was being made at four percent per annum. Now Mickey was positive that he had to hire her. He couldn't let her go into the world with that outdated letter. It had nothing to do with the present.

"Very nice," he said, handing her back the thin sheet that she was hoping would get her into the work force. He was trying hard to act businesslike, which always led him into a Joan Crawford imitation. "Basically, I just need someone who types. I'm a writer." Since her hair was so long, he wondered if she sat on it while she worked.

"I know. They told me at the agency."

"And I send out an occasional letter. I think the last one was in 1979. What else can I tell you? I need someone who will lie for me on the phone because I hate going out to lunch. And . . . I would like my secretary to adore me every working moment."

"I couldn't do that." His heart sank. He had no idea that it was capable of sinking this fast, this soon. "I couldn't lie on the phone." Did that mean she could adore him?

"Yeah, well, don't worry about it. If someone calls, I'll tell them I'm not in." She nodded in agreement.

"Does that mean I have the job?"

"If you want it."

"Thank you. I'm sure I will satisfy you." Mickey wondered if the Ohio Academy of Business told their students to tell their bosses that they would satisfy. He liked her attitude.

"So, great. So, when do I begin? I mean you . . . when do *you* begin?"

"I think it would be best if we discuss my salary so that there will be no confusion." She stood up to point out the rule that stated that salaries should be discussed.

"How much do you want?" Mickey was excited. He wasn't about to bargain with a woman who understood that adoration was part of the job.

"Well, the agency felt that I could start at three hundred dollars a week because I am extremely well-trained, but I felt that was too much . . ."

"I was thinking of three fifty." This offer was uncharacteristic of Mickey, who was insecure about money and cheap. He had a fear of being old and poor, and never reached for a check or paid a secretary what she deserved. He would have tried to clear this problem up in analysis if he had had the guts to talk about money while spending a hundred dollars an hour.

"That's not what you're supposed to say. You're supposed to say less than me, and then we get to negotiate." Mickey figured she had probably spent a whole day studying negotiating.

"I'm not good at negotiating. That's why I have to have an agent. I say we stick to three fifty. It's a nice round number. And on Secretaries' Day, I'll take you out for a nice hot lunch."

"I don't think you should pay me that much."

"I do. If I have a highly paid secretary then it makes me look more successful." She bought it. Astra Rainbow Blakely understood finance as well as she understood comedy.

"Fine. When would you like me to start?" They must have taught her to pin down and lock up the deal. He could see her practicing in class, taking turns at being the boss with another young woman. He figured she probably got it on the third try. She was very good at asking when she should start. Since he had never rehearsed, his answer was vague.

"Uh. I don't know. I mean, I want to do the right thing—to the letter. Did you learn about starting?" He faced her, waiting for his answer.

"It would be convenient for me to start tomorrow," she said, still the student pretending to be professional. A breeze came through the window and played with her hair, wrapping a few strands across her face. She brushed them back delicately and flicked her head. He watched this wondrous feat and considered it a ballet of the hair.

"And also, will this job provide me with any benefits, such as health and dental care?" Had she not been able to make her hair dance, Mickey might have been able to discuss medical advantages with a clear head. But he was pondering how her hair had done these magnificent leaps and was now back perfectly in place. He was willing to give her anything.

"Definitely. I definitely think I should provide for your teeth and your body and maybe a little life insurance, and free movies too."

"Thank you," she said, collecting her things. She put her purse across one shoulder and her briefcase on the other. Once she was up, he saw again that she was taller than he. This time he looked down to see how high her heels were. He had been tricked before into believing a woman towered over him, only to find that once she was barefoot she could look up into his eyes. This one was wearing shoes with hardly any lift. He had to hope she liked short men.

"I don't think you should go yet. It hasn't been twenty minutes. Maybe we didn't go over everything thoroughly."

She checked her list. Her face made lines when she did, but they were gone when her search was completed. Someday the lines would stay, but that was her future. Today they left. "We covered everything," she said. "I think it was supposed to take more time to argue about the salary, or maybe you were supposed to explain why you didn't think I should get dental insurance yet."

"Could we use the extra time just to schmooze?" She shook her head no. Mickey was surprised that the refusal came so quickly.

"I don't schmooze," she said. Her head was held so high, you couldn't miss her pride. "I won't be able to accept this job."

Mickey ran to the doorway to block her exit. He felt like a gay blade from another era trying to seduce a young Doris Day. "Wait," he shouted. Since his arm blocked the doorway, she had no choice. She wasn't frightened. Mickey Burke had never frightened any woman, and Astra Rainbow had never been scared. Since she had pushed that boy off that cliff, she had expected retribution. It had always been just a matter of time. "Do you know what schmoozing is? When did you get to New York?"

"Last Friday."

Mickey was impressed. "I've never met anyone who got here just last Friday. I once knew someone who had been here less than a year. But last Friday, that's really impressive."

"All I did was come here," said Astra Rainbow, not understanding why that should be at all impressive.

"Yeah, but so recently."

"Doesn't practically everyone come here from someplace else? That's what I heard about New York. I heard that there are a lot of new people here every day."

"That's true."

"So, a lot of people must have come here last Friday." Mickey was looking at her as if she were a newborn, and this adoring gaze made the girl extremely uncomfortable. She decided she had to get back to business. "I can't accept this job if you expect me to snooze with you." Her eyes broadcasted that she was insulted.

Mickey rushed to absolve himself. "I didn't say snooze. I said 'schmooze.' It's a New York word for 'talk.' "

She was so relieved, she actually leaned against the door frame. "Are there a lot of New York words?" she asked, hoping there weren't and that they spoke the same language.

"Not a lot. I'll point them out as we go along."

"Thank you, Mr. Burke, and thank you for the job."

"Don't thank me. I should be thanking you." He let down his arm so that she could pass into the hall. "Don't worry. There won't be a lot of work, and if there is we can just send it out to be typed, or I'll call the agency and we can hire someone to help you." He knew he wasn't sounding like the boss of her dreams, making all these promises and lacking authority in his voice, but he had to make sure she would be back the next day. She looked disappointed. Then he thought that instead of too much, maybe he hadn't given enough. "Is something wrong?" he asked, ready to take care of any of her needs.

"The agency. I forgot to tell you to make arrangements with the agency." For the first time she sounded like a girl and not a job applicant.

"That's okay. I'll do it. I'll take care of it. What do I do, call them and say I'm hiring you?" He worked hard to make her happy again.

"Thank you." She turned to leave, then stopped to explain. "It's just that Mr. Raphelson would be really angry with me. He said all I had to remember, once I got the job, was three things: ABC. A is for agency, B is for benefits and C is for 'Can I start tomorrow?' That's all." She was more dismayed than upset, but he took her dismay seriously and tried to rescue her.

"Would you feel better if I called this Mr. Raphelson and told him that I had just hired you and that you conducted yourself beautifully during the interview?"

"You would do that?" She brightened and then darkened again. "You don't want to do that; it's a long-distance call and the rates are highest during the day. That's what Granny told me before I came to New York City." God, she was beautiful. He loved women who had grandmothers that they quoted.

"Hey, no problem. This is a business here. I make long-distance calls all the time and I write it off on my taxes." Remembering that she wouldn't lie for him on the phone, he quickly added, "But this time, of course, I won't write it off."

"Well . . . I don't want to be a problem. We're not supposed to be problems. We're supposed to help you out so that you can concentrate on the important things. Mr. Raphelson told us not to be afraid to blend with the woodwork." He couldn't seem to tell her that she was not a very blendable person.

"Hey, this isn't a problem. This is just—just a situation we're having here. Believe me, if it was a problem, I'd let you take care of it. You give me his number and I'll call him and tell him how impressed I was with your businesslike . . . attitude."

She smiled and reached into her wallet for Mr. Raphelson's telephone number. "You should write down the number. I better keep Mr. Raphelson's card because I promised that I would keep in touch. I was the only one in the class who came to New York City and I think he wants to know how mean people are here. And the area code isn't on it so I guess nobody from out of Ohio ever called him before." She handed him the card and waited for him to copy the number down. "He's very nice but a little hard of hearing, so you're going to have to shout."

"No problem."

"Well, thanks," she said; one foot was already outside his office. "What time should I be here tomorrow? Oh, gosh, that was another thing I was supposed to ask. Please don't mention it to Mr. Raphelson. He said we'd make mistakes and not to worry, but I do worry. He also said that we wouldn't get the first job we tried out for. Gee, I don't mean 'tried out.' I mean, you 'try out' for cheerleading. I'll see you tomorrow."

Mickey waved goodbye. She was out the door before he realized he didn't know what time she should come to work. He ran out in the hall after her and caught her at the elevator.

"How about eleven?" he asked.

"For what?"

"For coming to work."

"Eleven isn't a time for coming to work. You either work nine to five or ten to six." She was obviously quoting Mr. Raphelson, since her voice had that businesslike quality again.

"Okay. Ten. Ten is great. And don't worry. I'm going to make that call now." She left assured. He ran back into his office and dialed Lorain, Ohio. When Mr. Raphelson got on the phone Mickey told him that Astra Rainbow Blakely had handled herself beautifully in the interview and that he had hired her for three hundred fifty dollars a week. Mr. Raphelson whistled and asked if New York needed any elderly male secretaries. For the first time in his life, Mickey didn't know whether what he was hearing was a joke or not. He was momentarily scared. There he was in New York, thinking that the people who didn't laugh at him just didn't know what was funny. This interview and phone call made him think there was a possibility that there was a whole country that *he* didn't get.

Mickey hadn't been in analysis for three and a half years, but he still felt free to call Dr. Talbot. Like all uncured narcissists, Mickey felt his ex-analyst would be happy to hear from him. He timed his phone call perfectly, knowing that the doctor always began his last hour before lunch at eleven and ended it at ten to twelve. Mickey had had that fifty minutes for close to eighteen months and he had tried many times to get Talbot to go to lunch with him. There was nothing he wanted more than to seduce his psychiatrist into giving him some free time. The doctor always politely explained that he ate his lunch at his desk. As Mickey left he would hear the phone ring. Today that call would be his.

"It's Mickey Burke and I've just hired a blonde," he said as soon as he heard Dr. Talbot's voice. He knew he should have asked how the doctor was and at least made an attempt at small talk. Admitting his problem in the first three seconds seemed like a simpler way to go.

"Ah, Mickey, how are you?" The doctor's voice was the most comforting one he had ever heard. It had the strength of a man's and the warmth of a woman's. No wonder his practice flourished.

"Pretty good . . . except I just hired a blonde." He was on this telephone for free advice. He wanted it quickly.

"I saw your show the other night." He had always hated when Talbot had watched one of his shows. He wanted to think of Talbot as studying large books with footnotes by Freud at night.

"You shouldn't watch that trash," said Mickey, meaning it.

"Yes, well. A good laugh here and there never hurt anyone. What's on your mind?

"It's just that I got a little panicked when I hired this blonde." A lot of the time that Mickey was in therapy was spent on the blonde problem. They touched on his uncontrollable temper while dealing with the network, the death of his father when he was three and his overblown fear of being old and poor, but the blonde problem took ninety percent of every fifty minutes. He wasn't the first Jewish boy to be tempted by forbidden fruit, but he was determined to be one of the first to be cured. By the time he went to Talbot it had been five years since Christy had divorced him and three since Mindy had left. (Christy had showed up in court in tiny jeans, cowboy boots and a cowboy hat and, despite this, had gotten the judge to wipe Mickey out financially. He was still willing to take her back and buy her a red fox jacket.) Mickey knew he was in trouble when he begged Lori, who was the fairest of the fair, to move in. It was becoming a bad habit. The more money Mickey made, the lighter the hair he fell for. Every session Mickey insisted that he was just attracted to blondes while Talbot tried to tie his patient's fear of Nazis and his desire to dominate the Christian world into the problem. Mickey never bought the Nazi or domination theory. He was willing to believe that the "Blondes Have More Fun" campaign, which had hit him as an impressionable youth, had had a large influence on him. Whatever the reason, Mickey had been left with a blonde syndrome even though he couldn't take their craziness. As he told Dr. Talbot, his blondes were so irrational, they broke expensive things. Although he never had been cured, he thought he had gotten this problem under control. He had actually had a two-year relationship with a Jewish brunette who didn't ever assume that he would pay her dental bills.

"You hired a blonde?" There was a smile in the doctor's voice. Obviously, he was trying to turn this into a social call.

"Yes." Mickey tried to sound desperate enough to get help. Since he wanted to sound as if he was drowning, he added, "And she's not age-appropriate."

"I have a cancellation at three. Did you want to come in?"

"No." Mickey didn't want to be sucked into therapy again. It involved the loss of too many hundred-dollar bills. "It's just that I got a little panicked when I hired this fair-haired girl."

"And?" Good old Dr. Talbot always knew what to ask. There was a reason he got the big bucks.

"And I'm going to love her from afar." Mickey calmed down and truly believed this was possible.

"If you want to work it through . . ."

"Yeah, well, I think I have it under control. All I have to do is remember Christy in divorce court in her two-hundred-dollar cowboy hat."

"Not all blondes are bad." Dr. Talbot had tried to convince Mickey of this all through therapy. Mickey preferred to think of them as poison.

"Yeah, I know, and not all fish is fishy, but there's a good chance if you order mackerel that it might be."

Talbot laughed. Mickey had stayed with him for close to eighteen months because the man laughed easily. "Let me know what happens." He would. He would call again at ten to twelve some other day.

Mickey tried to get back to the pages he was involved with when Astra Rainbow came in for the interview, but his concentration was off. Two sheets of paper were put in and pulled from the typewriter, crumpled and tossed into the wastebasket. Both wads went into the basket on the first try, since this was Mickey Burke's best sport.

For the next twenty minutes, he looked down at the people he made laugh. Even from eight floors above he could tell that they were sweating. Men carried their suit jackets and women wore dresses with no sleeves. Mickey assumed that he knew no one in sight, but they had all, every one of them, laughed at his jokes. These were his subjects. Without him their lives would be duller. It was only right that he was in an air-conditioned office while they fried in the street.

More time was wasted and more paper crushed into balls. Then there was another forty minutes spent on a phone call to his friend and lawyer, Jerry Milman. Mickey said he called to make sure Jerry had gotten tickets to the hockey game. Jerry never failed to get tickets, so it was just one of those reach-out-and-touch-someone calls. Mickey never mentioned his new secretary. Jerry had handled his out-of-control divorce, and Mickey had promised his friend that he would never let another blonde into his life. He swore that he had had it with Christian craziness and would never again marry someone he met at a stoplight.

Mickey Burke never relied on the muses. He counted on his mind rather than mythical forces for his creativity, but they were there for him that day. An idea came from nowhere. He ran to his typewriter and filled it with paper. He trusted his instincts. He punched out, "The Astra Rainbow Story (working title)" He indented and began. He had no guilt about stealing the young girl's life. The first thing he had ever written was about his mother.

> There's a story somewhere in what happened to one of those love children born in the sixties. There must have been thousands of them with names like Astra Rainbow, Moon Unit and Blue Star, and now they are filtering into society. Were they changing their names? These children who were conceived on mattresses on the floor in the East Village were now walking around taking dictation. Could they be applying to law school? Were there going to be lawyers named Heaven? Would anybody go to a doctor called Dog Moon? Did love children turn into love adults? What were their childhoods like? Did their mothers make them clean up their rooms? Did anyone else realize that the love children were here?

Mickey didn't mind this flood of questions. Many of his projects began like this. The answers came in the writing. He thought he was finished for the moment, but he only rested for a second before his hands were back on the keys. "One of these love children," he punched out, "comes to New York and drives a nice Jewish boy crazy."

Mickey leaned back in his chair. There was something there. This could get him out of television. He wanted to call Talbot back and tell him things were going to be all right. This blonde he was going to write about instead of love. She was going to pay him back for the others by getting him his first movie.

Astra Rainbow bought a pretzel on the street and, referring to directions written on the back of an envelope, walked eight blocks to the subway. It would have been nice if she could have had that good feeling one gets after securing a first job. She had deprived herself of good feelings while trying to strip away the bad ones. The most she could do was be practical about life. She hoped this job would carry her one step further away from her first years on this earth.

She took the A train to Brooklyn, where she was living on her great aunt's couch. She walked through Crown Heights, a neighborhood that was desperately trying to stay safe. There were always some bad guys hanging around, but she managed to get through their noises and shouts of "Come here, baby," and "Let me show you a good time." She wasn't scared of them. She assumed that she was going to pay for her sin and die young. Knowing that kept her brave.

# 3

## Shelly Silver
### Same Time, Same Place

DON'T blame Shelly Silver for anything. By the time she was thirty-five years old, the world had changed on her three times. When she was in high school she planned her wedding. She would wear flowers in her hair. Her groom would be gentle on their wedding night. At the University of Michigan she learned to pity girls who were given rings and promised split-level homes. Now, she was hoping for marriage again. She would wear flowers in her hair, but she hoped her groom wouldn't be gentle.

Even the concept of God had changed on Shelly. The God of her childhood was feared and loved and had a long gray beard and his hand on the ceiling of the Sistine Chapel. The joke at college was that God was a black woman. Then *Time* magazine declared that God was dead in blood-red letters on its cover. Now George Burns had taken the role. Don't blame Shelly Silver for anything.

Shelly stood in her vast closet, trying to decide what to wear to the funeral. Everything she owned that was black also showed cleavage and was not in good taste, even to mourn someone she had never known. The deceased was the mother of the man she had been dating for the last month and a half. She felt badly that Mrs. Goldblum had died, and she felt sorry for Barry because he sounded terrible on the phone when he had to cancel their date, but she found it really hard to cry over someone she had never met. She was going to the funeral because she hoped Barry could use her two shoulders to lean on. God forgive her, she thought that Mrs. Goldblum's untimely departure would be a good thing for her relationship.

Barry didn't ask her to come to the services, but she found out they

were at the Riverside Funeral Home and she knew that he would
consider it spectacular if she showed up. When he saw her in the
chapel, looking great, he would probably sit next to her and take her
hand. Aunts and uncles would turn their heads to see her there, striking and sympathetic, and they would be happy that Barry had someone to share his unhappiness with. When they drove to the cemetery
he would ask her to share his limousine. She knew that he would be
too grief-stricken to consider it a romantic ride, but it would get them
closer.

She'd better bring Kleenex for tears. God, she hated herself for
doing this. What kind of person would try to get a guy to like her at
his own mother's funeral? She knew the answer. A thirty-five-year-
old New York woman who was trying to get over loving Mickey Burke.
They had broken up over a year ago and he was still her first painful
thought in the morning.

So she was a louse for trying to look strong, yet vulnerable, at this
poor man's poor mother's funeral. So she was the scum of the earth
for digging into the back of her closet for her navy-blue Ralph Lauren
suit and her pumps. It was disgusting that on this black day she was
looking for her navy shoes, but she had faith that she would be forgiven. God would have to know how hard it was to be single, female
and scared. He must have seen the latest research that said only five
percent of women over thirty-five can hope to get married. Besides,
she wasn't going just to get the guy. She was going also because she
had gained a couple of pounds over the weekend and she was out of
control. A funeral was bound to take her appetite away.

The suit was tight. Why did a good Jewish boy like Ralph Lauren
cut his jackets so small? Surely he remembered that his people were
big-breasted. The shoes were also a miss. They were too short and
square for the lines of the skirt. She had developed an eye for style
since moving to Manhattan that wouldn't let her make the wrong
decision. These were her only navy heels. She had meant to update
them, but she always ended up buying dresses instead of shoes. For
one horrible moment she wondered what size shoes Barry's mother
had worn. She knew it was sick, but she had no control over sick
thoughts entering her mind. She knew Barry's parents were wealthy.
They lived on Park and Sixty-sixth. Women who lived in that neighborhood were known for their shoes. That's where all the Charles
Jourdans and Maud Frizons went to live. If Barry's mother wore an
eight B and if Shelly managed to become one of the family before the
beautiful shoes were given to Goodwill, maybe she could take them
over. Her new father-in-law might like the idea of his dear, departed
wife giving a legacy like footwear.

She was sure about the style of the black ones, which were sleek and narrow, but the color was throwing her. She was tempted to call her personal shopper at Bloomingdale's. Most of the time Paula Heft came through for her. She had picked out the perfect dress for Shelly to wear to that Gary Hart dinner. Shelly had thought it was corny to wear red, white and blue, but after an anchorwoman complimented her in the ladies' room she knew Ms. Heft had been right. Paula did wonderful, illegal things for Shelly. She put away clothes for her until she had the time to come in and try them on. Not just regular clothes that anybody could have, but forbidden sales clothes would be hidden in Paula's private closet, an area that most Bloomingdale's customers didn't know existed. Shelly was pretty sure that the black would work with the navy, but maybe she should just check it out with Paula. She knew it was pretty, but she never felt right unless the things she was wearing actually went together.

"Paula, I really hate to bother you," she said when she got her on the phone. She was always telling Paula she didn't want to bother her. She always felt she had to be careful about her disturbances.

"Who's calling, please?" Paula's voice was not at all friendly. Shelly got scared that she wouldn't be remembered.

"It's Shelly Silver," she said, the schoolchild waiting to be recognized. "Remember, I'm the one who you said shouldn't wear green. I'm the one from Rochester." This was, of course, the reason she had the need for a personal shopper. Shelly didn't yet believe that a girl from Rochester could dress herself.

"Oh, Shelly, darling. How are you, dear?" Shelly knew the "darlings" and the "dears" were a result of the thousands she managed to spend with Paula, but she liked them anyway. She felt fashion-safe.

"I have a question." By now she was feeling guilty. She was wasting Paula's sales time. She probably had three women in dressing rooms, waiting in bras and half-slips. "It's just a quick question." Her voice sped up, since time was money. "You know my Ralph suit?" As she said it, she realized it was much too egotistical of her to think that this woman remembered every detail of her wardrobe.

"Refresh my memory, dear."

"Uh . . . you sold it to me. It's a navy-blue pinstripe with a straight skirt."

"Oh, yes. Your question?"

By now Shelly realized that she had called Paula for too small a problem. Her mind worked quickly to redeem herself. "I have to go to a funeral," she said, knowing that would soften the saleswoman up, "and I'm just too upset to pull myself together."

"I'm so sorry, dear. How can I help?" There was sympathy in her voice. Shelly was relieved that she hadn't blown her relationship with Bloomingdale's.

"Do the black Bruno Magli go with it?"

"Of course, dear. You go right ahead and wear them, and I'm sorry."

"About what?"

"Didn't you say you were going to a funeral?"

"Yes . . . and I am. Thank you, Paula. Thank you." She was always sure to show Paula how grateful she was.

Shelly sat on the edge of the bed, thinking about the conversation she had just had. She didn't want to be the person she had become. She wanted to save thousands of dollars she spent on clothes because she might need it for her old age. She wanted to save the whales. She wanted to send money every month to an orphan. When she blew out the candles on each of her birthday cakes, she wanted to wish for world peace. Instead she was a woman who had wished that Mickey Burke would marry her. Shelly wanted to be one of the clean, shiny faces that smiled from the inside of *Ms Magazine,* the ones who climbed mountains instead of wishing to be married, but she wasn't there yet. It made her teary to think that she was going to a funeral to try to hook a man, but she had promised herself, her mother and her sister that she would do everything she could to eradicate thoughts of Mickey.

One would think there was a war on, the way they talked about the male problem. What no one talked about was how many single people died in the battle. The first few skirmishes might actually be inspiring, but eventually the confrontation would leave another fatality on the battlefield that was called Manhattan. Even knowing this, Shelly started to feel very guilty about going to the funeral. It seemed unfair to seduce a man under such trying circumstances. She was just about to put the navy stockings back in the drawer when she remembered that her grandmother had told her more than once that all was fair in love and war. What she hadn't said was that love was war.

Shelly's biggest battle, the one that almost killed her, had been fought with Mickey. She had met him three years ago, just after he broke up with that girl with no hips. He was so funny, she hardly noticed he was funny-looking. If one thing could make her fall for a guy, it was a good joke. She knew what all smart women knew: Laughter made you live better and longer. When she met him on the bagel line at Zabar's she had just broken up with a man she had lived with since college. He had insisted on continuing to work for Legal Aid while the rest of the world decided it was time to make money. Shelly admired his devotion. He hated her success. The eleven-year relationship that had started in school ended in a fight over a trip to Paris. He refused to stay at an expensive hotel even though she offered to pay for it. He screamed, "I don't want your dollars." Shelly had felt that he should have screamed, "I don't want your francs."

Shelly and Mickey had laughs in bed and out. She read everything he wrote and he tasted everything from her burgeoning catering business. He told her he could never leave a woman who bothered to stuff mushrooms. But he did leave. They nourished each other until the day he told her he needed a little more freedom. Those were threatening words. She knew "needing freedom" was the first step in a direction that she didn't want Mickey to go in. She cried. He said he didn't want to lose her, he just wanted some nights off. She panicked. Nights off meant other women, ones who weren't crying and talking about where the relationship was going. He said he had learned his lesson about being with just one woman, that it was dangerous for him. When he was married, he couldn't think of punch lines, he said.

She knew then that it was over. Oh, maybe the possibility of a meaningful relationship remained, but the probability of a permanent love was gone. She wanted to marry the man even though she feared that their sons might be short because of him and that the pictures of the wedding would never end up in the photographer's window because of him.

For over a year after the affair ended she had kept herself available for Mickey, in case he remembered how strong their love and deep their laughs were. Only recently had she faced the truth. Even though she woke up needing him and thinking about him, he could actually live without her. He could smile even when she wasn't there. He could walk the three rooms of his hotel suite without knowing that something was missing. He could face the Sunday *Times*, New Year's Eve and success alone.

Shelly became teary as she got into her panty hose, and she saw the irony in her tears. She was supposed to be sad over a dead person, not over her own life. She knew that the real reason she was crying was that she was trying to catch a man under such circumstances. More than once she had read articles on where to meet a man, but they all listed the same places, like sporting events and the take-out counter at your local deli. None had ever included the man who was likely to be vulnerable because his mother had died.

For several minutes she didn't have the energy to get dressed, but Shelly was a strong woman who had, in her relatively short lifetime, participated in a Hughes Aircraft lockout and also opened her own catering business. She recovered the energy that always came through for her. Soon her makeup, the slip with the lace, the pearls and the suit were all on. She put on the black shoes and knew Paula was right. They worked. She debated about a hat. She was always buying hats that she never wore. No. A hat looked too planned. Besides, men liked her curly hair and never knew she had to get permanents.

She transferred things out of her wine purse to a black one and stood in front of her mirrored closet door. She saw nothing but the sadness in her eyes. It was there a lot, reminding her of photographs of people in books who suffered much worse fates than she did. Those people were victims of war or poverty. All she had ever lost was an underweight, funny little man with hardly any hair on his chest. Unfortunately he was the thing she loved most. She wanted sparkle back in her face, but she was too weary to put it there herself. Yes, she could stand on her own two feet in expensive shoes. Yes, she could live alone and earn her way. But she couldn't seem to make herself happy.

She was more scared of the unknown than unhappy with what she had. She didn't smile into the mirror as she tried to help herself get ready for the world she had to face that day. Shelly's face was strong and by chance made her look proud. Not one feature took a back seat to any other. Her eyes were as dark as they could be. Her nose was prominent, but no more than her defined chin or definite eyebrows. Since moving to New York, she had made six appointments with plastic surgeons and had canceled all six of them.

In high school she was ignored. In a more mature world she was considered interesting. Capes had helped since she carried her extra six pounds in her breasts, although her thighs did a good job too. If she would be willing to give up her clothes and makeup and turn everything in for a well-fitting Israeli uniform, one could imagine Shelly against the skyline of Tel Aviv. She looked good in khaki shorts and had enough muscles in her legs to make you believe she had been on a ten-mile hike. She would have made a very good Sabra.

Before leaving her apartment, Shelly called her office. She ordered two of the most magnificent fish trays her firm had to offer, telling them to add extra Nova Scotia. Several of her competitors, attempting to be chic, didn't deal with basic lox platters. Shelly offered all the current raw fish and baby vegetables, but she also offered a Sunday morning special. She was smart enough to deal in whitefish heads and black olives, and it had paid off. Her Cater-a-Seder concept had launched her into the highest catering circles. "Food by Shelly" not only had been praised by *New York Magazine* as "good, basic and unpretentious," but also had given her the means to keep herself in frequent touch with Paula at Bloomingdale's.

She had the trays sent to Barry's father's apartment, reminding them to wait until late afternoon to try delivery. Then she asked if the squab that was needed for the Chase Manhattan branch board meeting the following Tuesday had been ordered. "I'll take care of it, Miss Silver," Seth, her manager, said reverently. She liked hearing the respect in his voice. Maybe he would work out. So far she hadn't been able to trust anyone. Not one of her managers had understood how thin the veal really had to be. Her spirits were lifted a bit. The next time she passed a mirror she smiled. Since her mood had improved, it struck her funny that she had almost passed up a funeral because she looked too sad.

Shelly took a cab to Riverside Funeral Home, arriving just moments before the service was about to begin. Barry spotted her as soon as she entered the chapel. He left the couple he was talking to and made his way toward her. He touched a dozen backs before they faced each other. His hug was so strong it almost hurt, but no woman has ever been unhappy with too strong an embrace. Shelly felt saved.

The funeral was as she pictured it would be. The mourners wept quietly. The husband tried to hide his tears behind bony fingers. The best friend delivered a eulogy that was full of love. The rabbi, who obviously didn't know the deceased, spoke in poetic generalities. He said she must have been a wonderful woman since her survivors were so wonderful. All through the service, Shelly's eyes were filled with tears. All those around her might have thought it was for the loss of Rose Goldblum, but even in her attempt to be supportive, Shelly couldn't have gone that far. She cried because on the other side of Barry was another woman whose hand he also held. Shelly surmised that the woman was in her early thirties. Her face was younger than Shelly's, and her body fuller and older. Here was a woman who had burned her bra and never retrieved it from the ashes. She wore an unusual black dress with billowy sleeves and a small black hat that purposely sat off center. It threatened to fall, but the woman's secret was that it never would. She had an abundance of hair, part of it prematurely gray. An attractive white streak started at the middle of her forehead and never stopped. Her skin was white, her eyes dark and her lips defiantly red. Shelly was hoping that she was nothing but an age-appropriate cousin, but her stomach was telling her that this sympathetic woman was another girlfriend. Shelly squeezed Barry's hand and he squeezed back. She had no idea how much squeezing was going on on the other side.

When all the words had been said about how great Rose was and the service had ended, Barry wiped his eyes and invited both women to accompany him, his father and mother's sister in the limousine. He went to help his friends and family, leaving the two women to face each other. They needed information, but neither one of them knew how to start, so they nodded politely and said what a lovely service it had been. When they ran out of accolades, they began to feel out their territorial rights. Each held her ground, knowing there was a great deal to find out before any moves could be made.

"Did you know Mrs. Goldblum well?" Shelly asked. That would let her know how ensconced with the family her enemy was.

"Well, actually, I never met her." Shelly was a little relieved and a little upset. If she didn't know Barry's mother, she was not very close to him. However, that also showed that she wasn't a relative.

"Did you know her?" The woman leaned against a pew and the real outline of her body revealed itself. She was large but firm, a worthy opponent.

"No, not really," Shelly responded, leaving her to wonder what "not really" meant.

"I'm Greta Weinstein." The woman extended her large, round hand. Shelly shook it carefully, as if danger lay in those fingers.

"Shelly Silver." She shook her head, indicating that she was giving accurate information.

"How well do you know Barry?" Greta asked, getting to the point. This was really what they had to find out. Greta had taken an elegant compact out of her purse and was checking her image. Shelly wished she had such a compact and skin that allowed inspection. Her own was olive.

"Pretty well." That was all Shelly wanted to reveal. "And you?"

"Very well." The words hit Shelly hard. If they had both known him "pretty well," that might have meant a fair fight. This news meant a lot more digging for information was needed. She took a few steps up the aisle of the chapel so that she could see where Barry was. Since he was still ushering people into cars, she knew there was a little time to sort things out. Her instinct, however, was to flee. She didn't want to hurt or be hurt by this woman who, she noticed, had the type of lips that lipstick clung to. Her own was always absorbed. She headed back to Greta and asked her to sit down. They sat with a space between them. The space was big enough to accommodate Barry, who had been spared this conversation.

"Why don't you go first?" asked Greta. Shelly nodded in agreement. She needed information as much as Greta did, but it didn't matter in what order it was given.

"Well," Shelly began, "my relationship with Barry is relatively simple. We started going out a little less than two months ago . . . I don't know . . . this is hard." She could see that what she was saying was painful.

"It's okay. I have to know."

"How much should I tell you?"

"I've been seeing him for close to ten months and I want to know everything."

"You don't want to know everything."

"Yes, I do. I'm the type of person who has to know details. Please. I'll feel better if I know it all. If I don't I'll make up the facts." Shelly, being a woman who also made up facts, fully understood.

"There's not much to tell. We've been seeing each other for a couple of months . . ."

"And you slept with him . . ." Greta seemed to be helping the story along, so Shelly was totally unprepared for what happened next.

"Yes."

"Did he call you sweetie?" Greta wanted to know.

"Yeah. He did." Shelly had no idea that her three words would cause the flood of tears. Evidently Greta was willing to share every-thing except what she considered to be her pet name. There was no warning, but once she started to cry, she cried for all the suffering she had received at the hands of men.

"I'm sorry," Shelly said, as if she were the guilty party.

"Was it just once or did it happen all the time?"

"We went to bed a few times." She tried to make this sound in-nocuous, since she could see Greta's hurt. Shelly had always mothered everyone around her, but the mothering had never happened this quickly before. The woman sighed and her breasts rose and then settled again. Because Greta was such a large woman, parts of her moved independently from each other.

"How many times did he call you sweetie? Do you think it was a mistake, or what?" Greta's dark lashes were long and wet. She looked like a hurt Bambi. Shelly took her hand and continued to feel that she had hurt this woman. She was just about to lie when she caught sight of the large, gold Hebrew letters above a stained-glass window at the front of the chapel. She had never been to Hebrew school and didn't know how to translate the language. However, their presence was strong enough to make her hesitate. Shelly was caught between God and human suffering. To lie would be a sin, but it seemed worth committing. She felt that the Almighty would forgive a lie that had to do with the soothing of a woman who liked to be called sweetie.

"It was a mistake. I'm sure it was just a mistake. Really, it just slipped out. He must have thought it was you." Greta stopped crying long enough to blow her nose into the lace handkerchief that was in no way designed for actual use. Shelly noted two things: that Greta was the type of woman who had accessories inside her accessories and that she, Shelly, was doing all the work. Shelly didn't doubt Greta's unhappiness, but she was suffering too. Greta's tears were such an effective device that Shelly was doing everything she could to stop them.

"Would you say your relationship with him was fairly insignifi-cant?" Greta asked, and waited for what appeared to be the most important answer of her life.

"Fairly."

Greta brightened a bit. Her compact was out again and she was checking for water damage. There was none. It was quite remarkable that so much emotion hadn't stained her. Knowing her mascara was still in place must have given her the freedom to cry again.

"Oh, hey, come on. He only called me sweetie once and then it sort of just slipped out."

"Yeah." This was accompanied by a large, heartbreaking sob that moved Shelly to take Greta into her arms. Greta allowed herself to be comforted, and the two women rocked back and forth.

"Really. He never liked me," said Shelly, giving it her best shot.

"He's a real bastard."

"Agreed. Only we can't tell him that today."

"You know, he probably peed in his pants when he realized we were both here."

"I wasn't invited."

"Me either."

"You think he knows we're talking to each other?"

"Yeah, and don't think he's not going to take advantage of his mother's death. He knows we're not going to attack him at a funeral. He's probably relieved that since we found out about each other, it happened today."

"Probably."

"I was beginning to think maybe this was it. I had it in my head that it was going to work out and that I could stop looking."

"Maybe it will. He probably just got together with me because he felt he was getting too close to you. I was like his last fling. A little nothing in the scheme of things." If this didn't work, Shelly was willing to apologize for having hurt someone she just met.

"Maybe," Greta said. She left Shelly's arms and went back to her compact. She sighed at her image as if she knew she had a rough job ahead. The tears kept coming and she mopped them up as quickly as she could, but there were still two attractive ones rolling down each cheek when Barry came back to get them. Apparently having imagined what had been going on, he walked with hesitant steps, as if he were in a minefield instead of a chapel. He knew that women could erupt even when you dealt with them one at a time. If the fuse was lit now, there would be no survivors. He had two choices: speak first and hope to get some sympathy, or take his medicine. He had never liked the taste of medicine, so he began with, "I miss her so much." On hearing his voice, both women turned to find him. He quickly sat down directly behind them in order to lessen the firing range.

"She was a wonderful woman," said Greta, pretending her tears were for someone other than herself.

"I know everyone thinks his mother is wonderful, but mine really was. I didn't call her enough."

"I'm sure you did. You were a good son. I remember one Friday night we couldn't get together because you went to visit her." The last remark from Shelly cheered up Barry but devasted Greta. He shook his head in agreement and managed a smile. Greta gave Shelly a hateful look.

"I just want to thank both of you for coming," he said, putting his head in between theirs. His hair, which tended to grow sideways, tickled both their cheeks. That seemed fair. "You're terrific. Just having you here has helped. I have to get out to the cemetery now. I'd love you to come with me, but I understand that you might not have the time. God, she was wonderful."

Greta was on her feet immediately, willing to go. "Of course I'm going to the cemetery with you. Do I have a minute to go the ladies' room?"

"Sure. Go ahead. I'll wait right here for you." Greta started off, then stopped. "You sure you don't want to join me, Shelly?" It was obvious that Greta didn't want to risk leaving a man with whom she might have a relationship alone in a chapel. Shelly, who was playing the role of healer, understood immediately. She went.

While they washed their hands, Greta became teary again. "You don't understand," she sobbed. "It takes me so long to find someone to like. I can go for years without really finding anybody I even want to go out with."

Forgetting for a moment her role as nurse, Shelly said, "You're not the only one. I don't go around falling for everybody. I go for long periods of time without being attracted to anybody. There have been only a couple of men in my life."

Just before they left the bathroom, Greta had one more question to ask. "Are you giving up, or what?"

"Giving up?"

"On Barry. Because if you are, this would be a good time to say that you didn't realize how late it is and that you can't go to the cemetery."

"I guess I'm not giving up," said Shelly apologetically. Greta lifted her breasts and walked out of the bathroom first. Shelly's chest was smaller, but her resolve was just as great.

The limousine was packed. The widower, Aunt Bea and Barry sat in the back seat, shoulders touching. Greta and Shelly sat facing them in individual seats on either side of a bar. Shelly felt as if the father and aunt were guard dogs ready to pounce and that she and Greta were guarding their own sanity. The ride was mostly quiet, punctuated only by remarks about what a wonderful woman Rose was. Barry told a story about being in the second grade when the teacher asked to see his mother. He was petrified. The meeting was after school, so he sat in the empty classroom at his front-row desk, overhearing the conversation between the two most important women in his life. He was sure he was going to be punished, but instead his dear, sweet mother was telling the teacher off. Her language was polite but strong. "Look," she said, "I didn't send my son to your school so you could make him nervous." And with that she grabbed little Barry's hand and marched him out. No teacher ever asked to see Rose Goldblum again. Barry, Aunt Bea, Shelly and Greta tried to laugh. Mr. Goldblum was too numb even to try. He watched the road in case the driver didn't know where he was going. Three times he yelled that the exit to take was Jericho Turnpike. He pointed with a finger that appeared to have too many joints.

Just when everyone thought they had arrived safely, Aunt Bea asked both women at once how they knew Barry. Greta managed to go first. She said that she and Barry were seeing each other in a way that made it sound as if they were just about to order invitations. Aunt Bea smiled, patted Barry's hand and said it was nice that Barry had someone. Shelly couldn't take it. She tried to look demure and said that she and Barry were also seeing each other. Aunt Bea thought that was terrific. "You are a lucky boy, Barry, to have these two beautiful young ladies as . . ." She became flustered searching for the right word and settled on "girlfriends." Shelly thought Barry was indeed lucky to have two people in his life, while she had none.

Shelly felt quite sad at the grave site. Mostly she was sorry for Mr. Goldblum, who looked so small standing there with his head bowed. She was holding one of Barry's hands while Greta held the other. His father was the one who deserved to have his hands held, but he was left to hold his own. He clasped them in front of himself as he repeated the words of prayer, keeping, almost, with the rabbi, his arms swinging to the rhythm of the words. It seemed so unfair that age had robbed him of attention. Aunt Bea did put her arms around him to guide him back to the car, but Barry clearly had the better deal.

They all went back to the Goldblums' apartment. Rose had left her legacy in her carpets, couches and drapes. The rooms and fabric she left behind were rose. With the exception of Greta, everyone was appreciative of the trays that Shelly had sent over. Shelly prepared Mr. Goldblum a plate, and he sat and ate it on a tall, straight chair that was placed against the wall of the dining room. It surprised Shelly that he could eat. She herself wasn't interested in food as nourishment. A black maid kept coming out of the kitchen to ask if he needed anything, and when she said she would be right there if he did, Shelly felt better. She thought that it would be a great idea for all widowers to marry their housekeepers when their wives died. Those were the women who had taken care of them their whole lives. They knew where the Alka-Seltzer was. Widowers might as well give them a respectable place in their homes.

About a quarter after four Shelly gave up. She saw Greta pop one of her fishballs in Barry's mouth and decided she didn't want a man who let someone feed him. She kissed both the Goldblum men on the cheek and was told again how nice it was that she came and was thanked for the food. She looked over her shoulder at the door and was happy to see the elder Mr. Goldblum being let into the bedroom by the housekeeper for a nap. He walked cautiously, as if he didn't know what to expect from the bedroom in which he had slept for the last forty years. It made Shelly feel good to know that at least his physical needs were being cared for.

Since she hadn't seen Greta make a move, Shelly was shocked to find her waiting at the elevator. "This could be the worst day of my life," said Greta, as if nothing counted but her own feelings.

"My guess is that funerals are never that much fun." Shelly pushed the elevator button three times, not trusting that Greta had already summoned it.

"I left because you did," Greta said. "I thought we could make a deal."

"A deal?"

"Well, yeah. At first I thought that you might back down about Barry since I've known him five times longer than you have, but it looks like you're going to hang in there, so I thought maybe we could go for coffee somewhere and talk." Shelly the businesswoman could not pass up the chance of hearing a deal, and they ended up in a Madison Avenue coffee shop. It was one of those places whose main business was lunchtime. From twelve to two the place was lively, with tuna salads and BLTs everywhere. At this time of day, the two minority waiters were impatiently waiting to go home, and the door was being locked to prevent further customers from coming in. Greta and Shelly sat in the empty luncheonette, their hands around their coffee cups. They had nothing to talk about but the deal.

"So, you have an idea?" asked Shelly, confronting the opposition straight on.

"Can I ask you something? Do you love Barry?"

"Is that important?" Shelly wasn't ready to reveal the whole truth yet.

"It's very important. Love should be worth something."

"You're right. It should be." They both were old enough to know love didn't count for anything unless it was mutual.

"Anyway, I figured if I love him but you don't, we should structure the deal differently."

"You want to tell me what deal you're talking about?" The middle-aged woman who was adding up the cash register receipts looked toward their tiny booth. She adjusted her black cardigan with a hostile move. Shelly felt uncomfortable knowing that she was keeping someone at her job longer than was necessary.

The place was closing, the waiters were putting on their jackets, the day's money was ready for the bank, but the conversation was too intriguing to stop, so Shelly suggested that they go back to her apartment. The cashier locked the door behind them, looking relieved that they had left.

On the large white couches in Shelly's perfectly decorated living room, they drank their Perriers while Greta worked up to her proposition.

"Let's see. You probably hit school in the early seventies."

"Right.'

· "Me too. I still have a scar from a police clubbing," Greta said proudly, pulling the shoulder of her dress down, revealing a "scar" that couldn't be seen.

"I have one, too, from the day we tried to lock the representatives from Hughes out." Shelly pulled up her skirt. They were excited about their war wounds. Out of kindness for each other they "saw" the scars that had long ago faded.

"I swear the C.I.A. had me on one of their lists," Greta said with pride.

"Times have changed."

"They sure have. The kids today don't know what we went through so they could sleep around."

Greta closed her eyes. "I voted Democratic last election, but secretly I was glad that the Republicans won." She then lowered the shoulder of her dress to find the imaginary wound once again.

"I wanted the Democrats, of course."

"Of course."

"But they would have killed me with taxes." Shelly made a mental note to deduct the Goldblums' tray as a business expense.

"Don't I know it? I'm a designer, you know." Greta left her couch to come over to Shelly's and showed her the label in her dress. On white satin, in block letters, it read GRETA'S SURVIVAL. "I'm not huge yet, but I'm growing."

"I was wondering where you got that dress. It's fabulous." Shelly perked up. Here was a designer in her own living room. That was almost as good as having a personal shopper.

"If you're willing to take the deal I'm about to offer, I can get you anything wholesale." This was almost too much for Shelly.

"So what is this deal?" Shelly liked the feeling of being intrigued. At thirty-five she always knew too much about tomorrow.

"I pay you to never see Barry again. The price is negotiable." Greta bent down, opened her pocketbook and brought out her checkbook. It was encased in a Bottega Veneta leather cover.

Shelly had to believe her. Greta even had her Mont Blanc pen out, on the verge of being poised. Shelly worried that it was going to leak. "The deal is you're going to pay me not to see Barry again?"

"If there wasn't enough red velvet to go around and I needed red velvet for next year's line, I would sure as hell buy all the red velvet I could get my hands on. There aren't enough Barrys to go around, so I'm ready to make a cash offer." Greta's gesture said, The ball is in your court.

"I don't need your money."

"I know. I was hoping that I was going to get to deal with someone a little less entrepreneurial."

"I can't believe you would be willing to pay money for a man."

"I figure you have to pay for what you want. This finding-a-man business isn't going to come cheaply. They're too rare in today's market. Barry isn't great, but since I'm willing to pay, it'll establish his price. Any suggestions?" Though they both knew a game was being played, they knew also that the reason for the game was real.

"How do you know I wouldn't take your money and then still see him behind your back?" Shelly smiled to let Greta know she wouldn't do such a thing. "Or what if you paid me, but Barry just kept hanging around?"

"I figure I have to take my chances. You look like a nice Jewish business girl, so how much are we talking about, fifteen hundred?" Greta opened her checkbook, but didn't start writing until she got approval on the figure.

"You're not really serious about this?"

"Yeah. I am. I've had a lousy couple of years manwise and I figure it's up to me to turn things around. Some things I can't change. I mean, my package is my package, and what I'm selling is over thirty years old, so if my boyfriend goes out with another woman, I can try to buy her off." All this was said in a friendly tone, with the checkbook used for emphasis.

"We've all had a lousy couple of years."

"I know. So, I'm into survival of the fittest. Those of us who start taking our lives into our own hands are going to come out ahead. From now on I'm going to run my love life like my business. Let's say Barry is the product. I'm willing to go for it, defects and all. I'm willing to go as high as twenty-five hundred."

"Maybe I could outbid you. I have a checkbook too."

"I'm sure you do. I just figured my ten months would give me the advantage. So, what do you want for him?" The pen was lifted. "Thirty-three-fifty is my top price, and you have to admit he's an inconsistent caller."

"You really want him that badly?"

"Yeah. I really want him that badly. I'm thirty-four years old. I need children. Barry is the type who would take them to their little league games . . . plus, I don't want to meet someone new and all his strange friends. And I'm scared of sleeping with someone new unless he takes a blood test . . . Yeah. I want him that badly."

"I couldn't take your money."

"Shit." Greta went into a funk. Her head was thrown back on the couch. Her whole body revealed her exasperation.

"Why don't we just let it play out its natural course?"

"Yeah. Yeah. Sure. That's what we've been doing for centuries, let it all just play out. That's why we're in so much trouble. There's not one relationship working out for any woman I know. So, what do we do; more of the same?"

"Did you ever think of joining the Vertical Club? It's this coed work-out place and . . ."

"I know all about the Vertical Club," said Greta wearily. "You get to work out next to a lot of nineteen-year-old models who have sequins on their leotards and don't mind the pain. I'm not going to gyms, or singles' bars or small dinner parties with somebody's nephew. I'm getting married this year and I'm on a hard-core manhunt. For the last time, how much do you want for Barry the lawyer? It can't be that much. Are you aware that he doesn't shower every day?"

Shelly was beginning to enjoy this woman Greta. Combined, her body, her dress and her exasperation took up the whole couch. She was resting for the moment, but clearly she was doing something about her life. "I couldn't accept money."

Greta awakened. "Plan two," she said. "We share him."

"What?"

"Like Arab women do. Did you ever see them riding around in limos, sharing the same American Express card?"

"In England I did," said Shelly. "I went there on a caterers' convention. Can you imagine having a convention dealing with food in London?"

Greta didn't want to answer food questions now. She felt she was on to something. She stood to make her pitch. She had taken off her shoes when she first arrived, but even in her stockinged feet she was at least five-ten. Shelly was sitting on the floor by now and was forced to look up at Greta as she energetically paced on large feet that were followed by large ankles and legs. "Look, there aren't enough men to go around. That's a fact. You know it. I know it. Every single woman in the country knows it, thanks to that cover of *Newsweek*. How dare they announce how little chance we have to be married, as if we didn't know. Did you notice that two weeks later *New York Magazine* had a cover story about depression? Maybe we're going to have to share." Shelly thought of Mickey Burke. She possessed only a fraction of him. He only called her every three months or so to make sure she would still talk to him.

"You could imagine sharing?" It seemed like one of those concepts that didn't factor in emotion.

"I've had a rough time with men. And I want to get married and have a baby. If you're asking me if I'd settle for half a man, I would." With this, Greta sank back into the couch. The deal was on the table. It was up to Shelly to reveal whether she could divide and conquer. Mickey was on her mind. Him, at least, she considered a man and a half. Sharing him would still leave her with three quarters of a person.

"You're not serious about this. How would it work? How do you know that any man would go along with it? Isn't it too Mormon for us?" The last two questions Shelly delivered over her shoulder. She was headed to the kitchen for a bottle of wine. She was going to pour Greta Weinstein her best Chardonnay. If this woman was willing to share a man with her, the least Shelly could do was share her booze.

Greta knew she wasn't expected to shout her answers into the kitchen, and she didn't have simple answers to complicated questions like, How would it work? All she knew was that life wasn't working as is and that two women had showed up for the same man's mother's funeral. She chose a sandwich from the tray that Shelly had brought out earlier and surveyed the room. She guessed right away that a designer had done the place. The rounded walls were the biggest giveaway. All those designing boys loved to round the walls. The fireplace was also a clue. It had been modernized and marbleized. The furniture was oversized, the lamps Italian, the paintings not dry yet. The room was not unpleasant, it was just too beige and too done for Greta's SoHo tastes. After being in apartments like this, she had always been happy to go back downtown where one's art, rather than one's decorator, determined style.

Shelly was back. On her way to the coffee table she slipped a bit because her stockings couldn't grip the bleached wood floors. The two wineglasses she had chosen clinked against each other, heralding, she hoped, good news. Greta settled down on her couch, and Shelly opened the wine with the expertise of a woman who'd been on her own.

"Who did your place?" Greta asked. She had already sipped the wine, since a toast seemed presumptuous.

"Two guys named Dirk and Dutch. They did a great job, but they fought over the recessed lighting and they're not talking to each other anymore." Shelly bothered to explain this, thinking that Greta might want to hire the team. Others had, but Dirk had moved to San Francisco, taking his color charts with him.

"It's well decorated," said Greta. She meant to be honest and less than complimentary without actually being insulting, but Shelly smiled and accepted the compliment that wasn't there.

"So, about Barry . . ." Shelly had a meeting with the Newleys at seven-thirty to discuss their daughter's bat mitzvah. Dirk, Dutch and her personal shopper at Bloomingdale's had taught her never to miss a meeting with a potential client. She was interested in this big, beautiful woman and wanted to spend more time with her, but she had time only to discuss the basics. It occurred to her that if only all her clients didn't demand to see her personally, her life might have had a better flow.

"I say let's share him. We tell him we're willing to do that. We treat him as if we have joint custody. He spends half his time with you, half with me. We alternate holidays, split vacations. I don't know exactly how it would work but I'm sure we'd have a hell of a chance of getting on *Donahue*." The sleeves of Greta's black dress were expansive. Both of her arms moved in a flightlike pattern, flapping in place. She was a big black bird. Even though the dress was dark, it would be unfair to say a hawk came to mind because hawks were sinister and Greta was not. When Greta became her friend, she would, with a variety of flapping sleeves and high-perched hats, always remind Shelly of a bird. This was quite an accomplishment for someone of Greta's size.

"I guess we have to get back to that important question again. Do you love him?"

Greta had to think too long for her answer. The burden of her thought caused her head to tilt, and her little black hat traveled with her. "I have loved three times. No, twice. Love is hard on me. I'd have to say I'm more interested in winning Barry. I merely consider him my last chance at happiness."

"Well, I don't love him either. But you were standing there feeding him today, and I figured that meant I should just back off. I mean, he was allowing you to put my fishballs into his mouth."

"I didn't know they were yours. I realized you sent the trays, but I didn't know they were your personal balls."

"Fish trays are one of my specialties."

"And you learned to cook at your mother's knee?"

"No. I started cooking because she didn't. We had this housekeeper who believed in casseroles, and I was a pretentious thirteen-year-old who was horrified by things like tuna fish and noodles. I asked for a cookbook for my birthday. I also wanted my family to be bilingual." Shelly smiled, remembering the days when she refused to speak anything but Italian. Her family had ignored her phases. That made it so easy to leave Rochester.

"You make a good sandwich. So, you cook for Barry. Don't make him fat. I'll pull his wardrobe together. I figure he's a forty short now. Let's keep him that way. And what do you think of the beard? I say we convince him to shave it before one of us gets a rash."

"I don't know. Whenever things don't work out for me I start thinking of . . ." Shelly had intended to say Mickey Burke, but she had learned it was better to keep his name inside her where it was more easily contained.

Greta was more than willing to finish the sentence that Shelly began. She pointed with the hand that held the sandwich. "You go right back to thinking about an old boyfriend. Am I right? I did that with Michael Rumpleman for years. You might as well go back to a familiar obsession rather than start a new one. Am I right, or what?" And what was left of the sandwich disappeared between Greta's perfectly red lips. Still her lipstick stayed in place.

"You're right." Shelly shook her permanent as if she could shake that man out of her hair. "If I could take a pill to forget him, I would . . . take half of it." She loved the man.

"I knew it. Believe me, I know what it's like to bear the pain of someone rather than let him go."

Shelly hadn't meant to tell the Mickey story, but it always poured out of her. "I tried everything to get him to marry me," she concluded. "I played hard to get, easy to get, friendly, suicidal. Nothing worked. I prayed to God for help and was embarrassed that I wasn't praying for world peace." It felt good to talk about Mickey again. Every friend Shelly had was tired of hearing about him.

They mourned for a moment over lost loves that they hadn't quite been able to lose. There were sips of wine before Greta launched into her plan again. "I swear it could work." Shelly was not taking her seriously, but she was enjoying the conversation. There were new ideas flying around her living room, and even though she had no intention of taking off with them, they were fun. She liked this Greta. She served up hope.

"How? How would you even approach Barry?"

"How? I don't know exactly how. I guess we tell him we're willing to both have a relationship with him. We . . ." Since Greta thought better on her feet, she stood again, taking her wineglass with her. She was slightly disheveled by now. The little black hat was heading in its own direction and the belt of her dress had also decided to veer to the left. "We know he'll be flattered. What guy wouldn't be?" The thoughts came quickly now, and Greta chased them around the room. "Of course we can't both marry him, but I never cared about rings and paper. Let's say, after a lot of work we both get the commitment. You can marry him, or not, depending on your politics. We both get babies." She landed on the hassock by the fireplace but was immediately on her feet again, this time to make a fire. Shelly was horrified. It was a working fireplace with the wood in place, but it was new and clean and ash-free, and she had no intention of ever using it. Fires caused soot. Fires caused whole buildings to burn to the ground. She blew out the match that Greta had lit.

"It leaks," said Shelly, not knowing the exact word to describe the inner workings of a fireplace.

"That's a shame." Greta didn't quite believe her hostess and stuck her head in the fireplace for a quick look. She saw nothing but a clean, unused space. When she turned back toward Shelly, one eyebrow was raised. She let it pass. "So, where were we?"

"You were outlining how we could share the man and you were saying how I could marry Barry."

"You could, you know. A man can ward off one Jewish woman, but two? One of us is smarter than he. Imagine the two of us together? We could have him eating out of our hands . . . maybe even gefilte fishballs off one of your delicious trays."

"I just don't think I'm ready to . . . settle for part of a person."

Greta emptied her wineglass, balanced herself into her shoes and said she had to go. With Shelly following, she found her way to the front door. "Think about my proposal," she said. "It might sound great to you on a Sunday morning when you have the feeling that everyone else is having brunch and getting engaged. Do you want to give me your telephone number?" Shelly did. She had an opening for a friend ever since Rochelle had moved to Brooklyn Heights, insisting it was just as good as Manhattan and you got more for your money. Shelly went to her white desk and got out her business card, and Greta handed over one of hers. "Sign of the eighties," she said as she slipped Shelly's card into her purse before closing the door behind her.

Shelly dreamed that Arabs were chasing her. The next day everything seemed to come in threes.

# 4
# Afterlife

MICKEY Burke liked peeking out of his office. He had developed this habit since Astra Rainbow had arrived. He loved seeing her lovely bottom molded to the chair. The chair was on wheels, and he thought about rolling her out into the hall and pushing her down it, giving her the ride of her life. He loved seeing the back of her head. Her hair waved and curled, or so it seemed, in rhythm with the typewriter. She and her instrument were one. Her eyes were riveted to the words he had written. Never once did she look at her fingers, and she hardly ever made a mistake. On rare occasions when she did, even her mistakes were a pleasure to watch. He had caught her making one once as he watched through the crack in the door. She made a fist and whispered, "Poop." He had barely heard it, but he was glad he had. He wasn't sure if anyone he knew had ever said "poop" before. He knew immediately that he would, before the morning ended, get out his Astra Rainbow Movie file and add that the heroine said "poop" when frustrated. Mickey Burke's fans said he had a good ear.

Every year of Mickey's life, he had mellowed. He had gone from being a raving maniac to being simply a maniac. His anger had developed when all three networks told him they didn't want his face on their airwaves. His job was to get his anger under control. Analysis had helped. Shelly Silver had helped. She had laughed him into becoming more confident. Just living helped. And now this new secretary, who had no hostility in her, helped. He hadn't had one tantrum since she arrived three months ago. If he thought about it, he would have known that she was having too great an effect on him. He hadn't thought about it, so he was still just interested in rolling her around the hall.

Mickey had mellowed, but not enough to trust himself. Today he had a network meeting, but he couldn't be sure that he wouldn't tell the head of programming to eat shit or something else equally appetizing. Therefore, his plan was to tell them his idea for a new series quickly. If they laughed as they should and told him how brilliant he was, he would never hand over the pages that Astra Rainbow was typing. He needed them only if they started asking their dumb questions, like, Did he think this show could last for seven years? In the old days, before he worked on his control, he would scream that he wouldn't fucking be there if he didn't think what he was presenting would be a hit. In fact, he shouted until his veins popped. Once he broke a window, even though it was an accident. His arms had a life of their own when he was upset. He could sense when he was starting to revolt and he now knew how to bite his inner lip and dig his nails into his hand to keep from throwing something that would shatter. The people he had meetings with were scared of Mickey Burke because, although he was short and less than a hundred and forty pounds, they knew that he could cause them to bleed. They saw him, took his phone calls and gave him time because he was funny, the kind of funny that made them and their audiences laugh. They would sacrifice the glass of their windows and even the pictures of their wives and children (Mickey was also known to throw frames) because he brought them funny shows that led to high ratings. Ratings translated into dollars for their networks and for them. If they kept Mickey happy enough, for long enough, and if they didn't worry about breakage, they could afford new pictures of their wives and children on bigger boats in larger frames. The guy had created three successful series in the last five years. If he wanted to yell, they would soundproof the walls.

Mickey was sure he could handle this meeting without going out of control. If he had to pull a hair out of his nose, he would do it. He would also have typed pages with him in case he did blow up. He would bite himself until he hurt and try not to tell them what assholes they were. He hoped this would be the last television show he would have to sell. If his Astra Rainbow movie worked out, he would never write for the little screen again.

The keys of the typewriter stopped. Rainbow spun her chair around and said she was finished. He was embarrassed. These past few months, had she known that he had been looking at her? He was like a child caught in the act. Reflexively, he slammed the door shut. Rainbow didn't question his actions. He was the boss and if he wanted to watch her and then pretend he didn't, it was all right with her. *Glamour* magazine was always suggesting that secretaries stand up for their rights, but Mr. Raphelson had taught her differently. He had never read *Glamour* or *Ms* or anything else that had to do with the twentieth century. His students were obedient, very marketable and virtually out of place in the modern world.

Mickey opened the door as if the slamming episode had never taken place and stuck out his head. "You finished?" he asked brightly.

"Yes. Do you want to check it over?" She was putting the cover back on the typewriter and still had her back toward him.

"No. I trust you."

"Oh, you shouldn't do that." She was scolding him.

"Why not?" He was briefly distracted, testing the weight of the pages she had just typed, as if he were selling ideas by the pound. The total seemed heavy enough to take into the network.

"You shouldn't trust me because you don't know me or my people."

Mickey, confused by Astra Rainbow's explanation, walked around to the front of her desk. He was about to get into one of his favorite positions, the one where he put his hands on the corners of the desk and leaned in so that he was eye to eye with his beautiful secretary. Today, because of his meeting, he was wearing a tie—nothing major, just a wine knit that wasn't jarring with his customary jeans and Brooks Brothers button-down shirt. There was a chance the tie would get caught in the move, but it seemed worth it. It was the only safe way he knew of getting close.

He hadn't expected tears. All the other times when he looked into her eyes he found them blue, clear and embarrassed. That's the way he wanted them now. Hadn't Mr. Raphelson told her not to cry? He knew he had to ask what was wrong, but he didn't want to. He felt sorry for her because obviously she was hurting, but he also felt sorry for himself because he was going to have to investigate this hurt. It wasn't that he lacked compassion, but rather that he had too much. A woman's tears could upset him for hours. Usually the woman stopped worrying about what was bothering her long before he did.

"What's wrong?" he was forced to ask.

"I'm sorry."

"It's okay. You don't have to be sorry to show emotion around here. I'm a writer. I thrive on emotion." He loosened his tie the way a Las Vegas singer did when he was about to bring home the big number.

"Could we forget I'm crying? It's really unprofessional."

"No. We can't forget." There were new tears replacing the old ones, small ones coming only from the corner of her eyes.

"This is the only unprofessional thing I've done, except asking you to ask Mr. Raphelson to call Granny about the cookies." She almost smiled. He was used to this, since Astra Rainbow almost smiled a few times a month.

"It's all right. Believe me, it's all right." Mickey noticed a tear land on the bow that she wore under her collar. He moved the pages that she had typed just slightly, to get them out of range of dampening.

"Maybe I'll stop soon."

He hoped so. He felt frustrated, not knowing what he could say that might possibly stop the flow.

But he just said, "It's all right. Sob as long as you want."

"This is my lunch hour, so you won't have to pay me while I cry." Her tears followed each other down the same shiny tracks.

"No. Consider this work time. You can have lunch when this passes over. I'll take you to lunch." He would buy her a fur coat if she would stop.

"It's not fair for you to pay me when I'm like this."

"Why not? This is show business. Actresses get paid for crying." The outer office was so tiny and Mickey was moving about so quickly that he reached opposite walls at least twice with each short sentence.

"Well, I'll have a quick lunch. I'll have liverwurst. They make that really fast because they don't have to cook anything."

Mickey hated liverwurst. He had never even seen it close up until he was twenty-one. The thought of it touching white bread and mayonnaise made him slightly ill. "You don't have to have a fast lunch. Have soup." He sounded like his Aunt Minn, a woman who thought soup cured depression.

"It doesn't matter," said Rainbow in a tone that would make a psychiatrist concerned.

"You have to tell me what's bothering you." In dealing with this girl Mickey had learned that if he acted like the boss, he usually got his way.

"I have to?" She bent her head down and rested it in both of her hands. She took his demands seriously.

"Yes. I'm afraid so," said Mickey, knowing he was winning. He sat down and stretched out his legs. They didn't get as far as he would have liked.

"It's just that what you wrote made me cry."

Mickey panicked. "It's a comedy."

"I know. It's probably very funny."

"I hope so. We all have to eat." At this point, Mickey wasn't speaking with just his hands in the customary Brooklyn fashion. His whole arm was involved.

Her head stayed down as she spoke. It was as if she was on the witness stand and afraid to look the prosecuting attorney in the eye. "It's just that I hope that what I just typed is true."

She had just typed a treatment for a television series he hoped to sell called *Afterlife* or *Whatever Happened to the Beckermans?* It was a comedy about Mickey's concept of afterlife. It focused on a family who died in a car crash and passed on to an afterlife where they lived among everyone in the world who had died so far. They had shepherds for neighbors. Mozart lived down the block in a split-level.

"What part do you hope is true?" he asked.

"The part about people living after they're dead." The tears kept coming.

"I don't know. I mean, I never died. It's just a silly idea." He was no longer in a casual position. He sat up straight in the chair, his arms outstretched, begging her to let it go.

"It's not silly. It's the most beautiful thing I have ever read." He hadn't expected her to defend her position so seriously.

"Thank you, but you can't take it so literally. It's just something I made up for television."

"Oh, I hope it's true," Rainbow said, reaching for a tissue. There was a box on the edge of her desk, exactly lined up with the container she used for paper clips. She wiped both eyes before continuing. "It has to be true."

"Universally, all religions teach an afterlife of some sort."

"I know, but yours is the best. I really want to believe it." Could this be? After such a short period of time, could he have become God to her? Did God sneak looks at the ones He loved?

He was cautious here. "You have a long life ahead of you. You won't have to worry about an afterlife for a very long time."

"It's just that I'm thinking of someone who died and I'm hoping that he's living like people do in your story."

"He probably is," said Mickey.

"Please let him be," she pleaded with Mickey, as if the control was in his hands.

"I'm sure that's where he is." He could think of no reason not to grant this sweet girl the assurance of heaven.

"I would be so happy if he was. And I hope it's exactly like you described it."

"Maybe it is. I doubt if I'll ever get there. There must be some other place for television writers."

"You deserve to be there, Mr. Burke. I'm sure there's another place for people like me." Mickey couldn't imagine any deed that this perfect secretary could have done that could send her to hell. Her skin was so shiny that she looked as if she had been born yesterday. A person so new couldn't have committed sins.

"No," was all he could say.

"Yes," said Astra Rainbow.

At the network, they were getting ready for Mickey Burke. David Weisner and Keith Connors were telling the new kid, Jennifer Ross, what he might be like. What she got from their warnings was that he would probably tell them a range of things that would filter down to "Go fuck yourselves." David had known when he hired lanky, attractive, Episcopalian Jennifer that she was a straightforward woman, and she knew that she got the job because she didn't take crap from anyone. They liked her having the guts to walk up to the head of programming and tell him where he went wrong. She had sat next to the chairman of the board at the last affiliates' dinner in L.A. and told him that he was slipping. "I don't think we're focusing on the right things," she had said, leaning forward in the kind of simple black strapless gowns that ex-debutantes wear. She went on to tell him that he was getting too soft. "This network is too interested in Emmys and not interested enough in advertising dollars," she warned him. "When we are number one for two years in a row, then I would like to see us put on some really classy programming, just for the sheer enjoyment of it." When the chairman asked her to meet with him the following morning, she said she couldn't. Her husband, a lawyer, and their three-year-old daughter were in California with her, and they were going to Disneyland.

When she got back to New York, there was a raise and promotion for her. She accepted the raise, saying that she had been worth more all along, but declined the promotion because she felt she had been placed correctly within the company ranks. She had impressed everyone from the chairman on down. She never perspired in her silk dresses.

Everyone considered Jennifer Ross a free-spirited woman who had it all. There was even a rumor going around that she was pregnant again. David and Keith were very careful in explaining why she would, like the rest of them, "take shit" from Mickey Burke. "His track record is getting better than Norman Lear's," David explained.

"He's pure profit," Keith added.

"You don't have to tell me about track records or profits. I read all the reports." Jennifer smiled, showing perfect Episcopalian teeth. The thing that these two men found most difficult about her was that she was nice. They were used to hating those tough broads who stayed until midnight and wouldn't let you compliment their legs. If you told Jennifer Ross she had a great body, she said thank you.

"We have to put up with him, even though he might throw something," said David.

"But don't worry. The meeting will be in my office, so only my glass is in jeopardy," said Keith.

"What about our heads?" asked Jennifer Ross.

"What?" came from both David and Keith.

"I assume when he throws things, he throws them at somebody. Do we duck or is it company policy to get gashed in the head?"

Neither man was sure if she was serious, but David raced to answer her question, hoping to put the young mother at ease. "He's not out to maim, he's just out to destroy." He said this as if it was good news.

"Anything else I should know—other than that we'd better like whatever he bring us or he'll get violent?"

"He likes us to laugh," said Keith.

"So we'll laugh, duck and eat shit," said Jennifer Ross.

"And he'll probably be late. No. He'll definitely be late."

"That's good. I won't be hungry enough to eat shit for at least another hour." The men laughed politely and wondered why she was being so easy to work with.

They were right about Mickey Burke's not being on time. At the time the meeting was supposed to start, he was sitting on his chair watching Astra Rainbow cry. He never tried to stop her because he knew it would be futile, as if she had a specific amount of tears that wouldn't stop until they had been shed. He was right. About twenty minutes after they began, the faucet that caused the flow shut off. She had used the entire box of tissues plus his hotel-ironed handkerchief. She stopped with one heavy sigh and then went back to business as usual. "Mr. Burke," she said, "you're going to be late for your meeting."

"You want to talk about it some more?" he said, indicating the pastel mountain of tissues that had accumulated in the wastebasket.

"Oh, no. I couldn't."

"Sure you could." The way he figured it, she could crawl into his lap and spill her secret into the fabric of his coat.

"No, please. I couldn't." She started to straighten her desk, closing the subject. She lined up the pencils in straight rows and made sure that the stamp dispenser was in its place next to the pen holder. When her desk was neat enough for military inspection, she reached for her jacket. "I'll only take about fifteen minutes for lunch on account of the crying," she said.

"I told you before. Take all the time you need." He awkwardly helped her with her coat because he had only one free hand. In his other were the pages she had typed.

"Well, in that case, I'll have my sandwich on toast. It'll take a few extra minutes. Thank you, Mr. Burke."

They went down in the elevator together. As the small area filled, the two of them were pushed closer together. He liked the intimacy that was being forced upon him. He realized that crowded elevators let you do things you would never dare if you had the space you normally needed. In the office, he would never have had his body against her, had the guts to crush, but here they were shoulder to shoulder, his right side touching her left. Since their arms were almost entwined, he wanted to hold her hand. He knew exactly where her fingers were. He wouldn't have to look to find them. But his life experience had taught him not to make moves at times like this and to stay away from blondes.

They parted on the street. He watched her, in her little navy jacket, until she went into the sandwich shop that was just a few doors from the Brill Building. He was sure that she was very polite when she asked for her liverwurst sandwich. She might even apologize for burdening them with the toasting.

The network was just a few blocks away. Usually he would be preparing what he was going to say at the meeting. He would be thinking of his opening remarks, something that would grab his small audience. An actor in a show had the chance to win over the crowds every night. A writer had only one chance to do his performance. He had to score and get out. He couldn't think of what to say. His mind was on Astra Rainbow. She seemed too fair, both in her attitude and her coloring, to have anything to cry about.

He was greeted by a short-haired receptionist who took him to the three standing executives. Since he had never met Jennifer, introductions were made, hands were shaken, he was asked to select a seat. He got first choice. "You mean I can have any chair in the room?" he asked. They nodded yes.

Mickey chose carefully. He scrutinized all the seats while the executives stood and waited. Since he was choosing, they wouldn't risk parking their bottoms until he'd made his selection. He chose the straight-backed one with the leather seat, picked it up and put it in the hall. "I always like to stand during these meetings, but thanks for the chair. It'll be great in my office." Keith laughed loudest. The chair was only a reproduction and now he had a good story to tell about that crazy Mickey Burke. "You're lucky I didn't take the couch," Mickey said, motioning for them to sit. "Come on, rest your asses. I'm going to lay the whole thing out for you and it could get tiring."

They formed a small semicircle around him. When they looked comfortable enough, he continued. "Look, I know we're supposed to do a little small talk here. I'm supposed to ask about your wives, husband, kids, and you're supposed to ask me if I still live at the Wyndham."

"I'm sure we can dispense wih that," said David.

"No. I don't think we should. I think we should have that petty conversation so that none of us gets hurt. David, I don't want you to go home to the little lady tonight and tell her that Uncle Mickey didn't ask about her. How old is she now, David? Let's see, you've been married this time for two years. I remember because you sent me an invitation to your wedding. I thought that was really strange because we have never spent one minute in real life together, so you must have been kissing my ass. Anyway, that's not the point. The point is that I was figuring out your wife's age. She must be nineteen by now." David laughed. "I sure hope you keep up with this one because I don't want to feel guilty about not sending you a present again." David laughed. Keith managed a chuckle and Jennifer smiled. Mickey hated himself for his vitriolic outburst, but he didn't have enough control to stop.

"And how are you, Keith?" he continued. "You still betting on the games?" This time there were low, polite laughs. They had to assume Mickey Burke was kidding or else they would be too offended to be in the same room.

"I have the Rams and six on Sunday." Keith leaned back, thinking his small talk was over.

"That's illegal you know, betting with bookies. It's really hard for me to do business with people who are defying the law." He smiled, confusing them, and then turned to Jennifer. She felt safe since she had no history with this angry little man.

"You don't remember me, Jennifer. But I remember you. You were in school up in Boston when I was. I spoke to you once. No—actually, I was dumb enough to speak to you twice, knowing all along that you had no interest in me. Both times you looked me over and said, 'I'm busy.' I remember because you said it so nicely. It was a sweet rejection, and that was all I could hope for at the time. The problem was, you said you were busy before I even mentioned a date. For me, you would have been busy night and day for the rest of your life." Jennifer tried to remember. She shook her head, as if actually shaking things around inside would make the episode clearer for her.

"I just don't place the incident," she said, sounding worried. Keith and David assumed her worry had to do with what Mickey would say next. They were right. She had told the world that she had graduated from Radcliffe, when actually she had spent her college years at Boston University.

"The past doesn't matter," Mickey said, dismissing his own story.

"Why don't we make it part of the deal that if the network buys this project, you have to go out with me."

"I'm married," Jennifer said, feeling safe.

"That means you don't date?" She smiled weakly. He let it go, but later that day he would call his agent and tell him that he wanted a date with Jennifer Ross written into the contract. She'd never know that he'd gone to Brooklyn College and had only been in Boston for three hours once in his life. He had found out about her lying past from his lawyer friend, Jerry.

"So, what do you have for us today?" Now that they all had been made to shake in their Italian shoes, David felt it was safe to start the meeting.

"Are we starting?" Mickey asked.

"Whenever you're ready."

"First, I want to apologize for my behavior here today. It was abhorrent. I regret that I have insulted you and your loved ones. And if it's any consolation, I'd like you to know that because of my behavior I don't sleep well at nights. I have been fighting my hostility problem for several years, but since it's the source of both my nerve and sense of humor, I find it hard to let go. I know this minor excuse should not give me license to attack those who are kind enough to do business with me. Please forgive me. Please." They were all moved by Mickey's words. Jennifer had felt manipulated at first, but his voice had become so hushed and small during the last couple of sentences that even she was on his side.

Speaking for all of them, David said reassuringly, "Hey, come on. You're forgiven." He turned to his two colleagues. "Is he forgiven, or what?" They nodded their approval to absolve him.

Mickey bowed his head as if he were receiving a blessing. "Thanks. You guys are great." Then he lifted his head and confronted them straight on. "I don't know if I apologized to make you like me or just so you'd buy my idea. I sure as hell know I did it only for my purposes—not to make you feel better. I hate you because you have the right to say yes or no to my idea, and I hate myself for even being here."

No one quite knew what to do. Keith and David had faced the violent Mickey Burke many times before. They could kiss off the past. This time he was getting too close to real feelings. They were willing to laugh with the man. They could take his ridicule. But they couldn't take his being genuine. They didn't want to feel with or for him. Jennifer, who was still involved with her own fears of being shown up as a B.U. coed, had removed herself to the outer circle of what was going on.

"Hey, come on. You're being too hard on yourself. We're having fun here," said David, in an attempt to get the business going.

Mickey became enraged. "Fun? You call this fun? I come up here and abuse you, and that's called fun? There's something wrong with me. We all know that, but I gotta tell you that you're really fucked up if you think what happened here today is fun. I manipulate and humiliate and I don't know why anybody takes it."

"We take it because it's good business to take it. When you come in here and sell us an idea, we invariably make money from it," Jennifer said. She was known as a straight shooter and she was right on target today.

"I don't get one thing," said Mickey. "Who's the hooker: you guys or me?" He had meant to ask a serious question, but they were desperate for something to lighten the mood, so they ended up laughing at the rhythm of the inquiry rather than its content. Mickey, who had been going for the laugh since he was four, was satisfied. He didn't question them further. What he had asked wasn't the deepest question he had ever posed, nor the most bothersome. He leaned his bottom against the windowsill and began trying to make his sale. As he pitched his idea, he sold it with his Brooklyn hands.

"Okay, here we go. Make believe I just walked in." They were all willing to do that in the hopes of hearing Mickey's latest idea. When he began, his voice became spontaneously more ethnic. He became a waiter in a kosher restaurant selling the chicken in the pot. "This is an idea for a half-hour situation comedy. Basically, it's about a family who moves to a new neighborhood. There is a mother, a father, a sister, a brother and a dog." He looked at the three approving. He knew in moments he'd frighten them. "So I have this typical American family. Everything about them is totally normal. Except they're dead." There it was, the bomb.

Still they sat: three people who were too polite and too scared of making the wrong move to leave. "I'd like to call it *Afterlife* or *Whatever Happened to the Beckermans?*" David knew it was time to laugh here. Although his laughter was not infectious, his listeners knew enough to follow suit. "Under the opening titles we'd show a head-on collision between this nice family and a guy and his bimbo. The guy is cheating on his wife when he's in this horrible crash, so he has to spend the afterlife with this blonde he was carting around. The body of the show is about what happens to these people. Everyone can relate because it's like moving to a new neighborhood. I figure the afterlife is not much different from Levittown except for the clouds on the floor. It's not an expensive show, a couple of sets, a cloud machine. Okay. So, after they realize they're dead, all these people are assigned to the same neighborhood, and the two drivers are still furious and blaming each other. You have a built-in dramatic conflict there."

The three network executives were growing interested. Mickey's words were luring them. They could have been repulsed by the subject of death, but here they were, in the hands of a good storyteller, being sold. "Now *Afterlife* is a place," he continued, "where everybody who ever died lands. Just to throw in an interesting statistic here, did you know that there are more people living today than have ever died? . . . Anyway, *Afterlife* is a world of its own, where your neighbors might be a family of shepherds who died years ago or even Freud or Shakespeare. Maybe the older Beckerman kid was studying *Hamlet* in school right before he died, and there's the Bard himself, living a few blocks away. Freud could be asked over to dinner one night because the family is having a tough time adjusting to death. As I told you, the family is typical. Typical in a fifties sort of way. She is the mother with an apron. He's the father in the cardigan sweater, the one who actually puts down the newspaper to talk to his kids.

"The boy is say, sixteen, ready to play basketball, confused about love. Since everybody in *Afterlife* stays the same age as when he died, he could meet his great-great-great-grandmother and fall in love. Also, maybe he wants to sign up for reincarnation, which horrifies the other members of the family since they would rather stay together as a family than take a chance on separating back on earth. We could answer the question, Is there life after death?

"The daughter, who is thirteen, isn't interested in reincarnation because she just can't bear the thought of being a baby again. The reason the family has to border on being stereotypes is that the situation is so weird that the audience needs something very familiar to relate to. They 'live,' and I use the word 'live' loosely, in a little house. The sheep from the shepherd next door keep coming through. The mother takes care of the family the way she would have done on earth. The father has some sort of job that would be death-related, such as working for the Bureau of Reincarnation. This is not a series about death. It's about adjustment to a new environment, although I think it would be reassuring to a lot of people to think that there is a place like this and that, with a good street map, they can find their dear, departed ones." Mickey went back to the window where he began. Before sitting on the ledge, he made his final plea. "Please buy this. I want to write a movie and get out of television because I can't stand it anymore. I need the television money to keep me going."

Customarily, after a writer talks about a project, the network gets to ask questions. Mickey wasn't going to allow for that custom. In the past he had, and that's when he'd thrown things. Therefore, when he finished, he silenced everyone by heading for the door. He turned on the way out. "Look, I know you probably want to know more, but I can't give it to you. It's all in here." He put the pages that Astra Rainbow had typed on the table near the door and left. All the way back to the Wyndham he wondered how offensive he had been. With his head down, shoulders up and both hands in his pockets, he looked like an old man who was fighting the wind. He wasn't old, nor was there wind on this mild October day. The people on the streets of Manhattan let him go by unnoticed. Several million of them would watch one of his shows that night. They would laugh at the people he created and never care about the man who made them happy.

Since Mickey Burke was not in touch with his feelings, he spent the night being lonely and not knowing it. He knew his stomach bothered him and that the corners of his mouth turned down, but he didn't know he needed people. He bought the *Post* from a kid who was screaming out the headline and read it on the toilet, staying in the bathroom, as usual, longer than necessary. (It had been his policy for years to read in the john. He always stayed until he finished the paper, as if reading had been his purpose for sitting on the toilet.) He made the mistake of looking into the bathroom mirror. He saw a sadder man than he would have guessed.

Luckily, there was *Monday Night Football*. He could call the Stage Deli and have a white-meat turkey with Russian dressing sent over. He could put his feet on the bedspread with his shoes on and no one in the hotel would complain about the black heel marks. He could call Jerry and bet on the Rams. He would probably lose, but it would make the game more exciting. Maybe later he would call Shelly Silver. Maybe. She aways sounded too hopeful when he called.

He wouldn't have found Shelly at home. She and Greta had become good friends since the day that Greta announced that she had the guts to drop Barry (after she had caught him with yet another woman). Greta had called at about five-thirty that day and had begged Shelly to come to a Park Avenue A.A. meeting. "You're a fool if you don't," she said. "It's in the best neighborhood, so it has the most successful guys. And if you know anything at all about ex-drunks, you know nine out of ten times their wives leave them. Now they're rehabilitated and just waiting for us. Throw on something red, sweetheart; it'll remind them of Johnnie Walker." Shelly wondered if Paula at Bloomingdale's knew what color to wear around alcoholics.

"But we don't have a drinking problem." The most either of them drank was two glasses of wine. Most of the time they had only one or maybe just a spritzer.

"Yeah, but we have a single-man problem. We go in. We sit down. We throw an eye on the men. There's no rule that says you have to stand up and say you're an alcoholic."

"I don't know. It seems like we're taking advantage of their unfortunate situation."

"We are. And we're way ahead of them. We'll be the only ones there who haven't killed some of our brain cells with scotch."

On the way to the meeting Greta was very excited. Even sitting in the cab, she was once again a massive bird. Her dress was green and the matching hat was green and blue. Her arms flapped, and Shelly had little doubt that she could fly if she really wanted to. "You have no idea how terrific this is going to be," she said, checking her blush in an Estée Lauder compact. "First of all, it's at this great old church, which means there will be tons of Jewish guys. Jews can't resist a good church. Secondly, and I swear on my mother's life about this, it's great that there's a football game tonight. It means that the really compulsive ones will be there, the ones who are determined to give up alcohol. I'm telling you, if they are that determined about one thing, they are determined across the board, and I'm talking money and sex."

Shelly wanted to tell Greta that she thought what they were doing was too desperate, that they should hold their heads higher. But she didn't say anything because some part of her wanted this to be the place where her search would end. Therefore, she too checked the blush before she followed Greta in.

Shelly stayed only twenty minutes. She couldn't lie to the one woman and several seemingly eligible men who asked her how long she had been sober. She waved to Greta to let her know that she was leaving. Greta caught up with her at the curb. "You're crazy to go. The guy I was talking to is worth millions. Really. I read about him in *The Wall Street Journal*. My subscription finally paid off."

"What do you say when they ask how long you've been sober? I can't lie to these people." Shelly's hand was up, summoning a cab. Greta applied the pressure needed to lower it.

"You say, 'It seems as if I've been sober all my life.'" Greta moved her back toward the church. "Come on. It's better than doing nothing about your life. On Thursday we'll go to a G.A. meeting. Those guys are really great. They were rich before they gambled and lost everything, and they have it in them to be rich again."

On nights like this Shelly tried to hate Mickey. How dare he not accept the love she had to give?

# 5

# A Suit the Color
# of a Stormy Day

ASTRA Rainbow woke up thinking about her boss. After typing his television idea, she had decided that he was a genius, or at least a prophet. She knew that he had made up the ideas on those pages that she had rushed to finish, but she had to believe it was all true. His *Afterlife* made much more sense than the heaven and hell the nuns and priests had taught. They were places as foreign to her as Africa. Mr. Burke's *Afterlife* was like Lorain, Ohio. It made sense. Why would people go to such strange places just because they died? Mr. Burke made more sense than the Bible.

In the sixth grade, along with some of her classmates, Rainbow decided to become a nun. Secretly, she told Jesus that she would be married to Him soon. One by one, except for Mary Jane Fortum, the other girls found boys, but Rainbow never wanted boys. Patiently she waited for Jesus to propose. She wrapped towels around her head to see what she'd look like as a Sister and practiced hiding her hands inside her clothing. She was warned that she had to be called to the vocation, so she listened hard, but the sign from Jesus never came to her. She thought He might have forgiven her for killing that little boy, but when He refused to ask for her, she knew she couldn't go into the convent. All during secretarial school she waited for the voice that never came. Obviously, Christ was too careful to take an accidental murderess for a wife. When she moved to New York, it was not only a move to a city, but a step away from the silence.

She was surprised to be thinking of Mr. Burke on a Saturday morning. Mr. Raphelson had said this wasn't necessary. Even at graduation, he reminded his students to work hard, but to clear their minds of business over the weekend so that they could better serve their bosses come Monday morning. Obviously, Mr. Raphelson hadn't counted on any of their employers being as enlightening as Mr. Burke. Since her unfortunate participation in the accidental murder, Astra Rainbow was willing to be shown the way. It didn't seem to matter to her if she were shown it via the Scriptures or via the script for a half-hour situation comedy.

Her thoughts left Mr. Burke when Aunt Emma came into the living room and stood over her. Norman Rockwell would have loved the old lady. She found material for her dresses and her aprons in prints that hadn't been seen since the Yanks won the war. Her thick legs were bound in heavy stockings. Her ankles poured over the black lace-up shoes she had worn for years. She looked as if she had just come in from feeding the chickens, but there she was, asking her niece what she wanted for breakfast right there in Brooklyn.

Astra Rainbow, who was hesitant to spend this kind woman's money, always asked for just a glass of milk. She had tried coffee, in order to be a real working girl, but it didn't do for her what it apparently did for everybody else. Aunt Emma coaxed her into bacon and eggs the way she did every Saturday morning. By a quarter to nine, they sat facing each other at the small kitchen table and were no less a family than anyone else.

"Do you have any plans for your Saturday?" Aunt Emma asked. She watched her niece eat as if she were watching a sporting event. With her loose arms, she cheered for the breakfast to be gone.

Astra Rainbow had plans. She had planned this day since she graduated from school. She was going into Manhattan to buy herself a blue suit and two blouses. Mr. Raphelson had suggested that blue was a good idea for a suit, but the one Granny sewed for her just didn't look like the other girls'. The blue was too bright and the skirt went out at the ends while everyone else's managed to go straight down. And Granny had always had a problem with bunching. For the last three Saturdays, Rainbow had gone to Saks Fifth Avenue and chosen the things she would buy when she had enough money saved. Today was that day. "I'm going to get that suit," said Astra while trying to get equal amounts of egg and bacon on her fork. She had always felt she had done a bad job when breakfast didn't come out even.

"How nice." Aunt Emma picked up her coffee mug in both of her hands. They were soft and puffy and seemed more like cloth hands than real ones. "I used to shop in the city."

"You did?" Rainbow was surprised. It seemed as if her great-aunt had never shopped.

"Oh yes. I've been to Saks Fifth Avenue quite a number of times. It's so big. It's an entire city block. Believe me, if you can't find what you need there, you're not looking right." Aunt Emma was good at remembering. She always had a slight smile that let you know she was picturing things exactly right. "I know Saks. Sure I know Saks," she said, remembering the large store where she had bought her sister a scarf for Christmas many years before.

"Do you want to come?"

"Oh, no, dear. You go. I have work to do." Aunt Emma always had work to do. Astra Rainbow had convinced her to let her help with the laundry, cleaning and grocery shopping. Still she always had work, some of it invented. Not one other person in the entire building scrubbed the hallway floor and walls outside his door. Rainbow had tried to convince her aunt to come with her on other Saturdays. It was futile. She always had work to do. Each week she refused loudly and with a laugh that said it was an absurd idea for her to take the day off.

When she was ready to leave, Rainbow checked her wallet three times to see that the money she had saved was still there. Maybe she would buy a pink blouse. Mr. Burke might like that, having a secretary with a pink blouse. Since she had started working, she had only spent money on the absolute necessities and managed to save the rest of her paycheck. She had offered Aunt Emma rent but had been consistently refused. The older woman stood by the sink, her head bowed over her pots as if at an altar. "Now what would I want your money for?" she said. "I've managed to pay rent on this place for a hundred years! I want you to stay as long as you'd like. It sure is comforting to this old soul to have someone next to me to watch the TV. So, don't you go and put any money near me. You understand, honey?"

Astra Rainbow soothed her conscience by buying things for the apartment. She bought flowers, and when she realized there was nothing to put them in, she ran to Lamston's and bought a little glass vase. She spruced up the bathroom by buying a new shower curtain, toilet-seat cover and rug. When she brought them home, Aunt Emma stood in the doorway of her old bathroom with the stained and chipped tiles and marveled at the minor transformation. "It looks right out of one of those beautiful magazines," she said.

These small, well-deserved luxuries didn't dent Astra Rainbow's bank account as much as rent would have. By the time she went to do her real shopping, she had three hundred and fifty-six dollars in her wallet. Since she had never accumulated any money before, she considered it a large fortune. Her intention was to spend it all.

On the way to the subway she ran into a sixteen-year-old neighbor, a black girl who came by with a bag of taco chips and gossip every once in a while. The girl loved lying on the floor of Aunt Emma's apartment, wrapping her brown curls around her finger and talking

about her latest boyfriend. There had been three since Astra Rainbow
had known her. They all started out as "really nice hunks" and ended
up as "dumb perverts."

"How're you doing, Mary?" The girl was leaning against the only
tree on their block. She wore a long wool scarf that was longer than
she was, and since it was wrapped around her neck more than once,
her head looked as if it were emerging from a purple tube and had
nothing to do with her body. She did the best she could to look
fashionable, but all her clothing was always dirty.

"I'm not doing so hot." When anybody inquired about Mary's well-
being, she was either doing "unbelievably fantastic" or "not so hot."
Even though Rainbow had heard these two responses frequently since
she had met the girl, she always responded to them. Her face saddened
immediately. Mary, being a child, did nothing to allay her fears.

"What's the matter, darlin'?" asked Rainbow. Mary loved to be
called "darlin'." Nobody ever called her anything but Mary, and when
they did they always sounded as if they were yelling. Even the boys
who tried to get into her pants didn't bother to call her "darlin'."
The ones who made their way in sometimes called her "baby," but
she didn't like that. It reminded her that what they were doing could
produce a baby. They trusted rubbers, but she certainly did not.
Balloons break.

"Eddie's the matter. Did I tell you about Eddie?"

"No. You told me about Carlos."

"Carlos is a fart. He tells me to meet him on the roof, which I don't
want to do 'cause who knows with all that kissing and rubbing when
you're gonna lose your mind and fall to your death. So, I meet him
up there anyway and we do it and it's okay. I mean it don't send me
to heaven like he say it would, but who am I going to complain to?
Anyhow, next thing I know he got his dick up Mary Flores. What he
think, just because we got the same first name, we both going to take
him in whenever he want? Like hell." Mary talked in an aggravated
tone, as if Astra Rainbow had suggested that Carlos was worthy.

"And that's why you're blue?"

"Fuck no. Carlos can leave it in little Miss Hole forever. I don't
care about either one of those shitheads, but if I catch Eddie around
here without his big-shot friends, I'm gonna cut off his dick and throw
the rest away." It dawned on Mary that this was a funny concept and
she laughed, bringing a mittened hand up to cover her mouth. She
was missing a bicuspid and never let her laughter go uncovered.

"So, what's bothering you, Mary? You want to walk me to the
subway and tell me about it?"

"Where you going?"

"Into Manhattan to buy some clothes for my job." They had started the short walk toward the subway. Mary walked backward, facing Rainbow. Since her leg warmers were stretched out and had a tendency to fall down, she pulled them up approximately every dozen steps. She never got annoyed with them and accepted their falling as if that was her fate.

"You're gonna pay double for whatever you're gonna get over there." She pointed in a definite direction. She didn't know exactly where Manhattan was from there, but pointing seemed necessary.

"But that's where the suit I want is. It's on the third floor at Saks Fifth Avenue."

"Saks? Are you crazy? You can get the exact same thing on the Lower East Side for like no money at all. Do you know how much they tack on for the Saks label? Like a hundred dollars or something like that."

Astra Rainbow had quickened her step, causing Mary to take fast little skips backward. She gave up on the leg warmers, letting them hang over her sneakers. Occasionally she tripped, but she always regained her balance and never broke stride. When they got to street corners, she waited, her back to the traffic, trusting Rainbow to guide them both across.

"I like Saks Fifth Avenue. I think it's a quality store."

"But they got the exact same stuff on Orchard Street," Mary pleaded.

"It couldn't be exactly the same because if it was *exactly* the same, why would Saks Fifth Avenue charge more? I've been there two—no, three—times now, and everyone there looked very honest to me. Of course I have never seen the owners, but it seems to me that they couldn't be bad people to have lasted this long."

"And I'm telling you, they're crooks."

"Then how come the government hasn't put them in jail?" Astra Rainbow stopped and waited for an answer, feeling that her question had made such a strong point that the argument was over. She had not counted on Mary's street smarts.

"That kind of crook never gets caught. All they ever catch are the little thieves, the black ones and the P.R.'s who go around lifting things without looking over their shoulder. I'm telling you, as sure as I'm born, those people from Manhattan don't never get theyselves behind bars." Now it was Mary who was sure that she had ended the argument.

"I'm still going up there," said Astra Rainbow. "It's a wonderful place. In this one building they have everything I would ever want. They even have bathing suits in the middle of the winter." Mary had not given up her fight. She pulled her dirty pink hat securely down on her head, hiding most of her hard, dark curls. She turned around to link arms with Rainbow and led her toward the subway.

"How about if we make a deal? I take you to the Lower East Side just so you can take yourself a look. They don't got what you like, and I keep my mouth shut." She demonstrated how shut her mouth would be by doing it, her lips held tightly together. It seemed to take all her energy.

"You're sure they have exactly the same merchandise? I want a suit the color of a stormy day." Mary, who was not sympathetic toward Astra Rainbow's poetic side, sighed as if she had a burden to bear.

"They got any color you want down there. You think they don't have the same colors downtown as they do uptown? It's the same exact stuff only the manufacturers, see, they got brains, so the stuff that's a little irregular, that the asshole places on Fifth Avenue won't take because their cunt customers would complain about a little missing button, they sell to the places on the Lower East Side and the smart people buy them." Astra Rainbow stopped walking. Mary, her arm still linked to her friend's, tried to pull her ahead, but Rainbow wasn't budging.

"I thought they had the same things and now you're talking about buttons missing."

"It's a big nothing. The signs say 'slightly irregular.' " She emphasized "slightly." The word took her twice as long to say as any other. Astra Rainbow became very serious. She hugged her purse in front of her and thought carefully about what she was going to say before she spoke.

"I don't want anything irregular."

"Why not, when it can save you real cash?"

"Mary, I would never want anything irregular in my life. Irregular is wrong. I just don't want anything damaged near me. You understand?" Astra Rainbow was as serious as Mary had ever seen her. She didn't know that her friend's entire quest in life was to be regular.

"Somethin' troubling you? You gotta tell me what."

"Nothing is wrong." Rainbow continued walking, hoping that would end the discussion.

"You don't sound like it. You sound almost crazy, and you gotta tell me on account of I tell you everything, like we was real friends." Rainbow's stride was long and Mary, who was only five-one and still growing, struggled to keep up.

"I can't tell you."

"Why? On account of it's so terrible?"

"Yes." And she saw the boy go off the cliff again.

"You'd be surprised at what's so terrible. There are kids in this neighborhood who got it from their daddies when they were nine. There are brothers who are up their sister's skirts every day, and practically everybody I know got themselves knived or burned or something just as bad, so don't go around telling me that what you got in your life is so terrible. The whole street has been in the hospital at least once."

"Mine is different."

Mary stopped and stood in front of Rainbow, preventing her from going on. "You think you're different or better than we all? I'm telling you, sure as I'm in this here street, that what you got to say is no better and no worse than anybody in the whole area can say." Mary was emphatic about this statement. And she was right. They lived on a street of hidden horrors where crimes were committed right in the home in front of, and often to, the children of the household.

"I think this is different because . . . well . . ."

"Yeah, so? You think I'm some kind of hero or something? One time, before I know it, I hurt my sister so bad, she hadda go to emergency. My whole family beens at emergency one time or another. She kept walking around on my things. She got her footprints on everything. I was supposed to be drawing a map of these here United States. I got this big piece of cardboard, only it was too big to put on the bed and so I put it right there on the floor and everything was going fine excepting I couldn't get Florida to look right. It kept looking like this big, long dick. It was pretty good though. I used to look at it all the time because I couldn't believe that I drew the whole United States. So, it was all good for a while excepting my sister Lucinda, she kept walking on it.

"She was only about six years old, but I know kids and she was old enough not to walk on something important. And the first few times all I did was like yell at her and hit her on the back. And she'd go running off to Mama, screeching about how I hurt her, thinkin' she was gonna get me in so much trouble. I tell you that was the one good thing about my old lady drinking. She would nod at the kid who was complaining like she was listening and sympathizing and all. But she never got up off her chair, so what good was it?

"The point of my story here is not about that fucking map. Lucinda done walk on it the day before I was going to hand it in and she got a big foot mark on California. And I got totally pissed 'cause I tell you, Rainbow, the whole country looked ruined to me. This time I went to my ma, and why I was expecting something different I don't know. She was sittin' in the only chair she ever sits in and she had a glass of ice in her hand. I guess the whiskey went fast. So what else is new? And I was crying and telling her how my whole school life was ruined and that she better do something about Lucinda, who would probably turn out to be a criminal because she was doing all these things purposely.

"And I got the answer I shoulda known I was going to get. She was watching *The Price is Right* and she didn't say a word. She just kept moving her glass telling me to get out of the room. So, I leave and I take a sock at Lucinda, which I do practically every day of our lives, but this time, I get her right in the throat and she starts gagging and making this funny sound and I start yelling at her to stop. A lot of dumb has happened right to me, but that's the dumbest thing I've ever done to another thing. I hadda take her to emergency, and they made her cough and swallow. She coulda died."

The story might have been some comfort to Astra Rainbow had the victim not recovered, but since her own story ended with a death, she was once more convinced that she was the freak. Everyone else had stories about accidents that left survivors. She had caused tragedy beyond repair.

"Well, I'm glad your sister was okay."

"Oh, yeah. She was okay. We had taco chips that night."

By now they were at the subway and Rainbow expected to descend into the underworld of transportation by herself. She was surprised that Mary was following her. A look in the young girl's direction brought forth an explanation.

"I'm going up to Saks with you. I'm gonna go because I ain't never seen anybody buy anything in one of those stores. It'll be like some kind of learning experience for me." When Rainbow hesitated, Mary quickly added, "And I ain't even tole you about Eddie yet." She flew past her friend and was down the stairs, heading for the turnstiles, before Rainbow could say no again. The older girl didn't bother asking Mary if she had told anybody where she was going. She had asked her once if her mother knew where she was, and Mary had said, "Most of the time my mother doesn't know where *she* is."

Eddie was dealt with on the train. As Mary put it, "He's a scumball. He fucks you one day and then he don't even let you copy his homework the next." Since it was Saturday and most of the commuters had the good sense to stick to their own neighborhoods, the train was almost empty. In their car was an elderly Puerto Rican woman who seemed happy enough with the shopping bag between her legs, a thin black man with a frightening cough, and four teenage girls dressed in short skirts and rhinestones. One would have to assume that they were going out that night and had dressed for the occasion seven hours early. Even though there were plenty of seats, Mary preferred standing. She was a sixteen-year-old girl with too much energy to sit. She clasped an overhead bar, swaying with the train, hanging over Astra Rainbow and entertaining her with stories of Eddie.

Since Astra Rainbow was a virgin, one would have thought that she would have disdained the idea of hearing the escapades of a

teenage girl who seemed to have a lot of fun but few morals. But
Astra Rainbow had spent the early years of her life traveling around
the country with her mother, a woman who not only believed in free
love, but also encouraged it. Rainbow had often awakened to sounds
of bodies making each other happy. Through the bars of her crib in
the light of dawn or dusk she saw her naked mother and the naked
man beside, under, or on top of, her, illuminated by the light. Her
earliest trauma was witnessing the sex act, a scene to which she never
became accustomed but always expected to see. There were always
naked bodies doing things to each other in her early life, sometimes
in darkened bedrooms, other times in the sunlight. Her mother had
made some small effort to avoid Rainbow's watching. She always
chose times when she thought her little girl was sleeping, busy or
focused on something else. But Rainbow did watch, and sometimes—
twice, in fact—she screamed. Other times she pretended to herself
that the two grown-ups were taking a nap together. It always frightened her. The men looked as if they were too big, as if they would
crush her mother. She wanted to tell them that her mommy would
get hurt and that they had better jump off. Once she did and both
her mother and the man laughed. They laughed for so long that Rainbow closed her eyes, pretending she didn't know what had caused
their amusement.

After that, the child closed every door that would shut her away
from the naked bodies. She didn't know why she didn't want to see
what was going on, but she didn't like any of it, not the strange noises
or the way the bodies looked or the smell of those cigarettes that
always made everyone silly. She didn't even like the giggles that
emanated from these beds. They were intimate sounds that didn't
include her, and she didn't get the joke. Most of the time her mother
had put her outside the room before this strange thing happened, but
sometimes it took so long she wandered in. The men didn't want her
there. Although only a couple yelled for her to get out, they usually
asked her mommy to get her to leave. "Go on, Astra Rainbow. You
be good," Helen Blakely told her daughter. Rainbow didn't exactly
know what being good was. She supposed that it meant not watching
what the naked people were doing. She tried to be good, but sometimes there were people she didn't even know in other rooms doing
the same things.

By the time she was four, none of this seemed strange. In her earliest
years she had been frightened by it, and although the fright continued
she had learned that the same people who were doing strange naked
things soon stood up, put on their clothes and paid attention to her
again. It was when she realized that things did go back to normal
when people stood up that she stopped grabbing her mommy's hand

and no longer tried to rescue her by pulling her out of bed. The acts of sex had become so much a part of the little girl's life that she learned not to worry about them and only interrupted her mommy when she got hungry. Astra was told that her mother would be out to help her soon, and she always was. Many times after the rolling around in beds, on couches and sometimes on floors, there was food for everyone. Immodest people, including her mother, stood around the refrigerator continuing to gratify themselves. Astra Rainbow ate with them. The sex always scared her, but out of necessity she lived with it. Her granny said that they lived like dogs, and she supposed they had.

Mary, who heard Astra Rainbow wanted to be a nun, was sure that she was shocking her. She loved telling her about her boyfriends and their successful attempts to have sex with her. She looked for a sign— a worried brow, a slight gasp, downcast eyes. But she looked in vain. "How come what I'm telling you doesn't make you think that I'm havin' too good a time or something? How come you not carrying on for me to stop?" Mary had once asked. And Rainbow had no answer. She had no restrictions for anyone but herself. When Mary asked questions like, "So, do you think Eddie is a fuck, or what?" Astra Rainbow didn't have the knowledge to answer. She had spent her first six years in a world where people exchanged flesh for no reason at all. Sometimes they just happened to lie down together. She had no idea whether to condemn Eddie.

"I don't know," she said when the train had stopped. Mary was pissed at her response. She had come to a friend for sympathy, and she was getting the truth instead.

"How can you not know? I'm telling you the guy is a fuck. I'm telling you that right to your face and you got all the facts, and here you is curling your face up and trying to think up the truth when you already know the absolute truth."

"I know that you wanted to copy his homework and that you really should do your own. Teachers give homework so that their students can practice what they learned in class." Astra Rainbow was not a righteous person. She delivered this speech without lecturing. Still, it made Mary itchy. Agitated, she arose and draped herself around the pole that was there to support passengers. Since she wasn't getting verbal help, she had to lean on something. She did everything possible with her body to let Rainbow know she was exasperated.

"You are some weird lady. Here I am telling you about all these guys who keep coming in and out of my body and even my friend Jeannie who is seventeen and a half thinks maybe I'm a little crazy in that area on account of once I did it with a guy who is twelve 'cause I really felt sorry for him. But you! You hear all my stuff and you never think it's wrong when the whole world talks about sinning and stuff. I haven't been to confession since I lost it. Can you imagine some priest sitting there and listening to all this junk about me lifting my skirt and pulling down my pants whenever some guy feels like it?" She left the pole now and stood right in front of Rainbow. She threw her scarf back over her shoulder before delivering the climax to her speech. "But that's not my point. My point is that all this time ever since we became friends, you don't tell me, 'Mary, you crazy to do that,' or 'Mary, you gonna burn in hell for that.' I know I'm gonna burn, but I forget when I'm doing it. What I'm asking is, how come you don't think I'm going to hell?" It was a serious question. Mary had found the one person who knew all about her and didn't condemn her. Astra Rainbow made her feel that maybe her soul could be saved.

"Maybe there is no hell. Maybe there's a place called Afterlife where everybody goes once they're dead."

"Yeah. Sure. Who says so?"

"Mr. Burke wrote about it, pages and pages. It's got houses and you get to meet famous dead people like Joan of Arc."

"Do you get to fuck?" The smile behind the ratty mitten was there again.

"I guess so."

"Do you have babies?"

"No. People are born alive and everybody there is dead."

"Wow, fucking without babies. What a great place. No wonder you crazy about this Mr. Burke." Astra Rainbow didn't know her caring showed. She turned her face toward the train window and looked at the passing blackness. Mary, who had learned how to tease before she learned how to tie her shoes, saw that she had embarrassed her friend. She had never before let an opportunity to tease go, and she wasn't mature enough to let it go now. She slid into the seat next to her victim.

"You blushing?"

"I was just looking."

"Yeah. Sure. It's real interesting looking at a tunnel with rats in it. I'm thinking that you're hot for this guy and you don't even know it." Mary enjoyed the thought of Astra Rainbow, with her puritanical blouses with high necks and long sleeves, being hot for someone.

"He's my boss."

"Yeah, but you talk about him like he's God or something. You even got him inventing heaven and hell."

"I didn't make that up. He wrote about it."

"I've been hearing 'Mr. Burke this' and 'Mr. Burke that.' Now you looking up, like into the sky, and telling me he knows more than Father Monte does. Father Monte, he thinks you can go to hell just for kissing a boy three times and letting him put a tongue in your mouth. So what makes you think that your boss knows more than Father Monte?" Mary challenged Astra Rainbow with her whole being. She hung on to her hat with one hand and pointed with the other.

"Father Monte was only taught one thing," Rainbow said simply. "He learned about heaven and hell, so that's what he feels he has to preach to you. Maybe Mr. Burke knows something that the rest of the world doesn't."

"There you go again. When you gonna admit you want to lay down for the guy?" Mary laughed like a bad actress.

These two girls from Brooklyn walked through the Saturday shoppers. Most of them were experienced and they balanced their purchases no less gracefully than native women balanced water from the well. They brought corners of their dresses out of the bags, just a sleeve of a dress, so the girl at the stocking counter would find the right color rust. They fought to get waited on, and, as in any jungle, the rule was survival of the fittest. Those with the loudest requests and the longest arms were helped first.

It was Rainbow's intention to go directly to the third floor. Mary followed behind, touching everything within her reach. If a bottle of perfume stood on the counter, she squeezed it. If a hat was on a rack, she tried it on. Rainbow took everything out of Mary's hands and urged her toward the escalator. On their way up, Mary reminded her friend, in a voice meant for the streets, that this place was full of robbers. "I could get any of this stuff for like nothing. You know that belt with the silver on it? They're asking a hundred and seventy-five for it and I swear to Saint Anne, I seen it for nineteen bucks on Fourteenth Street. They fuck you in this place." By the time they got up to the third floor, Mary had told everyone who was traveling with them on the escalator that they were wasting their cash. They heard her, but they tried not to look at this loud little black girl dressed in colors too bright for uptown.

Astra Rainbow went directly to the blue suit that she had saved for. She made sure it was a size six and that there were no damages. A young, somewhat ambitious salesgirl saw that she might have a sale and asked her if she wanted to try it on.

"No thank you. I've already tried it on. I was here last week."

"Do you want it?" the salesgirl asked, already leaving the black girl out of any conversation.

Mary made some clucking sound in the back of her throat that was supposed to tell Astra Rainbow that she was a fool if she did.

"I want it if it's exactly like what all the other secretaries are wearing. You know, if it's normal."

Both Mary and the salesgirl were confused by Astra Rainbow's answer.

"If it's 'normal'?" asked the salesgirl. She was disappointed. She thought she had an easy sale and now she was faced with this strange question.

"I just want to make sure that it's perfectly ordinary before I buy it." The clothes her grandmother made her were plain, but Granny wasn't a good enough tailor to make them look like everyone else's clothes.

"She could get the same thing for twenty-nine bucks downtown," said Mary accusingly. The salesgirl ignored her.

"I guess it's ordinary. I mean it's just a blue suit, with this normal skirt and this normal jacket. I mean there's nothing unusual about it. If you want something unusual, I can show you some really great things. We have this red jacket with black trim that's really different." The salesgirl headed for the red jacket, but Astra Rainbow stopped her.

"No, I don't want something unusual. If you're sure this is normal and ordinary, I'll take it." To Mary, she explained, "I just want to be like everybody else."

"You're too pretty, Rainbow. You can't be," said Mary. Astra Rainbow heard her, but didn't want to believe it. Being pretty had just given her the opportunity to be closer to boys, not to Jesus.

"Well, you're very lucky. It could have been sold," said the salesgirl, writing up the sale. Rainbow reached for her wallet. She had never believed she was lucky, and this salesgirl wasn't going to convince her.

"Yeah. Sure. It's real lucky to be robbed blind in a place like this," said Mary in a voice that threatened everyone who heard her.

While Astra Rainbow paid the hundred and sixty-seven dollars and sixty-four cents for the suit, Mary cradled her head in her arms in despair. She did this right in front of the cash register, moaning about the money and swearing about the bargains she could have gotten. Rainbow hadn't noticed that her friend looked shabby, but others did. To them she was a poor black girl who had lost her way in Saks. They checked to see that their pocketbooks were closed.

They didn't leave the store until Astra Rainbow bought two blouses, a skirt and a sweater. In each case, she wanted confirmation that the things she was buying were normal and ordinary. "I just want to look regular," she told Millie Morgan, who had been working at Saks for over twenty-five years. Millie looked at the plain white cotton blouse. "Darling," she said, "I started working here in 1962 and I've been here in blouses for eight and a half years. I'm telling you, this little shirt here—I must have sold thousands of them. It's a mainstay. It never goes out of style." That was good enough for Rainbow, who was happy to pay forty-four dollars for it. Mary said she was going to throw up because the one thing she knew for sure was that they were practically giving away white blouses for nothing downtown. She told Millie Morgan that they were charging four dollars for the blouse and forty for the label. Millie looked at the child and said, "So what am I supposed to do?"

Rainbow couldn't wait to get home. She wanted to release her new clothes from the paper and bags that bound them and look at them the way one would look at a newly purchased painting. She wouldn't wear them until work on Monday, but until then, her clothes would be watched and admired. She would lay them out on the chairs in the living room for Aunt Emma to see and she hoped they would stay there until Sunday night when the small apartment would be in order again. On Monday morning she would wear the suit with the white shirt, and for the first time in her life she would look like everyone else. Feeling ordinary would be her greatest accomplishment.

She had hoped to be home by six because Aunt Emma started looking for her when the sky darkened, and she didn't want the old lady to have any unnecessary fears. Rainbow never worried about the dark because she felt whatever harm was out there she deserved. She didn't make it home by six. Because of Mary Johnson she didn't make it home until midnight.

They had stopped briefly on their way out to watch a lady in a pink smock apply makeup to a young woman who kept saying that her husband was going to kill her. The makeup artist ignored her victim and approached her with royal blue on her finger tips. The woman in the chair recoiled from the luminescence of the color that was about to be placed on her eyelids. Unfortunately, she didn't have the courage to leave the high chair on which she was being displayed. The woman in the smock turned to Rainbow for confirmation. "This is the most subtle makeup in the world," she said. "The trick is to blend it in." Astra Rainbow, who wore only lipstick, understood. She nodded, giving both women the courage to go on.

As they pushed their way through the revolving doors and headed toward Fifth Avenue, Rainbow was thinking of whether they should buy two pretzels or share one. Her thoughts of pretzels were interrupted by the commotion she heard behind her. Mary was screaming about goddamn fuckers, but at first Rainbow didn't react because Mary was always screaming about fuckers. Rainbow turned around to see that two large men had each grabbed one of Mary's arms and led her back into the store. Rainbow had no idea why. She assumed that Saks Fifth Avenue had been insulted once too often by the brazen teenager and that they were going to ask her never to come back.

Astra Rainbow followed the man and Mary back into the store. This time they passed through the ground floor quickly. Mary was being dragged. She didn't fight her captors physically. She had learned in life that men were stronger than she was and they could take her where they wanted her to be. She did scream, however. Hundreds of Saturday shoppers heard her words. "Listen, you motherfuckin' crooks," she yelled. "You're the real crooks around here. They think you can get away with cheating peoples their whole life. Lady," she yelled to someone who was buying an expensive bottle of perfume, "lady, I can get that for you, no problem, for three bucks." On seeing the woman hand over her charge card, she fell apart. "Why you want to do that, lady? Why you want to give these robbers more than they deserve?" Astra Rainbow was not embarrassed. She knew the pain of sin but had never learned what shame was about.

The two men pulled Mary into the freight elevator and didn't seem to notice or mind that Rainbow came with them. Once they got to wherever they were taking the crying girl, Rainbow was sure she could explain that Mary was irritated. They would understand that the girl was poor and why she was being verbally abusive to their store. She would promise not to bring Mary there again, and they would have a pretzel apiece and go home.

They took Mary to an office on the sixth floor and, although they never acknowledged Rainbow, they let her stay. Mary was led to an office chair and told not to move. "I gotta go to the bathroom," she said, in the voice a pleading four-year-old would use. Her request was ignored. Rainbow was beginning to think that maybe Mary was right: The people from Saks Fifth Avenue were not a very understanding group.

Before Astra Rainbow could begin to convince either of the men of the importance of bathroom rights, they were joined by another suited man and a female officer in uniform. Rainbow knew it was time to speak up. "I don't think what you're doing here is fair. I understand that my friend shouldn't have gone through your store criticizing your prices, but you have to realize that she really believes she can get the exact same merchandise for less money. I don't think she talked anybody out of buying anything here. Most of the people she talked to just thought she was crazy. Why don't you just let her go now, and I promise I'll never bring her back?"

They weren't paying attention to her. They were putting handcuffs on Mary and trying to get some basic information from her. Astra Rainbow rushed on with her defense. "But I'll be back. I really like it here and I think you have fine goods at a fine price." Still they didn't listen to her. They kept demanding more details from Mary, her name, her age, how long she had been in the store. Mary was sobbing too loudly to answer. Rainbow was ready to take her friend by the hand, take her away from these people who were badgering her, when she saw why Mary was in trouble. The female police officer was emptying the girl's pockets. Mary may have hated the store, but she had apparently taken a lot of it with her. The first item Rainbow noticed was the blue eye shadow that the woman in the pink smock had been using.

Everything from the girl's pockets hit the table loudly, clanking against it, seeming to shout Mary's guilt. Even the gold chain made a louder noise than Rainbow would have expected. She became quiet and went to hold one of Mary's handcuffed hands, but she was intercepted by one of the security guards. The other one led her to the corner. He spoke so softly she could hardly hear what he was saying. "Miss," he said, "your friend here is in a lot of trouble. After we search your bags you'll be free to go."

"I wouldn't leave her." Rainbow spoke as softly as her informer.

"That'll be up to you, miss. I'm sure the store will press charges because your friend there took, by my account, this is not an official figure you understand, but I have a pretty good eye, and my eye tells me that she was trying to walk off with over five hundred dollars in goods. So, the problem is, miss, that we're not talking about petty theft, and my experience tells me that they are going to detain your friend for quite a while. I would just go home as soon as I can, miss, and maybe try to get your friend here some legal help."

"I'll pay for the things she took. I bought a lot of things today and if I return them . . ."

"They're not looking for payment. They're looking to do the right thing by the store."

"But she's only a little girl, and she's scared. I work. Maybe they would let me pay for everything she took. I could bring my check right over as soon as I get it."

"I'm afraid that won't be possible, miss. You see, the theft has already occurred." Astra Rainbow had no argument for this man. When he took her shopping bags away, she let them go easily. She knew he would find nothing unpaid for. She had been innocent most of her life and had once left a quarter in the street because the owner might remember where he lost it. Knowing this, each time she saw the guard remove the tissue paper from the things she bought, she felt violated. Her packages were supposed to be opened at home, the purchases smoothed out and enjoyed. Here they were in the oversized hands of a stranger. When the man put them back in the bags, he did the best he could, but he didn't know how to fold clothes the same way the salesgirls did. Before, she had felt she was carrying wonderful, new things. Now it looked as if her shopping bags contained laundry.

When he had finished his search, the man went back to the others and explained in his annoyingly soft voice that Astra Rainbow had not done any shoplifting. Heads nodded and instructions were delivered. "You are free to leave, miss," he said. "I will be happy to escort you back to the elevator."

"No. I can't. I've got to stay with her. Please. I've got to." Once again he went back to the others. There was another slow walk and long conference. She was far enough away from the others so that the investigation looked like some silent film. After nodding his head, he came back slowly; his gum-soled shoes made no sound.

"You can stay right here then, miss. If the store presses charges and they take your friend to the station, then you're going to have to ask the arresting officer for permission to go along. My guess, and I'm guessing from nine years of experience here at Saks and twelve at Klein's down on Fourteenth Street, is that they will let you go to the station, but not in the official car. You are going to have to take your own vehicle there at your own expense."

It took almost an hour to finish the business of charging Mary. Each item that she had stolen had to be verified and priced by Saks personnel, which sometimes took several phone calls to the various departments, and two sets of forms had to be filled out, one by the store and one for the City of New York. The girl sat quietly. Her head was down, her knees together, and her feet apart. Her toes faced each other. She mumbled that she didn't know how these things had gotten into her pockets, that somebody must have put them there. She spoke to her own lap, not making a plea to defend herself, but as if sending a wistful message. She asked to go to the bathroom again. This time her request was granted. The female officer led her past Astra Rainbow. "I was gonna give you the lipstick," she said to her friend as she passed. She was gone before Rainbow could thank her. She would have been grateful even for the unwanted gift, because Astra Rainbow was one of the few people on earth who could appreciate intent. Christ should have married her.

With Mary out of the room, nobody did anything. The suspect's leaving was a cue to take a break. That meant getting coffee in Styrofoam coffee cups from a machine down the hall and talking among themselves. The guards were concerned about the end of daylight saving time that night. They reminded each other that they would get an extra hour of sleep because you spring ahead in the spring and fall back in the fall. There was some confusion as to whether it would really be ten when it was eleven or if it would really be twelve. No one liked the idea of the days getting dark earlier. When the conversation ended, they finished their coffee and crushed their cups. Astra Rainbow felt it was time to put in a word for Mary.

"I hope," she said, "that the punishment will fit the crime."

They all thought they had heard correctly, but the male cop chose to verify it. "Ma'am?" he asked.

"I was just hoping out loud that the punishment would fit the crime. I was watching *60 Minutes* a couple of weeks ago, and a man had been in prison seven years for one marijuana cigarette. Well, maybe he had had more, but they only caught him with one. He was so severely broken that I've been thinking about him these past couple of weeks. And now that Mary is in trouble I'm only hoping that the punishment fits the crime, exactly." There was nothing more to say, and she didn't expect a response. Mary and her captor were back before she could get one anyway. The girl had regained a measure of her usual spunk in the ladies' room, and when directed toward her chair, she told the cop to leave her fucking hands off her. She knew her rights and she didn't have to get shoved around by no dyke copper.

By six o'clock, the arresting officers, Mary and Astra Rainbow were in the Seventeenth Precinct on Fifty-first Street. Rainbow had followed in a cab. "Get me a lawyer," Mary had screamed as she was taken for fingerprints. "Get me the best Jewish one who went to one of them big schools like in *The Paper Chase.* He's gotta get down here before one of these dykes uses a dildo on me, so get him fast." No one tried to keep Mary quiet. They did what they had to to book her and told her that she would be allowed her one call for legal defense. They handled her precisely, but not roughly. Her large gestures made it look as if she were being harassed. Rainbow read the situation correctly and didn't try to rescue her friend from the law. She obeyed Mary's instructions and headed for the phone, but once she got there she realized she didn't know a lawyer to call. She called Aunt Emma and told her what happened. The dear sweet lady misunderstood and thought the two young ladies were still shopping. Aunt Emma was happy they were having fun.

Her second call was to Mary's mother. Rainbow explained that her daughter was in a bit of trouble and that they were at the police station. She told Mrs. Johnson the address and carefully and slowly explained how she could get there. She spelled out the street names and told her how far she would have to walk. When Rainbow said she would see her soon and to please bring a lawyer, Mrs. Johnson said, "No. I'm not coming. I have no pencil." She hung up without saying good-bye.

There was only one other telephone number in the city that Astra Rainbow knew. Mr. Raphelson had told his girls never to call their bosses at home unless they were sure that it was important for business reasons. He cited an example of the secretary working late typing out a report. The boss has already left. The phone rings and a very important client needs to talk about a carload of televisions for sale at half price that must be picked up that night. In a case such as this, when the call related directly to cash, the boss could be called at home, but only by the secretary. She must never give his telephone number to anybody. On the final exam, question sixty-three had read: "You may call your boss at home if (a) you have a question to ask about the report you are typing. (b) you want to let him know you are finished and that everything is fine. (c) you want to ask permission to come in late the next morning because you worked so late. (d) someone called with an offer for your boss that means cash in his pocket."

Out of the twenty-three students in the class, only Carol Tyler got it wrong. She was sure that you could call with a question about the report. The other twenty-two future secretaries of America understood that you only called when it directly related to money. Now here was Astra Rainbow with a quarter in her hand trying to convince herself that Mr. Raphelson had never anticipated a situation such as Mary Johnson in trouble. Where she and he came from, teenagers stole only the smallest things from the drugstore. The small-town owner informed the parents, and the children, shamed, were forced to bring things back. The worst part was promising Mr. Bell, who smelled like rubbing alcohol, that you'd never do it again. None of the people back home would ever come close to understanding stealing from Saks Fifth Avenue and getting caught with gold chains in your pocket.

# 6

# A Bad Cold

MICKEY Burke woke up that same Saturday morning with a bad cold. He had to pee, but he couldn't find the energy to throw back the covers and he didn't want to freeze on his way to the bathroom. He needed a mother. What he wanted most was a hand on his forehead—a mother's hand, attached to a mother. She would be worried. She would fluff his pillows and give him the medicines he needed and not even ask him to talk. He needed his mother or Mother Teresa and neither one of them was likely to show.

Slowly, like a grandfather, he made his way to the bathroom, using chairs as railings as he went. When he returned to bed he was tired. He tried to sleep. Instead, he obsessed. He hated being sick on Saturday. When you were sick during the week, you got to stay home from school and run your cars over the mountains that were really your knees. Your friends were in school, but you never thought that anything went on without you. Time was suspended while you had your mother and your Aunt Minn all to yourself. If you got sick on Saturday, however, it was nothing but punishment because the sounds of Saturday were different. Ball games could be heard through open cracks. If you listened really hard, you could think you heard the sound of candy being sucked. Pity the child who was sick on the weekend and pity the adult who remembered what it felt like.

Mickey's room was on the eighteenth floor and he couldn't hear any outside noises. He never was aware of traffic until he hit the street. Today that worried him. Since he was going to spend the whole day in bed, he wanted reassurance that the rest of the world was operating without him. He was tired, but he forced himself to the window. He looked down and saw the lines of yellow taxis battling each other. Satisfied that things could move without him, he crawled back into bed and fell asleep, but he was restless and heard himself snore. He slept for less than an hour.

His depression came in a wave, clouding over the colors of the room. The tiny hotel suite that he hadn't minded before just didn't seem like home, and like the room, his life didn't feel like his. When he was sick, he was supposed to have a hand on his head and own the pillow that he slept on.

Mickey always dealt with his needs on a grand scale. If he were thirsty, he needed a dozen of something. He would call room service and ask for twelve Perriers. Today he turned his bad cold into dying alone. First he felt sorry for himself because he couldn't go out and play. Then he sneezed and was sure that he had the flu. The thought of that brought him to television commercials. In them, mothers hovered over their ailing children and worried about their fevers. They swore to the camera that the aspirin they loved worked on their precious child. Also there were the commercials with adults. In those, wives worried about their husbands. They stocked the medicine cabinet with the one bottle of the cold medicine they knew would work on the men they loved. On television no one ever suffered alone. There was always someone next to the sick person, standing by, ready to help with a cure. Single people, Mickey Burke knew, passed away alone, with understocked medicine cabinets.

By ten-thirty he had done a complete job on himself. He was convinced he was going to die young because both his father and grandfather hadn't seen their fifties due to massive heart attacks. He would eat right, go to the gym and not get involved with young blondes who drove you to your death. He imagined himself in a ward, on his last days on earth. The man in the bed next to him had a wife who held her husband's hand and fed him teaspoons of tea. Mickey had no one. He had heard that everyone died alone, but he didn't believe it. Some people died with hands on their foreheads. He realized that the hand would be attached to a body and that, if he married for that hand, he would have to adjust to the body behind it for many years. It would be the same body every night; maybe it would get larger or shrink, but in any event it would be there, over and over again, even if it wasn't needed. It would never go home, this body, because its home would be with him. Okay. It would be there when he was dying, but if he were lucky and survived this cold, it would also be there for forty years of waiting, making him move out of his hotel, making him own things like towels, making him have children who might be funnier than he was. These were the fears that were keeping him lonely. If he could be guaranteed that he was going to die soon, he'd get married right away.

About eleven, he sat in the chair while Bertha the chambermaid made his bed. He watched as her strong Swedish arms ripped off the old sheets and replaced them with cool new ones. Bertha was an elderly, large, peasant-type woman equally well suited to toil the soil or make the bed. She was relatively new to the Wyndham and good for a lonely man's conversation. As she punched the pillows into place, she was willing to answer the questions of the man in room 1811. She had been told on her first day of work at the hotel that Mickey Burke was a permanent guest and that for the four years he had lived there, he had been a big tipper.

"Are you married?" he asked. She was a very large woman and he wondered whose bed she fit into. She certainly didn't fit into the pink uniform that the hotel had issued her. Her bust refused to be held back by the thin cotton material. The buttons threatened to pop and the seams weren't going to hold for another week.

"Why would I want to do a thing like that?" she said, laughing as if she had told the best joke in the world. "I've been married once and that was enough for me, thank you. Mr. Jenkins was either home too much, sitting himself in that old chair while I went out the door to make a dollar, or you couldn't find the man. Too much or too little, that was Mr. Jenkins." She handled the king-size spread as if it were a handkerchief. It floated to the bed. Mickey momentarily thought of making this woman his wife, but he was rational enough to know that he would be getting the better deal and she would know it. "How about you, Mr. Mickey? Why is a good looker like you not hitched?" She removed used tissues from the ashtray. He wanted to spare her from touching the disgusting secretions of his body, but he didn't move. Anyway, Bertha had choreographed the disposals. The tissues went into the wastebasket. The contents of the wastebasket went into a large plastic bag that was safely pinned to her cleaning wagon, which she had wheeled into the room. Within moments his tissues had mingled with the garbage of the other guests. He didn't feel like mingling, but there was his blue tissue around the Marlboro box of a stranger. We get entangled whether we want to or not, he thought.

"I'm not married because I'm scared that I'll hate my wife two weeks after the wedding." He sat very still in his chair as he said this. The truth was out.

"You're a funny man." She had left to clean the bathroom, but her voice was strong and the conversation was easily continued.

"I'm also scared not to. I'm scared I'm going to get cancer and frighten all my friends away. A wife would have to stick around. You know what I mean?" Bertha, having left school in the eighth grade, might not have understood a discussion on the literary merits of Zola, but she understood fears. She wasn't scared of being alone or of dying or even of poverty, but she was scared of the devil taking her soul, and that was a fear that never left her.

"We all going to get cancer on account of what they're doing to the universe." He heard the toilet flush. It served to punctuate her point.

He turned his head toward the bathroom, just to make this talk as intimate as possible. "I don't want to decay alone. I want my wife to bring me fresh pajamas. Once, just once, I bought pajamas for myself and I didn't realize until I got home that they had a balloon bottom. You know what that is? The seat expands for comfort. Who wears things like that?"

"Sounds to me like you need help with your bottom, Mr. Mickey. Why don't you stop thinking about dying and blow your nose and have yourself a party? It's going to be nothing but Saturday night soon." She came out of the bathroom and handed Mickey a box of tissues, urging him to take one. She gave him the feeling that once he blew, his life would be different. She believed in symbolic gestures more than he did.

"You think I should get married, Bertha?" He was willing to obey her answer. In less than ten minutes, she had brought order and fresh smells to his room. There was no reason to believe that she wasn't a clear thinker.

"You should have a woman, that's for sure, but not for the reasons you're telling me. If you need someone sittin' there by your deathbed, you might as well hire someone. Anyone in my neighborhood would sit there and be your wife for five dollars an hour. You need yourself a life before death. Why do you want to sit around a hotel room with everybody else coming and going? The rest of the world is checking in and checking out, and you're here stuck. People aren't meant to be stuck. And they're sure not meant to be alone. It drives them crazy. I don't have a husband, but I do have a man in my bed. He's old and dumb, but he's there when I need my body warm. Why you want to make yours cold before it's really going to be cold?"

She convinced him. He moved from his chair to the freshly made bed. The cool, clean sheets temporarily made him feel cared for. Once he was settled, he felt he had to defend his masculinity. "I have plenty of girlfriends. Maybe not plenty, but enough." Why should Bertha think he was a loser?

"I know you've got women. I change your sheets each and every single day. You think I don't know when all these pillows have been part of the fun?" Mickey thought quickly. Bertha had been working at the Wyndham for a short time and he hadn't had a woman since . . . he couldn't remember exactly. She was protecting his pride with her trumped-up observations. He felt like telling her the truth, but he realized she already knew since she was the one who was doing the storytelling.

"I'm not referring to women who just make a dent in the pillow. I'm talking about how a human has to live. We have no right to be alone. We're just animals, Mr. Mickey, with apes for granddaddies. Animals don't go around deciding whether they're too scared to be with another hairy thing. They sleep with their own kind every night. You put them alone and they go crazy. That's what my friend Millie told me, and she cleaned up at Columbia University five times a week. She stopped, poor thing, because she didn't want to get spooked out by all those animals in their cages, and they were paying good money. They cry out at night. I think it's because they're by themselves. First they cry. Then they go crazy. You stay alone long enough, my friend, and that's going to happen right to you. You think you're any different from those hairy things who can do practically anything but talk?"

Bertha turned on the industrial carpet cleaner, a machine over whose motor anyone would have to scream. "So you think you any different from the other of God's creatures?" she yelled.

"I think I'm better," he screamed. His throat hurt when he talked that loudly, but he couldn't wait to defend himself until the rug was cleaned.

"Are you happier than they are?"

"Yes. I'm happier. I can go to the movies. I shit in the toilet, which I really enjoy. I have the privilege of spending money on things that are shiny. I can drive a car." Mickey and Bertha were not fighting, but the noise of the vacuum cleaner escalated them into a more hostile state than they had intended. Their voices rose and, as a result, so did their emotions.

"I don't mean any disrespect, sir, but when Judgment Day comes, you think our Lord has a better heaven for you than He does for the other creatures He created?" Bertha's head was below the bed as she cleaned. It was fortunate that she never got to see the expression on Mickey's face. He had stuck with her so far, but now that God and heaven had been introduced he was lost. His fears had to do only with his own pain on earth. He hadn't pictured Judgment Day or the gates of heaven since he was seven years old. It would be wrong to say he lived for the here and now, because he didn't. He lived because he had no other choice. And as long as he was living, he did everything to make himself comfortable.

Rather than get into a philosophical conversation about religion with Bertha, Mickey closed his eyes, hoping that when she emerged from under the bed, she would have the consideration to leave him alone. She did, finishing her cleaning quietly, following a routine that didn't need following since her rags and solutions had been in his suite the day before. Then she wheeled her cart to the door. Before she left she turned to ask if he needed anything. She spoke in a considerate whisper in case he was sleeping and not just avoiding her. He said he didn't. She had cleaned the inside of his medicine cabinet this past month and knew that it had contained the pharmacopoeia of a paranoid. There were bottles with everything she had ever seen advertised, over-the-counter drugs that promised to cure aches and pains better than the next guy. They were all new and improved and promised to relieve. She was sure there was some medicine that he owned that would take care of him.

"So, I'll be seeing you tomorrow. Felicia will be here tonight to turn down your bed. I sure do hope you feel better, Mr. Mickey, and— never mind. You just rest. You deserve it." He sat up, wanting to know what thought Bertha had been planning to relay before she canceled it.

"What? What were you going to tell me?"

"Just something that Millie knows from cleaning Columbia University." She started to close the door. Mickey's voice stopped her.

"Well, I want to hear."

"You might not like it."

"I don't have to like everything," he said.

"Well, she says that they've proven that married men live longer."

"Thanks for the information. I guess I'll get dressed and go find a bride." Bertha pushed her cart out of Mickey's room. She was slightly disgusted with the man she had tried to help. She didn't start humming until she was halfway down the hall.

Mickey had learned nothing new. He was aware of all the statistics, including the one that proved that men who were married lived longer. That one always made him reach for his heart. He was never comforted by its beat. It always seemed too strong and too fast. He always felt it was just about to stop. A wife could comfort him. She would make him live to be a hundred. It would be really smart for him to invest in one. Investments paid off for years. Maybe he should take a wife.

But people didn't take wives anymore. They did that in the days when you took a woman into your home or out to the Far West. Now the two of you took an apartment together and shared appliances. He didn't know if he could do that again. During the short time he was married, he hated co-owning a piece of Brie. On the other hand, he didn't want to die while his married friends went to the beach.

Mickey reached for his forehead and couldn't tell if he had a fever. He thought of calling room service and asking them to send up a mother. Every hotel should have one, he thought—a Bible in the drawer and a mother who came when called to press her lips against your face to check if you were burning up. At other times you could have her sent up to yell because you left your underwear on the floor. He bet the first hotel to put a mother on the staff would be jammed. Maybe it was a television series. A woman buys a hotel in New York with the money left by her dear, deceased husband. She is supposed to run it efficiently, like the queen who stands guard at the Helmsley, but she's just too nice a person. She ends up doing things for the guests that only a mother would do. She bakes cookies, brings in vitamins, laughs at their jokes. Maureen Stapleton could play the part. Mickey had no idea whether he had come up with a great idea or whether having a bad cold had made him incapable of sorting out trash. He coughed and sneezed and wished for a comforting presence.

He remembered that he didn't own slippers. Maybe he should make a commitment to slippers or to a woman who would buy them for him. She would give him children and the whole family would have slippers and take care of him in his old age, those golden years. By then he would have lost his sense of humor. He would bore his children by telling them stories of how he used to mistreat the network executives and they would have to listen or he would cut them off without a cent. "Laugh or you'll be out of the will," he would tell them. The will. Jerry kept telling him he had to have a will. For what? He didn't have a beneficiary. Jerry knew that Mickey had no one but his mother and his Aunt Minn to leave his money to.

Mickey tried to get up. Maybe if he took himself down to Barney's he could buy one of those seven-hundred-dollar Italian jackets that everyone said made him look taller. He dangled his feet over the side of the bed like a hospital patient who was trying to be brave enough to get out of bed. His mother did that in the hospital in Miami. Her feet had smelled like the feet of a sixty-eight-year-old woman. He wondered if his smelled like the feet of a thirty-eight-year-old man. Just as he was about to lift himself from the bed, the biggest sneeze of the morning came. He reached for a tissue in time and thought he was home free. And then he saw the blood. He had a bloody nose. That wiped out any hope of getting up. He lay back down, his feet still hanging. In his whole life he had never gotten into a fistfight or fallen out of a tree. He was a man who had always lived from the neck up. The sight—or even the thought—of blood was so foreign to him that he was always trying to force it back to where it came from. He took wads of tissues and pressed them tightly against his nose. Thank God this didn't happen in Barney's, he thought. I would have bled on something expensive and had to buy it.

The blood was a sign to him to stay in for the day. When you were Mickey Burke, you didn't take chances that your body might embarrass you. Since he was lonely and he couldn't get out, he'd have to bring a representative of the outside world in. He would have to call a friend and try to ruin his Saturday by having him come over and watch a sick man sneeze. It would have to be someone who wouldn't mind the risk of getting Mickey's germs on himself. That eliminated all the men in his life. Men were supposed to be sensitive these days. Well, they sure as hell weren't sensitive to other guys' illnesses. If you called them up and said you weren't feeling well, they would say things like, "Catch you later." Not one of those pricks would rush over with a thermometer. Women were definitely better people. The only thing they did wrong was make you live with them.

So now the decision remained: What woman? It couldn't be anyone he wanted to impress. There was a chance that snot would leak out of him. He couldn't invite Dory, the blonde who booked talent for *Saturday Night Live.* For her he needed a seven-hundred-dollar jacket, not a Fruit of the Loom T-shirt with some blood on it. He didn't have to think long to come up with Shelly Silver. She was the most nurturing woman he knew. She was the type of girl who didn't even mind looking inside of Band-Aids. He knew because she had looked inside his once and never complained about the pus. What neither of them knew was that was what had ended their relationship. Not the Band-Aid incident specifically, but things of that nature. They had started as two young lovers hungry for each other. They did what all modern lovers do: spent days in bed making love and telling each other that somebody was going to get hurt. And somebody did: Shelly. By the end of the first year of their relationship, she was no longer a lover. Without either of them noticing, she had become Mickey's mother. She saw to it that he ate. Most days she brought him food. She thought it was important that he got his sleep. These demands alone would have been tolerable. But she made the big mistake: She tolerated him when he whined. She understood. He could subject her to such noises ceaselessly, and she would let him. He asked her for unconditional love, and she gave it. But when she did, he didn't want to sleep with her anymore. Standing by the bed, she was his mother in a designer nightgown. They both knew that it was over, but neither of them knew the reason: Men don't want to sleep with women who forgive them.

Today he needed Shelly. He was uncertain about calling her. He loved hearing her voice—it brought up pleasant memories—but he felt guilty. He suspected his calls gave her immediate gratification followed by a day of unhappiness. The conversations started out warm and ended up uncomfortable, with Shelly, over a year later, still wanting to know what had gone wrong. She had asked the same question more than once. "Isn't my love worth anything?" And she had followed it with the single girl's familiar threat: "You'll never find anybody who loves you as much as I do." At the same time she worried that she would never find anybody whom she could love as much. Ask a man why he is unhappy when his affair ends, and he will tell you that he doesn't know when he will be so well loved again. Ask the woman crying in her queen-sized bed the real source of her tears, and she will tell you that she doesn't know if she can ever find someone to love so much again.

Mickey knew her number by heart. He lay there, looking at the ceiling, enjoying the molding that repeated its pattern around the room. He thought that knowing something "by heart" was an interesting concept. No one called it "knowing by head," which would have been logical. Knowing it "by head" would give you access to it, as you would have "access" to information in a computer; but knowing something "by heart" implied it might touch the very organ that keeps you alive. Also, since the heart was there to service the emotions, especially love, it was important for one's relationship to know things about one another "by heart." He knew Shelly's face, her height, even some of her thoughts. He phoned her, punching out the numbers, hearing the tones beep out a song he used to hear often.

"Hello," she said. Immediately he remembered all that was good about her.

"Hey. It's Mickey." He forgot to sound sick. He was disappointed with his voice. It sounded energetic when he was trying to evoke sympathy. He imagined Shelly on her bed, surrounded by the pastel pillows she loved to flop on. Perhaps he saw her there because that's where he left her last, crying into those pillows. Actually, she was in the kitchen having a Diet Pepsi for breakfast. She should have worn a robe over the light-blue nightshirt because now she was cold.

"Mickey! How are you?" She was still in love, damn it. Sometimes she felt cured, but look: Just hearing his voice, she was ready to rise or sink with each word. She needed a cigarette or she needed Mickey, even though she thought that she had given them both up.

"I'm great. Fine." He impulsively decided to be a big, strong man for this woman who loved him for his strength. It seemed awkward to tell her he was ailing right away.

"Yeah, me too. How's work going?" On many Saturday mornings she had wished that Mickey would call. In those fantasy conversations, he was the one asking questions.

"Work? More of the same," he said, introducing a cough for effect. "I'm doing a couple of pilots and I'm still mad at myself for not breaking out of television and getting into film."

"God knows, you have the talent. You're absolutely the funniest human being on the face of this earth." They had been on the phone for less than a minute and already they were into the old patterns.

She had told him he was wonderful, and though her bare feet were cold on the kitchen floor, she wouldn't leave the phone to get socks because Mickey was on it.

"Yeah, well, funny is one thing. Sitting down and writing anything longer than forty pages is another."

"You can do it. I know you can." She had no proof of his ability to write anything better than a half-hour television script, but she cast herself in the role of the head cheerleader in his life and gave automatic pep talks. She wondered why he didn't want her in his life every day.

"You always told me that," he said, remembering days when he would get depressed about his work and she would sit on her bed and cheer him up with her faith.

"Because it's true," said Shelly Silver. She was beginning to wonder if he had called just to get an injection of her support. He had done that about six months ago when he didn't think he was funny anymore. She had spent close to two hours on the phone telling him how wonderful he was. She hadn't heard from him since.

"I don't know, maybe I should just be happy with television. At least I have the feeling that all the doors are open to me all the time. Remember my idea for the show about afterlife?"

"Yes." She remembered everything he ever said.

"They bought it."

"That's great," she said. He could hear her enthusiasm. Maybe she had gotten up on her knees to shout her latest encouragement. "E.A.T. is buying my strudel," she said. When had they left him and started talking about her?

"What?"

"E.A.T. You know. The 'in' take-out. They're buying a couple of hundred pounds of strudel a week." She knew he hadn't asked, but she really thought he would be happy about her achievement.

"That's very nice." Mickey's voice was not unenthusiastic but not quite encouraging either.

"Yeah. Business is good." She thought she sounded like a middle-aged businessman. Her next line would be, "I can't complain." She was also angry at herself for bringing up her business and not letting the conversation flow. There was a silence, broken by the second cough from Mickey. "And what about the rest of your life?" she asked, not wanting to know. One day he might call and tell her he had married a blonde.

"I'm still at the Wyndham. I can't believe I checked in for two weeks four years ago."

"You'll have some bill when you check out." He gave her a polite laugh, but that was enough to let her know she'd made a point. Mickey was one of the cheapest men in the world, especially with his laughs. The chuckle turned into a third cough, which he didn't try to muffle. "Are you all right?" Shelly asked.

"I'm sick," he said, coughing again. It sounded phony, but it was real and, what's more, well-timed. He knew he'd get some sympathy.

"There's this horrible flu going around. Two of my waiters called in sick today."

Mickey didn't like her response. He wanted his to be a unique illness, not one that had struck down every waiter in the city.

"Mine isn't the flu. It's . . . something else."

"Nothing serious?"

Shelly's sister once asked if she ever wished Mickey Burke was dead. She said an immediate No, but after a ten-minute Talmudic argument, she had to agree that life would be easier for her if one day he would just step into some subway and never emerge.

"Nah. Nothing big. Just the usual coughing, sneezing, bleeding from the rectum." There he was, the good old Mickey she had known and loved too much. Shelly laughed. He always got her with rectum jokes.

"Do you have a fever?"

"I don't know."

"Don't you have a thermometer?"

"No. My mother took it to Miami with her."

"Can't the drugstore send one up?"

"Yeah, but I wouldn't know where to put it." He knew he had given her the best straight line in the world. He also knew she might be too concerned to use it.

"You put it in your mouth, asshole." Good girl. She got it. "Shove it up your ass" would have been the tritest way to go, and she didn't fall into that trap. On the other hand, he was slightly disappointed that she wasn't too worried to quip.

"I never could read one of those thermometers. Everyone in the world can make out the little red line, but I've never even seen it." A chill went through his body, and while he continued to talk, he got back under the covers and felt very sorry for himself.

"Poor baby," said Shelly Silver, and both of them knew she wasn't being sarcastic.

"There's no chance that you could get over here sometime today, is there? It would be great to see you again. We could talk. I could order in deli from the Stage. I promise I won't get any germs on you." He knew she would be there. Mickey had been refused by many women, but never by Shelly, especially when he could prove he had a cold.

Before saying good-bye, Shelly was already changing her day. If she hired a car she might be able to do it all. She would have to beg

Malcolm to blow-dry her hair. The permanent that he had given her for body had a life of its own, and she battled it every day. It was acceptable unless you were going to see an ex-lover. Then it needed Malcolm's touch. When he finished he always bent down and looked in the mirror with her. He asked her if she loved it. Not if she liked it, if she loved it. Malcolm was most comfortable with superlatives. One day she would realize that when she said she loved it that she was looking at Malcolm's perfect shoulder-length hair. She would have to beg him to squeeze her in on a Saturday. If he gave her a hard time, she would remind him that she had hired at least seven of his boyfriends as waiters. She didn't have to beg. Malcolm had lost his live-in lover at the same time Shelly lost Mickey, and they had great sympathy for each other.

Of course Paula had to be called at Bloomingdale's. The red leather pants would work. They had been worn and already molded to her body so they didn't advertise that they were a brand-new purchase. She needed Paula to locate the black sweater with the little pearl buttons that she had promised herself she wouldn't buy. That promise was made before Mickey Burke called.

She'd have to call her parents and tell them she couldn't meet them before they went to the theater. Her mother was in one of her having-to-get-cultured moods and had dragged her father down from Rochester to see Sam Shepard's latest play. They had expected to come over to Shelly's to see the daughter who was always too busy to see them. "Can we make an appointment?" her mother asked, with enough sarcasm to extend over the rest of their lives. When she heard Shelly was seeing Mickey Burke, Mrs. Silver would understand. After torturing her mother for years by saying she didn't necessarily believe in marriage and didn't necessarily think she needed children to be fulfilled, Shelly had tearfully confessed that she would die to marry Mickey and bear his offspring. Mrs. Silver cried with relief. Her daughter had returned from that dangerous decade they call the sixties. There would be no problem canceling. They'd have brunch tomorrow.

She couldn't get out of the Mendelburg bat mitzvah luncheon. Sharon Mendelburg had insisted that Shelly include in the contract that she would be there. Thank God it was a luncheon. They were always over by four since the bat mitzvah girl couldn't wait to get home and open her presents.

After calculating her day, Shelly assured Mickey that she could be there by five. She would have to change in the car, but if Paula came through, Shelly had faith that she could look as good as Mickey had remembered her.

When they hung up, Mickey got scared. It wasn't until he put the phone down that he remembered that he once had to run from this woman. Maybe he could work it so she only visited him when he thought he was dying.

Shelly didn't have the heart to roll out the cake early for the Mendelburg girl, so it was a quarter to six by the time she knocked on Mickey's door. She looked spectacular. Her dark hair was doing everything it was supposed to. The red leather pants had worked out great. The black sweater was long enough to cover the thighs she would rather not have. She had arranged for her portable oven to be in the arms of a bellhop she was planning to tip heavily. Unfortunately, he was a model type who looked beautiful in his issued uniform. She knew that Mickey was straight but preferred not to make an entrance standing next to someone of either sex fortunate enough to have a classically beautiful face and epic proportions.

When Mickey opened the door, her heart basically did what the poets said it would do. It leapt. They said a too-polite hello for people who had been serious lovers, and Shelly told the handsome bellhop where to put the oven. It wasn't until he was gone that they really faced each other.

"You're looking great," he said, the best remark he could have chosen. She had been complimented enough for her brains and success and was now going for something more. She had spent seventeen thousand dollars this year on clothes, hair and makeup. She was pleased it had paid off in a compliment from Mickey Burke.

"You're looking pretty good yourself." She meant it. Someone else might have felt his jeans were too new and too big in the seat and his nose was too red, but to her he looked like the man she wanted to be with. Clearly he had put no effort into his appearance, but he hadn't had a reason to. He needed warmth, not lust. He sat in an ugly chair while she plugged in the oven. She knew it was overdoing things by bringing her oven so that Mickey could have a good, hot meal. She knew no one would approve, including her sister, who once said she thought it was all right to make a man chemically dependent in order to make him incapable of leaving.

"I look like hell," he said. "This cold has me tired. Everything has me tired lately. Remember when I could stay up all night and work on a script?" She remembered. On those nights, she had wanted to be worth leaving the pages for. "I can't do that anymore. If something kept me up all night, I would tell all the secrets I know to the Russians."

"And what secrets do you know?"

"I know about a woman in a very high network position who says she graduated from Radcliffe but went to B.U."

"Do you think that will rock our national security?"

"Definitely. We're talking about lying in very high places. First they tolerate lies in the office and then they send lies over the airwaves. The next thing you know, we start believing the C.I.A. is doing a great job in South America."

"Well, so it's your responsibility to save our country." They had to quip for a while. If not, they might say something that really counted.

Surprisingly, it was Mickey who got real first. It happened just after beats of silence. First Mickey gave Shelly a look that made him appear to have been the injured party in their relationship. Shelly had no idea that he was just trying to stifle a sneeze. They were standing close enough for her to get sprayed.

"You know why I asked you over?" he said. Mickey was not without sentimentality, and it was coming through.

"You had a craving for catered food."

"I didn't ask you here just to feed me."

"That's good. Sometimes I think people are my friends because I make great cheese puffs." She appeared to be speaking casually, but her mood was intense. Mickey did that to her.

"You do make great cheese puffs."

"Yes, but I don't think that should be the basis of a relationship." She hated having brought up the word "relationship" this soon in the conversation.

"Well, I want to go on record here. I want you to know that I think there's much more to you than your puffs." She waited a couple of beats for him to list her virtues, but it quickly became evident that she wasn't going to get any more compliments at the moment.

"You're too kind," she said, though she knew that so far he hadn't been kind enough.

"I wanted you to come over because I was lonely."

Those were the magic words. She was melting faster than the frozen butter in the microwave.

"I never think of you as lonely. Ever. I always think that you can have whoever you want around you. Whenever you want." She noticed the large public telephone book in the end table. She considered it to be Mickey's personal directory. She had always thought it was unfair that he could have love if he wanted it.

"Sometimes. Sometimes I just hang around and feel myself getting older. There are times that I choose to be lonely on purpose." This was the complicated man she loved. Mickey with a cold was still more sparkling than any other man on earth. She wanted to hug his knees, but the smells from the oven stopped her and she rescued the food. That was her life, providing nourishment of one kind or another.

Shelly Silver had come prepared. In her oversized Sportsac she had dishes (heavy white ones that felt good in your lap), Pierre Deux napkins (large and inviting) and small silver forks (even though this was finger food). The same bag contained chilled champagne and glasses, the fluted ones owned by fine restaurants and childless single women. And to prove she really could perform magic, she pulled out flowers and a small, perfect vase. How could this man not love her? She had turned his sickroom into the French countryside.

Mickey looked at the colorful food in his lap and felt good. The plate had warmed his knees and taken the chill from his body for the first time that day. Although his taste buds weren't up to par, enough good sensations got through. He went from spinach to liver to glazed carrots, all in pastry, murmuring his appreciation between bites. He toasted her silently, and she sat on the edge of the bed, eating half the amount he did. Most of her pleasure came from seeing the man she believed she loved eating the food she created. At least something of hers was comforting him.

"How come a good cook like you who doesn't have any communicable diseases isn't married?" Mickey asked as he finished.

"I don't know," was her honest answer.

"We should have done it," he said, as if they had come close.

"When?" she asked, trying to deal with the romance of it. She wasn't sure if she had asked a question of the future or the past.

"When we first met. Before you could tell what a jerk I was."

"I could tell you were a jerk the first night I was with you." She transferred a ham-and-cheese quiche from her plate to his, a gesture meant to let him know she was only kidding.

"Then we should have done it after I said hello and before I made you pay for dinner."

"I guess we missed the moment." She wanted him to argue that they hadn't, that their life together was just beginning. She continued to forget that Mickey was an ordinary man.

"It's too bad we didn't know how to get together. You could have made me fat." He patted a stomach that didn't exist and popped the tiniest hot dog into his mouth.

"I could never figure out how you could be happy without me." It was the most serious remark of the evening, and it embarrassed them both. He ate yet another bacon-wrapped chicken liver, and she checked her oven. They knew how to avoid.

"Who says I'm happy?" said Mickey, swallowing his pride along with the bacon.

"I don't know. I thought you might be. It was just a guess."

"I'm not even sure I want to be." It made her angry that Mickey Burke could choose between being happy or not when the rest of the world didn't. She didn't show her anger. She had come to seduce him with red leather pants and enticing food. She wanted him to love her, and then she would decide what to do about it.

The phone rang. Shelly immediately assumed it was a woman and that the portable oven had made her look like a schmuck. Whenever she was with a man and the phone rang, she assumed it was his true love calling. While Mickey spoke she felt she had to wander around the perimeter of the room, as far away from the phone as possible. She pretended to pay attention to ashtrays and hotel paintings that she had no interest in.

Mickey's room was sparsely furnished. The drapes that hung on the windows were in hundreds of other rooms in the hotel. Obviously they were ordered in a nondescript bulk. The lamps said, "I'll work, but I won't be unique." There was a print of Venice on the wall that the hotel had provided. It just wasn't enough to hold her attention, so she started making promises to herself. When Mickey got off the phone she was going to lie to him. She would tell him that she had thought of him from time to time. That was true. He didn't have to know that the times were close together and that he was a constant consideration in her life. She would tell him that she had really loved him—once. She'd let him believe that was in the past, not that her love was the thing she still could think of first each morning. She would admit that she was happy that he called, but she wouldn't tell him that when she heard his voice a vital organ reacted.

She never had the chance to say anything. Mickey had begun writing on a small pad next to the phone. He was obviously taking down information, and he seemed concerned. She tried not to listen, but the room was small and his voice was animated. She realized he was getting directions and promising to be right there. Putting aside all her planned lies, Shelly had trouble believing that her evening was over. She had come to take care of a sick ex-lover, hoping to make him realize that he needed her. That required hours. She wasn't planning to leave until Mickey at least gave a sign of knowing what she was worth. None of this was fair.

"A friend of my secretary's is in trouble. I gotta go over there." He folded the directions into his pocket and then patted the shirt to make sure they were there.

"But you're sick." Her concern was real.

"I'll be okay." She was already reaching for him. There it was: the hand on the forehead that he had needed all day.

"You feel a little warm to me."

"I gotta get Jerry to go over to the East Side. This kid was picked up for shoplifting."

"Your secretary?"

"My secretary's friend, some young kid she went to Saks with." He was already dialing Jerry and taking the paper out of his pocket. "He's gotta be there. Come on Jerry, pick up! What good is it to have a lawyer for a best friend if he's not going to be there when a girl you don't even know is in trouble?" Mickey paced and coughed. Shelly could tell when Jerry answered because, having spent his energy pacing, Mickey sat down to talk. "Where the fuck were you? I know your place. No part of it is more than four giant steps from a phone."

Once again Shelly pretended she wasn't there. This time, at least she had things to do. It was her job to make all traces of the picnic disappear. Makers of magic are also the ones who have to clean it up afterward. During the call, she had collected everything except for the flowers. They could remain as proof that she had been there. Mickey hung up and coughed harder and longer than before.

"You really shouldn't leave," she said, trying to protect the man who was deserting her.

"I have to. This kid who works for me is . . . I don't know, she's like entirely new in the world. It's as if she had been born this year. I have to help her out. Listen, I'm sorry about this. I figured we would hang out tonight, talk about old times, new times. We hardly got started."

"Yeah, well, I guess I'll have to understand." She didn't have enough dignity at the moment to hide her disappointment. She stood with her oven under her arm, knowing her eyes were threatening to tear, yet still wanting to be an independent woman.

"You really should pick up that stuff on the way back," said Mickey, putting on his ski jacket. Since he hadn't been out all day he assumed it was colder than it was.

"On the way back?" She hadn't known there was a way back to Mickey Burke's room for her.

"Aren't you coming to the station?" He made it sound as if she would be abandoning him if she didn't.

"I didn't know you wanted me to." Damn it. She was revealing her neediness. She had wanted to be strong for the whole evening, but even with her hands full, she was clinging to him.

"Hey, come on. In a strange way, we might have fun. At least it won't be your ordinary Saturday-night dinner and movie." As he tried to persuade her, one sentence played over and over in her mind: *He wants me to come. He wants me to come.*

They picked up Jerry on the way. He looked so impressive in his lawyer's clothes that Shelly and Mickey whistled. The three of them had shared many cabs when Mickey and Shelly were going together. She had tried to keep in touch, but the ex-girlfriend and the best friend rarely continue to have a relationship. The friend doesn't really know what to say to her, and all she wants is information about the man who left. Jerry and Shelly had not seen each other in over a year. They sat shoulder to shoulder and hesitantly asked how things were. They expected a one-sentence answer. They quickly found out that each was a year more successful than when they had last spoken. Each had apartments two rooms bigger and worried about the new tax laws. By the time they got to the station, they were talking more easily. He told her it was just like old times, and she wished it were.

Jerry had questions for Mickey. "Are we really doing this?" He asked, "Are we really in a cab going downtown on a Saturday night?" The questions didn't stop until they got there. "You pay," Jerry said, opening the door to the cab.

The Seventeenth Precinct is not the largest in the city. The lights are too bright, the walls are too dirty and that night everybody was too put-out. In the half hour she had been there, Mary had told three cops to go fuck themselves, each in a different way. She told Officer Monroe, "Fuck off. *If* you still young enough to get it up." She told Sergeant Phillips, "Fuck yourself, 'cause no one else will." And she told Captain Elizabeth Martin, "If you had a dick, I would tell you to fuck yourself, lady." Astra Rainbow kept trying to restrain her from hurling insults, but Mary wouldn't be calmed.

When Mickey, Jerry and Shelly arrived, a lot of quiet conversations took place. First they whispered to Astra Rainbow, who explained what Mary had done. "She took what wasn't hers to take," she told them, never actually using the word "steal." Then all four of them moved over to Mary, who was sitting handcuffed and sullen on the bench. She was tired by now. Some of the fight was out of her. She was still angry, but she knew that this was the team that was going to help her and she tried to be polite. To her, "polite" meant not shouting and looking at her shoes. Jerry asked her if she had ever been in this type of trouble before. "My friend Julia had gone up to Alexander's with me once and put something in my pocket when I wasn't looking, and then we was both down in the station," Mary said, "only I don't know if it counted because it was my first time and we was real juveniles. When we got to court the judge blew this long speech out his ass, about growing up good."

Jerry sat on the bench next to his client and asked her to tell him exactly what had happened. Mary recounted the story in five too-fast run-on sentences. She was innocent.

"Look, I'm going to do my best to get you free on bail," said Jerry, writing lawyer's notes. "I have no idea how rough they're going to be. Maybe, and I want you to remember kid, I'm saying *maybe*, I can get you off on a technicality."

"Yeah, I heard of those," said Mary. She was interested enough to look up.

"You were picked up while you were still on Saks' property. The way I understand it, the security guard stopped you in the small area between the inner and outer door of the store because he was over-anxious for the arrest. If I play it right, I can probably get you off."

"Is he great, or what?" Mickey asked Astra Rainbow. He got nothing but her profile in return. Shelly had already noticed that this young, fair secretary got a lot of stares from her beloved Mickey.

"It's not going to be easy, but I think my case can be based on the fact that arrests are supposed to be made once the shoplifter is completely out of the store, proving their intention to steal. If they haven't left the grounds, the accused might possibly have intended to put the property back." Jerry looked for approval from the small crowd and got it from most of them.

Mary was ecstatic at this news. Only the handcuffs kept her from applauding, but she was able to laugh at the restraints now that she felt they couldn't keep her down forever. Mickey and Shelly joined in the minicelebration. They had come to free the prisoner, and Jerry had probably done the job. Astra Rainbow was shocked. She couldn't believe these people were happy at the prospect of evading justice. She had spent the last seventeen years of her life waiting to be punished for her crime and didn't understand why anybody would want to get away scot-free. When their cheers stopped she spoke up. "I can't believe what's happening here," she said, facing the united pack. She spoke like a lawyer giving her closing remarks to the jury. Mickey had never seen her this determined. "Why are we happy because of this technicality?" None of them could do anything but shrug. "I'm sure deep in her heart Mary wants her conscience clear," Astra Rainbow said slowly and clearly, taking giant steps between words, as if English were their second language.

"Shit," said Mary, thinking that she was losing her case.

"Mary, please. I'm only telling you this to help you." Rainbow was determined to win her point. She decided she had to touch on her unhappy childhood to convince Mary to do the right thing. "I know what it's like to go free for something when you should have been punished. I can't tell you the story because it's too terrible, but you have to believe me: Paying for a crime is the best thing you can do." Whereas the conversations up to now had been in hushed, private tones, she was now speaking loudly enough for a couple of law enforcers to hear. Nobody was ready to act on her confession, but she had a sizable audience. Soon she was down on one knee, not to beg, but to make eye contact with Mary, who was sitting.

"You is really crazy sometimes, Rainbow. You really is," said Mary, hoping that no one was taking her friend seriously.

"I know," said Rainbow tenderly for Mary's sake and her own. "I know I'm different. I try very hard to be the same as everyone else, but it doesn't always work, and that's because of the bad thing that happened in my past. I keep expecting something to fall on my head. Do you know what I mean?" Mary didn't, but Shelly thought she did. Mother to the world, Shelly felt very sorry for this angelic, pleading woman and wanted to comfort her, but she couldn't find the place to interrupt.

"Are you crazy enough that you 'spect me to go to jail where, as sure as you're born, they're going to gang-rape me?" Mary was not angry with Rainbow. She was doing her best to win her over.

"Being in prison isn't as bad as walking around thinking you're due to get hit by a car," was Rainbow's firm argument. Jerry was fascinated. Mickey, the writer, was memorizing. Shelly was feeling compassion for both sides. Mary was pissed. Just a couple of minutes ago she was home free and now her friend was trying to talk her into going to jail. "When you cross the street you probably expect to get to the other side," said Astra Rainbow. "When I go out into traffic, I expect to be run over. None of us gets away with the bad things we do. Even if my punishment consists only of me *thinking* I'm going to get hurt. Don't you want to go through life being able to dance in the sunshine?"

Mary at this moment asked the question in everyone's mind. "What the fuck did you do?" she said in a loud whisper.

"Something much more terrible than you did," said Astra Rainbow sadly.

"A long time ago?"

"A very long time ago."

"And they never caught you?"

"Nobody even knows I did it."

"Well, maybe it's not as bad as you think," said Jerry.

"It's very bad," said Astra Rainbow.

"If it was that long ago . . ." said Mickey.

"It was during my lifetime," said Astra Rainbow.

"But you can't live your whole life feeling guilty," said Shelly.

"I have to. If I don't then I'm not a person with a conscience."

"Then why don't you tell the cops what you done and *you* go to jail?" suggested Mary.

"I did that once. When I was thirteen and having nightmares, my grandmother, who knows what I did, took me on the bus down to the police station in Cleveland. She thought that maybe I could cleanse my soul.

"They were very nice to me. This policeman and a woman who wasn't even in a uniform took me into a private room and sat me down. They let my grandmother come in and sit off to the side. I was a little afraid because I had seen this movie once about a boys' reform school and I figured they were going to send me to some gray place like that. But I would rather have gone there than to never have my peaceful sleep again.

"I told the officer everything I knew about that awful day, and when I finished he asked me how old I had been at the time, and when I told him five he patted my hand once and told me I had nothing to worry about. He said that I had committed a crime before the age of reason, that police didn't arrest children, and that no five-year-old in our country ever goes on trial because a five-year-old doesn't really know what she's doing.

"But I did know. I didn't go to reform school, but I built a prison and I know that I am never going to escape. I don't think I'll burn in hell, but I'll never get to the other side of the street in peace."

Mickey couldn't help thinking what a great movie this would make. His writer's mind always made him leave the scene and stand aside. His emotions were always days behind an incident.

"That officer was right, you know," said Jerry. "Children's minds don't work the same as adults. They don't have the capacity to see the consequences." He was hoping his two sentences would absolve Astra Rainbow, who seemed to be in so much pain.

"I didn't know the consequences. That doesn't stop me from thinking about it every day of my life."

"Maybe if you see a really good psychiatrist," suggested Shelly.

"A really good psychiatrist would know that a person has to pay for a crime," said Rainbow. "All the talking in the world is not going to make me innocent." Still, to all of them she looked innocent. Even in the dim light of the police station, she appeared to have a halo.

"A good doctor can't absolve you from a crime. But he *can* help you live with it."

"I don't get nightmares anymore," said Rainbow, squeezing next to Mary on the bench. She hoped she had convinced the girl to take the harder path.

"Are we gonna get me outta here, or what?" said Mary. Like everyone else, she had been fascinated with Astra Rainbow's story, but she wasn't about to give up one day of her freedom. To her, peace of mind would come from beating the system.

"I want you to know, Mary, that I won't be mad at you if you decide to take advantage of legal loopholes. I just wanted you to know that, in the long run, the easy way out would be to serve your time."

"Yeah, well, I'd really rather not. I know this girl who was on the inside and she said you have to live in your own shit. If it's all the same to you, I'd rather not."

"Please think about it."

"Yeah, well, it don't need no more thinking, and I have a date with Eddie tonight. So if it's not too much trouble, I'd like to split soon."

"You're not going to skip bail?" Jerry interjected. He pointed his finger accusingly, as if she already had.

"Where you think a girl like me is going, to Chicago or maybe Paris? I ain't never even been to an airport." Mary looked smaller than before. She was the little black girl instead of the fighter that she liked to pose as.

Jerry left the group and negotiated for Mary's release. Two one-hundred-dollar bills were exchanged. Soon the five of them were on the street in front of the station. Mary felt good, and Jerry felt good. It had been a long time since he had practiced any type of law that didn't require a desk and a vest. It seemed cause to celebrate, and Mickey, who hadn't sneezed or coughed since the taxi ride, asked them all to dinner. "We'll go up to Joe Allen's, have some laughs," he proposed.

Mary had to rush off to meet Eddie. "He's gonna borrow a car." None of them really understood her explanation. They didn't understand what it meant for a young girl from the poor side of Brooklyn to spend time in a car.

Jerry had to go too. He had promised Laureen Spangler that they could discuss where their relationship was going. She had accused him of avoiding her because he had canceled out on this discussion before. He had to show up tonight. With any luck, Laureen would discuss the relationship for only five or six hours and then they could go to bed. She would talk on and on about how close they should be, but he always felt alienated by the talking and didn't feel close again until they had some really good sex.

So Shelly, Mickey and Astra Rainbow were left alone to have their first date. At first Rainbow didn't want to go. "I've caused you enough trouble, Mr. Burke," she said, thanking him and heading toward the subway. Shelly stopped her. She never had had this much sympathy for someone so beautiful. She knew the gorgeous young women who smiled at her from the pages of *Glamour* were not necessarily happy, but she couldn't help thinking that their perfect hair and baby-blue eyes insured party invitations and marriage whenever they wanted. Shelly was a brilliant woman who knew what all brilliant people knew: Looks count. She had nothing against beauty. She would have been perfectly happy to let beautiful women live in a roped-off part of the city with their own stores and restaurants. Then she would only have to see them in magazines, where they were flat and glossy and not able to steal plainer people's boyfriends. When she was in a position to meet one of these beautiful women, she usually felt uninterested in knowing them. She surprised herself by putting her arms around Astra Rainbow and bringing her back to Mickey's side. Shelly's intelligence helped her realize that this child who was appalled at the idea of crime would never attempt to steal anything, especially something human.

Mickey took over. He got them a cab and then a good table at Joe Allen's, pushing his small party ahead of others. Over the best hamburger in town, they smiled at one another. Mickey, who was very careful about money, surprised himself by pushing dessert. He reached for Shelly's hand under the table as the dishes were being cleared. His other hand wasn't visible. It might have been holding Astra Rainbow's. Shelly didn't care. In the presence of this young woman, Mickey was warmer to Shelly than he had been in a long time. In the strangest of ways, it was one of the best dinners with this man that she ever had.

# 7
# A Mercedes
# on Sunday

MICKEY shaded his typewriter. With his torso hunched over
it, there was no chance that the instrument could catch the
light. He didn't look like a comedy writer. He looked like a man doing
battle. The keys were aliens and he was attacking them one by one,
using a two-finger method. Not once did he smile or pause to savor
what he was doing. In fact, his only happiness was in seeing the words
accumulate. When he got to the end of a page, he was glad because
he liked knowing another bit of his work had been completed. Then,
when he rolled a new blank sheet into the typewriter, his mood darkened. He was never confident enough to feel that he had the ability
to fill a page correctly. When he ran out of letters to punch, Mickey
rolled back his chair. Without rising, he poured himself a cup of coffee
from the brewer that he kept on the windowsill. He faced his work
like a surgeon facing patients on the operating table.

*Further Notes on the Story of Astra Rainbow*
The girl has baggage. Either she really has committed a sin or
she thinks she has. This will work well because she looks so
innocent.

Incorporate idea of a Jewish man who has always wanted to
have a real Christmas. He always felt deprived because Chanukah
couldn't compare to the magic he thought the Christian holiday
held.

Astra Rainbow is a love child born on the Lower East Side of
New York to a young mother who has run away from home and
a father who is constantly stoned and deals in drugs.

The young family makes its way to a commune. Surprisingly,

the father straightens out and he's the one who takes care of the child. The mother wanders off and the father takes the infant back to his home in Ohio.

Since the father was a peacenik, he objected furiously to his father's gun collection. He argued with his old man about it all the time. When his father died, his mother wouldn't let him throw away the guns because they were a reminder of the old man. "He loved those guns," she says, as if they were all he loved.

The father enters the mainstream of society. He gets a job, let's say in a shoe store, and becomes an assistant manager. He marries a woman whom he never loves as much as his first wife, but who fits in with this part of his life. Astra Rainbow grows up. They move to the next town, but one day while visiting the grandmother, she gets bored and finds the gun collection. Naturally there is an accident. The five-year-old Astra Rainbow accidentally shoots her stepmother.

Nobody blames her because she was too young to know what she was doing, but she did know, and she feels guilty about it every day of her life. It is a very confusing situation because the father loves his daughter and at the same time he hates her for killing his wife. In order to protect the child, the father never tells anyone that the child herself had pulled the trigger, so everyone feels sorry for the motherless child. This drives the child crazy because she has always known it was her fault. The father remarries when the child is about twelve, and she goes to live with her grandmother because she makes the new wife nervous. When she's twenty-two, she goes to New York and falls in love with a Jewish writer. He manipulates her into inviting him home for Christmas. He is one of those Jews who wants to steal Christmas. (Note: Christmas will give me a good time frame for this.)

Because he doesn't know any of the background, he thinks he's going to have a great time in Ohio and a real Christian Christmas. When he first gets there, everything is exactly as he expected— all the Santa Claus shit, the whole thing. But after he's there for about a day and a half he sees the drama unfolding.

He learns about the accident at a confrontational dinner. The father blames his father for leaving a loaded gun as a legacy. The daughter blames the father for sending her away. The father blames the daughter for killing the one woman who made sense out of his life. The new wife goes berserk. (Note: The mother and the third wife are blondes. The dead wife is a brunette.)

The Jew keeps trying to get everyone to have a normal holiday. He wants everyone to go to church and sing "Silent Night." He doesn't want to ruin the one good Christmas of his life just because this crazy family has decided to have its moment of truth. (He doesn't want to be in the middle of *Long Day's Journey into Night*.) He can't believe anything bad can happen in a house with Santa on the roof, Rudolph on the front lawn, and the little baby Jesus in His manger under the tree. What he has to learn is that people in Ohio don't just kiss and make up. They do that in Brooklyn where you have to kiss your cousins even if you can't stand them. In Ohio, they end arguments with guns. And there probably is no 911 emergency number either, so those who don't die instantly bleed to death on the Oriental rug that's been in the family for generations.

The fatal shot has to come at night, on Christmas Eve, before the Jew gets to know what's inside of any of the bright green-and-red boxes under the tree. The family is sitting around the fireplace. Let's say they've just come home from church and they're warming themselves. Cookies are brought out by the grand-mother.

(Note: What great storage space these people must have. They have room in their homes for things that are used one day a year. They have boxes of ornaments and garlands and big Santas that are never seen for eleven months. His mother's small apartment could never have successfully concealed Christmas. It had a hard enough time with Passover and Chanukah. In Christian homes in Ohio they were able to conceal an entire reindeer, and that impressed the Jewish man.)

The grandmother feels she shouldn't let the family believe that she made the cookies, so in a speech that lasts much too long she explains that these are Janet Foster's cookies and wasn't she just the nicest woman in the world to bring them over, considering she has arthritis and all. The evening is supposed to be a typical Christmas Eve, but unfortunately the father's new wife has be-come obsessed with her husband's remark about his second wife being the only woman he ever loved. She finds the gun that Grandma keeps in case of intruders. (They do that in the mid-west—shoot intruders.) While the family members are gathered by the fireplace with hot cider and Jane Foster's cookies, she comes down the stairs and holds them captive.

The Jew panics. He's never been this close to a gun. He makes a fool of himself by crying, pleading, begging. No one else is even close to hysterical. They are trying to get the wife to put the gun down, but in the Jewish man's mind they are doing it all wrong. They're saying things like, "Put down the gun, Louise." He's screaming things like, "You'll be on *60 Minutes*," and, "I'll give you any amount of money to put that thing down."

She had meant to shoot her husband, but the Jewish man is so uncontrollable he gets the bullet instead. Just as he's dying, it all becomes very clear to him and he knows why he's been shot. Jews were not meant to have Christmas. He had to die young. Life with the guilt that he would have suffered would have been intolerable. He's learned his lesson and his only regret is that he can't give his message to other Jewish men: Don't go to Ohio for a Christian holiday."

Mickey wasn't sure about what he'd written. He felt safer with comedy and he knew there was a lot of tragedy here. He stuffed the pages into the folder and filed it quickly. His movements were fast, as if he were a jewel thief concerned about being caught in the middle of a robbery. He didn't know why he felt he had to bury the material quickly. He didn't want Astra Rainbow to see it, but she wasn't back from lunch yet. She couldn't sneak in because he would hear her dealing with the door, since he had one with a wooden frame and glass, the kind that private eyes should have. Probably he was hiding the pages from himself. If there was something there, he might have to write a screenplay. Also, there was the moral question: Could you write about a person who was bringing you corned beef on rye?

He tried to work on *Afterlife* or *Whatever Happened to the Beckermans?* He had promised it to the network by the third week in November, which seemed like a long way off at the time of the promise. Now that his mind was wandering, it felt as if he were facing an impossible deadline. He was in the middle of a funny scene. The members of the family are just starting to accept the fact that they are dead when the sheep from next door keep wandering through. The family had heard there were shepherds living next door and had thought the family name was Shepherd. Then they realize that the neighbors are actually shepherds who died centuries ago. Now they're deciding which is worse, living next to the animals they're scared to be with or being dead.

Writing was never easy for Mickey. He bled from his work. He left his desk and looked out the window. Seeing the lunch crowds dashing around eight stories below made him feel good. He knew that they were ordinary and he was creative. He could make more money than any of them from the things that came out of his head . . . when they came.

He didn't return to *Afterlife* but rather to the file that he had just tried to bury. Here was the gold. He would probably have to tone down the concept to make it commercial. The young man wouldn't necessarily have to be Jewish. He could be an Italian kid from Brooklyn who had never seen snow that wasn't dirty. That would work.

Mickey had waited for over five years for the right idea to come, and this might be it. Other writers didn't wait. They wrote one hack script after another, going for the jokes, not worrying whether they would be remembered or not. He knew that having no movie to his credit was better than having a bad, ordinary film. When he had something on the big screen, it would be monumental. He would get the good reviews and the big crowds. He would also go for the respect from Woody Allen. They would have dinners in his honor and his name would be used by charities to raise money. Those head-of-the-studio snots would pay for everything in his life. They would pick up his hotel bills all over the world, and he would charge suits to his room. The only mistake he could make would be to try to burst on the scene with mediocrity.

He forced himself back to *Afterlife*. He sat down at the typewriter and didn't get up until seven-thirty.

Astra Rainbow had brought in his sandwich and cream soda. She knew to walk softly and didn't need to be thanked. She placed the dollar-thirty-five change carefully on the corner of his desk, making sure the coins didn't clank. She didn't speak to her boss the entire afternoon. While he worked at his desk, she worked at hers. He would type a sloppy page and she would retrieve it and retype it, making it look as if it were ready to be handed in. She wished what she was typing was true.

It would help to know that there was an afterlife and that the little boy she had pushed to his death was living somewhere near the dead family. If Mr. Burke was right, when she died she would search for that little boy and tell him she was sorry. Of course he wouldn't forgive her. According to Mr. Burke's theory, since he had died as a child, he would stay a child through eternity and he would never forgive her for that. If his theory was correct, she would like to die at forty. She thought women of forty were very beautiful. Their breasts were full and they always knew what to say. They said the most beautiful things. She was sure that women of forty were the poets of the world.

Although Mickey knew that his secretary was typing his pages right behind him, he was surprised to see her still sitting at her desk at seven-thirty.

"How come you're still here?" he asked.

"Because you are," she said with secretarial devotion.

"Did you think it was funny?"

She knew her answer would be important to him and yet she couldn't form an honest opinion. He had asked her the same question for months now. Didn't he know what was funny? "I don't know," she said. She lowered her head, embarrassed that she didn't have an answer for him.

"How come you don't know what's funny? If it's funny, you laugh."

"I don't really laugh," she said. He hadn't noticed. He didn't really laugh either. He did when he was a kid, but ever since he had been paid to make others laugh, if he heard something he thought was humorous he would say, "That's funny." This was a typical response of many comedy writers. They make rotten audiences.

"Do you know when something is sad?" he asked. He sat down for her response, letting her know that he wanted a real answer.

"I guess so. Things make me cry. Like if there's a fire or a murder I'm always sad. I cry during Hallmark commercials too, especially the one where the little girl gives her piano teacher a card. I've seen it millions of times and it always makes me sad . . . or maybe it makes me happy." She got a bit flustered here. "I don't know, Mr. Burke. Maybe I'm not a good judge of sad either. Pardon me for saying this, but you really shouldn't ask my opinion. It just seems to get you upset." She folded her hands on her desk, the schoolteacher waiting for her pupil to respond.

"Of course it gets me upset. If I stop making people laugh, my whole career goes in the toilet. Naturally I'm going to ask the first person who reads it what she thinks, and naturally I'm going to be insecure if that person doesn't know."

"But it's not as if I know that some things are funny and other things aren't. Mr. Burke, I told you from the very beginning if that had to be part of the job, you shouldn't have hired me." She turned sad here and he quickly rescued her.

"Hey, it's okay. One of the best things I ever did is hire you." He wanted to comfort her by taking her into his arms, but he didn't. The one time he had put an arm around her, she had frozen.

"Really?"

"Really."

"But maybe you could get someone who types *and* laughs."

"Laughing isn't everything."

"But it's a lot. Did you hear about that man who was dying from cancer and he laughed night and day and he cured himself?"

"Yes."

"You did? You actually heard about him?"

"He's a famous man, Dr. Norman Cousins. He wrote a successful book about it."

"Well, I'm going to die of any disease I get because I don't know how to laugh. Oh, sometimes a laugh comes out, but not often. Once I laughed when someone fell down in the street. He didn't get hurt or anything, but all I saw was this big fat guy sitting there in the street, and I heard a laugh and I realized it was coming from me. Then I got scared that I could only laugh at other people's troubles, and from that moment on I really tried to control myself." She looked to him for approval, not realizing that she was going to get it.

"We all laugh at people falling down. Charlie Chaplin made a living falling down. He put banana peels everywhere you looked. The audience roared when Chaplin fell. That's not strange: We're so relieved that it's someone other than ourselves falling that we laugh."

"You know just about everything about comedy, don't you?"

"Well, it's what I do. It's how I can afford all those corned-beef sandwiches at full price."

"See, what I don't understand, Mr. Burke, is that if you know and they know, how come I have to know too?"

"You don't," he said. He had met other women who didn't know what was funny. He had fallen in love with each of them for no longer than a week and a half. He had married a woman who didn't know what was funny. It couldn't have been love.

Feeling the business of the day was over, she stood up and got into her coat. She did it gracefully, with no fumbling for the sleeves, without making him feel obliged to jump up and help her. Still, he got up to assist. Mickey always liked being part of the coat dance. Once he had learned how to do it, he thought it unfair to be left out of helping. He didn't think of Astra Rainbow as helpless, but did know that putting on women's coats was one of the most intricate things that men and women could do together.

When they got to the elevator, he asked her to dinner. Since the night they had helped Mary, this had become a ritual. He always asked and she always refused, saying it really wasn't a very good idea to go to dinner with one's boss. He had told her to think of him as a friend, but she insisted that they shouldn't be friends because it would ruin their working relationship. Mr. Raphelson had taught her about what happened when secretaries got too friendly with their bosses. Eventually the boss was embarrassed that his secretary knew so much about him. Then, since it was impossible for them to go back to a purely professional relationship, the secretary always got fired. He had sworn that he would never fire her, but Astra Rainbow stuck with Mr. Raphelson's advice. Tonight, as usual, she thanked him and went home.

Mickey started for his hotel. He bought six chestnuts for a dollar, mumbling to the salesman in the torn clothes and fingerless gloves that it was a gyp. He had bought the chestnuts hundreds of times and they were never any cheaper and never any better. Still, he complained to himself for blocks. When he got to Sixth and Fifty-seventh, a trio of telephone booths drew him. He was going to pass them by, but they looked inviting. In the night light the booths looked almost clean. The two end phones were both in use, one by a young male executive, the other by a young woman. They had both placed their hard attaché cases on the ground between their legs so their calves could protect their business. The man and woman looked like a matched pair. They should have been talking to each other. Glad he wasn't spoiling the symmetry, Mickey took the middle booth. He reached into his pocket, looking for a quarter. Again he mumbled, annoyed that in his lifetime the cost of a phone call had more than doubled. He hated that those phone thugs had made the price of a call twenty-five cents.

He had decided to call Shelly. If she were free, he would take her to dinner, somewhere nice, somewhere you had to have a reservation. He would let her pick it out since all he required of food was that there be enough of it. He hoped she would pick someplace brightly lit and unromantic. On this night he needed food and company, not hand-holding. His hands were tired from punching out words. He needed Shelly to laugh with him.

The phone rang three times before Shelly's recorded message told him that she was very sorry that she couldn't talk right now, but she would return the message as soon as possible. She added, in a voice that she had learned to use for business, that the machine was voice-activated and that the caller could speak as long as he wanted. Mickey had invested a quarter in the call, and he wasn't about to hang up without saying what he had to. "Hey, Shelly, it's Mickey," he said, trying to sound happier and warmer than he was. "I'm standing here on the street and I was kind of wondering if you wanted to go out and have a drink or something to eat. So, I guess you owe me one since I was going to pay tonight. Anyway, do you think this is funny? You know, I'm writing a pilot about this family that's dead. They all died together and they're living in a place which is sort of like Levittown with clouds on the ground. Everyone who has ever died lives there. Do you think it's funny if they have a problem helping their teenage son adjusting to death and they find Freud and invite him over to dinner so that he can help? Freud keeps trying to convince the family that death is the ulimate ejaculation. I'm going to grab a bite. Call me if you get a chance. Maybe we'll get together Sunday. We still didn't get to talk about the good times we had or aggravate each other about what we did wrong . . . And, by the way, did I tell you, you looked great both with and without the matching oven?"

While Mickey was leaving the message, Shelly was counting coconut balls for the Kesellman affair. "I swear—the only reason he's

letting me have a big wedding is that he loves your coconut balls,"
the future bride had told Shelly. She had promised that the groom
would not be without his balls. Since it was a Thursday-night wedding, the guests had left by eleven, the bride and groom were in their
suite at the Pierre by eleven-thirty and Shelly Silver had counted the
silver and was home by twelve. Naturally, once again, she didn't fail
to see the irony in the fact that she pursued a career that brought
people together and kept her alone. Making coconut balls and having
a relationship didn't mix well. Who but another caterer could put up
with her coming home at midnight at least a couple of times a week?
God, she was tired.

Mickey's message brightened her. She played it three times and
had memorized it by the time she called Greta. She had warned her
new friend that she would be home late, but Greta had insisted that
Shelly should call at any hour. "I'll be doing my sketches for next
fall and believe me, darling, I'll just be on the shoulder pads at two.
I'll be up all night and praying for interruptions."

Shelly played Mickey's message for Greta, and they both agreed it
sounded promising. "He needs you," said Greta. "I don't know what
he's going to do about it, but he definitely needs you. What I'm hearing
is a desperate man in a phone booth reaching out."

Shelly sank happily into the thousand pillows on her bed. She felt
really good. The man she loved so hard and so long had not only
called, he had mentioned a specific date. "So, I'll see him on Sunday,"
Shelly said, concluding the conversation, since they had analyzed
every word he had said.

"I put the ad in for Sunday," said Greta. There was always strength
in her voice. It never reflected the fact that the rest of the world was
probably sleeping.

"What ad?" Shelly vaguely remembered that they were going to
put an ad in *The New York Times*, but she was too tired from catering
and too excited from Mickey's message to remember why.

"The ad for the Mercedes." Greta fixed a neckline in one of her
sketches as she spoke. She was beginning to like the results. Now she
had to hope she could find enough red silk crepe and enough women
with cleavage who were willing to show it off.

"Oh yeah, for the Mercedes. I didn't think you were really going
to do that."

"Sure you did. You had your accountant send my accountant a
check for half the ad and half the rental of the car."

"That's right. He wanted to know what the hell I was doing and I
was too embarrassed to explain."

"There's nothing to be embarrassed about. Tell him we're just two
single women trying to beat the odds."

About three weeks before, Shelly had refused to apply for a pen pal in a white-collar prison. Greta was sure that writing prisoners was a great way to meet men. "It's not as if we're going to write to men who murdered their mothers," she said, trying to sound logical. "These are guys who embezzled or extorted from companies that probably cheat the public anyway. I'm not saying what they've done is right, but they are paying for their crime. You figure their wives tried to stand beside them in their time of need, but the pressure got too great. It's sort of the De Lorean–Cristina Ferrare syndrome. You start writing to one of these guys. I mean, we're talking white-collar, college-graduate executives who happen to be temporarily tied up, and they're just sitting there waiting for us. We go visit. A woman never looks better than when she's sitting on the other side of one of those prison grills. They learn to love us while they're still on the inside. We know they're not dating anybody else. We pick them up when they get out."

"And we support them for the rest of their lives because they can't get jobs."

"Don't be silly. Even Richard Nixon has been offered work."

Shelly said a definite no to the white-collar-prison scheme. She also said no to pretending they were reporters for *New York Magazine*. Greta tried to convince her that they could pretend to do a series of articles. "Here's the plan," she said, once more excited. When Greta got passionate, whatever hat she was wearing tipped, ready for take-off. It was a warning to those who knew her that she couldn't be stopped for a while. "First we say we're doing an article on the ten most eligible lawyers and we interview them. They'll all talk. What lawyer doesn't want that kind of publicity? After we either marry or totally exploit the lawyers, we move on to, say, the ten most eligible plastic surgeons. There's no end to it." Greta was so pleased with her proposal that she took a long, deep bow, the kind that is usually reserved for the star on opening night. "What? No applause?" she asked her audience of one. "This one has low overhead, short research time, and only a few phone calls. And maybe one of those little tape recorders they all use."

"And what happens when the articles don't show up in the magazine? Do they lynch us one at a time or do they form a vigilante committee?"

"I've been interviewed. Sometimes it makes it into the press, sometimes it doesn't. I never blame the reporter."

After saying no to the criminals, to the eligible-men series, and to the idea of bringing good-looking men to small-claims court and then apologizing, Shelly caved in on the Sunday Mercedes plan.

They would rent a small, two-seater Mercedes 560 SL for a day.

On the same day they would run an ad to sell the car. If a woman called, they would say the car had already been sold. If a man called, they would remind him that it was a two-seater and in no way a family car. If he didn't care, he would get an appointment to see the car. "It's really ingenious," said Greta. "For relatively little money, we are going to get to meet at least a dozen guys who at least have enough money to buy an expensive Mercedes. Chances are that some of them will be single. They're going to want to test-drive the thing, so either you or I get to spend some time with them, bumming around N.Y.C. and getting to know if we think they're a possibility."

"What if they want to buy the car, then and there, with cash?" Shelly's job was to point out the flaws in Greta's plans. Greta's job was to come up with ideas and to think quickly on her feet.

"We'll say that we have a previous offer and that we're just continuing to show it in case it doesn't come through. We'll take their names and numbers and let them know. I cannot believe how great this is. We actually get their names and numbers."

"What if we get attacked in the car?"

"We'll only go riding around with guys with good teeth and cashmere sweaters." That seemed to make sense to Shelly, who knew that rapists dressed poorly and probably didn't make regular visits to the dentist. Shelly finally had to admit there was some merit to the plan, and they put the ad in the *Times*.

Shelly returned Mickey's call and asked if they could get together Sunday night instead of during the day. That was fine with him, but he sounded confused. Apparently he hadn't remembered making plans. Shelly took a quarter of a Valium when she got off the phone.

The calls for the car started coming in late Saturday. "We're going to make it a bargain so that we get a large response," Greta had decided. Not being car people, neither of them realized how much of a bargain they'd advertised. The Sunday *New York Times* goes on sale around ten-thirty on Saturday night. It was particularly warm this early November evening and New Yorkers had not stayed home. On their way back from restaurants and movies they had picked up the paper, and those who were looking for cars turned immediately to the classifieds. They all wanted to find that big bargain, the car that had to be sold quickly and quietly because the owner couldn't keep up with the payments. Their fingers moved down the column of Mercedes and stopped when they got to the car that Shelly and Greta had put up for sale. Every one of them checked his watch and tried to convince himself that it wasn't too late to call. With one hand on the paper and the other punching numbers, each one hoped his dream car was still available and that the thirty-five thousand wasn't a misprint.

The first call came in at ten-forty, surprising Shelly. Greta had expected to come over at eight in the morning and be in plenty of time to start handling the phone. Neither of them had anticipated such overanxious buyers. Shelly stumbled through the first call, but by eleven-thirty, during the last call of the night, which included profuse apologies for the lateness of the hour, she was beginning to think that Greta had come up with an ingenious idea. She called her friend to tell her about inquiries and fell asleep forgiving Mickey for making her love him. This was slightly different. Usually she was angry at night and forgiving in the morning.

Greta was there by nine in diaphanous yellow. She didn't look as if she could fit into a sports car. They both went to the window to peek at the little red car parked across the street. They were proud of it, like parents checking a newborn through the nursery glass. "How many Jews?" Greta asked when they had left the window.

"What?" Shelly's father had always refused to buy a German car because of how the Jews had suffered. Shelly somehow thought Greta was asking how many Jews had sacrificed their lives for this car.

"Of the ones who called, how many are Jews?"

"I don't know. There was one Stein that I remember." Shelly ran for the list as Greta kept an eye on the car, as though there was anything she could do. If the car had been damaged or stolen, Greta wouldn't have been able to do anything from her viewing booth.

Like a child delivering a good report card, Shelly handed over the names of the people who had called. Times from ten to twelve-thirty were booked at twenty-minute intervals. ("Enough time for a good spin," Greta had figured.) Now she took the list to the light to examine it closely. Greta fished in her pocketbook for the Mont Blanc pen she both loved and feared, since it had once leaked, and checked off four names. "All right," she said, once the Mont Blanc was safely away. "We've got to remember to leave your answering machine on because there are bound to be calls all day.

Shelly patted the pillows beside her on the couch as if they needed comfort. The women yawned simultaneously, and then, affected by each other's yawns, they gulped for air again. "You know what we do? You know why we're so tired?" Greta asked.

"Because we work too hard." Shelly was sure she had the right answer. Overachieving had always been her style.

"Nope." Greta lifted the ends of her skirt the way a curtsying child would. She was still sitting and there was so much material in her dress that all her gesture did was widen the space she occupied.

"I'll bet playing football takes only half the energy of throwing a wedding where the bride wants everything in lavender."

"Well, heading up our minicorporations and also getting our eyeliner on in the right place is an exhausting job, but that's not what's knocking us out." Greta took a dramatic pause here. She had juicy information and she was going to dispense it slowly. "We've been on too many honeymoons," she said with authority. "You know what our mothers had? They had a wedding and then two weeks in a hotel room in Atlantic City or someplace Atlantic Cityish. It didn't matter where they went. They stayed in the hotel room exploring their husbands' bodies, wearing their best nightgowns, letting themselves be taken. I believe they were passionate for those two weeks. It's hard for me to picture my mother as passionate, but I think for those fourteen days she was hot. I've seen pictures of my parents on their honeymoon, and she had flowers in her hair. That's what women in heat do. You know what I think? I think those two weeks wore her out. I've been through three honeymoons in the last three years. I have spent two weeks with three different men. With all of them I tried to set up a love nest they would have a hard time leaving. They wiped me out. No wonder I'm exhausted."

"I've been on a lot of honeymoons also," Shelly said sadly. She too had memories of rushing home carrying flowers and candles, having to run back to the store because she forgot the guy's favorite juice for the morning. "It does take too much energy."

"Do you think these passionate interludes have ruined us? Maybe we became junkies for them. Real life can't be as exciting as a couple of weeks with someone new." And Greta threw her skirt wider than before. By now she took up half the couch.

"I think everything has ruined us. The sixties. The seventies. The eighties. Our mothers. Inflation."

The phone rang and they both perked up. A married woman forgets the thrill of a ringing phone. One call can make a life better or ruin it completely. Greta answered and scheduled the caller for twelve. When she hung up, the two women squealed like teenagers who have been told the school is snowed in. The phone was ringing again. This time Shelly took it and arranged a twelve-twenty.

Before they went down to meet the first "prospective buyer," they fixed their eye makeup with Q-Tips and ran lip gloss over their lips. Shelly pulled her sweater down so that the Polo pony went galloping directly over her left breast. Greta retied her scarf. They forgot that their lives had exhausted them.

The day held surprises. The ten-twenty man had a big smile and legs that almost didn't fit into the car. He laughed easily and wore short sleeves in November. He loved the color red. Shelly got to ride with him and she almost felt guilty leaving Greta on the curb. She hoped the next one would look just as good.

As he sped down Seventh Avenue, the man Greta had wanted asked Shelly questions about the car that she couldn't answer. She was a woman who had rarely been behind the wheel, and he wanted to know the size of the engine.

Her mother had infuriated Shelly by playing cute at the gas station. When she was no more than eleven she watched the woman, who she did not yet know was flawed, practically cry when smoke came out of her engine. Shelly's mother begged the man in the blue jumpsuit to fix the mess and not tell her anything about it. Unfortunately for both mother and daughter, Shelly had been reading a book about the first women flyers. The young girl was struggling to choose her role model. Even though she wanted the right to borrow her mother's sweaters, she was leaning toward Amelia Earhart and her friends. "Rough and rugged" seemed to have it all over Shelly Silver's style. That day in the gas station, Shelly vowed never to be helpless with a machine. Still, a little less than three decades later, here she was, giggling through the technical questions. She was her mother, saying, "You'll have to ask my friend about that, and when you find out, don't tell me." A small flirtatious laugh escaped her lips. She was in the forties, a decade she hadn't dipped into before.

"Do you have the service record on the car?" He looked at her as she spoke, and she felt he had his eyes off the road for too long. Mickey always looked at her while he drove. He drove her to the Hamptons once, telling her an entire idea for a pilot and looking straight at her the whole time. She kept putting her foot on an imaginary brake, which is what she did now in the little red Mercedes.

"Am I making you nervous?" he asked with a smile. People who were otherwise nice often enjoyed making you nervous in moving vehicles. The fact was, he *was* making her nervous, driving too fast, asking questions she couldn't answer and referring to things she never heard of. To her, a service record was something military.

"I can't really fill you in on things like service records. My friend, the woman you met at the curb, knows all the technical details about the car. I know the basics, like color and where the rock stations are." He threw his head back and laughed. It was too large a laugh for such a small car, and Shelly noticed his head was too far back for driving.

As he screeched around corners they asked each other what they did. He was a history teacher at Princeton, which gave Shelly about two blocks of fantasies of living in a stone cottage, having teas and dinners with intellectuals who loved her baked chicken with the wild-rice stuffing. It had been a long time since Shelly had met a history teacher. Many of the boys she had known in college stayed on to study history and avoid the war. The graduate schools were filled with boys preparing themselves to pass the secrets of the ancient world on to others. They were as much a part of her past as campus violence and bell-bottom pants.

"If I buy your car, even if I hear something rattling, I'd like you to cater a dinner for two sometime and I would like you to be one of the two." He looked at her warmly. She liked his look. She hated that it appeared he was about to hit three pedestrians. She gasped. He stopped on a dime and thought nothing of it. "I'll be happy to pay all your normal fees. I'd just like you to drive out and see my place. I'll provide the wine." Shelly looked at the clock. Ten-forty. She couldn't believe how well this silly little scheme was working. This was her first ride of the day. Usually she wasn't even out of bed by now, and here she was being invited to a stone cottage in a state she ordinarily didn't like but now considered beautiful and possibly blooming with bougainvillea.

"That would be fun. I have a portable oven." She realized most women traveled without this cumbersome accessory, but she had always considered it one of her assets. She never minded being with her portable womb.

He suggested all this should happen next weekend and since he had her number, he said he would give her a call. As he drove back to the West Side, she watched the road and his profile and couldn't imagine that the rest of the day would be any better than this. He flew down West Seventy-seventh and then, with one sharp turn, they were back in front of her building and headed toward the parking place, which was thankfully still available. Standing there were Greta and the next man. He was graying, nice-looking and trim, one of those guys with good muscle definition. He probably had a personal trainer. Perhaps Greta would get her man too. Maybe all four of them could go abroad every summer. Everything was fine until Shelly and her future date got out of the car.

"If my mechanic says there are no problems, I'm going to take it," said the professor, lifting the hood to take a layman's look.

"Maybe you should think it over," said Shelly, hoping to avoid the sale.

"No. I'm going to give you a check now." The professor reached in his pocket for a checkbook and pen.

"It's just a deposit. His mechanic could nix the whole thing," said Greta's man, heading for the driver's seat.

"You've got to give me the first shot at this," said the professor, turning his charm on Shelly, acting as if they had been lovers for years. She wasn't sure he had winked, but he might have. Shelly looked toward Greta for help.

"We're not going to accept any money now, but if you give me your number, we'll call you at the end of the day." Greta took the list of men and her Mont Blanc from her purse.

"That's not the way you sell a car," said the professor. He closed the hood. It was hard to tell whether he slammed it out of anger or merely to shut it.

"It's not?" said Shelly, interested in keeping things light.

"No, it's not. This isn't some sort of contest. If I went into a store to buy something *and* left a check they wouldn't tell me they'd let me know." He started writing. The gray-haired man honked the horn, ready to start his test drive. He was already fooling around with the automatic windows. Greta put her hand on the professor's arm, which interrupted his writing. He wasn't at all happy. Shelly felt she could forget about the baked chicken.

"We decided last night that we weren't going to take any checks on a Sunday," said Greta.

"Are we going or not?" asked the gray-haired man. He was starting the engine.

"Get him out of there. I'm buying the car." The professor started writing again, and Greta turned to Shelly. She had had the answers up to now. This time Greta was silent. She played with an escaped hair. She looked to Shelly for help. The man in the car blew the horn.

"Uh, that check is going to take a lot of zeros," Shelly said, hoping to shock him into stopping.

"I know how many zeros are in thirty-five thousand. I'm not in the math department, but I know my zeros." He gently took her by the shoulders, a gesture that usually precedes a kiss. Instead, he turned her away from him in order to lean his checkbook on her back to facilitate his writing.

"You realize this is a Sunday and we'll have to wait until tomorrow to call the bank. And God knows where the pink slip is. And aren't you going to have to get a loan from the bank?" Greta was doing her best to halt the process.

"My check will clear," the history professor said. Shelly figured he was one of those teachers with family money.

"You realize that we'll have to keep showing the car, just in case you don't have sufficient funds." Greta had found her boss-of-the-business voice.

Shelly looked toward the professor to see just how angry he was. He was as pissed as she expected he would be. The man in the car was angry too. Finally, the professor pointed one finger at both of them, yelled that was no way to do business and stormed off without a word about dinner.

"We can write that one off," Greta said, as she got in the car. Shelly never got the chance to tell her she had almost had the chance of another little honeymoon.

By two o'clock the comedy had turned to farce. It seemed that most men needed more than twenty minutes for a test drive and that they all spent too much time looking under the hood. By twelve the appointments were a half an hour late and by two there was a line of men waiting, seven in all: three short, one exceptionally tall, three holding jackets, scared that the New York weather wouldn't hold up for them. They were all trying to be patient enough to get their hands on an underpriced Mercedes. They wore varying combinations of khaki jeans and purposely faded work shirts and spoke to each other as if they were a committee called together to put down the broads who were selling this car. They were angry because of the line. Had they known the truth about the car "sale," there might have been, at the very least, verbal abuse.

When she realized things were out of control, Greta dragged Shelly to the curb to tell her they were in trouble. Shelly already knew that. Five men had tried to leave deposits. "What we have to do next time," Greta said, "is rent a Rolls and schedule the appointments forty-five minutes apart. And no more bargains," she added, as if they were actually selling a car for less than the market value.

The basic problem was no longer whether they could seduce these men. They couldn't. Everyone was too hostile to be flirtatious. The real problem was crowd control. Shelly got out of the car once to find the two-twenty and two-forty appointments ready to swing at each other. Both were weary from waiting and overheated. Impatient, sweaty men could be nice to each other for only a limited amount of time. Unfortunately, they were both A-types and the taller one was also a sporadic user of cocaine. The shorter one had tied his brand-new K-Swiss sneakers too tightly and felt it too much of an effort to loosen them. They had begun to discuss the national budget, but that was not the real reason the disagreement escalated into a fight. It was that one man had taken the position that the defense budget should have been cut. Had he played by the rules of a gentleman debater all would have been fine. Instead he riled up his opponent by saying repeatedly, "Yeah. Sure. You know that because you were there when they decided that." First there was an accidental brushing. Then a gesture turned into a shove that was forming into a possible punch by the time Shelly intervened. Like a good camp counselor, she stopped them with cookies left over from the Saltzmans' boy's sixth birthday party. Although the men on line ranged from twenty-five to sixty-five, they were all boys. With the right leader, they could have been marched off on an overnight hike. She would have told them all to go if she hadn't been scared that Greta would have considered it a waste of seven men.

"How come the car is so cheap?" said the first man in line. Since he was first, he could afford to be a skeptic.

She thought quickly. Her explanation would have to satisfy seven nodding heads. "For a couple of reasons," she said. "We wanted to sell it quickly because the place where we garage it used to have very reasonable rates and now it's about twenty dollars a minute. I don't know if you know the place, it's at Forty-second and Tenth. There's also a rumor that they're going to tear the place down, and I'm in no mood to buy a condominium for the car. Did you see that in the *Times*, how they're selling condominiums for cars?" Since nobody challenged her, she didn't have to continue but, facing seven angry men, she felt she should. "And my friend and I found we were using the car less and less. At the beginning, when it was a brand-new toy, we . . . uh . . . drove out to the Island all the time, but you know how it is, you get used to a thing and you take it for granted. Like when I first got my exercise bike, I swore that I would get on it every day, but do I? Are you kidding? It can sit there for months and I don't even look at it." Her mouth was going, but her mind was praying that Greta would return before she was hung. "So, my friend and I chipped in for the car and then it kept sitting there and we wanted to get rid of it fast because she needs the cash for a loft." She didn't dare take a breath. It was to her advantage to keep up this pace. At least no one was maneuvering her neck into their hands. "I guess we didn't realize what a bargain we were offering. We asked a couple of people and they felt that thirty-five thousand was fair." No one looked any happier, so she rushed to add, "Anyone who wants to leave, can." She said this as if she held them by force or will.

"I'll give you thirty-six," said the second man in line, who had been fairly quiet and very short up until now.

And so the auction began. The tall loud one shouted, "Thirty-seven!" and the troublemaker in the middle was up to thirty-nine-five by the time Greta returned with the car. Shelly thought the sight of the Mercedes would calm everyone down, but they continued to shout numbers. None of them realized their offers were in vain. Greta took a turn at trying to reason with them. It wasn't easy. The man who had just test-driven the car was writing out a check, which both the women and all the men waved away. Shelly was happy to escape to the interior of the car with just one of them.

"So, what do you do?" she asked him when they were far from the crowd.

"I'm in real estate," he said. The old Shelly from the University of

Michigan would have felt obliged to ascertain that he wasn't a slum-lord. The current Shelly smiled and asked him what he thought a two-bedroom co-op on West Seventy-seventh between Central Park West and Columbus would go for.

By six o'clock the car was safely back to the rental agency, and the two women sat facing each other on the same couches that they had occupied that morning when their mood was optimistic. They had slipped off their shoes and, now safe from the angry crowd, they could laugh. They laughed without inhibition, as few men can. They had thirty-five years' worth of laughter apiece. They laughed because they couldn't believe what they had just done, and they laughed because they had survived it. When they wiped their eyes and sighed, they laughed again because they had been successful. They had made contact with fifteen men in one day.

"I got one exterminator," Greta said, struggling to get words out.

"An actual exterminator?" After the strain of the day, they found this particularly hilarious. They could hardly speak for howling.

"You know what's really funny?" asked Greta. "To hear an exterminator brag. If a lawyer wants to be showy, he drops the name of his clients or who he dragged to court. All a doctor has to do is tell you where his offices are. If an exterminator really wants to impress you, he has to let you know who has rats and roaches."

"Did he name names?"

"No. I tried to get him to, but all he kept saying was that I would be shocked and surprised if he told me who. And when I really pressed, he said that one of his people—he didn't call them clients, he kept referring to them as people—"

"To differentiate them from the rodents, I guess."

"I guess . . . Anyway, one of his people was on the cover of *Time*. What was so crazy was that for about a block and a half I was impressed with him."

"Did he ask for your number?"

"Yeah, he did. And I didn't know how to get out of it. Oh, God. I gave my number to an exterminator. Me! Who once marched for wildlife." With this, Greta threw herself onto the couch. Her bottom half was still sitting, but from the waist up she was lying down.

"I have to admit it was an interesting day," Shelly said.

"It was. I couldn't believe there were seven of them there at once."

"And what about the guy with the hat who was talking to you so long? You know—the one with the cap. He's probably bald."

"Oh, him. He kept warning me about this scam where people give you a phony certified check. He kept breathing hot air on me and telling me to be careful." Shelly now lay down on her couch, feeling she'd earned the rest.

"Did he want to get together?"

"Yeah. I think so. He said he'd call."

"I'm telling you, this has to be the greatest thing we ever did."

"There were problems. We lost a lot of the ones who had to stand in line."

"Maybe we should hire a couple of successful single architects to draw up plans for a summer house. We wouldn't have to build. It's a hell of a way of meeting architects."

"You're out of control."

"No, Shelly. Don't you get it? We're in control."

"We had a mob scene out there. They hated us."

"No more than the men we've actually dated. Next time we rent a Rolls and space it better."

"Give me time to get over this one." Shelly closed her eyes. It had taken a lot of energy just to refuse the checks. She knew she could sleep but she had to try not to.

"One month. I'll give you one month, and if you're not married by then, we go for the Silver Cloud."

They both closed their eyes. Greta smiled. They had pulled something off. They had fooled men with checkbooks and had been in control. There was more than one dance in high school that nobody asked her to. Today the boys stood in line for her.

On her couch, Shelly calculated the effort it required to get ready for Mickey. It didn't seem possible to get dressed and out the door. "I'll never be ready for Mickey," she said to herself, her friend and the neighborhood. It was more than a simple statement.

"You're kidding."

"I told you I was going to see him." Outfits danced through her head. The red leather pants kept swirling in, but when Shelly remembered that she had worn them when she last saw Mickey, she forced them back into her closet.

"I knew you were going to see him, but I didn't realize it was tonight." Greta sat up, pouting like an eight-year-old child.

"What's the matter?" Shelly asked. She sat up slowly, exhausted. They faced each other again.

"Nothing," said Greta, looking down. She wiggled her toes, making sure she still had control over them.

"Come on." Greta's pubescent behavior brought out the mother in Shelly once again.

"It's just that . . . Oh, it's not important . . . It's just that, I don't know. I understand that you have to go out with him. Believe me, I'm the first one to say dump your girlfriends when a guy shows up. That's an unwritten rule between single friends. You can always cancel me out at the very last minute, the last *second* if you have to . . . It's just that today we had this major experience together and I wasn't ready to let you go yet." Greta wasn't crying, but she might as well have been. Her voice was shaky.

"I'll call him and cancel." As she said it, Shelly hoped Greta would try to talk her out of it.

"No," Greta said. She put her head in her hands. She was weary, not just from today, but from the ongoing chase. "I'd be too guilty for the rest of my life if you didn't go."

"I'd be guilty for the rest of my life if I did."

"Is this a guilt-off? Are we going to sit here and outguilt each other? Because if so, I want to call my mother. My brother is forty-two and she still tells him she's sorry he didn't become a urologist."

"So, what do you want me to do? I'll do whatever you want. Mickey Burke has been around for years. He's not going anywhere. I'm sure I can squeeze another date out of him."

"You're too nice, Shelly."

"Nah."

"Yeah. Your job is to go out there and mate."

"But I don't have to do it tonight."

"Yes, you do. Analysts go nuts when their female patients moan about being alone and then don't get out whenever they can. So. Here's what's going to happen. I need about five hours of sleep, which I'll get on your couch once my makeup is off. You're going to go out there, smelling sweet, intending to seduce. If you come home tonight, I'll be here. If you don't, I'll be jealous." With that Greta lay down again, freeing Shelly to go.

"Yeah. Okay. And I'm sure I'll be back tonight. We're not into touching each other yet. We're still reminiscing about the past."

"Shelly?"

"Yeah."

"I'll be real happy for you when you land a guy, but only if I land one the same month." Greta spoke softly; her words were more serious than she had meant them to be.

Shelly called Mickey to tell him that she couldn't make it. It surprised him. She had always made it before. She got a little scared when he didn't reschedule their dinner, but back in the living room she felt her future was safer with a woman with plans than with a man with none.

If there are turning points in life, this might have been one of them.

# 8

# A Head Injury

WEEKS ahead of time, Mickey started hinting to Astra Rainbow that he would like to go home with her for Christmas. He needed to see and feel the turf that he wanted to write about. He could write about New York. He had walked the streets of Manhattan, memorizing them. The roads of Lorain were something he would have to learn.

At first he worked on his secretary's sympathy. When she returned with his corned beef on rye one day, he told her how lucky she was to have a family to go to for the holidays. She didn't allow his hints to register. Right after Thanksgiving, he talked about how he would love to be someplace where they actually knew the turkey before they ate it. Still nothing. At the end of November, when she finished typing a draft of *Afterlife*, he gave her two hundred-dollar bills and told her to buy some decorations for the office. "It's the only Christmas joy I'll have," he said, as if he were orphaned and living in England in another century. He bowed his head and tried to look homeless whenever he could.

One day he asked her what the Christmas dinners of her childhood were like. Astra Rainbow confirmed his fantasies, describing even the Jell-O mold salad in the shape of an angel. After explaining that there was always more than one kind of pie for dessert, the girl got wistful. "Oh, Mr. Burke," she said, her hands in the prayer position. "It's too bad I won't be home this year. Sometimes there are two kinds of pie and chocolate fluff for those who want something lighter." There must have been something about remembering the fluff that really got to her. She made a gesture that erased the whole thing from the atmosphere and tried to return to her typewriter, but she had nothing to type and looked to Mickey for pages. Since he had none, she realized that the conversation was going to continue. She showed her dislike for this by assuming her most businesslike posture. Her back was straight. Her hands were folded. Her eyes looked nowhere near his.

"You can't go home? You've always been home." At times like these, Mickey's voice tended to rise in volume and pitch. He started to sound like an adolescent boy who had every problem that puberty brought with it.

"I don't have vacation time coming." Her attitude was cocky, as if she had already won. Her fingers tapped out her victory on the edge of her desk.

"I'll give you vacation time. I'm the boss. I can do things like that. Call Mr. Raphelson if you don't believe me." He handed her the receiver, which she quickly replaced in its cradle. She handled it as if it were hot.

"Mr. Raphelson told us not to expect a vacation until after we had worked a full year."

"What about holidays? Are you supposed to work on Christmas? You want to make me into an ugly man?" He folded his arms in front of his chest. It would have helped if he were taller.

"I expect to have from noon on the twenty-fourth to Monday the twenty-eighth off." Since each one of them was interested in winning, Astra Rainbow once again tried to end the conversation. This time the cover on the typewriter went on. There was no reason for this other than to punctuate her attitude.

"So, go home for a couple of days." Mickey didn't understand the difference between Jewish and non-Jewish plane commitments. Jews flew to Miami for the weekend.

"Oh, no. I couldn't do that, not for a couple of days. It would cost too much money. It cost me one hundred and seventy-six dollars just to get here. I'm paying Granny back twenty-five dollars a month." Here she counted on her fingers. "I have a lot to go," she said.

"Look, I've been thinking about what to get you for a month now—I never know what to get women—so how about I give you a ticket to Ohio as your Christmas present?" Mickey expected her to behave like a puppy. He thought she was supposed to jump up and down and eventually land on his lap. He didn't expect to be licked, but a kiss on the chin seemed appropriate. Instead she became solemn.

"You are the nicest man. You really are. It would be wonderful to see Granny and Mom and the boys and even Joe, but . . . but no thank you, I just couldn't. It's too big a gift." She was proud to refuse.

"Sure you could," said Mickey, digesting this new information.

There were a Joe and boys in the picture. He had figured the plot wrong. Maybe the gun would have to be in the hands of a stepfather, if that's what Joe was.

"No. I couldn't leave Aunt Emma alone on Christmas. She was so nice to let me use her couch all these months and, as if that wasn't enough, she's making me a blanket." Mickey had no idea that his secretary slept on a couch. He knew she lived with an aunt in Brooklyn, but he had always pictured her in a bright sunny bedroom with lacy curtains with tiebacks and a vanity where she brushed her hair a hundred strokes before retiring. The room he had in mind was not unlike Judy Garland's in *The Wizard of Oz*.

"What if . . ." Mickey paused. Since he was a lover of cash, the following question came slowly. "What if I pay for Aunt Emma to go too?" The offer was made, though he hoped she would leave her great-aunt at home in the bosom of somebody else's family.

"No," said Astra Rainbow. She was getting embarrassed by the offers. She arranged the script on the desk so that the pages aligned perfectly. She hoped her boss would stop being generous.

"Why not? How long has it been since Aunt Emma was home?" In his family a question such as this would provoke enough guilt to get people packing.

"She hasn't been back home in eight years. The last time she came there was such a big snowstorm, we could hardly get to church." He wanted big snow, not New York snow, which seemed to be under the city's control. He wanted snow that you knew came from God, the kind that forces people to form human chains in order to get anywhere.

"So, why don't you let me send her home for Christmas? Eight years is a long time to be away from your family. And at her age, who knows how many more times she's going to get to go back to Lorain." Mickey had no idea how old Aunt Emma was. She could have been thirty-six. Since she made blankets, he took the chance that she was at least in her sixties with enough gray in her hair to look old.

"I just couldn't let you be that generous. It's not fair. Mr. Raphelson told us that our bosses would probably give us Christmas presents. He thought we would get a scarf or maybe even cash bonuses, if that was the company policy. He told us that we were in real trouble if the gift was lingerie." She said this as a fact, rather than a warning. She had never felt threatened by Mr. Burke.

"He also said never to give your boss anything personal. He told us how an ex-student of his, I think it was Barbara Sue Marshall but he never mentioned any names, gave her boss pajamas and how he chased her around his desk for January and February and then fired her in March. I don't know if you know this or not, but according to Mr. Raphelson, March is the hardest month to get a job, next to December." Since she had recited the Rules of Gift Giving According to Raphelson, once again she considered the subject closed. She emphasized this by sitting back in her chair, folding her arms and taking in more air than she needed.

This attempt at stealing Christmas hadn't worked, but he would try again. Quickly Mickey backed into his office and got *The Astra Rainbow Story* folder from its resting place. He scribbled across the bottom: "Note: In the real story, there's a mother and boys; who is Joe?" He had to get to Ohio this year. There weren't many things that nourished your soul and your career at the same time. He couldn't leave the gold unmined.

On December fifth, Mickey handed in a draft of *Afterlife* to the network. He thought they were lucky to get such a wonderful script and that they should let him do exactly what he wanted for the rest of his life.

On the eighth, David Weisner called to say that they all loved it. The secretaries were laughing out loud, he said. Jennifer thought it was the best script she had ever read, and he thought it was the best script that Mickey had ever done. When could he come in and get notes?

"Notes? Notes for what? You just said you loved the script." Mickey was facing his office window and saw himself screaming. He was scared by the reflection of the raving maniac he had become. The man he faced was the angriest human being he had ever seen. Had Mickey run into him on the street, he would have run the other way.

"We have a few notes. Nothing big. Adjustments." David paced as far as his phone cord would take him. He knew there would be trouble. He asked Jennifer to make the call, but she had some luncheon that she was speaking at. Fucking women. They could escape into these cockamamie organizations, leaving the men to deal with the Mickey Burkes. She was probably delivering a speech about how all these women would have to stick together. They did. At luncheons.

"Adjustments?" Mickey spit out the word as if he were saying "assassins."

"Yeah, so when are you free? We'll be available whenever you are." David had learned that the only way to get anywhere with his writers was to ignore the negatives. None of them wanted to rewrite. They all thought what they handed in was perfect. Often he had to coax them into his office to talk about changes even though their contracts called for a second draft.

"You cocksucker," Mickey yelled. "Don't tell me what I've done is great and then ask me to change things."

"Just a few minor things. You'll see. You'll be in and out of here in fifteen minutes."

"Why don't you take the script and shove it up your ass?" Mickey always wished that he could be more creative with his insults, but when he was angry, ass, cocksucker and fuck were the main things that came to mind.

"Okay. I'll tell you what I'll do. You make the changes, and believe me, they're minor, and I'll shove it up my ass. How about you come in tomorrow at three-thirty?"

Mickey took the same route to the network that he had taken when he sold the pilot. The crowds he passed then were dressed for fall and happy to be outside. Now, although it wasn't officially winter, the weather had turned on them. Patches of ice on the sidewalk threatened to bring them to their knees. The wind was so strong you had to walk backward into it. Mothers insisted that their small children hold their hands, hoping that together they would have enough ballast not to be blown over. The elderly stayed home. Everybody said it felt as if it were going to snow.

The first snow of the season delighted people. It proved to them that the heavens were working correctly, but now, though it was only December, it had already snowed a few times and New Yorkers were tired of being blanketed.

Mickey Burke was one of those people who never get cold. He wore his sports jacket unbuttoned. His scarf wasn't tied and wasn't the type that would really help anybody anyway. Shelly had once said that Mickey's anger kept him warm, and there was probably great truth in that. Explosions generate a lot of heat, and Mickey was always ready to explode. He was particularly explosive on his way to the meeting. Those fuckers! If they didn't like it, there were reasons for change. But the fuckers *liked* it! They just wanted to get their hands on it so they could tell their husbands, wives, children and superiors that they were fixing the new Mickey Burke script. Television had to be the only business in the world where they didn't leave perfection alone. They were always telling him to make the characters more likable because they had to come into people's living rooms. That was bullshit. People were always inviting unlikable friends into their homes. When he softened his characters, the network guys were bewildered. Where had the funny, hard edge gone? What the fuck did they think comedy was? It ain't funny when everybody is saying please and thank you. Fear is funny. Yelling is funny. Being nice is what nurses are to the patients in the next bed.

He was already forty-five minutes late and still walking slowly. Usually on the way to the meeting he would think about the script about to be attacked. The more firmly planted in his mind were the words, the more ammunition he would have with which to fight back. They would say, "Shouldn't the daughter show us she's happy?" And he would smugly point out to the assholes that she had done that in the first act. He would point to the stage direction ("*Daughter beams*") and then accuse the assholes of not being able to read. Today he was thinking ahead, beyond *Afterlife* and into his escape from television. He hoped more than ever that *The Astra Rainbow Story* was his ticket to artistic freedom. He would pretend to hear the network's notes, say yeah, yeah, give them some of what they wanted so they could feel they had their hands in, and then he would leave television forever. It was time to make his mark on the big screen. He had to get to Ohio.

This time they met in Keith's office, but Keith was democratic enough not to sit behind his desk. David, Jennifer and Keith formed their semicircle around Mickey. He felt he was up for parole and if he controlled his emotions long enough he might be able to get out of this place. He refused to take his jacket off, and when Jennifer, who stood ready with a hanger, asked why, he said he thought he wouldn't be long. They liked the script, so how much criticism could there be? It wouldn't hurt to stay in his jacket for some minor adjustments. David said he didn't want Mickey to get overheated and catch the flu, there was a lot of that going around. Mickey said he would rather have the flu than their asinine notes, and all three of them laughed. He wanted to tell them they were too free with their laughter, that they were laughing shits, but he was afraid they were going to laugh again, and Mickey Burke believed laughter was soothing to the soul and made you live longer. He was totally uninterested in prolonging the lives of these three.

Jennifer took over. Obviously she had been elected to deliver the notes. She had confidence and delivered her criticism without fear. She wasn't about to sweat in a new silk shirt.

She told him they thought that the characters needed to be a little nicer. He told her that this was as nice as they were going to get and if they didn't like that, she could go to hell. She told him that they felt the characters needed to grow. He told her that the business about characters who grew was one of the all-time dumbest comments he had ever heard. He had heard that drivel before. But he couldn't believe he was hearing that shit on this project.

"Let me get your fucking comments straight," he said. "You want these people to be nice and then grow? Into what? Fucking saints?" They thought at this point that he was going to smash something. Actually he did look around for something to break. There was nothing that was going to satisfy him. He walked over to the door and they thought he was leaving. Instead he deliberately banged his head against the door frame. The cracking sound was loud and scary and no one, including Mickey, knew whether the door frame or his head had been broken. With this one blow, he'd created blood and fragments of wood. Jennifer mothered him to the couch and made him lie down. He held his head and told them he had to learn some control.

"I don't know why we put up with each other. I hate you. You must hate me." Here Mickey paused due to the throbbing in his head. The three people in the world he would least wish to have nursing him stood by. He looked up at them and knew that he should never be in the same room with these people again. The last thing he said before blacking out was, "Fuck Lucy." Nobody knew exactly what he meant, but once Mickey was in the hospital, they paced the halls and analyzed his words.

The doctor on duty said he had a concussion that was severe enough to keep him under observation for a few days. The three executives by then had come up with a diagnosis of Mickey Burke's words. Lucille Ball had been the mother of situation comedy. If it hadn't been for her, Mickey wouldn't have been subjected to the network's notes. Poor guy, he was so brilliant and had such a hard time working within the system. The characters should grow, they told each other as they hailed cabs to go home. They sent Mickey a huge clown made of candy and balloons that told him to get well. The card read, "Take your time. Don't worry about the script until you're completely well." He knew what that meant. Their comments still stood. They had probably figured they would win. They were a network with many door frames and he had only one head.

Mickey's first visitor was Astra Rainbow. He had a nurse call his office to tell her where he was in case of emergency. (He knew, even during his most severe pain, that it was sad that there was no one to notify. He didn't want to worry his mother and aunt, and Jerry would give him a lecture using legal language.) Astra Rainbow rushed right over to be by her boss's side and to warn him about hospitals. "They are not good healers," she told him sincerely.

"It's just a concussion," he said. He saw a concussion as a friendly thing that children got when they fell off their bikes. "And this is a good hospital."

"I know it's a good hospital," she said with more impatience than she had ever displayed. Her hands were fists and her eyes narrowed. "But just because it's a good hospital doesn't mean they are going to make you whole again." He smiled. She had thought him whole before. He wondered if anyone else did.

"They're not doing anything. They just told me to lie here." He'd been told not to move and he had no intention of disobeying. Even if he moved slightly it felt like an express subway was running through his head.

"No, Mr. Burke. You have to heal, and healing takes a lot of hard work and you can't do it here."

"Then where?" He wanted her to say Ohio.

"I don't know." He was disappointed. She had come to rescue him but lacked a place to run to. She was as disappointed as he, since she was failing as a white knight.

"It'll be okay."

"Maybe we could get you back to the hotel . . . if only the Indian lady was here. I swear, all she would have to do is touch you with her hot hand. Her hands get hot when she heals and you'd be fit to run around the park if you wanted to." He didn't want to run around the park. He wanted to close his eyes and hear stories about snow. If he could bury his head in enough country snow, the agony would be gone.

"Who is the Indian lady?" When Astra Rainbow gave him any information, he tended to grab it.

"She was a real Indian who my mother took me to when I was very little and hurt my leg. Maybe we were in the West on a reservation or something. It's hard for me to remember because we were in so many different places." He had figured it wrong. Her mother hadn't deserted her.

"And she healed you?"

"Yes. She really did, Mr. Burke. She put her hands on me and they were hot. I got scared. A lot of people we knew dressed up like Indians, but she was the real thing. I didn't cry, though, and I swear my leg felt a whole lot better. I wish she were here with her healing hands." The girl touched her own hands together, hoping they would at least be warm. They weren't. Astra Rainbow figured it was just one more talent she didn't have.

"You and your mother must have seen a lot." Mickey tried not to show his hunger for information. He tried for a "passing the time of day" sort of attitude.

"Yes, we did." She stiffened. There was no way that she was going to be chatty about her youth.

"Tell me about Christmas," he demanded. Even on his back, he could be the boss.

"What about Christmas?"

"Christmas in Ohio." His eyes were closed by now. The house he had built in his mind was there, its multicolored lights outlining the roof, commanding the visitor to enter. To him it said, "All who enter here love Jesus." But he was there as an observer. The saints should understand that.

"I already told you everything about it, Mr. Burke."

"Tell me again." The cold was soothing him. The snowbanks on either side of the path to the house would ease his pain. He could lie down on the ice. It would numb him.

"It's not that interesting. Really. All my Christmases at Granny's were just like everyone else's on the block. We would start by making the cookies. They always came first because we made so many to give away as gifts." The cookies of his childhood were Fig Newtons. They came out of a box, and his mother was convinced that since they contained figs, they were healthy. He never saw any trays with circles of dough ready to spread in the oven. There were never any cookies shaped like angels or otherwise decorated in any way except for a few with red and green sugar that were in bakeries around Christmastime; but those were just for the Gentiles. He imagined Astra Rainbow's grandmother had Christmas cookie cutters in the shapes of trees and stars, and she had tubes of icing and hard silver balls to decorate them. Granny's cookies must be something to see, lying side by side on trays, forecasting the celebration of the Savior's birth. "We made dozens of cookies," Astra Rainbow said, remembering the magical task. "Granny would roll out the dough really fast, sprinkling everything with flour so they wouldn't stick. And she had a whole set of cookie cutters. I used to love the Santa Claus head because it didn't really look like anything until it was all finished and you'd put the beard on and the eyes in.

"We would work all weekend, and Granny knew how to do it just right. She used to cut one shape right next to another, sometimes even upside down so more would fit. And nothing was wasted. If we were doing snowmen and there was just a bit of dough left, she would press out a little bell." Astra Rainbow thought Mickey had fallen asleep, and she was sure her speech had done it, but when she stopped talking his eyes popped open and she had to go on. She was his medication. She told him about the year they were snowed in and they couldn't get to church; and how one of her stepbrothers, the one who had always hated church, cried bitterly because they couldn't go. Mickey empathized with that little boy. The painkillers were taking hold, taking his thoughts away. He wanted to cry because he couldn't go to church either. He asked her to go on and promised to pay for her cab home.

She told him about how Granny took her into town and let her choose one new ornament for the tree each year and how she remembered each of them. Her earliest choices were determined by size. The young Astra Rainbow wanted the biggest ornaments she could find. Her goal was to be able to stand at the top of the stairs and see her ornament from there. When she got older, she learned two things:

Save the best for last, and bigger isn't always better. Mickey smiled. He remembered learning to save the best for last from his cousin Ellen. They went to the candy store with enough money to buy the wax teeth and enough left over for two pretzels. Ellen taught him to break his pretzel in half and put it in his pocket. He had never saved anything before. When they'd sucked all the green liquid from the teeth, had provoked every single adult to tell them to take those crazy things out of their mouths, Ellen and the very young Mickey sat on the fire escape and ate the rest of the pretzels. He never completely got the salt out of his pocket, but it didn't matter. The lesson was learned. He never did learn that bigger wasn't necessarily better.

"More," said Mickey when Astra Rainbow stopped talking. He was a child fighting sleep. She told him how the dates on the calendar were crossed off and how presents were secretly wrapped, never to appear until the tree was up and decorated. Mickey Burke again felt sorry for himself. The best Chanukah present he ever got from his mother was a Dodger baseball jacket with a warm lining when he was eleven. He had asked for it every single day for a year, and then there it was, just lying on the worn couch. His mother made him try it on a week before Chanukah because she didn't want to throw money out by getting the wrong size. Aunt Minn stood there for a second opinion. Since it fit, the jacket hung in the closet, although he wasn't free to wear it until after the holiday. After he lit the Chanukah candles, Mickey looked around for a wrapped present. He got nothing but a big, wet kiss. The next day he wore the jacket to school, but he never forgot that he had had no wrapping to rip into.

That was the year Mickey made up the story of his father. Every day of his life he had seen a picture of the very young man who had died of peritonitis in the third year of Mickey's life, but he had never thought to ask what the man was really like. Mickey's relatives had indicated that he was scholarly. When he reached puberty, Mickey made up fantasies about him. He was sure that his dad would have been a giver of surprises. His father would have hidden the jacket under the bed after wrapping it in the silver and blue colors of Chanukah.

When Mickey finally fell asleep, Astra Rainbow watched him. She didn't trust that he would sleep for long and he might need her to talk about Ohio. She wondered what Mr. Raphelson would say about her bedside devotion. He had never really discussed what to do if your boss was in the hospital and asking for stories. She knew she was supposed to handle office business when he was away. She had turned on the answering machine. There was nothing to type and there was nothing else to take care of. Maybe she would call Mr.

Raphelson long-distance and discuss a few things. She had been warned by him not to develop any emotional ties to the man she worked for. But now, here she was, deeply concerned about Mr. Burke's well-being. She had thrust her hand over her heart when she had heard what happened to him. Surely good secretaries didn't do such a thing.

Mickey slept for about a half an hour, and not once did she tire of looking at him. He was a dynamic man, as interesting asleep as most people were when they were awake. When he did awaken, he didn't even turn to look at her. He trusted that she was still there. "We have to go home for Christmas," he said, looking at the ceiling, which he felt might press down on him.

"Well, I can't this year. It'll be okay, I guess. I was on Fifth Avenue the other day, and I saw all the beautiful store windows. They were the most fantastic displays I have ever seen. I wanted Mary to see them, but I didn't dare to take the chance of bringing her uptown—even though I truly believe she's reformed. And the tree at Rockefeller Center is really the most beautiful thing I have ever seen. I wrote to Granny about it, and the only way I could describe it was for her to think of the biggest tree in the forest."

"What forest?"

"The one behind our house."

"You have a forest near your house?"

"Yes. Sure," she said, implying, "Doesn't everyone?"

"I had a subway near mine." Mickey was weary. He wanted her to take him to Ohio, and she had become enchanted with New York just because it knew how to decorate itself. Mickey figured he had to try to win her sympathies. He had the advantage. Hospitals were good places for asking favors.

"I thought maybe you should take me to Lorain." He'd said "maybe" to keep from sounding pushy.

"I can't," said Astra Rainbow.

"Why not?" He put his hand to his head to remind her that he was in pain.

"I can't afford it."

"I'll pay."

"I told you that's much too big a gift. I haven't been with you that long. You should get me something like a change purse, something in the small leather area." They spoke to each other but avoided eye contact. He kept his eyes on the cracked ceiling, where he could, he thought, make out the face of an old Indian.

"I don't want to give small leather goods. I want to take us all home for Christmas." Astra Rainbow frowned. She would have to refuse again. She couldn't let him pay for her trip and she couldn't let him find out things, like that her mother walked around naked.

"I'm sorry, Mr. Burke, but that's really not possible."

"Why not?"

"Because. Because a boss and a secretary shouldn't share one roof."

"Nonsense."

"Really. It's not a good idea. We have a good working relationship that shouldn't be forced off balance."

"It won't be. Don't you see? I have to heal in the country. I need Granny and Jesus and all the other people you know. My head hurts."

"Should I call the nurse?"

"No. You should take me home. I need to go someplace where there's a forest nearby."

"Maybe you won't be well enough to go all the way to Lorain. You should go to Pennsylvania or somewhere like that."

"I need a hearth. Does Granny have a hearth?"

"Well . . . yes."

"I need it."

"You're going to think we're weird."

"I hope so. I like weird people."

"I don't even know my father. I found this picture once in Helen's bag. It was at the very bottom, you know, the flat part at the bottom? The picture was protected by cardboard on both sides that was taped together, but it slipped out easily so I didn't think I was sneaking looks at anything I wasn't supposed to. The photograph was of four naked men, although one held a frying pan in front of him. There was a question mark over three of their heads, and even though I was only seven at the time, Mr. Burke, I knew that my mother thought one of those three men was my father. She was guessing; but I didn't have to guess. I knew immediately which of those men was my dad. I still think I'm right."

"Was it the one with the frying pan?" Even with a concussion his mind worked well.

"Yes. His eyes were just like mine."

Mickey had only studied one semester of psychology at Brooklyn College, but he knew that the young Astra Rainbow had to have chosen the modest man as her father. Since she never could have tricked her mind into thinking that her mother was pure, she picked herself a daddy who had the decency to hide behind a cooking utensil. Having figured that out, Mickey went back to sleep. The next time he opened his eyes it was almost midnight, and Astra Rainbow was gone. His head felt much better; some of the pain was suppressed. He was hungry for food and for news of the world. He needed to nourish his body and expand his Astra Rainbow file. Food was already there. It had arrived when he was sleeping, and Nurse Fiscus had left it getting cold and hard for him. When she came back to pick up the tray, she saw Mickey reach for it. She moved it closer to him, said something about what a good rest he had had and left. The tray was on a stand right under his chin, and since he wasn't supposed to move, he could only eat as if he were either very old or very young. He sipped lukewarm chicken soup directly from the bowl. He rolled peas into his mouth. He dribbled in the fruit cup. If he had a wife, he thought to himself, she would have fed him.

After consuming a very little food, he found a new worry. He calculated that Astra Rainbow, because of her age, was one of the oldest love children around. There were bound to be thousands more, and this one had never laughed at his jokes. None of them would laugh. They had spent their formative years dancing by the banks of rivers and eating pumpkin products. How the fuck were they going to know when something was funny? He wrote comedy about fathers and sons, mothers and daughters. Those children didn't even know about those things. They knew about photographs of naked men with question marks over their heads. His career was over. The love children were coming and they would own television sets. He wondered if the executives at the networks realized this and were planning for it.

Maybe he should call Jennifer Ross and let her spread the word. He would tell her that he had the first of that generation working for him and he would spend the next couple of months trying to get Astra Rainbow to laugh. There must be something that she found funny. And when he pushed the right button, he would know what the rest of her peers thought was a laugh riot too. He could be the first writer to write specifically for a particular generation. Of course they would love *The Astra Rainbow Story*. The girl would have had a body that had been so free in her formative years that now she wanted to contain it in proper suits.

If he could get to Ohio, he would meet Astra Rainbow's mother. He expected to find an aging hippie who still wore long dresses and had waist-length hair. Most of those women had changed with the times, but the real earth mothers hadn't. One saw the real ones even on the streets of Manhattan, mainly in summer, mainly in sandals, their hair still growing. Last July he had stared at one who was selling jewelry in the street, little pieces of silver that she had hammered into earrings. He was reminded of an aunt of his who had never changed her style. Throughout her life she wore her hair swept up and her shoes open-toed. This street jeweler wore a long skirt and must have played the guitar. When she was twenty-five, everyone was like her, but now she stood out as someone who clung to an era. In his movie, he would make Helen an aging hippie too. She would be an annoying character, pushing granola and playing a guitar when no one wanted to hear one. She would not know that the guitar was not the sound of Christmas. She would anger everyone, not only by singing all the wrong songs—her types always played songs to which only they knew all the words—but also by dressing as if she had been a contemporary of Christ's.

By his fourth day in the hospital, Mickey couldn't be kept down. His doctors would have preferred his staying still for another twenty-four hours, but his head told him that they were being overly cautious. True, he was not a man who was in tune with his body. For all of his life, he had existed only in his mind. From the time he was nine and had put his head inside the empty television, he never needed the rest of himself again. He never exercised. Most of the time his pants didn't fit right because he had very little idea about the size or type of his body. But about his head he was an authority. He was too scared to actually leave the hospital as a result of their warnings, but he no longer could lie still. He sat up and was in business again. His first call was to Shelly. He knew that since she had canceled their date, the dynamics of their relationship had changed. Since he was an excellent manipulator, he knew that a call from the hospital would be a big help to him. Women were lenient with men in hospital beds.

"Hello," she said warmly. When she realized who it was, she cooled down rapidly. She desperately needed to keep her stronghold.

"Listen, Shelly? I'm sorry I didn't call sooner. I would have liked to have gotten together." That was the truth. He enjoyed being adored.

"Yeah . . . well." She wanted to hang up to show strength. Yet she wanted this conversation to go on forever.

"I would have called by now . . ." He sensed that while he hadn't been forgiven yet, he soon would be." . . . but I'm in the hospital." Shelly dropped the phone—a sure sign that she loved the man.

"Wait, wait. I'm here," she yelled, retrieving the instrument that linked them. She sat down on one of the chairs in her eat-in kitchen and held the phone firmly in place. "What happened?" They were too young for illnesses. She correctly assumed that he had had an accident.

"I did a stupid thing," he said. He had always known it was stupid to use his head, the part responsible for his livelihood, to make a point. "I had to go to a meeting for notes on a pilot." She pictured him entering a tall glass building, wearing his gray blazer and the wine scarf she had given him. "You know, the whole thing is so fucking stupid. When they make the deal with you to write a script they assume that you're going to louse something up. That's why when they make the deal they ask for a first draft and revisions." He stopped here. Three days of lying down had robbed him of some of his strength. As his energy came back, so did his anger. "They fucking *expect* you to fail, and if you don't they want their money's worth anyway. They'll find something wrong with your script just so they don't feel cheated."

"Mickey, are you in the hospital for your nerves?" She was scared to ask if he was having a nervous breakdown. She doubted it. He had been difficult, but he was basically rational. He was in the class of a Talmudic neurotic.

"No. No, I did this stupid thing. There they were, telling me how to improve this script and I felt—I'll tell you what I felt—I felt like hurting them, really hurting all three of them. I wanted to kick them in the shins because I was beyond words. Anyway, I didn't want to give them any more of my mind, but didn't have the nerve to throw a punch. Even as a kid, I didn't get into fights. I got a water pistol every spring, and spraying someone was the most hostile thing I ever did. So when I couldn't talk anymore and I was seeing red—I actually saw red—I knocked my head against the door. I was planning to knock my head against the wall as a symbolic act, but when I turned around, the door was there. Those fuckers sent a stupid clown with a card saying not to worry about the notes until I'm better: They're going to give me another chance to kill myself!"

"Oh, Mickey, I'm sorry." There it was, the pity he needed.

"It was dumb," he said. "We all know who got hurt. The network isn't sitting in the hospital."

He let her continue to soothe him. He had called for comfort and reached a comfort expert. Before she hung up, she promised to visit him that afternoon and offered to take him home the following day. He knew he would be happy resting on her bosom.

Mickey had calculated correctly. His head was healed, ready to go anywhere with him. He went to the window and looked out at the Hudson, a river he had learned about as a child. His history books had showed the mighty Hudson with early settlers on its banks. He knew New York was a port. Its rivers surrounded him yet had nothing to do with his life. He knew they were there, but he had never thought of himself as living near water. He was not a sailor or even a swimmer. He enjoyed the view less than others would.

Jennifer Ross was his second call. He waited until after ten, a time you could assume that ambitious executives were sure to have arrived. He got right through to her. Usually he would have had his end of the conversation mapped out in his head. Today he just knew that he had to make contact. He counted on the words having a life of their own.

"How are you?" she asked. He knew she was more well-mannered than concerned.

"Better." He still wasn't sure why he had called. Maybe it was just to see how fast he could get an executive on the line.

"Well, that's good. We were all very worried around here." He imagined she had her feet up on the desk, legs crossed at the ankles. He was wrong. She sat straight in her chair and played with a pencil, turning it continuously from point up to eraser up.

"All of you? Did you have a big meeting over there in the large conference room, all of you sitting around that big table? Did the memo that drew you there say 'Meeting at two. Re: Mickey Burke. All personnel required to attend'?" Maybe he had called just to rile an executive.

"It was actually more casual than that. Groups of twos and threes meeting informally in hallways and whispering about that crazy, lovable Mickey Burke."

Whispering in hallways? He liked that. He especially liked the idea that people he didn't know knew him. " 'Crazy'? 'Lovable'? Is that what they think of me? That I'm crazy and lovable?"

"And talented and a lot of other things."

" 'Talented'? Did you say 'talented'?"

"Yes. No one ever said you weren't talented. You know you're talented."

"Let's just say I have a talent for television. That's a whole lot different from actually being talented."

"You're too hard on yourself."

"No, Mrs. Ross. You're too hard on me. I hand you my best work and you tell me how to improve it."

"There's nothing that can't be improved."

"Oh, really? Why don't you guys take a look at *Death of a Salesman* and call Arthur Miller in and give him some notes?"

"All right. I see what you're getting at."

"You don't know what I'm getting at because I didn't know what I was getting at until now. Now, I know. I'm calling you, Mrs. Ross, to blackmail you."

She laughed. Obviously this was crazy Mickey Burke at his frightening best. Talking to him was far more interesting than sitting in one of those boring development meetings, which was where she was supposed to be. Everyone at the network tolerated her wandering in and out of those meetings because she was "a find." "Blackmail me? I'm clean," she said, forgetting that she wasn't. She had lived with the lie so long, she had forgotten she invented it. Sometimes on the train back to Connecticut it came back to her, but each time it was fainter. She was successful now. She had a baby who had caring in-home help and a husband who defended the law. Surely no one any longer cared that she had made up her college education.

"You're pretty clean, Jennifer. Too bad you never went to Radcliffe." He was sorry now that he had done this over the phone. He would have enjoyed seeing her stiffen up.

"Who told you that?" She gave the pencil hell.

"You did. Don't you remember all those interviews you gave when you first got your job? You talked about dear old Radcliffe." This was fun. He sat up and let his legs dangle from the bed. Nothing hurt.

"I remember. Who said I didn't go there?" Her accent had changed slightly. It was more cultured, now that she was being challenged.

"My friend, Jerry. He's a nice guy. We went to Lincoln together and became friends because we were both superior to everyone in the class." He took a breath. These had been a fast couple of sentences to a man who had been lying down for four days. Jennifer was quiet while he paused. There was nothing she wanted to say at the moment. It was too early to defend herself. So Mickey went on. "Anyway, Jerry saw your picture in *Daily Variety* one day. You must have been really proud of yourself: attractive, young, female executive, ready to rise. And good old Jerry, he called to tell me you were a liar. It said right there that you graduated from Radcliffe, and Jerry remembered that he knew you at Boston University—a very good school, mind you, but it's no Ivy Leaguer. You probably only need B minuses and lousy SATs to get into B.U."

"How do you know Jerry is right? Ross is my married name. Maybe he confused me with someone else." Her voice was calm. She had set out to deceive and wasn't planning to reveal the truth now.

"That's exactly what I said. 'Jerry,' I said, 'I know Jennifer Ross. She really doesn't look like the type who would lie.' You know what Jerry said? He said that's just the type that does it. Smart guy. He's got street smarts. So what if he didn't get the best education in the world? At least he doesn't lie about it."

She was looking for cigarettes. She had given up smoking over nine months ago, but now she was opening every drawer. Her secretary came in to deliver the mail, and Jennifer gestured for a cigarette by puffing an imaginary one. The secretary was nice enough to refuse at first, but when Mrs. Ross put her hand over the receiver and hissed, "Get me one," the secretary rushed to obey. Jennifer hated "situations," and this was an impossible one.

"You know, Mr. Burke, I don't think anybody cares where I went to college."

"You do. If you didn't care, you wouldn't have lied about it over ten years after graduation."

"Yes, but I still maintain nobody cares."

"I do. I'd rather not work with a woman who has trouble telling the truth. Maybe even all your colleagues would. I don't think they would have cared where you were from when they hired you. They

needed someone exactly your type, an athletic sister. You were made
for them. They needed a girl who wouldn't get hurt when she fell
down. They especially needed someone who could win sometimes,
who owned her own racquetball racquet. You do own your own
racquetball racquet, don't you, Mrs. Ross? It's known that you come
from a wealthy family. Don't tell me you made that up too. If you
were that inventive you'd belong on the other side of the desk with
us writers, getting notes."

"I'm from Philadelphia."

"What's that supposed to mean? Nobody poor ever came from
Philadelphia?"

"Mainline Philadelphia. If you don't believe me, ask your friend,
Jerry. If he's the Jerry I think he is, he came down to the house a
couple of weekends."

"You didn't say you got a master's, did you?"

"No," she said wearily.

"So it's just a four-year lie."

"I really don't think this is relevant to anything."

"No. See, that's the thing: If you were some underprivileged minority, I would have understood your behavior. It might have opened
doors for you. But you're practically blonde and may have even had
a pony. Doors have been open your whole life. I'll bet you had a show
dog."

The match was struck, the cigarrette lit. It didn't have the calming
effect Jennifer had hoped for, since the problem was still talking to
her. She couldn't hang up. Network people didn't hang up on one of
their most successful writers. "I don't think anybody cares that I told
a minor lie. They're running a business here. You writers never stop
to realize that the networks want to make money. I have made plenty
of money for them. That means dollars, Mickey. Do you think they're
going to get rid of a dollar-maker just because she made up a little
bit of her past?"

"Probably not. Probably they'll hang on to you with all their might.
They'll probably give you all kinds of raises and throw stock options
at you. So, what you're telling me is that you wouldn't mind if I told
everyone where you really went to school and produced the yearbook
to prove it." He lay back, though not for his health. His head felt fine.
The conversation was fun, and he was going to relax through it.

"Of course I would mind. I would more than mind. It would be a
major annoyance and it would embarrass me and my family." She
tried to sound sweet, like the kind of person who didn't deserve to
be embarrassed.

"That's great."

"Why?"

"Because if there were nothing at stake, you couldn't be black-mailed."

"You're going to blackmail me?" She took this as a Mickey Burke joke and tapped out a tune with the pencil she had been playing with before. "How?" she asked, still not worried. This was still a game.

"I'm not sure. I've never blackmailed anyone before. Do you have any ideas?"

"You want me to come up with something you can squeeze out of me?"

"Sure. You think you're creative. If you can develop projects for the network, you can think of one thing to offer me that you don't want to give up."

"How about my firstborn?"

"What would I do with a kid? I don't want the kid of someone who falsifies an education. It might be an inherited trait."

"Money?"

"Yeah, I would like some money. But it would be too trite just to bilk you out of some cash. Think, Jennifer. Think."

"You're the writer. You think."

"I don't want to. I really believe that part of your suffering should be coming up with the torture."

"All I can think of is money. I'll drop some of it off in a brown paper bag at the phone booth of your choice."

"All right. I like cash, but we have to say an exact amount. I would be a stupid crook if I let you throw an unspecified amount of cash at me."

"How about two hundred dollars?"

He thought about this for a minute and liked the idea. Jennifer Ross's money was bound to be clean. She probably only dealt in new, crisp bills. "Yeah. Sure. I could use two hundred dollars. And then in a couple of weeks, I could call you up and ask for more. Isn't that what blackmailers do, keep asking for more?"

"Yes. They always do, until they're caught and shot in the back of the head."

"It's not very nice of you, Mrs. Ross, to mention heads when mine is in the hospital in pain."

"Sorry."

"That's okay. Next time I call it'll be from a phone booth with a handkerchief over the receiver."

They hung up together. She thought it was one of crazy Mickey Burke's crazy ideas. He was already thinking of what he could do with two hundred bucks. By ten-thirty he had decided to use it toward a new VCR and was sorry he hadn't made the drop-off date and time specific.

Mickey's last full day in the hospital turned out to be one of the most enjoyable days of his life. Just as Nurse Judy Feely was wheeling in his lukewarm lunch, Shelly arrived with her portable oven and hors d'oeuvres. His bedspread became a picnic ground in the English countryside. He was fed, pampered and loved. For the first time, he realized how symbolic his life was becoming. People threw notes at him so he knocked his head against the wall. Shelly, the woman that logic dictated he should be with, carried her oven—which had to be her womb—with her. Into the oven went little hot dogs; and out came warmth and little baby food.

Shelly worried about him and kissed him when she left. She had meant it to be an innocent hospital kiss, but Mickey, ecstatic from the stuffed mushrooms, grabbed her and kissed her passionately. It didn't quite work since he was lying down and she was leaning over him, but it was good enough to keep her fantasizing. She would be sure for weeks that Mickey's true inner self wanted her and that the safety of the hospital allowed his feelings to explode. Maybe she should bring him home with her. She could put a hospital bed in until he was well enough to realize that things were working out well. The bed would be expensive, but passion didn't come cheap.

Mickey took a short nap after lunch. Nurse Feely awakened him as she removed a chair from his room to bring to 1237, which had more visitors than seats. The chair was light; she could easily have whisked it out of the room, but she chose to drag it instead. "Why are you doing this to me?" he said before he was fully awake. It was the right question, but a coherent person wouldn't have bothered to ask.

"They need this chair next door." She said each word as if it were a complete sentence.

"You could lift it."

"*You* could lift it. I ain't takin' chances with my back for nobody." Mickey thought that she would have made a good gang member. She was built for the streets and was exactly why sane people stayed out of the Bronx even during daylight hours, even when they really wanted to shop at Loehmann's, a store with designer discounts.

"Florence Nightingale would never have carried the chair out."

"Oh yeah? You know that for a fact?" For a moment he thought this strange combination of healer and brute was going to take a swipe at him with the chair, but she left with just a dirty look.

Astra Rainbow and Mary showed up about four. Mary was sure that her coming was a gift to Mickey. He had helped her stay out of jail, and now she was returning the favor.

"How you doing, Mr. Mickey?" Mary asked, her face too close to his. She had been dragged there by Rainbow and had expected gore.

Her only experience with hospitals up to now had been with emergency rooms. She had taken younger brothers and sisters in for things as minor as third-degree burns and as major as being hit by a truck and having most of the life knocked out of them. Before Mickey could tell how he was, Mary was yelling at him. She pointed a finger within her torn mitten. The small hole at the top didn't quite let the finger out. "Now I don't want you to think about dying, Mr. Mickey. The good Lord will only take you if He sees fit, and I done lit a candle for you, and that's got to count for something."

"I'm feeling fine. I'm going home tomorrow."

"Tomorrow?" Mary gave Astra Rainbow the dirtiest look she had. She had come all the way into Manhattan because she thought Mr. Mickey was in some stage of dying. To her, everyone who wasn't sent home from the emergency room was very ill and in danger of leaving this world. God and Jesus had to be put on the alert. Now here was Mr. Mickey looking fine and telling her he was going home tomorrow. Things sure were different uptown.

"Mr. Burke is feeling much better," said Astra Rainbow, defending her boss.

"Yeah. I sure can see that with my own eyes. He looks like he could go dancing tonight." Mary didn't bother to hide her disgust at having had to visit a well man. At this point, Rainbow asked her friend if she could see her in the hall and virtually dragged Mary out of the room. The younger girl pretended that her arm was hurt, but she got no sympathy.

"Why are you acting like this?" Astra Rainbow asked in the loudest tone she dared to use in a hospital. There were signs warning her to be quiet, one with a 1940s nurse with a finger warning, "SHHHH."

"Like what?" She had tried the play of innocence with her mother and teachers for her entire life. If you pretended not to know what you did wrong, the crime didn't exist.

"You came up here to cheer up Mr. Burke, and you're in there behaving as if you're disappointed that the man can sit up."

"Sit up? That man looks like he's ready to get maximum pleasure. It cost me one whole dollar to light that candle at St. Matthew's. You got that?" Mary felt she had made a great point. Who from her neighborhood wouldn't understand wasting a whole dollar?

"How can you think of a dollar? Didn't Mr. Burke come and help you that night when you were in real trouble? Didn't he give up a lot of his time for you?" But that failed to impress the girl with plenty of time and very few dollars.

"Yeah, he helped me out by getting me that lawyer guy. That guy was the one who really helped me and will help me on January twentieth when he's gonna get me off scot-free."

"If it wasn't for Mr. Burke, you wouldn't have that lawyer. I don't think you should be angry about visiting the poor man in the hospital."

"Poor man? Where do you get your ideas? That man is not poor and he ain't sick and he didn't need that candle lit. You know something? Eddie wanted to hang out with me this afternoon and I didn't go with him on account of you convinced me that I had to visit this guy. All I'm saying is that he don't look like he needs visiting to me."

"The man is in the hospital."

"Yeah, so? I'm in the hospital, too." It was evident to Astra Rainbow that the young Mary had not developed a sense of responsibility. She had seen Mary taking care of her family, but she had always worn a scowl. Now she was sour about having had to visit a man who looked too well.

Mickey couldn't see the scowl, nor did he hear the argument. From his point of view, he saw Astra Rainbow looking exasperated, her hand constantly pulling her hair back—a gesture he had seen her use when she was exasperated before. From this small glimpse, his writer's mind completed the story. He was sure Astra Rainbow had dragged Mary with her, convincing the girl that she had the responsibility of visiting the nice old man who helped her with her shoplifting problem. He had seen Mary's face when she saw that he was okay. He had stolen her time and manipulated her out of some sympathy. She had wasted her prayers. This time Mary was the one who had been ripped off.

Astra Rainbow convinced her friend that she had to go back into the hospital room without her scowl, and Mary returned to Mickey with a smile on her face. Some would say that she was a good actress. Anyone who understood the life she had led knew that she had to act to survive. She acted as if she didn't mind that she didn't have a father; and she acted as if she didn't care that her mother frequently slapped her across the back of her head. She did a lot of acting with boys. She acted as if she didn't care about them; and she acted like she didn't care that she wasn't their permanent girlfriend. Most of the time she acted as if she didn't care about anything, especially what was happening to her on rooftops and in dark hallways.

"Mr. Mickey, I'm real happy that you're doing so good," Mary said, giving one of her best performances.

"Well, I'm not feeling so wonderful now." The truth was, if he felt at all bad, it was only due to being too rested: He was itchy to go. However, he was in a benevolent mood and didn't want Mary to feel she had wasted candle money or subway fare on him.

"Really?" It seemed to both Astra Rainbow and Mickey that Mary had brightened. At least she had not made the trip in vain.

"Yeah. I see two of everything and my head hurts."

That rated another smile from the young black girl. Mickey was sorry he hadn't told her he was terminal. He might have gotten a large laugh.

"Wow," she said, getting excited, since real pain was something she understood. "I'm gonna go to church for you tonight again." Mickey was happy. Nobody had ever gone to church for him. He liked the idea of Mary among the black-garbed widows, lighting candles handed to her by a nun who smelled from Lysol.

"Do you want me to get the nurse?" Astra Rainbow asked. If her boss was hurting, she was going to get help.

"No. It's all right. They have sicker people to tend to." He was a perfect martyr. He even raised his hand to his heart and closed his eyes at the right time. The sigh was placed nicely.

"Well, can I do anything for you, Mr. Burke, before we go home?"

Mickey's instincts were good. It was time to take advantage. Like a good chess player, he knew it was going to take a few critical moves. "You want to do something for me?" That should at least get him in place.

"Sure. Do you need something typed or filed? Do you want me to call someone, or pick up any medicine?"

"No." He had to be careful here. Astra Rainbow had rarely allowed anything but business to pass between them. The night she called him to help Mary was the one exception. Even her visits to the hospital were businesslike. "This favor has nothing to do with work," he said as casually as he could.

"Oh." Mr. Raphelson's warnings filled her head. He had raised his voice and both of his eyebrows when he told them about poor Frances Monroe, a girl whose boss asked for small favors at first and then big ones.

"It's just that the doctor told me it would be a good idea to take a vacation."

"That's a good idea, sir." She rarely called him sir. He could be in trouble.

"I never had a vacation," said Mary. "Nobody in my whole family ever had a vacation except for my sister, Lily, who went to one of those camps and hated it." Mary shrugged her shoulders. She didn't know why Lily didn't like camp. She hardly knew what a vacation was.

"Granny took me to Chicago once and . . ." Rainbow had meant to go on, but she saddened before she did. She put both of her hands into the pockets of her sweater. The weight of her arms dragged the sweater down, misshaping it. She needed something to hang on to.

"And," she continued, "when I was very little I was on vacation all the time."

Mickey, the writer, perked up. He had known when he met Astra Rainbow that he was meeting a more interestng character than he could conjure up. As she revealed pieces of her past, they were like gifts to him, but the information came slowly, since she refused to violate their employer-employee relationship. He didn't enjoy her agony, but he was anxious to hear about these early vacations. "Where did you go?" he asked. He raised himself up high on the bed, letting her know it wasn't a casual question.

"All over. Even Texas. My mother and I just kept traveling around. She was like one of those hippies."

"Sounds good to me," said Mickey.

"I don't know," said Astra Rainbow. She let the anxiety go and her hands, which had turned into fists, came out of her pockets. Mickey wanted to know more, but he wanted to make his move while she was relaxed.

"I told the doctor that I might not be able to get away because I didn't know where to go." This was Mickey's second big move. The hint was big enough. Why was Astra Rainbow not rushing in to rescue him?

"There must be someplace. If I had some cash I sure would find me someplace." Mary was remembering television commercials she had seen with planes traveling past the sun.

There was his opening. Mickey had never been big enough or brave enough to play sports. If he had, he would have found the clearing and made the touchdown. "There's only one place I'd like to go." He turned and gave Mary his plea. It seemed more dramatic and less threatening that way. "I'd like to go to Ohio with Astra Rainbow for Christmas."

Mary thought it was a totally reasonable request. "So, what's the problem?" she asked her friend.

"I don't have the money to go." This was directed at Mickey. She was reminding him that they had had this argument.

"I told her I'd pay." Again, Mickey spoke to Mary. He had found an ally.

"If he's gonna lay out the bucks, go." Mary was too young to have anything but the simplest solutions to problems.

"I can't accept such an expensive present."

"Are you crazy?" In Mary's world you took what you could get.

"It costs a lot," Astra Rainbow said, knowing that this was not an argument that Mary could understand.

"I can afford it."

"He can afford it."

"Still, it's not right."

"What if I told you that I just came into some extra money?"

"How?" Astra Rainbow's eyes narrowed. The challenge was there.

He should have known better than to tell the truth. He told her about Jennifer and the money that could be in the telephone booth of his choice. He ended with, "So actually, it's a free trip."

Astra Rainbow picked up her purse and the sensible coat that she had bought on sale at Lord & Taylor. (She was still too afraid to go back to Saks.) "I'll take you home to Lorain if you promise not to blackmail that lady, Mr. Burke."

He promised.

He was going home for Christmas.

# 9

# Shelly Lies Down

IT wasn't the bad permanent that sent Shelly to her bed. Those who didn't know her, her mother included, might have thought so, but Shelly Silver was too smart to let too-tight curls wreck her whole holiday season. Nor was it Mickey's telling her he was going to Ohio. She expected him to disappear at times and knew he would return. Their lives were too tangled for them to lose one another completely. It wasn't her business either. Business, in fact, was good. She had the chance to prepare the food and order the plates and napkins for other people's fun. She had the opportunity to do eight Christmas parties and four in celebration of the New Year. She could witness young, successful men with fifty-dollar ties toasting each other and young businesswomen on their way up, wearing necklines that were on their way down. It was cleavage season.

On December twenty-first, for the first time since her fight with the flu, Shelly Silver took to her bed. The cause of her malady was Greta's news. Greta was Shelly's newest friend. She had made her presence strong and her attitude offered hope. Greta had come over to tell Shelly her good news. They sat on their matching couches, though as a result of the strain of the season Shelly reclined further than her friend. Shelly had had a battle with a linen rental place only minutes before Greta arrived. They wanted to send her red and bright green napkins and she was insisting on rose and dark green. Her clients came back because of details like this. She had insisted that they come up with the colors she needed if they had to comb every linen rental in the tristate area. She had won. The victory was small if you considered only the size of napkins, but a big one in terms of taste. "If it's the wrong rose," she warned, "heads will roll." Since she always fought with these people, she never celebrated her minor victories. The battle might have been won, but the war would go on as long as there were caterers and rental linens.

Before Greta arrived, Shelly had changed into a tailored, black wool robe with pink piping that she had thought would be great to wear the morning after sex when the man lingered on. The robe was three months old and had never been worn. She tried to remember the last time but couldn't while she was standing. She had to sit on the edge of the bed and think hard, too hard for a woman her age. The face of the man eventually appeared, but the lines in her forehead deepened as she tried to remember his name. It came in shifts. Gary something. Yeah: Gary Minsk, lousy lover. He was the one with such a light touch that her mind wandered to the sale at Bendel's. It had taken Gary so long to work up a sweat that she had mentally gone through the entire Sonia Rykiel department. Still, she would have given light-handed Gary another chance. Too bad he had taken her to lunch and apologized for going back to his wife. As Shelly worked her way around the outside of her seafood salad, she felt sorry for the past and future of Mrs. Minsk.

She had enjoyed—well, tried to enjoy Gary on the Monday of Labor Day weekend. Now it was cold and December, even colder because she had no prospects. A quick replay of her sex life reminded her that this was the longest she had ever gone without a bedmate. She preferred to think of her plight as a sign of the times rather than an individual failure. People were not as promiscuous out of fear of disease. Still, she hadn't even had the chance to turn down even an unreciprocated passion. Here was a new problem. Up to now there had always been someone to seduce her. The depression that sometimes hung over her threatened to show up.

The doorbell rang before Shelly could get upset. She rushed to let Greta in. Her newest friend soothed her soul and made her feel that the hunt was almost as much fun as the capture. Unfortunately, the second Shelly opened the door, she feared this wasn't going to be the cozy evening she had planned for. Here was Greta in her mink coat, either en route from someplace important or on her way out.

"Where are you going?" Shelly asked, trying not to show her disappointment.

"You're not going to believe this," said Greta, removing the fur. She folded the coat over a chair, then refolded it because she felt she didn't do a good job the first time. Greta was not ordinarily neat, but she took care of that mink, which she had bought for herself. She had cited that the biggest difference between herself and her mother was that her mother had cried for her fur. Greta remembered hearing her mother's voice through a closed door, words and sobbing intermingled. "Sid," she cried, "I'm the last one on the block without a coat with all male skins." That night Greta might have promised herself that she would never wait for a man to buy anything for her if she hadn't been concerned with knowing what male skins were. She feared that her mother would get her wish and then embarrass Greta in her puberty by wearing these male skins everywhere. Later, when Greta was successful, she headed for the furrier on her own. When she got there, a couple was already in the showroom, and the woman swirled in front of the mirror as the husband took out his checkbook. Jack, the furrier, tactfully asked Greta if she wished to show the coat to anyone. "No," she said proudly, thinking she would never cry for a fur.

"You want me to hang it up?" Shelly asked. Her own mink was on a satin hanger. Although she didn't know Greta had a fur when she first met her, she had noticed that women with similar coats flocked together, as if they were part of a herd.

"No. It's fine here. Really." Greta stood close to the chair, making sure it wasn't going to slip. She didn't want to see it lying in a pile on the floor.

"I have a great hanger," Shelly offered one last time.

"No. I'm sure it's fine," said Greta, willing to let the coat stay. She wanted to be the type of woman who treated fur casually, but she hadn't learned to do that yet.

Shelly didn't have to ask her friend to sit down. By this time, Greta knew what couch was hers. Hers was the closest to the door and Shelly's closest to the phone. Shelly had tried to convince her world that there were no emergencies in catering, but someone was always on the line screeching about dry teriyaki or forks with bent prongs.

"You want something to drink?" Greta didn't, a sign their time together would be less than half an hour. Thank God it was Wednesday and *Dynasty* was on.

"So what's new?" Greata asked. At least she wasn't rushing things.

"Everything is a disaster. I called my lawyer this morning to see if you could sue for a too-tight permanent."

"It's not bad."

"You're just saying that because I feed you all the time. I told them to use bigger rods. Malcom kept telling me to leave my head in his hands. I should make him pay for all the hats I'm going to have to buy. I didn't need to plunk down a hundred bucks for frizz. Frizz I can grow on my own . . . Let's see. What else? Oh, Mickey called to say he's going to Ohio for the holidays. Why do I know he'll be back to torture me again? My guess is that he's going there with a hard-on. Also, some business hysteria, but that doesn't drive me crazy anymore. My mother called and felt I was old enough to hear that my father wasn't affectionate enough. She said she wanted me to read between the lines. I didn't want to compare notes because I'm sure she's gotten more than I have this year . . . How're you doing? It better be good. There's only room for one of us in the toilet at a time." She actually was not expecting Greta's news to be better than her own. Unfortunately Greta forgot that misery loves company, especially when the company is sitting on one of your couches.

"I don't know where to begin." You couldn't miss it. Greta was beaming. Shelly wanted to put up a protective shield, but it was too late. The beams would have penetrated it.

"You met somebody." Shelly tried to smile as she said it. The smile was stiff. She had a good heart and wanted Greta to be happy, but not exactly now, when the man she loved was on his way to the Midwest for holidays that would leave her lonely.

"I met him a little over a month ago." Worse. This wasn't some new romance that could play itself out in a date or two. A little over a month ago meant the relationship had had a chance to turn sour, but hadn't. Shelly kept her stiff grin as Greta continued.

"Remember the day we rented the Mercedes? Well, I ran into one of the guys who came to see the car. There I was, desperately trying to hail a cab, knowing I had no chance since it was five o'clock and raining. Out of nowhere, there he was. He drove up in a little red two-seater, just like the one we were pretending to sell. Heaven knows how he recognized me under an umbrella and everything. Thank God he did." Greta not only thanked God. She covered herself by knocking wood, bending down to use Shelly's bleached wooden floors. Before Shelly could summon up some fake good wishes, Greta rushed on with details, the kind the happy friend can't wait to tell and the depressed one would rather not know about.

"Anyway," she said, looking at the ceiling, recalling the good times, "we went out to dinner that night and the next and the next and he kept saying things like, 'I'm never going to let you go,' and I kept thinking, What am I doing with this guy? He's not my type. The last thing I wanted to do was fall for some guy who wasn't my type. Believe me, I tried to pull away but he kept showing up with calla lilies, you know those gorgeous flowers that Warren Beatty kept giving to Diane Keaton in *Reds*. They have always been my favorite flower because they're so hard to get. One night he had to go to four florists just to get a bunch. How can you not like a guy like that? Still, I didn't love him. To be really honest, I was trying desperately not even to like him. He comes from New Jersey. I've never gone out seriously with anyone who didn't live in Manhattan or wasn't at least making steps to move in." Greta paused just long enough for Shelly to jump in.

"I know what you mean. There's something about men who don't live in the city. I used to think of them as failures." Shelly hadn't meant to burst any bubbles. She was just trying to keep an exclusive hold on her friend. The holidays were coming up, and a man with off-season lilies could be a dangerous opponent.

"He would move for me." Greta took a Virginia Slim from her enameled cigarette case. Her red nails worked hard to get it packed and lit.

"He would move? It sounds serious." Shelly tried to sound happy while being devastated. This had happened before to her. Girlfriends had gone in and out of relationships. She had done it herself. But never before had it hurt as much. Greta had shown her how to attack the situation aggressively. Magazines were full of advice, but no one played the game as well as Greta. She was out there looking, searching the world while everyone else was hoping to be found. She made it seem possible that mere women could hunt the men down.

"When he said he wanted to move, at first I felt this overwhelming responsibility. I mean, you just don't let someone move from one state to another without feeling you have to help them line their shelves or something."

"And his shelves are the ones you want to line?" Shelly was a lawyer, sitting up straight, confronting her defendant. She had no intention of wrecking her friend's life, but if she happened to utter the combination of words that made Greta realize that this man was not right for her, that would be forgivable and the two women could continue to search together.

"I guess so. I don't now. I'm crazy about him." Greta giggled. The laugh was incongruous with her sophisticated look.

"How come I didn't know about this? We've been on the phone practically every night. I mean, I'm very happy for you. Very. But how come?"

"I wanted to tell you. I almost did about a million times, but I didn't want to jinx anything." Shelly understood. She had had secret lovers, the too-good-to-be-true variety that she had kept to herself for fear that the world would upset the relationship.

"You sure you don't want something to drink? I mean, this is an occasion. Shouldn't we toast your happiness or something?"

"Not yet. I'm still insecure about this lasting. All I know is that we're set through New Year's Eve." Shelly hadn't celebrated a New Year's Eve since her catering business took off. This year she had to do four parties. She took a moment to envy everyone in the world who was able to spend a holiday normally.

"If he's willing to move, you should feel a little secure."

"Yeah. I guess. It's just that, well—you know these things. In the end there are only two ways to go. Either you get married, or it falls apart. There's the let's-be-friends situation that you and Mickey seem to have worked out, but I can't do that. When they say, 'Let's be friends' to me, I can't help thinking that they're taking from me only the parts they want and I'm letting them discard the rest.''

"It's a shame that women always end up thinking about the end at the beginning.''

"Yeah, well, that's our training. Since none of them work out until the one that does, we get used to endings. I can be fickle. I know it. I can leave a guy because of his underwear or because he doesn't read the really good books. Still, it hurts. I've been dating for twenty years now—it's been a series of good-byes, all with tears and hurt. No wonder I'm happy and scared to death at the same time.''

"Maybe this is the one.''

"Maybe," Greta said sadly. "Or maybe tomorrow night I'll be crying on your shoulder.''

"You can have both of them.''

"Thanks.''

"I can't believe you met the day we rented the car," Shelly said, in an attempt to brighten things. Thinking of relationships ending had put them both under clouds.

"Yeah. He was right in the middle of that long line.''

"The one with the pipe?''

"I wish. If he were the one with the pipe, I wouldn't have to convince him to get a whole new wardrobe, which he is, by the way, perfectly willing to do. He was the one with, oh God, the yellow shirt.''

Shelly searched her mind for the right man. She couldn't find one with a yellow shirt. "I don't remember. They're sort of blending together. I think I was too scared that we had done something illegal to remember any shirts.'' Shelly leaned back and smiled, remembering that day, but the good feeling left once she thought about her future. If Greta had found her man there would be no more days like that Sunday. Shelly would lose her pal.

"I really don't know how to describe him. You couldn't say he was good-looking. He's sort of medium height, light brown hair, receding forehead, a little bit of a potbelly—but so what; right?''

"Right. I would never let a pot stand between me and happiness.'' Shelly had been looking at Greta during the whole conversation, so she saw the first tear appear at this point. It was large and perfect, like a tear in a cartoon. It was wiped away by the back of Greta's hand, but immediately there was another in its place. Greta had her handkerchief out before Shelly could run for a tissue.

"Oh, God, I'm so shallow," sobbed Greta. Shelly walked over the coffee table to join her friend. She put her arms around her, knowing she would have to convince Greta she wasn't shallow.

"You're not. I don't know one other person who actually supports a couple of foster children. Really, Greta, we all think about doing it, but you got around to it. And you visit your grandmother. Nobody does that with such regularity. And you designed and made the costumes for the Henry Street Settlement Christmas Show. And . . ."

"You don't have to make me sound like such a goddamn Girl Scout." There seemed to be no end to her tears. By now, not only her face, but Shelly's robe, was soaked.

"There's nothing wrong with being a Girl Scout. You're generous. And you're a sensitive tipper. Shallow? You subscribe to *US News & World Report*. I won't have you calling yourself shallow in my home." Greta almost smiled. The tears almost stopped. There were a few silent moments before Greta could speak again. A sigh preceded her words.

"I don't know. I really like this guy. It's great when we're alone. He rubs my back. The sex is good. He's a giver in bed, you know what I mean?" She looked to Shelly for an answer to her question. Shelly nodded. She knew how valuable givers were.

"Most givers, I'm not saying all, but most—are either short, or have small things, or are in the age group of men who want to be sensitive. They're givers and criers and act like they have premenstrual syndrome every day of their lives."

"I know. That's the crazy thing. Hank is none of those things. He's just a nice guy."

"So it sounds like you got a really good deal."

"I do. Really I do. So why am I crying? Because as long as we're behind closed doors everything is great. I mean he rubs my back with care. The problem is I can't take him out in public."

"You can't?"

"I lied to you before when I told you that I didn't tell you about him because I was afraid of jinxing the relationship."

"That's okay."

"I've told all my friends that same lie." At the mention of other friends, Shelly was a bit hurt. She was jealous of anybody else in Greta's life. "The truth is that I'm embarrassed to be with him."

"I once liked this guy with a mole and I took him to my cousin's wedding and, I swear, the whole night I felt that everyone was looking at that mole. I didn't want to care, but I did. Sometimes I think I'm not married and a mother because of that growth. Talk about shallow. To this day I can't look at my cousin Rita's wedding album."

"This isn't physical. The problem with Hank is that . . . Oh God, he's the one we made fun of that day. He's the exterminator." Having said it, Greta rested her head against the back of the couch and closed her eyes.

"I remember . . . the exterminator."

"He's really nice. He's even very careful about the way he exterminates. He uses traps that don't make rats suffer one second longer than they have to."

"Sounds like a terrific guy."

"You don't find guys like that every day."

"I know. I know. I've been looking for one my whole life."

"Why does he have to be a fucking exterminator?"

"It's his own business, right?"

"Oh yeah. It's his own. He's even got a dozen guys working for him. They have squirrels on their shirts and they ride around in trucks with big roaches on them." One day they would find this funny. But now, since Greta was clearly suffering, they passed up the laugh.

"So he's more like an administrator," said Shelly, trying to be reassuring.

"That would be better, but he says he never wants to sit behind a desk and send others out to conquer termites. He says he always wants to keep his hands in." Greta said these words with great pain. Shelly guessed that she and the exterminator had had discussions about this delicate matter and that he had won.

"I'm sorry. I still don't see insurmountable problems."

"I keep thinking I smell rat poison."

"So you get him to throw on a little Canoe."

"Yeah. But I keep coming back to the big one, the outside world."

"Have you tried it with him?"

"Oh yeah. I've tried it. Remember that party down at Reva's Boutique in SoHo?"

"No. Yes. That was the same night as the Bernstein bar mitzvah. Come to think if it, Lilly Bernstein still has my vases. Why doesn't Seth remember to do anything?" Shelly wrote a note to herself. She did this while still looking at Greta, pretending to give all her attention.

"We went to Reva's and everyone was there—Kit, Jeremy, Cheryl, every up-and-coming designer in the city wearing one-of-a-kinds. You could feel their talent. It was strange, but I was proud to be there with Hank. Maybe it was because we had made love that afternoon. I just felt I was with a real man, a regular guy. I liked seeing the hair on his arms, and I proudly introduced him around."

"It sounds good."

"It's not. We moved through the crowd with our white wine in our plastic cups and everything was fine. Then Christie Lunney caught up with us and told Hank that she knew him from somewhere. She asked him if he was in Aspen last Christmas and wondered if he belonged to her tennis club. I was getting a kick out of it until, of course, she put her finger on where they had met. She poked him in the chest and yelled out, 'The rat man. You're the rat man. I was at my sister's in South Orange and we saw this major rat run across her kitchen floor. Your ad was the biggest so we called you and begged you to come and rescue us even though it was a Sunday night.' Then Christie grabbed her heart like some goddamn romantic and started complimenting him as her hero. I wanted to die. I knew at that moment that the man who I had adored that afternoon would never work out. There would be other parties and dinners and chance meetings in movie lines, and I would be waiting for the next person to know I was with an exterminator. I'm just too shallow for this mixing of worlds."

"You don't think you could ever say, 'So what?' to the Christies of the world?"

"Could you?"

"Me? You're looking at a woman who was scared that her children would have moles."

"You read the articles. They keep saying if you really want a relationship, you realize that nobody is perfect and there are things you have to overlook."

"It's hard to overlook fifteen trucks with roaches on them."

"Maybe it'll work."

"Maybe we're just too picky."

"We don't have to settle. Who says we have to settle?"

"You have some wine?"

"Of course I have wine. Caterers steal wine." Halfway through their drinks, Greta mentioned that she had run into Barry, the man who had introduced them.

"He was with a very leggy woman," Greta said with disgust. They both put him down as a man who was just interested in going out with visuals.

Greta stayed longer than she had expected to. When she had enough wine, she remembered that she was beginning to love the man who gave back rubs. "I better go. He's waiting for me," she said wearily. She looked at her coat and sank back into the couch as if the mink was too heavy to bear.

"Am I going to get to meet him?" Shelly was trying hard to be the supportive friend. She would swing her mood in any direction Greta wanted to go.

"I don't know if I'll ever cart him out again."

"Maybe it'll . . ." was all Shelly could say.

"Do you want to share him? We could do a joint-custody routine."

"No, thanks."

"You're right to say no. There's no value in half an exterminator."

They hugged at the door. They hung on to each other longer than usual since they were both in trouble. Greta slipped into her coat, slipped into the elevator, slipped into the night, and eventually slipped into the exterminator's arms. Everything was all right when nobody was watching.

Shelly turned all the lights in her apartment on and got into bed. She wondered where all those boys from high school were who tried to get into her pants. For the first time since puberty, she felt no need to shave her legs.

# 10
# Flight Toward Christianity

ASTRA Rainbow looked out of the window for the entire flight. This amazed Mickey. As a child, Mickey had always insisted on sitting next to the window when he, his mother and his aunt flew to Florida. He looked out as the plane took off and when the plane landed. The clouds in between bored even a five-year-old. Rainbow watched this blanket of white almost the whole time they were in the air. She turned only when the stewardess asked which meal she wanted. Astra Rainbow told Sally Meadream that she wasn't hungry. Mickey almost immediately regretted buying first-class tickets. Not only was the girl not going to eat, she really didn't understand that she was in first class. He had wanted to impress her, but didn't get his chance. She must have thought the rest of the plane was exactly like the front. Knowing that he had spent close to five hundred dollars for these seats, he asked her if she would like to take a walk. His intention was to show her the crowded conditions and inferior meals in the back of the plane. She preferred to look out the window. It was not a flight to remember except for one bumpy section that was ferocious enough for Mickey to grab on to the solidness of his chair.

"You scared?" he asked into the strands of her hair.

"No. Do the bumps mean anything?"

"Not to the crew. To them it probably just means that we are in a bit of turbulence. To me it's a sign that death is imminent." Still she did not turn.

"Do you really think you are going to die?" He thought it interesting that although they were in the same plane, she felt he could go while she might stay intact.

"Not exactly. I'm just having thoughts in that area because the bouncing around of the sky here made me feel a lack of control. What is death, if it isn't total lack of control of everything in and about your body?"

"And that scares you?" Her hand had been pressed against the window. She examined it for traces of dirt.

"Yeah, but believe me, Rainbow, we're not going down. It's just my own private neurosis that keeps me from enjoying being thrown around in the sky."

Here the captain's voice interrupted him. It was one of those soothing, blue-eyed voices that reassures you that you are flying with someone who would drop bombs on Nazis if he had to. Also there was something in his tone that said he was a family man. He probably had bought the wife sexy underwear while he was in New York and wasn't about to fail to deliver it. "Ladies and gentlemen," he began, which was standard enough. (If they were about to crash he probably wouldn't have been so polite.) "I have turned on the seat belt signs because it looks like we're experiencing a storm front here. We should be out of it in another twenty minutes. Until then, please refrain from walking about in the cabin."

Mickey couldn't take this for another twenty minutes. He was sure he was being punished for seeking out Christian worlds. The air got worse. The plane bounced more. Astra Rainbow watched the clouds, which they were in the center of now. Mickey watched his life pass before him. It was filled with too many network meetings. On one spectacular bump he thought of Shelly. Her world had always been safe for him. He had never had to go flying off into storms with her. He and Shelly would have stayed home, facing only bumpy cab rides, machines that you could get out of whenever you wanted. It was only for women like Astra Rainbow that he risked his security and allowed himself to be scared. Of course, no one ever felt alive while he was feeling safe. If Mickey weren't so sick to his stomach, he would have this thought through further. The safety of Shelly could make his stomach upset in a whole other way.

He tried to look death in the eye just so he could write about it someday, but even though Mickey Burke had a trained imagination, he also knew he had a trained flight crew who would get him there. Instead of facing death, he asked his God to please make the bumps go away. He had a Jewish stomach that was meant to be grounded. His prayers weren't answered. The captain kept apologizing, and Mickey tried to get into a man-against-nature mood.

"We think we know it all," he said to his companion, "but when it gets down to it we can't control the wind." Astra Rainbow, who had grown up where crops were ruined by storms all the time, had known this for her whole life and wondered why the grown man next to her was making such grand statements about the weather she had grown up with. She had never experienced the wind this high up, but she had always known it was there and that generally you had to do more than fasten your seat belt to keep things intact. Her family was always running out into their small fields to throw blankets on animals and tarps on crops.

In New York Mr. Burke had seemed very smart. She had never been that close to such intelligence. Maybe she should tell him that when they got home it would be better if he left the wind out of his conversation. She didn't say anything for fear of hurting her boss. She sure hoped he was only peculiar on planes and had this man-against-nature stuff out of his system by the time they landed. She had some passing fears of being embarrassed by her family. Granny could talk an awfully long time about nothing, and her stepfather always seemed to be passing gas and trying to make a joke about it. Her mother was naked too often. But those embarrassments faded into the clouds she was watching. Now she worried about being embarrassed by the city boy. She hoped once they landed he would discontinue his philosophizing.

When they landed, Mickey's first surprise was seeing the pilot who emerged from the cockpit. He was shorter and darker than his voice had led the passengers to believe. Mickey thought he had been flying with a general when all the time he was in the hands of a second-generation American whose wife probably bought her own underwear. Mickey Burke was one of those rare individuals who was practically free of prejudice. The only people he hated were those who had the potential to change his scripts. He just didn't like to go flying with anybody whom he perceived to be shorter than himself.

His second surprise was Granny. He had expected a white-haired woman who was gently attended to as she sat by the hearth. In fact, she was in her fifties, driving a '66 Mustang and her only silver hairs were among the blonde. She was classy. She might have had only one Sunday dress, but it was the finest one she could sew. Her hair was neatly secured behind her ears by a large tortoise-shell barrette, and her posture was too good for her to be anybody's grandmother. Her handshake hurt him. Her eyes were so clear they must have seen clearly. Her only flaw was lacking warmth—even for the granddaughter she raised. Granny brushed off the hugs and kisses she received from Astra Rainbow, actually backing away from them.

Mickey had very little luggage and a small shopping bag of presents that he had brought for the family. When he started to pack the trunk of the car, Granny took over. It was a trunk she knew, and she directed every bag. He offered to drive but she refused. She said the old car knew her touch and besides, she knew where she was going. Mickey should sit up front, she said, so he could see the beautiful countryside. Astra Rainbow sat in the middle of the back seat. She was happier than he had ever seen her. "It is good to be home," she said, and bounced even when the car didn't.

They went from city to suburbs to rural communities to farmland in less than a half an hour. Mickey Burke was not disappointed by the old homestead. The house was a mile away from the main road. He calculated that the mailbox would be on Twenty-ninth Street while the house, in Manhattan terms, would be on Forty-ninth. In New York one would have to go through several distinct neighborhoods just to get a letter. They followed a road with hills of snow on either side. As they did, Granny continued to be their tour guide. In the city she had made a point of telling Mickey that they had a historical society, a country museum with Rembrandts and Renoirs, and their own symphony. Now that they were on personal ground, she talked about the Newfields who started it all. "My great-great-great-grandfather built our house for his bride. He was among the first to settle here, and if you don't believe me, you can check it out in the library. Yes, Mr. Burke, we have a local library. We may be country people, but we haven't forgotten the importance of the written word." Her tone was cross. She was accusing Mickey of thoughts he never had. She reminded him of those stern teachers in Brooklyn who gave homework the first day of class just to prove who's boss.

"The original house was built in 1836, just sixty years after our independence. Of course there have been additions and modernizations since then. We Newfields keep up with the times, and folks around here will tell you that we were the first to have indoor plumbing." (Mickey hoped it had been kept up well. Strange toilets were never friendly toward him.) "My own grandmother saved her egg money and paid for the electric lights. In those days we harvested wheat, with chickens just as a sideline. It wasn't easy to put those pennies away, but Grandma did so that she could take a bath and see what she was doing. We've sold off most of the land, and the chickens are not much to talk about, but there she is, Mr. Burke, the family seat."

Mickey didn't know quite what to say about the house. It was not distinct enough to call it wonderful. One could see where each addition had been made since each new Newfield had chosen new materials with no regard to the original. It looked to Mickey like a stone house with an addition from Queens and another brought in from Las Vegas. There was a very blue bird in the snow that helped Mickey to say the house was noble. This pleased Granny, who never minded compliments.

The inside was as eclectic as the exterior. The roaring fire he had expected wasn't going to happen, since there was a television set sitting in the fireplace. There were worn, comfortable chairs next to ones that looked like they came from the nearest Hilton. Most of the wallpaper was old and comfortable, but the downstairs powder room, of which Granny was particularly proud, had gold paper with red flocking on it and two fixtures that had different-colored clumps of glass that reminded Mickey of restaurants where you could buy steak for a dollar fifty-nine. Although the home had its good points, wooden beams and a terrific newel post, Mickey had the feeling that it wasn't worth photographing. He had packed his camera first, remembering to include his wide-angle lens. Now as they walked from room to room, still with the tour guide, he found himself looking out of windows. He decided that the outside was what he had come for. There was an untouched barn that he made sure was still there from every window. He had expected Christmas decorations, but the only sign of the holidays was a package of store-bought cookies. The cellophane window on the package let you see they were green-sprinkled trees that had broken before they arrived home. Before abandoning his fantasy completely, he held out hope that the attic housed a box of overflowing wreaths and angels.

Mickey was shown his room, one that he knew had once housed boys. The wallpaper was a faded blue-green and had all kinds of old cars, boats and planes on it. There was a definite transportation motif going on. There was a small desk that a small boy must have done homework on, and there were bunk beds. To Mickey Burke, an only child, the beds were the most romantic thing in the room. He figured he would try both top and bottom before he left.

Astra Rainbow ran to her room, excited to be back among familiar things. What she had left behind was all still there, including the half-used container of talcum powder. Clearly, hers was the room of a girl who had hoped to enter a nunnery. It was sparse and predominantly brown. The bed looked as if it were too small for an adult.

Rainbow opened her closet and saw the clothes of her past. How simple they were. The clothes of a girl learning to type. There were prints that the girls of Manhattan left behind. She pushed them aside to make way for the things she had brought with her, even though her suitcases were still downstairs. She sat on her bed and let the feelings return. She remembered going with Granny to pick out the paint in town. There was an excitement about getting to pick out a color for her world. She had studied a large box of Crayolas on the day of the decision. Paint was like spring. It offered a new beginning. Unfortunately, the girl never got a choice. The dark beige was on sale and Granny fell for it, paying with folded dollar bills that came out of a black cotton change purse. The paint was a disappointment. Even Mr. Robards, the handyman who did the job, disliked it. He frowned when he opened the can, and although he tried to make the best out of a bad situation by whistling while he worked, it clearly pained him to have to use such a drab color.

The other memory that pervaded the room was one connected to the small porcelain ballerina that was made in Japan. It had been given to her by her mother and her new husband when they came to visit after the wedding and before they had their two horrible sons. Astra Rainbow, who was only eight at the time, had thought the gift was an invitation to join their family. She was sure that they would come and get her as soon as they had a house. During their visit they talked about getting one. They never did come and claim her, and the ballerina, who had one shoe off and one shoe on, stood and waited too.

The small statue no longer made her happy or sad. Astra Rainbow picked it up and moved it to the other side of the dresser only because she wanted to make a change. She had been to the big city and, in the stark room of her childhood, moving the small dancer was the only change she could make.

Mickey had expected to be alone when he unpacked, but there was Mrs. Newfield, her hands filled with Ivory soap and worn towels. "Might I come in?" she asked. "I've come to stock your bathroom." It was evident that she wasn't going to make a move unless he gave her permission.

"Yeah. Sure. You want me to take those?"

"No, young man. I'll just put them where they belong."

"Be my guest," said Mickey, fully aware that he shouldn't make jokes for people who didn't know his rhythm.

Mrs. Newfield spent a few minutes putting her things away and then once again stood in the doorway. "Might I have a word with you, Mr. Burke?" Mickey thought for a moment she was going to instruct him about washing his ears.

"Yeah. Sure. Come on in." She sat down in the desk chair, which he didn't expect. If they were really going to have just a few words, they were strong enough to stand. He sat on the lower bunk, banging his head on the upper one as he did. He knew he was going to have to lie about the pain.

"Did you hurt yourself?" She sat quietly, acting very differently than the Jewish grandmothers he had known. His own mother would have not only soaked his head, but also her own, just to keep him company.

The sound alone should have revealed that there was some pain going on, but Mickey knew he had to be manly enough to cover. At least he had hit the back of his head, missing his concussion. "No, no problem. I just grazed it. The noise was worse than the actual bump, which is probably rising, but I'm positive I won't have even a slight headache." He realized that he was working too hard to convince a woman who didn't care if he had been hurt that he hadn't been.

"Why are you here, Mr. Burke?" This was not a question Mickey expected. He had expected to be invited into the womb of the family and, so far, things had been fairly cordial and on schedule. There was something strange about receiving towels and then being asked why he took them. Since he couldn't tell this upright woman that he was there to steal Christmas and Christianity, and still have time to compile notes on Astra Rainbow's background, he would have to stay away from the truth. Fortunately, he was a writer who could think on his feet.

"The city was closing in on me," he began. He realized immediately that was a bit too dramatic. The one thing he knew about Mrs. Newfield was that she enjoyed simplicity. "I needed to have a little country in my life. I wanted to see snow that hadn't been walked on by French poodles." (He had wanted to say that he wanted to see snow that hadn't been peed on by French poodles, but he knew when to censor himself.) Since he wasn't getting any response, not even a nod of the head, he pushed forward. "I thought it might improve my writing if I got close to nature again . . . not that I was ever close to nature before. The only time I ever left the city was for a couple of weeks of summer camp. I hated it and my mother had to come and pick me up, but not because of the birds and trees."

He was quick to apologize to this grandmother and didn't want to knock her nature. "There was a counselor who kept picking on me because I was a wimp. It also didn't help that I was underweight and my mother sent up a special protein drink that I had to have at every meal. So, naturally, the kids picked on me, too. I just hope they know that I grew up to be a writer and they didn't." Mickey knew he was far away from Mrs. Newfield's question, and he fought to get back. This time he would try for sympathy. "Actually, I came because I was in the hospital recently, nothing catching, just a concussion, and I needed the rest, not that I'm not perfectly willing to help with the chores. I'd like to do chores. I've never had any real chores that I could do with my hands." He was happy with this answer and looked for approval from Mrs. Newfield. Her eyes were clear, but he saw no emotion. Strange, these people from the middle of the country. They were too hard to read.

"So you did not come here because of my granddaughter? The truth, Mr. Burke." Mrs. Newfield was not showing any anger. She had come with the soap and stayed for the facts.

"I like your granddaughter very much. She's a lovely girl." Mickey had chosen to stay on the most neutral territory he could find.

"And beautiful."

"And beautiful. She's very beautiful. It's impossible to miss her beauty."

"Do you have designs on her?" He loved the question and would have to remember it for *The Astra Rainbow Story*.

"Designs? I'm not exactly sure what you mean." At this point Mickey thought that Mrs. Newfield was asking if he planned to marry Astra Rainbow. He felt he had to steer clear of promises.

Although Mickey couldn't read Mrs. Newfield, she seemed to know exactly what was on his mind. He would have to learn a straighter face. "What I mean is, do you lust for her?" was Granny's next question. Mickey had the feeling that this woman would know if he was lying, so he decided he had to tell the truth, but soften it. He bent his head before answering, partly because he thought it was a good idea to show modesty, partly because a vein was throbbing and the change of position felt nice.

"No. Absolutely not." His old voice had come back, the one he used to have before it changed. "I mean, not that she's not beautiful, she's a girl any guy would lust after and I'm just an average guy. Not that I'm going to do anything about it. I didn't come here to . . ." He searched quickly for words. Since he had never spoken in the Bible Belt before, he had never before realized that conversation didn't flow the way it did back home. "I didn't come here to bed her down." Mickey couldn't believe the words he had chosen. He felt minutes away from talking about this year's crop and Mim's rheumatism.

"Mr. Burke, I don't know if you know or not, but my granddaughter is waiting for her calling." Mrs. Newfield looked at Mickey to make sure he understood what she was saying. Astra Rainbow had warned her that Mr. Burke was a Jew and not to bring up religion. Mrs. Newfield wanted to know how they could do that when they were celebrating Christ the Lord's birthday, and Astra Rainbow patiently explained that they should just remember that her boss was Jewish. The young woman stressed that her grandmother should be sensitive. Mrs. Newfield, who had never been sensitive, said she would try. Her method of trying was to speak more slowly than she normally did. Since Mickey looked confused, she bothered to explain. "Astra Rainbow has wanted to be a nun most of her young life. She is waiting for some sign to let her know she has chosen the right vocation. I am not going to let you or any other man spoil that for her."

"Excuse me, Mrs. Newfield . . ."

"Call me Granny."

"Granny?" Since the woman clearly didn't like him, this request seemed out of context. Up to now, he had been sure that he was going to "Mrs. Newfield" her until he went home.

"You're in my home, Mr. Burke. You will sleep on my sheets and eat from my dishes. I think that gives you the right to call me Granny." Since Mickey wanted to get back to Astra Rainbow becoming a nun, he decided this was not the time to go against orders.

"Well, if I'm calling you Granny, you call me Mickey."

"What gives me that right? You are, after all, my granddaughter's boss. I would feel funny addressing you in such a familiar way." This woman was tough.

"I'm giving you that right. As you said, I'll be sleeping and eating on your stuff. The least I could do in return is give you my first name to use whenever you want."

"Do you mind if I think about it?"

"No. Think about it as long as you want."

With this she stood up and moved to the window. He hadn't expected her to think about it right then, but obviously she was going to. The light that hit her was bright, and he could see every line on her face. It was Astra Rainbow's face forty years from now. He wondered if the girl knew that those wrinkles would one day be hers. She stood by the window for only seconds, but time was expanded in this room of silence. Mickey became uncomfortable over the internal debate that Mrs. Newfield, now Granny, seemed to be having. He could not imagine the pros and cons she was weighing. By the time she faced him again, he learned that she was not an impulsive woman. She spoke as she went back to her chair.

"I think that Astra Rainbow should continue to call the man she works for by his full and proper name. I also believe that during your stay here that Astra Rainbow and I should address you in the same way. Therefore, I feel it is best that I continue to call you Mr. Burke." By now she was seated. They both knew there was still unfinished business. "Now, where were we?"

Mickey knew exactly where they were. She had been talking about delicious mysterious things like vocation and callings. He felt it was safer to shrug than to bring up the thoughts that had already been thrown at him. There was another pause, briefer this time. She now addressed her real reason for coming to his room. The soap and towels had been the excuse.

"We were talking about my granddaughter. I know she is a beauty and a highly sexual creature. I know that it is wrong for one adult to guard another's virginity, but I assure you this is a special case.

It is absolutely imperative that this girl devote her life to the church. We are both very sad that she hasn't received her sign yet."

Mickey needed information, but it was clear that he wasn't going to get it. He sat there on the bed rejecting things to say next. He wanted to ask if it was more the grandmother's idea that her Astra became a nun. He concluded that there was nothing he could ask and not much he could say.

"I'm sorry, too," he offered. He shook his head and closed his eyes, trying to look as sorry as possible. Truthfully, more than anything he was intrigued, but he wasn't about to reveal that.

"Yes, well, we all are. I just don't want it to be the greatest tragedy of our lives." Apparently feeling she had made herself clear, she stood and extended her hand. When Mickey stood to shake it, he knocked his head on the upper bunk again. This time the blow was more severe. Curse words floated in his head right near the pain. When he opened his eyes, he saw silver spots. Still he would lie about the damage.

"Are you okay, Mr. Burke? Blows to the head shouldn't be taken lightly."

"Yeah, well, fortunately my concussion was in the front and this is in the back area." He was sure he was going to throw up blood and hoped she would get out of his way in time.

"Well, that's good. I would hate to think that our beds were attacking you." She almost smiled. Obviously she felt she had struck a deal with him. Mickey wanted to ask what they would do if the calling never came, but she was already leaving the room and he didn't feel it was the type of thing that he should say to his hostess's back.

The first thing Mickey fished from his suitcase was the notebook he brought to take notes on *The Astra Rainbow Story*. He got his pen from his jacket pocket, and after entering the date, he started recording the mystery. All he had for the book was a series of questions. Why did the grandmother feel it necessary to tell him anything? Why was it absolutely imperative that Rainbow devote her life to the church? Should he save her from it? Did it have anything to do with what the young woman referred to as "something terrible in her past"? Did the girl know that her grandmother had spoken to him? Was he seeing typical life on the farm or was he in the middle of the most bizarre circumstance? Before he could continue, Mrs. Newfield had intruded again. She had probably left the door open so that she could return. He was in a boy's room, and his privacy was being invaded. His own mother had never understood that she should not put her head into his private space. Like all mothers, she left her body on the other side of the transom to prove to herself that she was not an intruder. When he saw Mrs. Newfield, Mickey felt obliged to hide his notes. In too jerky a movement, he moved them behind his back; then he felt he had to explain. "I'm a writer, so I fool around with thoughts all the time."

"Oh, well, how nice. To think there's a real writer doing his work right here in my house." Mickey couldn't tell whether or not she was being sarcastic.

"Just a few notes." He didn't want her to think that he was in the middle of an epic novel.

"Well, I'm very impressed. I used to write some darn good poetry, but Lord, I haven't done that since I was a schoolgirl. I saved the poems if you'd care to read them."

"I'd love to." He tried to sound as impressed with her as she was with him. They would be poems that rhymed, with dried flowers pressed between them.

"I'll try to dig them up. I'm going to the market now. Is there anything special you would care to have, Mr. Burke?" Mickey translated this question as, "I waited until you got here to ask what you Jews eat."

"No, nothing special." I'm just like you and all the other Christians around here. Bring me bread you can make holes in.

The woman was perfectly willing to go now, and Mickey should have let her. Instead he tried to clarify things so that she could have a perfectly happy shopping trip. "I don't want you to worry about me and your granddaughter, Mrs. Newfield. We're not . . . we don't . . . We've never had any physical contact. We're just basically good friends." Here was Mickey's mistake. The good-friends concept was known in the cities. Here on the farm, where animals and man had to have offspring, the concept of good friends was a foreign one.

"I've never known a man who didn't do what nature told him to do." And Mickey knew she was right. He never knew a man who didn't try to do what nature told him to.

"I have no intention of touching Astra Rainbow," he said nobly.

"Yes. Well, we'll see. My granddaughter knows the steps she must never go beyond. Let's just hope the devil doesn't decide to pay us a visit." She said this straightforwardly but it felt to Mickey that she hadn't let him be noble.

This time, she shut the door tightly when she left. Mickey had the feeling that intrusions were over. With his notebook still in his hand and his suitcase still unpacked, he lay down on the bed to sort out the conversation. Mrs. Newfield didn't want him touching her granddaughter—that was clear. It was possible that she had made up the part about Astra Rainbow wanting to be a nun just to keep him away. It was also possible that Mrs. Newfield was protecting herself. Maybe she simply wanted her child back. Preferably she was guarding a black secret. His movie would be better for it.

He looked out the window and saw Astra Rainbow walking through the snow. Quickly his camera was out, and he photographed her, enjoying her colors against the snow. Through the lens he fell for her again, and by the time his camera was back in its case, he was hoping that Mrs. Newfield wasn't serious about protecting her young ward and that one day Mickey and Astra Rainbow would be living on Sixty-seventh between Madison and Park.

Mickey had expected the drawers in the room assigned to him to be empty, but they held remnants from somebody's boyhood, among them a child's tie. He remembered having one just like it and his mother calling him her "little man" every time he had clipped it on. With that tie on and his hair slicked down, he was sure that everyone in the neighborhood was staring at him. He imagined they were saying to themselves that they wished they had a little boy just like him. Mickey smiled, remembering what a cocky child he had been encouraged to be. Only now did he know that nobody noticed whether he was wearing a tie or not.

In the second drawer there was some child-sized underwear, modern and white enough to have been worn within the last few years, and a toy gun that was so realistic that Mickey jumped. Grandma Arnold had once given him ten dollars for an excellent report card, marred only by a U for effort in physical education. He had made ape sounds as he attempted to climb the ropes. He never could climb them, but neither could Larry Solomon, who got an S. The U was for those sounds that made the other boys laugh. Mickey sometimes hoped that Mr. Ryan had seen one of his televison credits and realized that the really good rope climbers were probably selling insurance.

Mickey had wanted desperately to spend most of Grandma Arnold's money on a cap gun, but his mother forbade him. "They look too real," she said. "And what if somebody thinks we're sticking them up?" Mickey promised never to point the gun at anyone, but his pledges weren't effective: He was persuaded to buy a magic set instead. It was okay making sponge balls disappear under plastic cups, but he never stopped envying every cap gun in the neighborhood. Now here he was, holding the toy gun of his youthful dreams, and he wanted to shoot everything. He aimed it at a tree, pulled the trigger and heard the click he had been waiting for all these years. He went into the bathroom and shot himself in the mirror right between the eyes. Hearing footsteps, he spun around and aimed the gun at the door. When Astra Rainbow stuck her head in, just as her grandmother had, he found himself hiding something behind his back for the second time that day.

"Do you have something behind your back, Mr. Burke?" Astra Rainbow asked in a frightened voice. Mickey revealed the toy and she jumped back, shielding herself with her arms as if that would stop an oncoming bullet.

"It's only a toy," Mickey said, a naughty boy caught in the act.

"Gosh. I was really scared," she said, catching her breath as she spoke. "I thought maybe you had come here to kill us all." Mickey felt as guilty as a homicidal maniac.

"You did? You thought I had snuck into your granny's home for the purpose of shooting the whole family?" The boy who wasn't even allowed to buy a cap gun was astonished that anyone could think him capable of violence. "Do I look like a killer to you?"

"Killers come in all shapes and sizes, Mr. Burke," she said in a tone that Granny would have used.

"Yeah, but you know me. I'm the guy who brings you lunch if I happen to be in the neighborhood deli." He was using his nice-guy defense, which he realized had very little chance of holding up in court.

"I don't know if I know you," said Astra Rainbow, holding out her hand for the gun. He handed over the weapon, sorry his fingerprints were on it. She put the gun back into the drawer, as if she knew where it had come from. He was slightly embarrassed at the glimpse she caught of his underwear.

"I came to ask you if you wanted to take a walk," she said, once she was back at the door. "It's really glorious out there," she added, selling the excursion.

"Yeah. Sure." He moved quickly, taking his Timberland boots out of his suitcase. Astra Rainbow waited patiently as he dressed warmly, with a sweater and a down jacket. She wore jeans, sneakers, and a light cape. They didn't look as if they were in the same weather at the same time.

Mickey loved the virgin snow. In New York snow fell from the sky already dirty. Here the only damage was made by his own footprints. He liked the pretty girl by his side, but the real romance was between him and the impression he was leaving behind. He thought of his work and compared it to this walk. Writing for television was like walking in the fresh snow. You could see where you had trodden at the moment, but even as you made your mark, you knew it would melt. He thought of how he had to write his film. Films were preserved for future generations.

"My granny came to talk to you?" Astra Rainbow asked. Unfortunately, she asked just as Mickey, the city boy, was losing his balance. He was embarrassed since he wanted to be as surefooted as the girl he was trying to impress. Astra Rainbow read his embarrassment but didn't know that it was the slipping that had caused it. She worried about what Granny might have said. "She didn't say anything serious, did she?"

Mickey, who was by now walking like an old religious man, didn't have an easy time with the girl's last question. What Mrs. Newfield had said was serious enough, but he didn't feel like getting into it. He was too scared of falling down and didn't want to have to concentrate on anything beyond not breaking any bones. "We had a nice talk." Another slip in the snow and Mickey reached for Rainbow's arm. He had no intention of letting go. He hadn't felt so feeble since he had tried to climb the ropes.

"Granny can really talk. I'll bet she gave you her 'No man should ever touch me' speech." Either his unsure footing or Astra Rainbow's words left him flat on his ass. He was lying in the snow, looking up helplessly at her. The pain wouldn't come until later. The embarrassment was now.

Astra Rainbow looked grander from his point of view, a large heroine filling most of the sky, arms extended, offering help. This scene would never make it into his film. His hero had to be a real hero. If he couldn't stand in the snow, his Warren Beatty would. The cold penetrated the real Mickey Burke, but the one he put on paper would leap snowdrifts in a single bound.

"Are you all right?" she asked, bending over now and wondering why he was refusing her help.

"I think so. It's just that I have this trick knee." He didn't. He needed an excuse to be lying there. No real man would be flat on his back just because of new-fallen snow. He refused her offer of help. Feeling awkward, he turned away and managed to get on all fours, then into a kneeling position. Finally, his back still rounded, he stood. He knew he had just done a short portrayal of the evolution of man.

Astra Rainbow suggested they return, but Mickey had to prove that this white stuff that they were walking on wasn't going to tell him where he could go. But they walked even more slowly and as they did, he made some calculations. Now she was twenty-two and he was an old thirty-eight. When she was fifty he would be using a walker, and when she was sixty-five he would be dead.

They walked silently for a few steps, both listening to the stumbling sounds his boots were making. The guy on Thirty-third Street had sold them with the guarantee that they had the best tread on the market. "These are like snow tires for your feet," he had said. Mickey still believed the guy. The boots were gripping. It was his legs that were insecure.

"You want to hang on?" Astra Rainbow asked after a couple of slips that could have turned into falls. Mickey wondered if it was possible to be macho and let a woman carry you through the snow.

Finally he took her arm, pretending it was a friendly gesture rather than a desperate one. Depending on her center of gravity seemed to help his own. Mickey decided to think of the way they walked as a new closeness they were forming. "We all need someone to lean on, especially in this cold world." She was his cane out here where there was too much sky, but he could be hers when they got back to his turf. She might be surefooted here, where she could follow the footsteps of her youth, but she didn't know enough to ask the guy behind the counter to cut the fat off the corned beef.

Once he was sure he wasn't going to fall down again, he didn't mind getting back to the conversation. A squirrel in the snow could have been distracting, but not to a man who was dealing with two generations of women, both of whom had mentioned the same provocative words. "Your grandmother is quite a . . ." He paused. Mickey had originally intended to say "character," but he knew that Astra Rainbow idolized the woman. He came up with "lady," which he felt was safe enough.

"Oh, no," said Rainbow. "She would hate to be thought of as a lady. Actually she's very naughty. She's had lovers, you know, and I'm not talking behind her back. She tells everybody."

"She didn't tell me. Mainly we talked about you."

"Right. Her 'Astra Rainbow is going to be a nun' lecture. I know it well. She gave it to every boy I ever knew." Mickey liked the idea of being called a boy. Too often he was reminded of middle age, especially now when the top half of him was trying to lead him home.

"Have there been many?"

"Not really. A few neighbors drifted by and there were some from town, but I didn't pay any attention."

"You must have been popular in school," he said, his words interspersed with heavy breathing. He made himself another promise to join a gym and get in shape.

"Oh, no. I went to an all-girls Catholic school. Granny said when she saw that I was getting breasts, that was the safest thing to do."

"So you didn't take any of the men . . . or boys seriously?"

"Mostly they were older like yourself, Mr. Burke." He didn't like hearing he was an older man. He had forgotten that when he was in his mid-twenties and working as a staff writer that he was often angry at the "older guys" on the staff for not getting his humor. Time had made him one of the older guys. "I like older men," she said before he had time to become really insulted. He thought of pointing out to her that thirty-eight in any society was not considered older, but he didn't want to lose the use of her arm.

"And I'm sure older men like you," he said, wanting to stay in the ballpark.

"Yes. They seem to. Mr. Raphelson once asked me to come into his back office, and when I did he showed me one of my papers with a strikeover. We were totally forbidden to do strikeovers, but I couldn't help it. Somehow I put an 'h' over an 'i'. I could hardly remember doing it, like I was in a trance or something, but there it was and I recognized it as my work. The second I saw it I started to cry, and then there was Mr. Raphelson consoling me and kissing my cheeks and my neck and trying to open the buttons of my blouse. I had to bite him."

"You're not talking," said Astra Rainbow after they had walked a while in silence. Women always pounced on you for not talking. Some became angry when he got quiet. Others became scared, wanting to know what was wrong. Women. Didn't they know that sometimes there was just nothing to say, or in this case, there was too much to say and no one to say it to? He was lonely for Jews.

"I was just thinking," he said. He tried to smile so that the girl he was leaning on wouldn't worry about the silence.

"About what?" she wanted to know. He should have known she would ask. They always wanted to know what you were thinking about.

"I was thinking about what your grandmother told me about your becoming a nun, and I was wondering if it was her idea or yours."

She thought he was silly not to know how things worked. "It wasn't anybody's idea. It's something she prayed for and I waited for. She's still praying and I'm still waiting."

Before either of them spoke again, and just as Mickey was worrying that they had gone too far and he wouldn't have the energy to walk back, they reached the front door of the house. They had made a circle in the snow without his realizing. He recognized the footprints he had made when they left. They were near Astra Rainbow's but separate. When he looked at his most recent marks, he saw how dependent he had become. His feet never left her side. Mickey was surprised to see a wreath on the door, the first big sign of the holiday. When Astra Rainbow let them in, bells rang. This is what he had come for.

Rainbow went to make them hot chocolate, and Mickey went upstairs to take off some of his layers of clothing. When he looked out of his window, he could see where they had traveled. It wasn't as far as he thought it had been.

Things began to brighten. Mrs. Newfield was back with armloads of groceries. Mickey carried them in, wishing he had offered to pay for them. A tree was delivered by the closest neighbor. He and Mickey shook hands and then each of them took one step back to talk. The shaking of hands was the only moment of trust between these two. There was talk about the tree being too tall for the living room, but when they stood it up, they found that it could have been custom-made for the room. The decorating wasn't going to be done until the following day, when Helen and her family arrived.

Mickey was assigned to test the lights, and he didn't tell them that Jewish boys don't know about electricity. Each time a string of lights lit up, he was amazed. When one didn't and he alone found the bulb that was the culprit, he was even more amazed. He read the faded instructions on one of the boxes and figured out how to make a string of lights blink. He felt converted.

At dinner Granny produced a tuna casserole that she had prepared beforehand. This, to Mickey, was a miracle, since his mother would never serve anything but solid blocks of meat, starches and vegetables, nor would she prepare anything in advance. Cooking was done just before eating. Somehow Mrs. Newfield had managed to freeze her dinner, and she made Astra Rainbow and Mickey guess the ingredients while they ate. Mickey knew that the whole thing must have been held together by cream of mushroom soup, but Granny was so thrilled to have disguised everything in her Corning Ware that he didn't participate. After they had given up, she told them her secret about Campbell's Cream of Mushroom. Mickey acted as if she was a cooking genius.

They finished the meal, and Mickey helped clean up. He did things for these Newfield women that he had never done for his mother. By seven o'clock, just about the time that he was usually thinking about where to go out to dinner, they were already finished. Granny suggested that they watch a little TV. Mickey didn't quite know what she meant by this. There was a big television set in the kitchen and a little one in the living room. Either she was suggesting that they watch television for a short time, or that they watch the smaller television, or both. Since Granny headed for the living room, it looked as if they were going to have their television experience there.

Watching television with two other women was something he hadn't done since childhood. Once in a while Jerry came over to his hotel for a basketball game, and when he hung out with Shelly they flicked the remote control together, but generally his television viewing was a solo experience. Now the three of them sat on the couch and Mrs. Newfield reached for the *TV Guide*. Mickey wanted to suggest that they move the television from the fireplace before the children got there and worried that Santa Claus wouldn't make a proper entrance with a Mitsubishi in his way, but he decided to keep quiet about it.

He had been successful with the tree lights, but he had never even been able to turn on an unfamiliar television. He had no confidence that he could move a television and install it elsewhere.

Just as Mrs. Newfield was choosing a program from the magazine she had relied on for years, Astra Rainbow remembered that one of Mickey's shows, *Two Is One Too Many*, a series about a confirmed bachelor, was on that night. Not realizing that he was surrounded by farmers, Mickey had thought that the show was on at nine, but he found out that it was on at eight and that everything was on an hour earlier for people who ate casseroles and had to get up to milk the cows.

"You wrote this show, Mr. Burke?" Mrs. Newfield asked, pulling over some type of needlework. She was making dozens of different-colored wool squares that looked as if they would be joined together one day.

"I didn't write this one," said Mickey, and before he could explain further, Astra Rainbow jumped in.

"He created it, Granny. He wrote the first one. The people liked it, and then other writers wrote some more, using Mr. Burke's characters and suggestions." She had started her explanation strongly, but as she went on, she became unsure of exactly how the system worked. Her voice weakened, and she looked toward Mickey for verification.

"That's exactly right," said Mickey, making Astra Rainbow feel sophisticated in her knowledge of the inner workings of the network world.

"Well, let's see what this is all about. I usually watch my *Cagney & Lacey* right about now, but I think I could forgo it this week in honor of our guest who is such a creative man." Granny stood, and for the first time that day, showed some age. It took her a moment to straighten out. When she did, she checked her *TV Guide* for Mickey's show and went over to the television, choosing the channel first, then turning it on. She stood and waited at the fireplace, making sure before she sat down that the picture for which she had paid three hundred and fifty-nine dollars would be there. When she was satisfied with the reception, she sat back down and pulled the crocheting toward her.

The show wasn't on for another seven minutes. With Mickey in the middle, they sat through the end of *Family Feud*. Mickey had always liked that show because it proved to him that he really had the I.Q. of which his mother was convinced. The Newfield women identified with the contestants. He could feel the women's strain and then their joy when the Reisses got to take home ten thousand dollars. Granny shouted answers to them when they were slow, and Astra Rainbow applauded the victory. Mickey, who had been writing television for

Americans for years, had never watched television with them. He had, himself, shouted at football and basketball games, coaching the players to their victories and defeats, but he had no idea that *Family Feud* raised emotions.

Then came the show—the title, the theme song, his name. Unfortunately Mrs. Newfield dropped her needle right before his credit appeared, and even though Astra Rainbow was shouting, "Look, Granny, look," Granny didn't look in time. Mickey was slightly upset that she didn't see his name. He believed that she doubted he was the big shot Astra Rainbow told her he was. Rainbow got so upset that her grandmother had missed this important moment that she removed the basket from Granny's lap, forcing her to watch.

And watch she did, with none of the enthusiasm she had had for *Family Feud*. There, she had laughed and fought with them. Now she sat expressionless, arms folded, concentrating. She didn't laugh once, never even smiled. She might have been watching Jacques Cousteau. Occasionally she would ask a question, such as, "Are those two married?" and Mickey, who was sweating out her reaction, would hurry to explain. "Yes, that's his brother and sister-and-law. They keep wanting Hank to get married even though they have a lousy marriage themselves."

"Why?" Granny asked.

"That's the comedy. On one hand you have a guy who is unhappy and single and trying to convince his brother to give up his rotten marriage and on the other you have this unhappy married couple who want their brother to settle down." This he said in a whisper, in order not to drown out the TV, and with the hope that Mrs. Newfield would at least laugh at one of the funny lines.

"And that's funny?" asked Granny.

"Well, twenty million people think so." At this point Mickey found himself defending his most successful show.

"That's very nice." She still hadn't smiled. Mickey was about to ask her what type of programming she liked when Astra Rainbow leaned forward and defended her boss.

"Granny, it's a big hit," she said with a great deal of passion. Her face had reddened before the words came out. It was she and not Mickey who wouldn't rest until Mrs. Newfield acknowledged that the show deserved to be on the air.

"Well, what do I know? I don't really watch much television, just some of my favorites." Another dig. She would turn the machine on to see shows she wanted in her home. Mickey's wasn't among them.

"It's really not important whether you like it. I mean, I don't take it personally," said Mickey, who took the weather personally. He had once asked why it had to rain on him.

Rainbow was up and standing in front of the television. She picked the center of the room to make her final stand. "It's a great show. It really says everything about what's going on in America today. You like to keep up with things, know what's happening in the world. This show tells it like it is. It really does." She punctuated her sentences by pointing at the set, even though the final credits were over by now.

"I'm sure it's interesting and I'm going to look at it again in the summer when they rerun it." Mrs. Newfield worked hard on the square in her hand. "As far as keeping up with things, well, I try. I subscribe to *Reader's Digest* and read *People* magazine when Molly cuts my hair. They tell you absolutely everything that's happening in *People*. Did you catch the issue with Princess Diana on the cover? They said that she and Prince Charles weren't getting along and that she was causing all sorts of trouble around the palace or the castle or wherever it is they live. I prayed for her to find peace." Granny yawned, causing her to check her watch. "I've been up since five," she said by way of explaining why she was nodding off. "We go to sleep early around here, Mr. Burke, but feel free to stay up and enjoy my Mitsubishi television." She kissed Astra Rainbow lightly on the cheek, the way a much more distant relative would. Then, still yawning, she headed upstairs. "Don't waste electricity," she said as she disappeared. Once she was halfway up the stairs she couldn't be seen anymore.

"I'm sorry," said Astra Rainbow once she had heard her grandmother's door being closed.

"She didn't have to like my show." Mickey moved from the couch to the chair closest to the television and wondered how he would get through the next four hours of life. He had brought three books specifically for nights like this, but it took too much energy to start a book.

"Yes, she did. And here's the crazy thing. I'll bet she did like it. I'll bet she's just afraid of you."

"Me? No." He always wanted to be feared. He couldn't believe it was finally happening.

"Yes. If she likes you, then in a roundabout way, she gives me permission to like you and she knows that should never happen. First of all, you're my boss and . . . and we better leave it at first of all." Astra Rainbow was almost flirting with him. She had bent down and put her hands on his knees as she spoke. It was the closest they had ever been physically. It would have been easy to kiss her had he been feeling brave enough. Unfortunately, the whole Newfield experience was leaving him meek. And the only feelings he had at the moment were paternal ones.

"Would you like a glass of milk?" Rainbow asked, as if milk was the most exciting drug in the world. Mickey hadn't had a glass of milk in about ten years, but he said he would and he followed her to the kitchen. There they sat at the table with nothing to say to each other. They hadn't really shared experiences, and now it appeared that they were forbidden to have anything but a "Mr. Burke" relationship in the future. Mickey had no intention of fucking around with a future nun.

Breakfast had been Mickey's mother's weakest meal. She bought little packages of dry cereal and never even thought to get the assortment. If she bought cornflakes, Mickey had cornflakes eight days in a row. The worst week of his childhood was the eight straight days of shredded wheat. In those days he thought pancakes were pure magic and waffles so wonderful that they must have been the work of special food artists. When he was on his own, he always ate breakfast out, indulging in the strongest coffee he could find. Lox, onions and eggs could brighten his entire weekend.

Granny's breakfast was endless. It was as if she were a short-order cook. She asked him what he wanted and when he wasn't sure if he was hungry, she suggested a list of things he could have, most of which came from animals. She seemed happy when he settled on bacon and eggs.

When Granny went to the pantry to get jam that she had put up last summer, Astra Rainbow whispered that she would explain everything on their morning walk. This was the first he heard about their taking a walk that morning, but he was willing to go. It would be worth slipping in the snow in exchange for information.

Mrs. Newfield went to pick up the rest of the family at the airport. Mickey offered to go even though he knew it would deprive him of his walk and the information it would bring. Astra Rainbow insisted that Mrs. Newfield could go alone. He was surprised at her vehemence, which revealed a side he had never seen before. She was working hard to get to be alone with Mickey, and it was wonderful to see his angel flapping her arms around the kitchen and coming up with reason after reason why Granny should go to the airport alone. The car wasn't big enough for everyone. Granny already knew the way. Mr. Burke didn't know how to drive her temperamental car. Finally Mickey gave up being gallant and Granny said Astra Rainbow could sit down and eat, she was intending to go alone all along. She had to do errands on her way and she wouldn't subject young people to that on their winter vacation. Astra Rainbow was satisfied and settled in her chair and spread butter on toasted bread, thicker slices than he had ever seen before. It was at this point Mickey realized he hadn't said anything funny since he got to Cleveland. He was hoping his sense of humor was just temporarily gone and that he could be in Ohio and funny at the same time.

Their path from the day before had been covered by fresh snow. Mickey hadn't realized that it had snowed during the night, but it must have since there was no trace of their walk from the previous afternoon. It was warmer than yesterday. The sky was a strong blue and the sun didn't hide. Before taking his first steps, Mickey grabbed Astra Rainbow's arm. He tried to make it a warm, masculine gesture, but they both knew that he was hanging on to her.

They walked silently at first. Astra Rainbow had a tendency not to talk when she didn't have to, and Mickey, who hadn't stopped talking since he was two, had come to listen. Sounds of nature occasionally filled the void, but instead of pleasing him, each distinctive sound frightened Mickey. He figured the wolf was at his door and out there, away from the house, he had no door. When it seemed to him that she had forgotten that she was going to tell him everything, he couldn't help asking questions. "So what were you going to tell me? Remember, you said you were going to explain everything? Don't you think now is the time?" He never could let a conversation take its natural course.

There were a few quiet beats before she began. He heard his footsteps packing the snow as he walked. Her sneakers didn't make the same impact his heavy boots did, so the crunching was solely his. He thought she was going to speak several times. Once even her lips started to move, but they had walked a dozen steps before she was brave enough to talk.

"Mr. Burke, I think you're the first normal person I've ever met in my life. I used to think Granny was when I was little, but I've known for a long time that she isn't. And Mr. Raphelson really isn't either. He used to beg me to let him touch me and then two seconds later he would cry and beg forgiveness. We belonged to the same church. He never did touch me. I think the asking part was normal, but the crying was a little crazy." Just then an animal raced across the snow. At first Mickey was scared. Involuntarily, he squeezed Astra Rainbow's arm. When he saw the harmless creature, he was embarrassed about his unwarranted fear.

"It's only a little rabbit." This was said kindly, but he felt that inserting the word "little" was a bit cruel.

"I just didn't expect it," he said. He had no experience anticipating animals that might surprise him.

"Don't worry, Mr. Burke. There's nothing around here that's going to hurt you." He realized she was wrong. In less than twenty-four hours he had grown dependent on her. He loosened his grip, signaling that he was brave again, and she went on with her story. "I guess I might as well start at the beginning. That's the only way the whole thing makes sense. Please stop me if I say anything upsetting." He didn't expect that she could. "As you know, I never had a father. I mean, I must have been fathered by someone, but my mother really didn't know who did it. She was a hippie and I was a love child. My mother and I traveled all around the country, sleeping all over the place, sometimes even outside. I remember very little of that part of my life because I was so young at the time. I think when I was really little that she carried me on her back. I can't remember, but I think so because I remember seeing grown-ups from high up.

"When I was about five we ended up in Seattle. We always just ended up in places. Helen would decide to go there and we would hitch rides and somehow get there. I guess you should know, Mr. Burke, Helen smoked marijuana. Please don't hold it against her. A lot of women did in those days. Seattle was supposed to be a wonderful place, and I guess it was. It's hard to know if I'm thinking of the right city, since we traveled so much. Am I boring you?"

He hadn't expected her question and he took a few steps before realizing that she was waiting for an answer. "Boring me? No. Absolutely not. I always wondered what happened to all those love children."

"I hope they had better lives than mine," she said rather dramatically. She sounded formal, as if she was being interviewed by a reporter. "When I got to Seattle, something terrible happened. We went to a park and a boy started pushing me and I pushed him back. None of the grownups were around. This is something only Helen and Granny know. I pushed that little boy off a cliff to his death. I . . . I never even knew his name."

Mickey never would have guessed that this was Astra Rainbow's past. He would think about what it meant to her. Now he rushed to defend her. "It wasn't your fault. You were a child," he said, as if two simple sentences could erase all her years of guilt.

"I was a child. That's why I was never even punished or taken to jail. I also know that I killed that little boy. Mr. Burke, I've robbed him of over a dozen of his own Christmases so far." He couldn't bear Rainbow's sadness. He wanted to find the words that would make her feel better, but he had never consoled a child murderer before.

"You didn't know what you were doing. You didn't understand the consequences."

"I did know what I was doing and I also knew that people who did bad things were punished. Once when I pushed a little girl away from her doll, I was hit on the hand and told never to hurt anyone again. When I peeked over the cliff and saw the boy lying there, I thought,

Oh gosh, I'm really going to be in trouble for this one. But the trouble never happened, at least not in the way I expected."

Mickey continued to be amazed. During all those times he had worked on *The Astra Rainbow Story*, never once had he suspected the tragedy that had occurred. He had always imagined Rainbow to be the victim, and he was right. He had only known Jewish guilt, the kind that blossoms when you don't do your homework or you're mean to your mother. This was bigger than anything he had suspected or knew. He wanted to help this girl, but he knew she felt that was God's job. His curiosity led him to ask what happened next. Just then the sun disappeared behind a cloud that he hadn't even known was there. He was so unfamiliar with nature and so accustomed to creating fiction that he took the change in the weather personally, as if a supreme being had the time to change the sky for the benefit of two people on a walk.

"The problem is, nothing happened," Astra Rainbow said. "The little boy was buried, and nobody blamed me. I expected the police to come and take me away, but of course they never did. Actually things got better for me. My grandfather had died by then, and Helen and I came here to live with Granny. My mother even tried being normal until she left us, just after my seventh birthday.

"I thought about what I had done a lot and it kept me from playing with other children. You can imagine how scared I was that I would hurt or kill somebody else. None of us ever mentioned it until I started having nightmares when I was about twelve. I would scream out in the middle of the night and Granny would have to run in and calm me down. The dreams were violent. I would throw one tiny baby after another over a cliff." She stopped here and became as upset, as if she had actually killed the babies rather than just dreamed about doing it. He hugged her then and believed she was crying into his shoulder because her body shook gently. But when she moved away, he saw there wasn't a trace of tears. Instead there was fear.

"You're not going to tell anybody this, are you?" To calm her he answered so quickly that he stumbled over his first few words.

"Uh . . . no . . . no . . . absolutely not. I wouldn't tell a soul." He knew he had to make her believe him quickly, so he hugged her again. "I promise. Really. You have my word," he added. While she was still in his arms he couldn't help thinking about his screenplay. The gold he had collected so far would have to be buried. With his promise not to tell, he had signed himself up for more years of television writing until his next chance of escape presented itself. He gave all his feelings to the girl in his arms, but he couldn't help feeling sorry for himself. His movie was dead.

"It's really important that nobody knows. Granny made me swear on a Bible that I would never tell anybody."

"You have nothing to worry about. Your secret is safe with me." He crossed his heart as proof and Rainbow relaxed.

"Good. I'm glad. I wanted to tell you before because I felt you had a right to know about the person you hired."

"I do know about her. She's honest and wonderful."

"Really, Mr. Burke?" Obviously she was going to believe him.

"Really." She smiled. He wished it was that easy to make everyone happy.

"I was wondering, since you think I'm all right, if you could do me a favor?"

"Sure."

"I wouldn't ask, but you're the most important person I know."

"It's all right. Ask."

"Well . . . I was wondering . . . I was wondering if you could do something about getting me to be a nun. Now that you know the story, you can understand why I might not have been called. I have to become a nun, Mr. Burke. How else am I going to get into heaven?"

"Me?" What a favor for a Jewish boy.

"I was just hoping you could use your influence." Didn't she know that he had no influence with Christ?

"My influence?"

"Well, you know how you can get things that nobody else can get? Like you said it was a miracle that you could get those theater tickets for your lawyer friend. Believe me, I know this is harder, but . . ." She put her hands in her pockets and looked down at her foot, which was making a semicircle in the snow.

"I'll do my best." He looked at the heavens while she looked at him.

"Thank you. Oh, thank you, Mr. Burke," she said, and then quickly added, "We should stop talking now." With these words Astra Rainbow ran from him toward the house. He thought it was miraculous that she could run in the snow. Afraid of falling at first, he stood immobile. Then, when it became apparent he would have to make it back on his own, he inched toward the house, using the footprints he had made just that morning as his security. He was proud to have made it back by himself, but concentrating prevented him from thinking over what she had said.

The front door was open, but no one seemed to be at home. Actually Astra Rainbow was upstairs getting the guest room ready for the arriving family, but he didn't know that until later. Mickey sat in the most comfortable chair in the living room, and since he was a Jewish boy who had been in therapy, he used his amateur's knowledge of psychiatry to sort out what he had just heard. He knew Astra Rainbow as a child had accidentally murdered and so felt guilty. The adults around her at the time didn't have the knowledge of her "crime"; this had made things worse. That little girl was waiting to be punished, and the punishment never came. Her confusion must have been overwhelming. He had once taken ten dollars from his mother's pocketbook. It was standing open on her dresser, inviting him in. He had to have this supercolossal magic set that cost fourteen ninety-five, and the stolen ten would get it for him. He wanted to perform the magic for his mother. He had learned how to make paper flowers appear from a can and how to make sponge balls disappear under plastic cups. If he did these and a dozen more tricks for her, she would ask where he got the set. So he kept it in his closet and performed his magic in his room, sometimes thinking that his mother would be amazed at what he could do. For more than a week, he waited for her to discover the loss of money. At first he thought she didn't miss it. Then he thought she did notice, but was waiting for him to confess.

When he could no longer hold the guilt and when he had perfected the disappearing quarter trick, he finally found the moment to tell his mother. She faced the sink with the water running. He faced her back. "I took ten bucks from your purse to buy a magic set," he said. Although she had never hit him, he shielded his face with his arms, expecting at least a slap. "Next time, ask," she said, never turning around. He would have preferred the slap. At least the sting would eventually have faded. He never enjoyed the magic set again. Astra Rainbow must have never enjoyed her life again. He thought about the nightmares. Just as she was reaching womanhood, she dreamed about killing babies. She feared children, first as a child, later as a burgeoning adult. In her mind, she was harmful to kids. If she left the real world and became a nun, she wouldn't have to face a life that might hurt her. And of course there was that extra bonus. Nuns went to heaven. The poor kid thought Mickey had enough pull to get her in. He had friends in high places, but not that high.

He pushed himself out of his chair and shuffled into the kitchen to make himself a cup of coffee. Astra Rainbow was there emptying the dishwasher. Funny, he hadn't heard her come down the stairs. When she saw that he had come into the same room, she fled. She left the dishwasher open and half-filled. Not a word was said. Her only concern was to escape from Mickey.

He started after her, then stopped, knowing that wherever he found her, she would run from him again. He knew she had fled because she was embarrassed by her confession, but Mickey didn't know how to deal with it. He wanted to stay and help her. But just as strongly, he wanted to pack and go home. Unless Rainbow relaxed, staying would be impossible. Mrs. Newfield and the others would have to notice that she was avoiding him and they would want to know why. If he didn't tell them, they would just assume that the Jewish boy had ruined their Christmas.

Before he could figure out what to do, he heard the slamming of car doors and the high-pitched voices of a family arguing about suitcases. He met them at the front door, smiling, pretending that they were entering a normal situation.

Helen's family was a grim, unattractive group. Helen herself was a pale version of Astra Rainbow and looked old for her age. Her two sons, named Tad and Brad, aged thirteen and fourteen, looked underfed and underclothed. The legs on their pants were too short and the sleeves on their shirts exposed too much arm. They were also overexposed to the weather. Neither one wore a jacket. Joe, Helen's husband, struggled with his height. He had been squeezed into the car and he had to stoop to get through each doorway. Mickey, who was barely qualified as "full-grown," resented his stature.

What was apparent from the beginning was that no one in this family ever smiled or attempted to be charming. Helen herself led the group in sourness. Her lips remained stiff. The only clue that she had once been a hippie was the length of her hair. It had once been the color of Astra Rainbow's. Now it was half-gray and faded and down to her waist, uncombed. He had been right about Helen's hair in his *Astra Rainbow* file. The file would have to be burned.

Mickey greeted them as if he were the host. He helped with the suitcases, made small talk about their trip and tried to get the boys excited about Christmas by pointing out the decorations. Since none of them responded, his cheerfulness grew to television proportions until he became the father out of *Father Knows Best*. The only things that seemed to interest any of them were the presents that Mickey had brought. Instead of apologizing for her uncharming family, Mrs. Newfield made excuses for Mickey's behavior, the biggest one being, "He writes for the TV."

Once all the luggage was inside, Granny gave out the room assignments. Helen and Joe were to have the guest room, and to Mickey's surprise Tad and Brad would, as Granny put it, "bunk in with Mr. Burke." They would take turns using a sleeping bag on the floor, and for a few minutes Mickey thought "they" included him. He knew the house wasn't large, but there was a sun-room downstairs with two faded couches. He saw now that both boys were too long for them, but he still felt they should suffer rather than ruin his privacy. He wanted to say that he had always had his own room and wasn't good at sharing, but good guests didn't blurt out such things. Just as everybody was heading up, Astra Rainbow appeared at the top of the stairs and forbade anybody to take another step. "Mr. Burke has to be alone," she said. "He is a writer and needs his peace night and day in order to create." Not one of them argued with her, and the boys were sent to the sun-room, both complaining that they were too long for the couches.

He had imagined a Christmas full of joy, but as they decked the house with boughs of holly and other green and red objects, Mickey knew it was unlikely. The sour children and their somber parents refused to get with it. Mickey, or Mr. Burke, as they all called him, tried to get the spirit going, not so much for these too-tall children with the dirty fingernails as for himself. He was probably going to get one shot at this down-home Christmas thing, and he didn't want it blown away. Maybe he wanted it for Astra Rainbow too. Although she didn't mention her tragedy again and gave no indication of bringing it up, her story had gotten to him. He wished he had the power to fix her up with Christ. She needed that more than any present under the tree. For now she had been able to suppress her sadness, but if you looked closely, which he did, it was there behind the eyes and at the sides of her mouth.

The tree was trimmed without much ceremony. The event was actually like a family free-for-all. Even the angel on the top was placed by Joe in a matter-of-fact way. That's where it went, and he was tall enough to get it there. The boys showed some delight in poking around the packages, but even that was done with hostility. They shoved presents in each other's faces, hoping to destroy the wrapping in order to see what was inside. This sure wasn't the way it was on the Perry Como specials. Mickey thought more than once that he missed his mother and Aunt Minn and that he would visit them in January. He needed their sort of hugs to recover his soul. Most of the time his mind went back to what Astra Rainbow told him in the snow. He knew he had heard something that day that he would never forget. His job was to absorb it into the rest of his life, so that it would never be as prominent again.

On Christmas Eve they dined on supermarket cold cuts and took a vote on whether to go to church or not, with Mickey abstaining due to last-minute guilt about praying to the wrong God. The vote was two in favor, four opposed. Helen's entire family made it very clear that they weren't going no matter how the vote turned out. "We don't have clothes for it, Ma," Helen said, making it clear that there was to be no religious outing.

They watched television for the second night, and the only Christmas relief Mickey got was from a Dolly Parton–Kenny Rogers Christmas special. He missed his mother, his Aunt Minn, the colors of the

Israeli flag, laughing with Shelly Silver, his hotel room, his remote-control television, Zabar's, his own blanket and pillow, his privacy, his fantasies about Christmas, his terry-cloth bathrobe and his typewriter. He was also constipated.

While he missed his world, this alien family fought over what television shows to watch. Astra Rainbow kept insisting that Mr. Burke would be the best judge because Mr. Burke wrote for television. She made her stand more than once, and finally Helen said something like she didn't care what he did, she wasn't going to miss Tom Selleck. This seemed to make Joe jealous, and Helen fanned his jealousy. She obviously had been telling her husband for years that she loved Tom Selleck and was able to convince Joe that if Tom, as she called him, ever saw her he would immediately want to make love to her. While Mickey could understand her love for the star, he couldn't understand how she convinced her husband that the feeling would be mutual.

"Mr. Burke has met Tom Selleck," said Astra Rainbow proudly.

"No," said Mrs. Newfield, as if she were Mickey Burke's biographer.

"Really, he has. Tell them, Mr. Burke." Astra Rainbow had presented him with the stage and there was no getting out of it. Everyone turned to listen, even the two boys who were simultaneously picking their noses. This was the moment at which Mickey, the Jewish boy, would enter their lives.

"It was no big deal," he began, knowing it was the biggest deal that would ever happen to them. As a boy, he had met someone who had claimed to know Jerry Lewis. He had so many questions to ask: What did Jerry eat? Was he always funny every minute of the day? They tried to quiet the young Mickey with marble cake, but the questions continued. That night in bed, he had been mad at himself because he forgot to ask if his favorite star had children.

"Go on. Tell it," urged Rainbow.

"We might as well hear it," said Helen, not willing to be nice yet.

"Like I said, it's no big deal. He was going to do a television special with Carol Burnett and they wanted me to write it, so we got together a couple of times."

"A couple of times?" This was Helen warming up. Mickey understood what could happen. When he was a fan of Jerry Lewis and so far removed from the star, he actually became a fan of the man who knew him. Helen inched closer to Mickey as Joe stiffened. He looked like the type of guy who could grab you by the neck and say, "Stay away from my woman." Mickey had expected to be singing "Silent Night," not irritating family sore spots.

"I was just with him a couple of times. When you're going to get involved in a show, you usually sit around and talk about what the show could be about." He had to admit there was something about this that he was liking. His show business connections always helped make him the center of attention. His mother and Aunt Minn always had questions and made him repeat all his show biz stories to their friends. They asked him every time they saw him if Elizabeth Taylor had a face-lift.

He expected Helen to ask endless questions about Tom Selleck. Instead she asked the ultimate one. She inhaled no less dramatically than Bette Davis and asked, "Do you think he would like me?" She sat on the edge of the couch, her legs crossed, her long, thin arms hugging her body. She was hunched over, showing off her bad posture and ratty hair. Mickey immediately felt the web he was caught in. If he said no he would unnecessarily crush a woman who lived for *Magnum, P.I.* If he said yes, Joe might pop him in the mouth.

"Why don't I ask him, if I ever run into him?" said Mickey, thinking he was safe.

"You said you know him, so what do you think?" persisted Helen and, before he could answer, Joe made several loud rumbling sounds in his throat. By now he had stood up and was standing in front of the television, blocking everybody's view. No one seemed to care, since Mickey had become the evening's entertainment. Although it was perverse, he found it very funny that Helen felt he could think for another man on the basis of two meetings.

"I would think that any man would find you lovely," said Mickey, the diplomat. He knew if he could learn to tell lies like this to the network people, his life would be easier.

Helen wasn't going to settle for Mickey's diplomacy. She was out for Tom Selleck's muscles and she was determined to get them, even if she had to take this skinny little man's word for it. "Do you think he would be attracted to me?" All heads turned toward Mickey.

"Sure, why not?" He tried to sound very casual and wanted Helen to stop pushing.

"Do you think Tom would like to have an affair with me, Mr. Burke?" Mickey loved that he was "Mr. Burke," while a man she had only seen in his celluloid form was "Tom."

"Sure, why not?" had worked the first time, so Mickey used it again. Helen sat up straighter and for the first time since he had met her, her shoulders were not rounded. Joe whispered something that Mickey couldn't quite hear, but he thought it might be, "Shit." He immediately felt guilty. He and Joe were men together in a world where women often caused trouble. They had been born on the same team and here he was, selling his brother out. Maybe Helen would be hell to live with, thinking that Tom Selleck could be hers if only she showed up in Hawaii. She might make demands on Joe that he couldn't meet and then hint that the movie star would be happy to take his place. Of course one could never say that Mr. Burke meant to cause trouble in paradise because what he had seen of this family bore no hint of paradise. Still, he did feel that he had tampered with the balance of a marriage. Joe's shoulders were the ones that were rounded now.

They all watched *Magnum, P.I.* silently. There was even silence during the commercials. Mickey thought of talking, but talking had gotten him in trouble that night. Mrs. Newfield continued crocheting her endless squares. Mickey understood now that they would all one day be attached to form an unattractive blanket. He had seen one on the sun porch and it was ugly. Astra Rainbow had pulled her chair next to his, and although she didn't talk to him, he felt he was there to protect her. He realized he was watching television with the two women who had mishandled her life.

Surprisingly, there was an ounce of gaiety after the television was turned off. Granny served eggnog straight from the carton and cookies straight from the box, but things were more festive than they had been all night. Mrs. Newfield even made an attempt to bring up Santa Claus, saying that they had all better get to sleep early so that Santa could come. Nobody was buying it, especially the boys, who long ago had outgrown not only their clothes but also their expectation of miracles. At least neither boy had been fresh for most of the evening, and they were willing to go along with Granny by going to bed on their too-small couches. "Don't you dare wake us in the morning," Helen said as she ascended the stairs, ruining the mood that had been so hard to achieve. Mickey figured she must have smiled at one time. She had been a flower child, and they had spent most of their time smiling.

Mickey chose to sleep on the top bunk that night. He had a bit of a struggle getting up there, but he knew he should grab the opportunity now, as he would probably never have another. He and Rainbow were supposed to leave on the twenty-sixth, but Mickey was homesick and he was going to try to talk her into leaving the night of the twenty-fifth instead. With another family he would have had a very different Christmas. All families had their baggage, but this couldn't be the way holidays were meant to be. If it were, they would have died out centuries ago. Maybe he would someday try to get the experience from another group. Right now Christmas wasn't for him.

On Christmas morning they all gathered around the tree. They stayed in their nightclothes to open presents. Tad and Brad's pajamas were predictably too short. Granny wore a grandmother's robe, one of those thick ones that look like bathroom rugs that no one could or would want to see through. Helen's nightgown was a shiny bright blue, too ill-fitting to be sexy. Her terry-cloth robe hung from her once again rounded shoulders. Astra Rainbow was in bridal white. Her gown was heavy cotton, almost Victorian, and seemed to be ordering the world to stay out. The only surprise was Joe. His pajamas were red. Who would have thought of him as Santa?

"Who's going to hand out the presents?" asked Granny, as if she weren't in charge. She was seated in the most comfortable chair with her supplies beside her. By her slippered feet was a wicker waste-basket for discarded wrapping and on the arm of her chair was a large pair of scissors that she had brought from the kitchen. Obviously she felt that there was going to be some rough ribbon to handle.

"I think Mr. Burke should be Santa Claus," said Astra Rainbow. She looked at him as if he were the real Santa Claus, there to give them a merry Christmas. Mickey at first declined, but Rainbow begged, and when everyone else also declined, Mickey was pressed into ser-vice. He was actually dragged to the tree by Helen's two mean boys. They laughed as each yanked an arm.

The presents were festive enough, wrapped nicely in the kind of Christmas paper he had seen all his life. Mickey's gifts stood out. Not only were they wrapped in silver, but they were neater and more compelling.

Mickey remembered a conversation he had months ago with Astra Rainbow. He had asked her if she had always gotten everything she wanted for Christmas, and she said yes. Now that he saw the packages he couldn't imagine that any one of them held the potential for a great amount of happiness. His own gifts were very generous, but even they couldn't contain everything anybody wanted.

The first present he picked from the pile was to Astra Rainbow from Granny. She wanted to rip off the wrapping, but Granny stopped her. Mickey didn't know it yet, but Mrs. Newfield had a story behind every gift she gave. The story had to do with Astra Rainbow actually looking at the gift in a store before she moved to the big city. Granny went back to get it for her that night and had been saving it all these months. She was very excited about it because she knew Rainbow would be surprised to see it again. At this point, the girl made several wrong guesses about what was inside the package. Mickey was getting anxious about the contents by now and was surprised that the family was tolerating the delay. Helen had lit a cigarette. Although she wasn't exactly interested in what was happening, she didn't mind that it was taking so long. Finally Astra Rainbow gave up and ripped open the package. Mickey couldn't see what it was, but he could see the girl's delight. She screeched, "I don't believe you really got this for me," and went to thank her grandmother with a tight hug and a sweet kiss.

"Were you surprised?" Granny asked.

"Completely," answered Astra Rainbow. She took a deep breath as if she still couldn't believe it.

Mickey walked over to this magical gift that had brought so much delight. He couldn't believe it either. There on the couch, where Astra Rainbow had placed it, was a Word-A-Day calendar. He thought it was very sweet that the stationery store item could elicit this much gratitude. He now understood not the meaning of Christmas but the meaning of a Newfield Christmas. Their wishes did come true because they were so modest.

The gift stayed under discussion for much too long. Granny bothered to explain to the family how it worked. "You put it on your desk—Astra Rainbow has a desk now that she's a secretary—and every day you learn a new word. It starts at the first of the year." Rainbow sat down again and placed her calendar in her lap. Mickey worried about his own gifts. If this calendar had caused delight, his might cause hysteria.

One by one the presents were handed out—puzzles, underwear, pot holders. (As a dramatic move, Mickey had decided to hand out his own gifts last.) Each one was examined and discussed. Its history was given. Everyone was thrilled with what he had received. This ordinarily quiet family got high as a result of these presents, and Mickey found it comforting to know that this was how things really were. Before this visit he had no idea that five ninety-eight could make a person happy. Both boys got toys that they had really wanted. Tad got the horn for his bike, and Brad got a Nerf ball. They were willing to forgive the boxes with the pajamas in them for these two items.

Eventually the only presents left were the ones wrapped in silver. Before handing out his gifts, Mickey felt compelled to make a little speech. He never would have imagined that he would want to communicate with this family. But there he was, in their midst, feeling happy for them because they had gotten what they wanted. "Before I give out my gifts," he began, "I just want to thank you all for having me here. I wanted to know what it was like to have a real Christmas, and I thank you for letting me have one today. It was really very nice of you to take me in." If he had stopped there, he wouldn't have gotten into trouble. Something drove him on. Probably he didn't think it was a dramatic enough ending. "And I just want to tell you that I think it was great that everybody was happy with his gifts." And here was his big mistake. "It taught me that somebody doesn't have to spend a lot to make another person happy." Mickey Burke had no idea that he was being an insensitive schmuck. (Nor did he know that no one understood what he was talking about. They *had* spent a lot.) If this had been another family or another day, he probably would have added, "So next time I won't be such a schlemiel and spend so much." But he never even came close to saying those words. These days his mind was censoring humor without his even knowing it.

He was excited to give his gifts. He started with Granny, who couldn't imagine what was inside the box. In Mickey's family, anyone from age five would have known that it was jewelry, but to the New-fields the contents were a mystery. She attacked the box aggressively, cutting off the ribbon with the scissors she had brought for that purpose. While she carefully opened the paper, she said it was a shame to harm such beautiful wrapping. She had said that for every gift she opened. Everyone looked from her face to the package since they were curious about both the contents and her reaction. Finally, there it was: the two-hundred-dollar watch. She nodded, but she had nodded at other presents. She put her hand to her heart, but she had done that when she got the paperback version of *The Joy of Cooking* from Helen. What Mickey got was her same set of reactions for a lot more money.

"It's absolutely beautiful, Mr. Burke," she said, then added, "but I already have a wristwatch." She held out her wrist to prove that she was telling the truth. With the other hand she was giving him back his gift. He didn't take it. He was going to argue her out of this. The duel began.

"Everybody in New York has more than one watch," he said.

"This is not New York, sir."

"What if you need a watch when you dress up?"

"I don't dress up much anymore."

"It's a quartz watch. You never have to wind it."

"Lord, I don't mind winding my watch. It's as natural to me as brushing my teeth." They were both working hard by this time. Sparring was never easy.

"What if yours breaks and you have to take it in and have it fixed?" Mickey knew he had an edge when she hesitated here. Her head tilted, telling him that there was some merit in the broken-watch argument.

"Well, we'll see," said Granny, slipping the gift under her chair where she stacked her other presents. His beautiful watch rested on the new egg timer she had loved so much.

Mickey had five more watches to give out. He knew now that he wasn't going to be the hero he had anticipated being. He was just another of the Santa Clauses who had come there that day. He gave out all five at once, but still the family opened them one at a time in a pecking order related to how well they knew him. Astra Rainbow was first. She loved her watch and took a lot of time with the instructions that came with it. He never read instructions and was bored with her recitation of "Care and Cleaning of Your New Time Piece." She was impressed, but not impressed enough to put it on. Her watch too went on the pile of gifts she had collected. As she put it down, she caught sight of her Word-A-Day calendar and sighed with pleasure for it once again.

Helen was the only one to give him a hug. She was a strong hugger. A little gasp of air escaped from him. Clearly it was designed to make Joe jealous. She put her new watch on, depositing the old one in Granny's wastepaper basket. Mickey gazed at Joe, who looked poorer and sadder to him than he had the day before. Mickey was sorry to have given Joe's wife a gift she had liked. Joe was next. By now it was no secret what was in the boxes. He opened his, stood up and shook Mickey's hand, said thank you and politely sat down again. He threw away the box and slipped the watch into his pocket. His laconic style was attractive. There was a little Sam Shepard in him. Both boys emulated their father. They were quiet and polite, and the second they were finished, they went back to the Nerf ball and the bicycle horn.

Most of the day was spent with the menfolk watching one football game after another and the womenfolk in the kitchen getting Christmas dinner ready. It was evident in the one afternoon that equal rights had not hit the Newfields. It wasn't as if the women weren't interested in the games. Helen often yelled from the kitchen for the scores, and Astra Rainbow ran out whenever she could to catch the halftime show. "I always wanted to be in a marching band," she said. It was, of course, the perfect wish for her. There she would march like everyone else. With a hat covering her magnificent hair, and a trumpet in her hand, she could disguise the fact that on the inside she was different from her fellow marchers.

Dinner was magnificent. Everything that was supposed to brown had browned. The greens were vibrant and the smells were enough to entice a hungry man away from the endless games. They were eating in the small dining room with the best china. Granny sat at the head of the table, surrounded by Astra Rainbow and Mickey. Before she let anyone eat, she thanked Jesus Christ, our Lord, for the food. Mickey once again asked himself what the fuck he was doing there. He had come to steal Christmas, but it didn't feel as if he had gotten away with it. He had paid heavily for this experience with his sense of humor.

# 11

# The Prodigal Lover
# Returns

MICKEY came back to New York hungry for a really good knish and for Shelly Silver. (The easiest explanation for this phenomenon was that he had overdosed on Christianity.) He had the feeling that they would both be easy to get, but when he called Shelly, he found that she had a meeting about a future brunch that night. He said he'd call her again the next day, but within five minutes his hotel phone rang. It was Shelly saying that the party had been canceled at the last minute because the hostess's kid had chicken pox. That was, of course, a lie. For the first time in her successful career, Shelly had lied to the customer, saying that her mother was very ill. She thought that God would punish her by striking her mother down, and the second she got off the phone with Mickey, she called Mrs. Silver to make sure she was alive. When her mother said that she was going to Atlantic City that weekend, Shelly, with an unprecedented show of emotion, begged her mother to be very careful.

By seven-thirty, Shelly was dressed. She stood there in front of the full-length mirror in the jumpsuit that Paula of Bloomingdale's insisted she have, and realized she had become a Cosmo girl. It might have been less obvious if the zipper hadn't been pulled down to reveal the cleavage she had had since she was sixteen. She had once hated women who pushed their breasts, but here she was selling her physical assets. She had been late growing them and had prayed to God for them to come. Once she had them, she hid them under loose sweaters and crossed arms because the boys in high school might want to touch them. She burned her bra in her freshman year of college and was warned by her mother that if she didn't give them the proper support they could drop. Fortunately, her family had enough money so there was one for burning and four more for supporting the future. College was, for the most part, a braless era for her, although her mother's words worried her. Once when she went running across a field in just a T-shirt, she didn't feel the joy of nature, she heard her mother's voice and felt the bounce. At the advice of *Glamour* magazine, in an article on the right way to dress for a job interview, Shelly wore a very good bra while she was job hunting. She knew she was trading underwire support for independence, but during the four years she spent at school it seemed important not to wear underwear. When she graduated, it seemed important not to let her breasts stand in the way of her career. Putting on the bra made her feel not only that she was harnessing herself, but also that she was a traitor to the cause. It was a confusing time because it appeared that the world demanded that she go braless and get a good job at the same time. There were warnings that in order to enter a man's world, something she and all her contemporaries were trying to do (simply because there was no woman's world), you had to act like a man. Strangely, behaving like a man meant wearing a bra, since bouncing between nine and five was strictly forbidden. Cleavage was also forbidden. The bra had to be the right style, none of those push-up numbers. It wasn't until after the eighties had begun that Shelly resolved the issue and wore fancy underwear under her pinstripes.

Her breasts were one, or two, of her best features. Men had said so, her mother had said so and Shelly knew from girlfriends how lucky she was to be able to go braless and also wear those backless styles. Now she was offering them to Mickey. Of course, she could have zipped the jumpsuit up, projecting more of a NASA look than a sexy one, but she preferred to remind him of these two things that she had prayed for at thirteen and he had played with only a short time ago. She always felt dumb when she tried to look sexy, but when an old boyfriend was coming by on a cold winter night, she knew it was smart to be dumb. Once she'd thought it over, the zipper came down even further on those proud beauties. It would be so nice to have him back.

When she finished with her body, she started on her hair. It was important to her that she have more than just a full head of hair. She had been tricked by the media into thinking she had to have a mane. She shook out the curls and bent over from the waist, brushing with her Mason Pearson brush. Animal-like things started to happen, since she was blessed with an abundance of hair. It was hard to know why she felt it necessary for her scalp to sport this junglelike appearance. Her date for the evening had only thought to run an old comb through his hair.

The bell rang. Her heart stopped and there he was, not tall, dark and handsome, but short, dark and funny. He would never be Ken, but then again she was no Barbie. They were real people who happened to be able to laugh together. In his hand was a rose wrapped in cellophane. "I bought it from a twelve-year-old gypsy," he said. "I was scared her mother would beat her up if she didn't sell enough of them."

"Do you think they do that?" They both knew that they were just talking gypsy filler while Shelly hung up his coat and got used to having him in her apartment again.

"Do what?"

"Do you think gypsies beat up their kids?"

"Yeah. I do. If I were a really nice guy I would have bought twelve of these." He gave over the rose with no ceremony, making sure the flower was not a symbol of romance.

Shelly headed for the kitchen for a bud vase and Mickey followed. She worried about the lighting in the kitchen. Overhead fluorescent was good for cooking, but the least flattering light to be seen in. She had to get back to the soft light and candles in the living room quickly.

If only Mickey and Shelly had known what each other wanted, they could have saved hours of seduction and verbal foreplay. First there was the wine-and-pâté part of the evening. Then there was the listening to music portion (Springsteen before he was married), the watching-of-a-tape portion (the middle of *Body Heat*) and even the pretending to look at television portion (laughing at Joe Franklin.) Shelly used her entire home-entertainment system that night. Finally they were on the same couch. It was after one A.M. when he made his move. She loved his move but hated that they were on the white couch. One dug-in heel and she might have to reupholster.

When it was obvious that they were going to do more than fill each other in on how they spent their Christmas vacations, Shelly squeezed out from under Mickey, took his hand and led him into the bedroom. It seemed worth it to break the mood and save the couch.

Unfortunately, her bed was nothing you could just flop onto. Dirk and Dutch had insisted on a white spread with over a dozen pillows in graduating shades of apricot. They had promised her *Architectural Digest* if she only listened to them. "We're not asking for carte blanche," they said, adding quickly, "although God knows we would love it. Everybody we know gets carte blanche but us." By this time Dirk was beating his chest and Shelly gave in to the family of pillows. Since then she had never gone to bed spontaneously.

Mickey helped her remove the pillows and turn down the spread. This eliminated all chances of being simply thrown down and taken. There was also that brief interlude when Shelly went into the bathroom, put in her diaphragm and took off her lipstick and mascara. Dutch had talked her into the Pratesi sheets, and why take chances with sheets that cost enough to feed a family of five for a month?

Mickey was already in bed by the time Shelly came out of the bathroom. When he saw her he was happy. Here was the woman he wanted, the one he could talk to, the one who understood what he wrote and calmed him and fed him so he could be funny, the one who didn't have to be a nun. It was good to be home.

Shelly sighed when she climaxed. It wasn't necessarily a sigh relating to this particular climax. It was more a cumulative one that said, "Mickey's back and I've got him." He too was happy. It felt good to be in the right place at the right time. They made love like two Jewish kids. They weren't the best athletes in the world, but they were considerate of each other's bodies. They didn't sweat, but they got everything accomplished. Nobody got hit in the eye and, most importantly, they knew not doing it would be a sin.

There was breakfast in bed the following morning, a magic trick produced by a maid who was happy for her boss. (Shelly at first had a hard time having a maid. She felt she was exploiting a sister. The feeling left when Lucinda made it clear that she would rather vacuum than waste time talking about women's rights.) While brushing her teeth, Shelly promised the mirror that she wasn't going to get hurt by Mickey again. This time she was going to play it smart. She would remember what Greta had taught her and play Mickey like a valued customer. She wouldn't be anxious. She would give him the impression that there were other men in her life and that she could live without him. She would tell him she couldn't see him sometimes even when she could. It had taken her thirty-five years to realize that people want what they can't have. She had promised herself in earlier mirrors never to play games, but those mirrors were probably broken by now.

She never kept those promises. Over the next few weeks, every time Mickey left she was scared and every time he asked to come back she was hopeful. She wore her insecurities on her jumpsuit sleeve and she carried the fear of his departure in a matching purse. She worried even after Mickey moved his toothbrush in.

"It's just a toothbrush," she told Greta. "I can't think of it as anything more."

"How many toothbrushes does he have?" Greta, ever practical, wanted to know.

"I don't know. This one is electric."

"Electric?" Greta was truly excited about this information. "You know, of course, what electric means."

"It means he has good oral hygiene." Shelly was too scared to think of anything as good news.

"A man can have many toothbrushes, Shelly, but only one electric one. Where does he send his shirts?"

"Why?"

" 'Why?' she asks. Don't you know how to read anything? If his shirts are going to your laundry, you can pick out bridesmaids, and don't expect me to wear pink. I loathe and detest it. And I'm not dying my shoes to match anything."

"Lucinda takes his shirts to my guy, but that's only because they were lying around in a pile in the corner."

"Forget the shirts for a minute. When he leaves work at night, where does he go first—your place or his?"

"He stops off at his and then ends up at mine."

"Forget where he goes straight from work. Stopping off shows a dependence on being independent, if you know what I mean." Shelly knew.

Shelly and Greta had several of these "trying-to-figure-out-Mickey's-intention" conversations before they came to the conclusion that he was moving in slowly and that Shelly and Mickey would be living together by May. They figured this out mathematically, both using pocket calculators to factor in how many items he was bringing over and not taking back per week. Since there had been an acceleration factor, that was built into the equation. Shelly would have rather had a firm discussion with Mickey about living together, preferably over brunch in one of those "fern" restaurants where all the waiters wore one earring, but it didn't look as if that was going to happen. It looked as if they weren't actually going to talk about it. She would never have that moment when they kissed over the croissant.

Naturally, she was in pain. So was Mickey. So was Astra Rainbow. Shelly's pain was in remembering a time when she had been deserted by this man whom she was letting back into her heart. Each time she saw his Braun toothbrush, she thanked God it was there, but she also suffered the hurt that she was sure would follow. She looked everywhere for protection but couldn't find it. Even her personal shopper at Bloomingdale's wouldn't abe able to come up with a shield strong enough to make Shelly feel safe. Greta kept telling her to go with the happiness, but that advice was hard to follow if you were a woman who had already been rejected by Mickey Burke, or anybody else.

Shelly worked hard to keep the affair happy. She laid out impromptu picnics on the bed. She didn't initiate any discussions about where the relationship was going. And in an attempt to keep the honeymoon going, she didn't use the same bathroom he did. Still, she walked under a cloud and waited for it to rain on her parade. When it did, she planned to drag out the Burberrys umbrella that she had bought on Fifty-seventh Street but knew it wouldn't help her aching heart.

Mickey's pain had to do with Astra Rainbow. There were times that he missed her. She still sat at his typewriter every day, ready to turn the pages he scribbled into viable television scripts, but he missed the few days of intimacy he had shared with her. He wanted to protect the child who had told him about her sin, but he knew she would never talk about it again or allow him to help heal her. It was Astra Rainbow who had made it clear that they were back at business now and that it was best for him to be simply Mr. Burke again. Since he had never been allowed to touch her, he could only use words to try to recreate the intimacy. He had tried to use them all. Words like "us" and "feeling" and "supportive." Astra Rainbow ignored this intimate vocabulary. She needed this job and remembered what Mr. Raphelson had said about mixing work and anything personal. She apologized more than once for asking him to use his influence to try to get her into a nunnery and begged his forgiveness for overstepping into his world. He wanted to apologize for taking advantage of her inability to know what was normal.

There was also the pain of wanting her. He was sinking into love with Shelly. He liked her curls and recognized her value to his writing. He told her his jokes and she laughed in all the right places. She made his words come more easily. But Rainbow's office was situated so that he could watch her back all day if he wanted to. He wanted to. (He could go from passionate to paternal in a matter of seconds.) He realized after staring at her for about an hour that the trouble with his dealings with women, aside from the fact that he always seemed to need more than one of them, was that he had to deal with their fronts. He fell for their fronts. He talked to their fronts. He was forced to deal with their fronts, but what he felt most comfortable with was their backs. With their backs—just hair and shoulders, waistlines and legs—he was safe. There were none of the problems. He would never tell anybody those thoughts because they would be embarrassingly chauvinistic. They weren't. They were just the thoughts of a man who never learned how to deal with women's fronts. His mother and Aunt Minn had never taught him. They couldn't have. They had fronts, but he usually watched their backs too, as they leaned over ironing boards and sinks. He needed a father to teach him how to deal with the face of a female.

Astra Rainbow's pain might have been the strongest of the three.

She had come back to New York promising herself that she would be a good secretary again. She had felt it was permissible to be getting close to her boss far away from where they worked. She never counted on feeling anything for the man whom she had brought home to Ohio. Now, every morning when she saw Mr. Burke, her heart did something funny. It didn't stop beating, but it did let her know that it was there. Rainbow knew that Mr. Burke was going off to see Miss Silver all the time. She had liked Miss Silver when she met her at the police station when Mary was in trouble. Sometimes she was happy that her boss was with somebody. He was writing a lot these days, and sometimes when he talked to Shelly Silver on the phone he laughed very hard. She hadn't heard him laugh like that since she had known him. A man couldn't laugh that hard and be unhappy.

She imagined that they did all those things that she would never be able to do with a man. Of this, Astra Rainbow was not jealous. Even in her fantasies of being close to Mr. Burke, she never went to bed with him. It must feel good. Too many did it in too many books and movies for it not to feel good. But since she was not going to let that particular good into her life, she wasn't jealous of Miss Silver in bed. She hoped that they had intercourse.

She thought of Lorain as her Camelot, that one shining moment in her life. What she missed most was Mr. Burke caring about her. She had held him up in the snow, but he had held her up for three days. Not once was he too weak.

It was unlike her to confide in anyone, but she felt there were too many tears forming at all the wrong times. So one night when her aunt was asleep, smiling and snoring, Astra Rinbow let Mary into the apartment and told her the Mr. Burke story without once mentioning her childhood tragedy. Mary heard about the walks in the snow. The girl described what happened with poetic accuracy. As she told it, she realized how powerful she felt. She had actually taken her boss home. She was expecting Mary to have a solution for her heartache, but when she had finished, the girl's first words were, "What century you living in, anyway?"

"It's just that I don't ever want to be involved with a man." Astra Rainbow realized that what she had just said was true. The girl had never played with dollhouses. She wanted Christ or a father and nothing else. The times she liked Mr. Burke best were the times he watched her from behind. She would like him to continue that. Sometimes she would fling her hair just for his enjoyment.

"Who's talking about not getting involved, girl? Where you living, the planet Claire?" Mary was lying on her back on the couch that Astra Rainbow slept on. She had an extra-large bag of taco chips on her stomach and she ate the chips nonstop. The crunching became part of the conversation and made everything seem less important.

"People get involved and then they get married," Astra Rainbow said to a girl whose own mother had or hadn't been married three or four times.

"My old lady sure hasn't. She said she has, but I don't see no ring to prove this. I don't seem to remember *you* mentioning no father that you had as a kid." Mary's world had women and children in it and the occasional man who took you to the roof. She had seen plenty of weddings with brides in cheap lace and grooms in rented ruffled shirts, but too often the grooms were soon missing and the brides became mothers who were married to their children. "So, what's the problem here?" she asked, pausing for another taco chip. Then came another question. "You want this guy as a boyfriend, or what?"

That answer came simply. "No," said Astra Rainbow. "I can't have him that way because he's my boss and I'm going to be a bride of Christ, I hope."

"You good at this typing that you do?" Mary wanted a simple answer. She wasn't going to get one.

"I'm very good at it. The last time I was tested, at the agency who sent me to Mr. Burke, I typed eighty-eight words a minute. I did make two small mistakes that could be easily corrected, but they subtracted for those and I still ended up with eighty-eight words a minute. And here's the interesting part."

Mary didn't believe there was an interesting part. All this talk about words flying across the paper was so boring that she had doubled her chip intake. "I never would have believed that I could have improved from there, but I actually did. Sometimes I think I'm capable of burning up the paper because I'm going too fast. I may even be doing over a hundred by now." She was as proud as a race car driver.

Mary knew that Aunt Emma was sleeping in the next room. Therefore, when she yelled, it was in a whisper. "I'm not asking for a report on the history of typing. I just have to know if you could maybe get yourself another job somewhere, thereby getting your ass out of your boss's office and then maybe you could be his girlfriend. I say maybe because if you use as many words talking to him as you talk to me, I don't know how long he's going to hang around." With this Mary shut her eyes to show she was running out of patience.

"I don't want another job," cried Astra Rainbow, as if Mary had just fired her. They were both surprised at her outburst since she was usually a quiet girl with well-controlled emotions. "Jesus. You must really like this guy. Everyone in the neighborhood yells but you. When I first saw you, I didn't think you lived around here on account of you're so light and in case you haven't noticed, this here is a primarily P.R. neighborhood with a little black thrown in. And the second reason I thought you must be living in some other part of the world is that you didn't holler like the rest of us. So where was I? Oh yeah. I was thinking that you probably are hot for this guy. Did he try anything yet?" Since the conversation was headed toward sex, Mary was willing to sit up.

"No."

"No? Is he normal, or what?"

"He's very normal. Very." Astra Rainbow was unusually defensive. She would defend Mr. Burke's normalcy to his death. "He didn't touch me because my granny asked him not to."

"What, is he gay or something? He's old. He's at least thirty or forty. Nobody that old listens to anybody's granny. They listen to their fuckin' gonads. A guy wants one of us and he'll do anything to get in our pants." Mary felt she had made a convincing argument and she punctuated it with blowing up the now-empty taco chip bag.

"She made him promise not to touch me, and he's a very honorable, *normal* man, and he didn't." Astra Rainbow was also punctuating her speeches by punching the arm of her chair. She was a farm girl, and the punching had muscle behind it.

"You make him sound like a priest or something. So where's the heat? I say you don't know what you're getting into until you let him into your hole. Then you come back to Mary and talk about love." She made "love" into three syllables, mocking the word.

"That's never going to happen. I'm never going to do it, even if I don't get my calling."

"You ain't never going to do it? Never is a long time."

"I just can't risk having a baby." With this came a small shiver, revealing her terror.

"You see me having a baby? No. I ain't gonna have one either unless I'm lucky enough to get some guy who isn't a minority to fall in love with me. And what are the chances of that? There isn't one on the whole block. But who says that has anything to do with anything? You never heard of protection? You never heard of condoms and diaphragms and foam and a lot of other things you put up there so you don't get pregnant?"

"I know all I have to know since I'm not going to do it anyway."

"You know Ginny who lives over there by the school? Anyway, when we cut out we always go by her place on account of her mother has this job in the cafeteria over there by St. Mary's. So one day Ginny starts crying because she's sure she's pregnant and she's swearing that Ray, that's her boyfriend, always wore a rubber. I can't believe it because I know Ray and he was the type who would do his

homework, or at least until fifth grade, when everybody stopped. So
we all come to the conclusion that the rubber popped, and Ginny is
living with her mother now and this little baby, and they both working over there in the cafeteria."

"It wasn't wise to take chances."

"I would take them. If a hundred-percent white man wanted to go
to bed with me and I knew for sure that he would marry me or give
me the money, I would. That's just dreaming, though."

There was a moment of silence now in which they both dreamed.
Mary thought of a man who wouldn't desert her, although she didn't
fantasize about anybody in particular. Astra Rainbow thought about
Mickey Burke. "I can't stop thinking about him," she said. "Maybe
I am in love or something." She hoped it was something other than
love. Love would mean giving up the church.

"Maybe," said Mary. Although she knew everything to know about
sex in Flatbush, she knew nothing about love.

"I want him to love me even if I don't love him." This time Astra
Rainbow punched both arms of her chair.

"Yeah, well. You want that? Then you gonna have to let him put
it in," said Mary, hugging what was left of the taco chip bag.

When Mary left, she pleaded with Christ to take her. "I need you,"
she whispered into her pillow, not really knowing whether she was
praying to the mortal she worked for or the Son of God who had died
for her sins.

What Astra Rainbow didn't know was that she was not the only
one helping her cause. Mickey had made a promise in the virgin snow,
and he was either immature enough or mature enough to honor all
promises to women. The one he made in Vegas to his ex-wife was the
worst. He wondered if she was still driving around in that baby-blue
Mustang convertible.

Two days after he got back to New York, after drinking Shelly's
orange juice and before going to the office, Mickey made a call to
Jennifer Ross. She was ready to play the second she got on the
phone. "It's taken you an awfully long time to find a booth," she
said.

"I decided that there wasn't a booth in Manhattan that was worth
receiving cash. They all have sticky floors." Mickey had just gotten
out of the shower and had chosen too small a towel. He didn't feel
like making negotiations while trying to be modest. Shelly had gone
down to the Fulton Fish Market to personally select the best shrimp
of the day for the Chase Manhattan lunch, but the maid was wandering around the apartment and he didn't know whether she was
willing to see more of him than she ever had before. He made an

arrangement whereby he covered his front and used whatever was left over to help his backside. The maid never showed up. She wouldn't have appreciated his attempt.

"Where would you like the money then?" Mickey thought Jennifer was having too good a time with this. There was nothing in her voice that indicated that this was an uncomfortable call. He felt she should at least have had the courtesy to squirm a little.

"I am no longer interested in cash, Mrs. Ross." Mickey desperately tried to get a certain formality in his voice. He imagined she was leaning back in her chair and he wanted her sitting upright.

"Well, if you don't want cash, what do you want?" Jennifer was rearranging her Filofax. She was getting rid of a section, making room for more telephone numbers. Obviously she felt her contacts were about to expand.

"I want you to arrange a meeting with me and the highest Catholic official in New York that you can get your hands on."

"I'm Episcopalian," Jennifer said, feeling she wouldn't have to deal with this request.

"I know you're an Episcopalian. Of course you're an Episcopalian. You get to have all the ceremony with about half the sin. I bet you have uncles who have pants with pheasants on them."

"They do, and they go to the country club and get drunk, but not as drunk as the Catholics get." Jennifer was trying to joke with him. One of the things Mickey hated most was a nonprofessional trying to quip.

"Look, Jennifer, you get one of your uncles to get one of their friends to get me a meeting with a Catholic in high places. I want one of those guys who has worked his way up from choirboy and has a good chance of taking over Manhattan. If they can get me to one of the five closest to the Pope, I'll get my ass on a plane to Rome. If not, I'll need less than an hour."

"Are you serious?"

"Perfectly serious." His towel fell off at this point, which didn't help him keep the authority in his voice.

"Is this for research? Because we have people."

"This is for personal reasons. I expect you to get back to me today."

"And if I can't?"

"You can. If you can lie about where you went to school, you can find me one priest." He had started to say one fucking priest, but he decided not to. It might have taken her longer to find one of those. He hung up without saying good-bye. He had always felt that good-byes ruined the impact of a hostile conversation.

Mickey didn't mind doing anything in the nude with the exception of bending over. He had to pick up the towel and when he did he reminded himself of Neanderthal man.

Jennifer Ross came through. Supposedly, Monsignor Rosetti was third from the top. She tried to set the meeting up at the monsignor's office, but the clergyman's secretary assured Mrs. Ross that her boss would rather meet at the network. The monsignor was very interested in how a television studio worked. When she told Mickey where the meeting would take place and why, Mickey said, "God Himself would try to get close to show business."

Rosetti and Burke met three mornings later in the network conference room. Jennifer arranged for tea to be served, and although the room was modern and stark, Monsignor Rosetti, weighing in at two hundred and eighty pounds, gave the room all the religious flair it needed.

The meeting got off to an unfortunate start. Because of the monsignor's excessive weight, none of the chairs in the room could handle him. Jennifer had to call maintenance, and an old, large piece of stage furniture was carted in. It gave the monsignor a chance to tell Mickey that he was a fan of his show and that he tried not to miss it. It was difficult for Mickey to accept a compliment from this man. He had three large chins that all moved under a tiny mouth. One had to wonder when the chins would drop and there wouldn't be enough facial muscle to bring them back up.

Because of the size of the man, everything was out of proportion. The prop department was warned to bring in the largest chair they could find, and it turned out to be a throne from a comedy sketch from long ago. The large chair forced the conference table to be moved off center. Rosetti moved as if each step could bring him a heart attack or find him a minefield. His breathing sounded as if it were on an amplifier. The tea was a joke. His hands were twice the size of the cup. When the two men were finally left alone to talk, Mickey felt as if he were having an audience with a king. The chair the monsignor sat in was not only larger, but higher. Mickey's head didn't even come up to the third chin. The humble Jew had come to ask a favor of the church. The monsignor was going to wait to speak until Mickey presented his request. He knew this Mr. Burke had something to ask for. Since it took all his energy just to live, he was going to sit and wait before he had either to grant—or not grant—a wish. He thought he was smiling reassuringly, but the folds of his face didn't allow his emotion to show.

"I have a friend," Mickey began. He realized these fellows often heard members of their flock begin with "I have a friend." The monsignor managed a nod of the head. Things on his face shook much longer than on most people.

"She's my secretary, a beautiful girl, about twenty-two, a good Catholic and . . . here's the hard part. She wants to become a nun." There was no expression on the clergyman's face, or at least none that could be seen.

"What is her problem?" This was said as if this whole meeting was an annoyance. Mickey would have preferred, "What is her problem, my child?" He felt he was entitled to some clerical benevolence. Also the New York accent didn't help. It was from the streets, and Mickey felt that he could get yelled at.

"She's wanted to be a nun ever since she was a girl, but she's never gotten her calling."

The monsignor understood. His little eyes disappeared behind his heavy lids. "We lose so many of them because they expect some great sign from heaven. They think there's going to be skywriting or something." He paused here to catch his heavy breath. "They wait for some voice to talk to them or the face of our blessed Virgin Mary to appear on their sheets." He was clearly disgusted with these crazy kids. "And it's not only the girls. The boys are hanging around waiting for the miracle, too. If they see someone walking on water, they'll consider joining up." A Jew would have said a nice, big "oy" here. Rosetti attempted to throw his arms in the air. They didn't fly freely.

"So what you're telling me is that the calling to the vocation could be more subtle." Mickey leaned in for an answer. They were getting somewhere here.

"It could be next to nothing. I'm not saying, mind you, that Christ Himself can't come down to Queens and sit on some kid's bed and ask him to come into the priesthood. I'm just saying that's a million-to-one shot."

"What's in the 'next to nothing' category?" Mickey took his pen and index cards from his back pocket. They were usually in his jeans, but out of respect for the clergy, Mickey had worn a pair of gray slacks to the meeting. The pants were expensive, but just as ill-fitting as everything else. The man had no ass.

The monsignor was fascinated by the blank cards. He leaned in for closer inspection. Here's where Mickey got to smell the man. He was overweight, perspiring and had no need to impress women. Mickey couldn't come close to guessing the date of his last shower. "You write funny things on those cards?"

"I write funny things, telephone numbers, things I don't want to forget." Mickey moved back. He tried to make the motion casual, making it look as if he needed the support of the chair in order to write. It was the odor that drove him away.

"And what are you going to write now?" Because of Rosetti's size, Mickey had figured he was in his seventies. Now that he was listening to his voice, it was clear that he was dealing with a much younger man.

"I thought you could tell me some of the more subtle ways that my friend can feel her vocation. Maybe she missed one." Mickey's pen was ready to write.

"Well, for example, I got mine in the bathroom." Mickey wasn't sure he wanted to hear this. He imagined it could happen through a good bowel movement, but Mickey didn't want to be talking about the bathroom area with this man. "I was twenty at the time," the monsignor continued, "and had just cut myself shaving. I realized, at that moment, that my blood was so important in the scheme of things. I wanted to become a part of a universal blood. I was seeing my own mortality and the importance of it at the same time. That story has impressed many young boys. Of course my mother was thrilled. She had told me I was going to be a priest since I was four."

Micky had nothing to write down. He couldn't tell Astra Rainbow to start shaving. He did understand what Rosetti was saying. It was the small, insignificant moments that tended to lead to the inspiration.

The monsignor was willing to give another example. "Sister Kevin is one of our modern children. She got her calling at a Michael Jackson concert. She just knew that she could do what Mr. Jackson did, on a different scale, of course." He sat back on the throne that props had provided. He was confident that he had gotten the church's point across.

"I understand what you're telling me. It's not this big thing. It's just a feeling . . . a thing . . . like sometimes I know there's a story inside me and I have to tell it."

"You do understand. As you know, our church needs these young people. We have fewer would-be priests and nuns every year. I have to wonder how many are missing the subtle things. Maybe we should send more of them to those rock-and-roll shows." Since this was Rosetti's big effort at comedy, Mickey was gracious enough to laugh. "You want funny? You come have dinner with me and the boys. It's funnier than anything you could write." Mickey wondered if the man knew he could be just as insulting as inspiring.

He put the cards back in his pocket and then started his pitch for Astra Rainbow. "This girl is really special. I was just wondering if you could . . . I don't know, talk to her. You'll see how serious she is. Maybe this one small thing about having to have a calling could be looked over, just this once. I mean, you yourself said there was a shortage . . ."

"When they do television shows about religion, do they put guys like me on to see that everything is technically correct?" Could it be that the monsignor was ready to make a deal? Mickey had learned a long time ago that everyone wanted something to do with television.

"Sure. The network is always hiring what they call technical advisers." Here was Mickey's chance. "Now that they know you . . . is there any chance that you could use your pull and help this girl get in?"

"If she's as good as you say she is."

"She is. And beautiful too . . ." Realizing that the church didn't actually need beauty among its ranks, unless they intended to put more nuns on *Donahue*, Mickey loudly added, "Beautiful, inside and out."

"I'm sure I can do something. If it's one thing I have, it's a little pull with the Lord."

Mickey's business had taught him to close the deal. "Are you telling me this girl is in?"

"She'll have to meet with the mother superior, but if she isn't insane or doing this for all the wrong reasons, I'm sure there'll be no problem." The monsignor may have winked. Small moves were hard to tell on him. "Just make sure she mentions my name and gives the mother superior my card." Mickey was impressed with the church. He was glad that it hadn't completely left earth and that pull could get you in. He loved that they carried business cards.

The men were supposed to stand up in unison, but even moving slowly wasn't going to get any choreography going with Mickey and a man this size. The good-byes were too loving for the deal that had just transpired. The monsignor gave Mickey his card and then tried to hug him. It was an impossible move. All Mickey really got was a little warmth and a big whiff of the clergyman's underarm. He pretended to have business so that they wouldn't have to go down the same elevator.


The following day, Astra Rainbow found the monsignor's card set against a small bunch of white roses. It might have been a bridal bouquet.

Mickey explained that the monsignor gave his word that Astra Rainbow could join the church. It was just a matter of paperwork.

"I don't think so." She politely put the card in her top drawer. "Thank you for the flowers. They're beautiful. I love baby's breath. My mother used to wear it in her hair."

"I thought you wanted to be a nun." He pointed to the top drawer with the card in it. "He can get you in."

"Maybe I was put here on earth to do your typing." It was a heady thought for a narcissist like Mickey.

"You're not giving up on becoming a nun, are you?"

"It was just wrong of me to have you intervene. Don't worry, Mr. Burke. If Christ wants me, He'll let it be known, and I'll give you two weeks' notice."

Mickey backed into his office. There was something exciting about this girl. She had just put him in competition with Christ.

# 12

# Trying

OVER dinner one night in February, holding hands around the candlelight, Mickey and Shelly decided to try to make their relationship work. They both knew the operative word was "try." By morning Shelly was scared and Mickey was panicking. She wasn't so sure she should trust him with either her fragile furniture or her fragile heart. He was remembering what it was like to have to lie in bed next to the same woman every night and have to ask when he wanted to change the television station. She was determined to make it work and, although he didn't know it, he was determined to make it fail. He didn't mean or plan to be annoying. He just was.

The same night that they committed to trying, they talked about where they would do this trying. His place was out because he had no place. Her apartment was the logical choice, but he felt that he would always think of it as her home. She thought of it as an invasion. She wanted Mickey Burke in her life safe, secure, every day, but there seemed to be two things she wasn't prepared for: letting him share the apartment she had decorated for herself and getting rid of an apartment in a rent-controlled building. These were her things that she and Dirk and Dutch had put together. It was her first real home as a grown-up. These were her walls, with her carefully chosen fabric on them. She couldn't move. There was no one in the world who deserved to benefit from what she had done for herself. Unfortunately, that included Mickey, the man she genuinely loved.

Over one piece of cheesecake with two forks, they decided it would be best to take things one step at a time. Mickey would move into Shelly's place. If everything worked out, they would consider getting a place together. They held hands and smiled at each other while he got sick of the idea of their incomes commingled and she thought of his invasion into her space. They both thought they were in love. They just happened to be thirty-five years old in a complicated decade. That night, after making love, they gave each other their accountants' telephone numbers.

The next day Shelly told Greta that she was happy, but not as happy as she thought she should be. Wise Greta replied, "Nobody is as happy as she should be. Shut up and have babies. I might have one with the exterminator." When Mickey told Jerry he felt he was doing the right thing, Jerry patted him on the back and told him he couldn't lose. "If worse comes to worst, you can always go back to the hotel." Jerry was smiling, but Mickey wasn't. He didn't know if he could make it night after night with Shelly, but the hotel was looking worn, dirty and depressing to him. He was, for now, a man who worried about going forward yet knew he was burning dingy, unusable bridges behind him.

He assured Jerry that they would still watch *Monday Night Football* together. He pictured them, sprawled in Shelly's beige den. Shelly could leave them incredible sandwiches with notes with hearts on them. Maybe this was going to be all right.

Two things happened in March that proved to Shelly that she loved her man. On March seventeenth (Shelly remembered the date because she had to cater a St. Patrick's Day party at Citibank, and the meat looked green instead of the dessert), Mickey spilled an entire glass of grape juice on one of the white couches and managed to get the rug too. The catering business had made Shelly intimate with spills. She was always rushing for the club soda and calming down hostesses by making horrible, Rorschach-looking stains disappear. But this was her couch and her stains and there was Mickey, looking guilty with a purple mustache and an empty glass. She told him over and over that there was no harm done, but they could both see that there was. The club soda faded the purple to lavender, but there it was, a stain signaling that Mickey Burke had made his mark on Shelly Silver's life. He really loved her when she hugged him and said it didn't matter. She looked over his shoulder at the matching blotches on the rug and couch and thought her life might never be as pretty as it used to be. Nobody ever told Shelly that a woman could be too nurturing. But from that night on, their lovemaking tapered off and they never knew why. They hugged more but there was less sex, which worried them both. (Not enough to get help, but enough to tune in to Dr. Ruth when they thought no one was watching.)

Worse than the stains were the things that Mickey brought with him. Shelly had only known Mickey as a resident of hotel rooms with hotel furniture. She had no idea that he had bought some funky art-deco pieces with the money he had first earned as a writer. He had them in storage and he had been waiting all these years to unveil them. He told her that he was having a few of his beloved belongings delivered to the apartment. She expected books, maybe a clock. The old things turned out to be a tasteless assault on her apartment. There in her living room stood a large, ratty, rust suede chair that needed repair, a desk that was too large for Manhattan, some posters that only very young men would buy (she recognized them as nouveau and rotten), and about twenty-five to thirty objets de junk. They were meant to be funny when purchased by Mickey, the young comedy writer. He wasn't looking for art at the time, he was looking for laughs; now the tired laughs were among Shelly's newly acquired refinement. Since his things were larger than he was, and had less class, they were the ultimate intrusion.

The den became Mickey's lair. His things were squeezed among hers, occasionally touching. She was sure she would never again garner the compliments she once had. She knew living together would mean sacrifices, and in her head were lists of pros and cons. She loved him. She needed him. Not for the solid things like furniture and walls, but for warmth and to have a hand to hold in the elevator. She wanted this to lead to marriage and children. The only real negative was that he was there all the time and with all his things. Unfortunately, under these conditions, positives tend to stay the same while negatives grow. She had heard of a couple once, both psychiatrists, who had apartments next door to each other. They spent time together only when they wanted to. She pictured the husband in a dark green silk bathrobe knocking on his wife's door, asking permission to come in. She imagined them dancing, just the two of them, to an old Victrola. This to Shelly was ideal.

There was no doubt that Mickey loved Shelly. (Or that he would soon.) He loved to sit on the high white stool in the kitchen, sipping wine and watching her work. He had spent all those childhood years watching his mother make the same chicken over and over again. Even though he was no longer inside a make-believe television set, he was good at entertaining any woman who was pounding meat for his dinner. His mother had used shortcuts and was proud of it. "Store-bought" was a phrase without shame in his childhood home. But Shelly made everything from scratch and often wonderful things happened before Mickey's eyes. Not only did ingredients turn into desserts, the woman he cared for ended up with flour on her nose. This he knew to kiss away.

Mickey, who had never cooked, was always comfortable in the kitchen watching the women he loved turn raw things into something wonderful just for him. Again he was watching a back, this time

Shelly's. He spoke to her from behind, just as he had entertained his mother and aunt from that same angle and watched Astra Rainbow. He noticed that Shelly had a gray hair among the very brown ones, and that made him care for her more. If he was very good and didn't cause any trouble, maybe they could grow old together. Maybe they were growing old together now.

From Mickey's point of view, only one thing was going wrong. Before he moved in, the sex had been sweaty. Now, even the thought of bed made him sleepy. He had always gone to bed late, sometimes as late as two in the morning because of a great Katharine Hepburn–Spencer Tracy movie or a plot point he was trying to figure out. Since he had moved in with Shelly, he was tired at night. He had always envied those people who bragged that they could fall asleep the minute their heads hit the pillow. Now he was one of them. A few times he had felt Shelly press up against him, giving him all the body language he needed to know she wanted to make love. His body wouldn't permit it. Even when he tried to stay awake and respond, sleep overcame him. One Tuesday he fell asleep with his hand on her breast. In an attempt to keep the lines of communication open, they were going to talk about this problem as soon as possible. Mickey pretended that he was just as anxious to "work it through" as Shelly was, but in reality he would have been happy to let lying dogs sleep. There was nothing he could say except, "I love you. My hand gets tired." Shelly was sure they could work it out during brunch on Sunday. Mickey, who hated discussing sex over eggs, remembered that he had to visit his mother and Aunt Minn. "I promised them I'd come down there this weekend."

"Are you sure you're not avoiding?" Shelly asked.

"I'm positive. We can go to Café Des Artistes next weekend and talk for hours about how inadequate I am. I swear I'd stay and do it this weekend, but you know how long it takes to get a good brunch reservation. I say we put our sex life on hold while I go to Florida, and when I get back we can talk everything out over the best eggs in town."

"You won't stay long?"

"I'll just let them squeeze me and I'll be right back. You know I'll be back soon. I can only write the *Afterlife* script around you." Shelly tried to accept this as a compliment. It was nice to know that the creative man in your life created well around you. The only problem was she had his ink marks all over her bedspread and a long line of black ink on her thigh.

"Why aren't I depressed to see him go?" she asked Greta.

"When we have them, we don't want them in our faces all the time. Who would you rather go to Europe with, him or me?" Shelly hesitated. "Me. You'd like to go to Europe with me. Then, when we're finished shopping, looking, knowing enough to sit down and eat those gorgeous little sandwiches, then and only then, you should let him come over for the weekend. Believe me. There's nothing worse than going to Europe with someone who actually wants to see the sights. We'll go to Paris next year and you can invite what's-his-name over for a Friday night. Now, as for this weekend in Miami with Mom, use the time to enrich your soul and bleach your mustache."

Mickey's mother and Aunt Minn were more interested in who this Shelly Silver was than in the Hollywood gossip they usually craved. They still wanted to know whether Linda Evans and Joan Collins really liked each other, but "How's it going with that girl?" was still the main topic. He told them that he thought he loved her. When they asked if he was going to marry her, he reacted as if he were too young to do something like that.

It was a short weekend, with a lot of coffee cake. Freyda Burke was a strong believer in three meals a day. All meals, including breakfast, had some sort of dessert attached to them. Breakfast ended with sweet rolls and stewed fruit. Lunch and dinner had different forms of Entenmann's cake. Usually they were content to watch him eat squares of whatever they put in front of him. Both of them were on strict diets ordered by their doctors. They watched each other more carefully than they watched themselves. Minn would catch Freyda sneaking something and fight her for it. Eventually the forbidden item would end up in the garbage disposal. When Mickey was there, they delighted in feeding him everything that they couldn't have.

He was due to leave on a ten-P.M. flight. According to Freyda Burke, that would give her son a full day in Miami with nothing to worry about. He understood the full day in Miami part. He never understood why, if he took that late flight, he would have nothing to worry about. Mickey spent most of the weekend telling the two women who raised him that they looked beautiful at their new slim sizes. They modeled new size-twelve dresses that they bought. As he complimented them, they complimented each other. Aunt Minn said she felt healthier than she had in a long time and that life would be wonderful if the Cubans would just stop having rallies.

Freyda suggested that they have dessert on the terrace the last night Mickey was there. The women balanced their Jell-Os, and Mickey had his square of coffee cake. They removed the plastic from the chairs, rubbed the mosquito repellent on and made believe that it was more pleasant outside than in the air-conditioned apartment.

Both women posed against the railing, showing off the silhouette of their new bodies. His mother wore a deep pink blouse. His aunt's was a lavender. The dark air robbed them both of their color. Their jewelry took them into the night and could have safely brought aliens in from space. He thought the show was for him, but rather suddenly his mother was talking about something she felt he was old enough to know. His first thought was that she was going to tell him that he was adopted. He was sure he wasn't. There were baby pictures of him all over Bensonhurst, and he had his mother's fierce nose. His second quick thought was that his mother was trying to tell him she was dying. This was news he couldn't bear. He loved her. He didn't want to have to deal with the mysteries of the universe. He wanted her there, in the flesh, always asking questions about people in Hollywood. He wanted to hold her when he wanted to and to smell the too-sweet rose perfume that she used too much of. What could he possibly be old enough to know? Not that his mother was dying.

Minn nodded at Freyda, giving her permission to go on. Mickey, the only audience, sat in fear. The news he hadn't heard already hurt.

"Your father was a wonderful man, a scholar." He had heard this sentence about his father many times. When relatives were around they nodded their heads in agreement. Young Mickey had inherited all his books and didn't know what to do with them.

"Such a brilliant man," said Minn. Mickey couldn't see the path they were leading him down. Did brilliant men leave their sons genetic diseases? His father was too young to die.

"After your father, I couldn't even get interested in another man. They couldn't compare." Mickey had heard this too. There were times when he wished for a father, but more often than not, he didn't want to deal with a stepfather who had ideas about how to treat little boys.

"There really was no one to compare," Aunt Minn said apologetically. Were they telling him they were sorry he had grown up fatherless?

At this point his mother found a little pool of light on the terrace and, like an actress, stepped into it. Minn waited in the wings. Freyda swallowed twice before she felt brave enough to tell the boy what really went on. "Your Aunt Minn isn't really your aunt, by blood, I mean."

If this was the news, it was perfectly all right with Mickey. He never did manage to match her up with any blood relatives, but there were other aunts and uncles in his childhood that couldn't officially be sewn into the family tree. "I somehow knew that." Mickey smiled at his ladies. Minn put her arm on Freyda's shoulder for a second, encouraging her to go on.

"Since I would never, ever take another man in your father's bed, I took Aunt Minn." She took the long, deep breath she needed. "We love each other, like men and women do."

Minn rushed in. "We didn't plan it. It just happened."

Mickey was full of joy. He was on his feet immediately. He kissed one, then the other. He held them tightly, not letting them out of his family circle. He danced them in a line through the apartment, a dance that resembled those done at religious weddings. "We're going to have a party," he said. "A big one with all our friends—a big party just to celebrate us." They all cried and hugged again and got out the family albums. So many of them showed the two women with the little boy in the middle. "No wonder I'm fucked up," screamed Mickey. "I had two Jewish mothers."

"I told you he'd be fine," said Freyda.

"We should have told him years ago," said Minn.

"I am fine." He couldn't help laughing.

"How come you're taking it so well?"

"I don't know. I guess because for years I've been worried that you didn't have anybody to love." He said this to both of them.

"We shouldn't have worried him," said Freyda.

"I'm glad you have each other. I'm really happy for you guys."

"And one more thing," said Aunt Minn. "Since this is a day for confessions, I want you to know I'm not a natural blonde."

"She's been dying her hair for years," said Freyda.

"And now you know everything." Aunt Minn was right. He felt he knew everything.

Mickey called Shelly to tell her he would be spending another day in Miami. He and his mother and his aunt had plans to make. Shelly tried to understand. He was only asking for a day.

The boy slept well. The mothers did too. On the plane home the following day, Mickey smiled and wondered if they actually kissed each other. When he really got used to the idea, he realized that although it was interesting, this couldn't be his screenplay either.

# 13

# The
# Red Herring

J UST as Mickey was spending more time looking at Astra Rainbow's back than Shelly's and Shelly hurt her toe on Mickey's ugly deco Easter egg that had accidentally found its way under the bed, the miracle they hadn't even thought to pray for happened. Shelly got the red herring.

For about six months there had been rumors that the building was going co-op, and there were signs that the rumors were true. The owner had put carpeting in the elevator and had given the doormen new uniforms in an attempt to make things look classier. Every New Yorker knew that these attempts at upgrading meant that the building was up for sale. Tenants who had never even nodded at each other stopped at their mailboxes and asked each other if they were going to buy.

At the beginning of May, just as the tenants with balconies put out their plastic pots of flowers, everyone in the building got a notice that the owner was intending to sell the apartments on a noneviction plan. This notice was known as the red herring, although it was neither red nor fish. It was appropriately nicknamed because of the surprise it brought.

Since Shelly worked at home that morning, Lucinda brought in the notice of intent with the rest of the mail. She knew she had brought in a letter of substance when her missus ran for her glasses and closed the bedroom door behind her. It didn't matter to Lucinda that the building was going co-op, so she began her day as always. She sprayed for the cockroaches. Although she hadn't seen a roach in over three months, she thought it was a good idea to do some preventive spraying.

Shelly was shocked at the notice. She and the rest of the tenants had expected a financial break. If you were lucky enough to be living in a building when the red herring came, you were supposed to be able to get your apartment at bargain rates. She had calculated that hers would be no more than two hundred and fifty thousand—a hefty amount for a woman who, before the revolution had never expected to pay for her own shampoo. Here it was listed on the schedule at three hundred and forty thousand. She counted the zeros and cried. She had no idea whether she could afford it or not. She just felt sad to have all those zeros on her shoulders.

Everyone in the building thought he was being ripped off, and a tenants' committee was formed. (Greta, upon hearing about this, told Shelly that if they were ever looking for men again, they could go to tenants' meetings all over town. "Nobody would know we didn't live there. We could go to the best buildings in town. It wouldn't be bad to meet guys who are buying their own apartments.") Over Danish and coffee in the Lawrys' apartment, 5B, two bedrooms, no view, the tenants voted to hire a lawyer and fight back. Since there were already sixteen lawyers living in the building, there was no problem in finding one to go up against the big guy, the owner they had never seen.

Mickey offered to buy the apartment with Shelly, and that seemed scarier than the price. She could share her body more easily than she could share her walls. She could let him in as an invited visitor, but the shell had to be hers. What if they separated again? They'd have to sell the place and split the profits. Shelly didn't want profits. She wanted the roof over her head to be her roof and to be there as long as she needed it to protect her. It said a lot about the times she lived in, times when a woman felt more secure with an apartment than with a man. She had learned that the apartment offered better protection.

All sixteen lawyers worked hard to get the owner to reduce his prices by twenty percent. Shelly Silver, although she was hyperventilating about the price, could afford to buy her apartment. More importantly, she could once again afford to take care of herself. If Mickey Burke ever walked out, Shelly would only be destroyed. She wouldn't be homeless.

Mickey, however, was. There he was, a second draft due on his script and no real place to hang his Emmy. He felt his toothbrush was in jeopardy. The decorators had convinced Shelly not to have clutter on the sleek bathroom counter. Whenever Mickey found a good corner for his toilet articles, the items were buried by Shelly, Lucinda or both.

The morning that Mickey couldn't find his razor, Mrs. Schimmel from 14D made it known that she was moving to Arizona for her health and was willing to sell her co-op for a ten-percent profit. Mickey heard about it from the doorman, who throughout the conversation was the most accurate source of information. By lunchtime, Mickey ran his hand across his facial stubble and was able to convince himself that it was a good investment, and by three that afternoon, Jerry, who had been Mickey's lawyer even before he finished law school, got Mrs. Schimmel on the phone and told her he had a firm offer.

Mickey wasn't planning to live in 14D. Terms like "tax shelter" and "hedge against inflation" were used. Fortunately, Mrs. Schimmel wanted out as soon as possible, and by July of that year Mickey's things, including his Emmy, his objets d'art and writing files were sent upstairs. There was an old single bed up there just in case Shelly's caught on fire. Mrs. Schimmel never knew she had saved their relationship. It had taken twenty-two hundred square feet, down payments of a hundred and fifty thousand dollars and a woman moving to Arizona for her health to make Shelly Silver and Mickey Burke feel safe with each other.

Mickey ended up spending half the week upstairs, sometimes writing in the middle of the night while lying on Mrs. Schimmel's faded pale-green carpet. Shelly called the whole arrangement very romantic. "I never know when he's going to surprise me," she told Greta over cold salmon with the green sauce on the side.

"It's everybody's fantasy," said Greta. "Who doesn't want some nights just to get into a bed with a Valium and a full-time boyfriend upstairs? You're living like royalty. Kings and queens have separate wings. It gives you a chance to fart. I would love that, but do you have any idea how many rats Hank would have to kill to move into my building?"

"How's it going with you two?"

"We're still having a wonderful private life and a rotten public one. The four of us should get together for dinner."

They did. They dressed up and went to the Ginger Man. While Hank was in the bathroom, Greta apologized for Hank's polyester jacket and his behavior. He had ordered four domestic beers and had tried to talk Mickey into doing a situation comedy about an exterminator. He offered to split the profits fifty-fifty, which was more than he offered to do with the bill.

Mickey and Shelly were smug after that dinner. They saw how unfit Greta and Hank were for each other and how perfectly matched they were. They drank champagne in Shelly's kitchen and giggled about the rest of the world. It's hard to say at what moment they fell in love. It was a peaceful happening rather than a passionate one. Maybe it happened as they sat tiredly on stools, leaning on the butcher block. Maybe Mickey realized that he had been facing this woman

for over an hour rather than just studying her from behind, and maybe
Shelly didn't notice that Mickey was digging his heels into her enameled stools. They loved the world that had brought them together.
She could laugh at all the things that people did who were less hip
than they were, and he could get them down on paper. They felt if
they really had wanted to go to Sean Penn and Madonna's wedding
they could have, and they could choose to read about it or not in
*People.* They knew what to wear and at the same time look as if they
didn't care what they put on. They knew what to eat and how wonderful cheap wine could be when you could afford the good kind.
They brought their cans of Coke to the table because they knew not
to and they put ketchup on everything for the same reason. Their
instincts told them when to be political. She sent money to NOW
whenever they asked, and he made jokes about Falwell whenever he
felt. They both dreamed of being delegates to the Democratic National
Conventon. He was going to work his way in by writing material for
candidates, and she was going to supply the hors d'oeuvres. They
both knew they had received from society and that they would feel
beter if they gave back. Together they were always one year away
from being altruistic. Until then they would be using their platinum
American Express cards on themselves. They could be Yuppies because they were Yuppies with their eyes wide open.

"I think I love you," said Mickey, who didn't purposely qualify his
statement. Shelly went straight into his arms and felt that there was
some sense to the universe. She had waited for this and couldn't help
leaning on the man she had wanted for so long. When love blossomed
on the Upper West Side, it was easy to spot. The area was filled with
struggling relationships, but the real thing was hard to find. Any
observant person could have spotted the love in Shelly's kitchen on
that hot August night. Greta and Hank might have sparked it, but it
didn't come to a full blaze until a little after one that morning, when
Mickey knew that he was comfortable. They were too tired to make
love, but they celebrated by sleeping in the same bed. They fell asleep
with their arms around each other and felt lucky.

When Shelly Silver was nineteen and still believing everything she
had learned, she had been proud to tell her mother that she didn't
need a piece of paper to prove her love. "So if you don't need it, you
might as well get it just so your father won't have a heart attack."
Mrs. Silver was always using her husband's heart as a means of
keeping her daughters in line. They were, of course, talking hypo-
thetically, since Shelly's boyfriend at the time took baths too infre-
quently, even for someone committed to existentialism. This attitude

of not needing marriage ended up being more than a stage that that crazy girl was going through. In fact, seven years later Shelly was scared to marry the lawyer from legal aid. She was in no mood to pay alimony. It wasn't until she was thirty-one and feeling mortal that she longed for marriage. She and her friends had decided by then that if the rest of your life was different from your mother's that it was perfectly all right to take a husband. She had gotten conservative about the same time she started decorating. *Time* and *Newsweek* did cover stories on herpes and everyone got scared of fooling around. Then there were the AIDS stories, buried at first, covers later, and everybody who didn't want to commit suicide was careful about whom he slept with. There were more engagements, more weddings and more women looking for love, marriage and children, even if it meant admitting to their mothers that they had been right all along.

By now Shelly realized that she had always flowed with the tide. As soon as Marlo Thomas married Phil Donahue, she had longings to marry, preferably to someone she didn't have to support. Now that Mickey was in love with her, she wanted him to satisfy her longings. Her marriage campaign began on a Sunday while she and Mickey shared *The New York Times*. (She had the Business section. He was into Arts and Leisure.)

"Look at them." Shelly slipped the picture of a happy family over his paper.

"What?" He had no idea what this very happy, very young family had to do with them.

"I just think they're a nice-looking family," she said, withdrawing the group. She sounded like a grandmother showing off her offspring.

The following week, she walked him past the windows at Bergdorf's where each window featured fantasies for brides. She made the mistake of asking him which gown he liked best. She had hoped he would say, "You would look great in that one. Let's get married the first Saturday the rabbi is free." He didn't. Mickey couldn't decide which gown he liked best and he really thought she was asking his opinion.

Her hints turned into questions. "Do you think we would be selling out if we got married?" she asked on a long phone call. With the protection of the phone, the questions got more direct.

"Shelly, are you still worried about what your sorority sisters will think?" And she knew she had lost him for this call. They would now talk about peer pressure rather than about whether the wedding invitations should come from Tiffany's or Cartier.

Once when they were in bed she asked, "Do you think people who are married try harder?" and Mickey said a sleepy no before rolling over and going to sleep. He believed single people who lived together tried harder, but he was too tired to have one of those three-hour relationship sessions that ended up with both parties trying to start their sentences with, "I feel . . ."

Mickey didn't realize what was happening until the questions turned into proposals. Usually they came late at night when Shelly was finished with work and Mickey was finished with basketball games. Often they were said in Shelly's bed, and since she was tired of hinting, the proposals were very direct. "Will you marry me?" she asked, giving him very little chance to escape.

At first he tried acting Talmudic, answering a question with a question, "Will I marry you?" he asked back, knowing that would give him at least two more beats before he had to compose an answer.

"Yes."

"Who knows?" he asked, worming his way out.

Soon Shelly learned not to let him off easy. "You can't just say, 'Who knows?' I need an answer," she said while he wondered why she was attempting to ruin their perfect lives.

Mickey didn't want to be the type of person who couldn't commit. He had created a show about an asshole who was destined to live alone because he couldn't give his heart away. Mickey put pain into the guy's life and clearly made him look as if he were missing something. He had grown up watching movies about bachelors and the wonderful lives they had, but in his own life he only saw one unmarried man, Uncle Seymour, a man who never looked as happy as his celluloid counterparts. Uncle Seymour had a smelly cat and might have been gay if the world had let him be. Mickey knew commitment was better. He just happened to choke on it. Every time Shelly proposed, he avoided answering and stayed away for a day. Then he was back wanting more love and warmth in her big bed.

Greta and Shelly sat on the twin couches, legs crossed, minds opened, talking about what turned out to be Shelly's latest problem, which was, as she explained it, her inability to keep her mouth shut. "I just can't stop," Shelly said, as if she had an addiction. "Every night I promise myself that I'm not going to talk about marriage, and the next day there it is. I'm proposing again."

"Exactly how bad is your habit?" Greta asked, taking yet another Hershey's Kiss. They had been at the candy quite a while now, and a pile of little silver balls lay between them.

"I would say that now I'm up to once a day. No. That's not fair. Let's say that there are some days that I'm able to control myself. There are times that I have gone as long as thirty-six hours without even hinting. It's hard, but sometimes I manage to suppress the urges.

There are other times that I'll do it two or three times in one hour. He retreats to his typewriter, of course."

"What a wimp," said Greta, on her twelfth Kiss. She popped them the way others might pop illegal drugs.

"He is a wimp. I mean, here I am, I'm not saying I'm the bargain of all time, but I have good hygiene, a mother who not only lives out of town but is scared to be intrusive, and I know nouvelle cuisine. He could do worse."

"He could do a lot worse. Where else is he going to find someone who comes as fully equipped as you do?" This, of course, is what girlfriends were for. Greta knew how to stroke an ego.

"Even my teeth are in good condition. I'm not one of those women who gets married just so her husband can pay for her dental work."

The fun of the conversation left when the candy was gone. They had gone through a seven-and-a-half-ounce bag and had enjoyed some badly needed silliness. Now, knowing that constant proposing could be harmful to a relationship, they had to figure out how Shelly was going to keep quiet. Greta worked hard on finding a solution.

"Okay. So we know that asking him to marry you isn't doing any good, right?"

"Right. I mean, it's not as if he's accepting and shouting yes. What I'm really afraid of is that I'm driving him away. One of these days he's going to ask me to give it a rest. I just have to learn to shut up."

"Who can shut up? The minute you look at him, you're thinking of marriage. I know. I've been there."

"I don't even know why. It's like I'm possessed. Me, the girl who thought it was disgusting that Laurie Singer got engaged to that resident in her senior year. I felt sorry for Laurie. Love was one thing. Love I could understand, but marriage just was something society wanted you to do. So why am I pushing for it? Why aren't I leaving this good relationship alone? I have him. He's mine. You want to tell me why all of a sudden I *have* to have a marriage license?"

"You probably had a bride doll when you were a kid. That doll walked down the aisle that I had made between the folds on my blankets. And Ken and Barbie didn't help either. They got married at my house every other day."

"You're telling me that Ken and Barbie were a bigger influence than the entire sexual revolution?"

"Oh, yeah. Absolutely. They had a great life. Mine got married after she went to the beauty parlor."

"You know what I've thought of doing?"

"What?" said Greta, still trying to think of a solution.

"You're not going to like me for this," said Shelly. "It's very embarrassing," she added, knowing it was absolutely necessary to qualify what she was going to say.

"Go on," said Greta. Now she was leaning back and looking up. She knew there was something juicy about to happen.

"Promise you won't think of me as a . . . conniving little bitch?"

"You're looking at someone who forced you to rent a Mercedes in order to meet men. How conniving is that? And I promise."

"I stopped using my diaphragm about two months ago. My mind has clicked into an era when women tricked men into marrying them by getting pregnant. Before you say anything I want you to know it's disgusting and unfair and archaic and I can't help it." Shelly slid off the couch and sank to the floor where she felt she belonged.

"It's . . ."

"Don't you think I know it's a dirty trick? And who even knows if it's going to work? He could put his arms around me, kiss me on the cheek and promise to stand by me for an abortion."

"So it's a dirty trick. Dirtier would be telling him you're pregnant when you're not, getting him to marry you so that the three of you will be a real family and then pretending that you fell down the stairs and had a miscarriage."

"I'd rather be a real family—oh God. This wasn't supposed to be my life. I was supposed to be chairman of the board of Chrysler or governor of New York."

"We just didn't know what it would be like not to propagate the race."

"In the meantime, I've got to stop proposing. The proposing is driving him away."

"Whatever you do, no matter how frustrated you get, don't give him the ultimatum. Never say the following: 'Look, if we don't get married, we're wasting each other's time. We shouldn't see each other anymore.' Men can pack fast."

They both could have predicted that the ultimatum would eventually come. It started out as an ordinary night. Shelly had an early cocktail party to do, so she planned to be finished by eight and knocking on Mickey's door at eight-thirty. The party had one too many drunks, a waiter who didn't show and a host who tried to seduce her. (Greta had always thought that Shelly could have made better use of her profession to meet men. "You really should specialize in giving expensive parties for male hosts," she said one day when Shelly was trying to pull together a lavender bat mitzvah.) The seduction took place in the bathroom, her least favorite place to be seduced, and ended with him teasing her by holding her check high above his head as if she should jump for it. When he saw she wasn't going to play, he followed her into the kitchen, making it known that he was watching her closely in case she had any intention of taking the leftover clams that he paid for.

It was exactly nine-twenty when Shelly reached Mickey. She had told the cab driver to drive fast, and Max, a good Russian cab driver, was happy to fly her home. He tried to get her into a discussion about how beautiful a man this Mayor Koch was, but Shelly was too tired to do anything but agree.

Mickey greeted her warmly. At the door, his body became an envelope for hers and she slipped inside his arms, knowing before she got there how good it would feel. He asked her if she minded if he watched the rest of the game. There was only ten minutes to go. She knew that that was a trick. She had learned years ago that ten minutes meant ten minutes of playing time and that could take a good twenty to twenty-five minutes. She didn't mind. Did he mind if she lay down on his bed? She just wanted to give in to her exhaustion for a while. He didn't mind. She made it perfectly clear that a short rest would rejuvenate her. She wanted more of him and wanted him to know that she wasn't gone for the night. She vaguely remembered that this was the eighteenth, a good time to conceive, and she wasn't about to waste the night with exhaustion. She told herself to stay awake, but she fell into one of those deep sleeps reserved for the very tired. When she opened her eyes Mickey was standing over her. She hadn't heard him whisper her name so she thought he had been watching her sleep. This embarrassed her because she was sure she had been drooling. She wiped her mouth and was relieved not to feel excess moisture. She pulled down her skirt just in case there was too much thigh showing.

Mickey looked taller from Shelly's angle. Although his head usually was a little lower than hers, now it looked as if it were touching the ceiling. She liked him towering over her. The one thing she always managed to warn her family about was that he was a petite man. "He's very successful," she would add quickly, as if that would forgive his lack of height. It was a case of one kind of stature covering for another.

She lay there, too tired to talk, and appreciated this new heightened Mickey. "You fell asleep," he said, telling her nothing she didn't already know. She was too tired to tell him she knew, so she just shook her head and waited to wake up. Had she been awake she would have nodded once, maybe twice. Since she was in that twilight area, her head didn't stop nodding in agreement.

He must have told her what he was going to do. He wouldn't have just left. They must have had some plan for Shelly to sleep on the single bed in Mickey's place and for him to go down to 3C. She never heard any arrangements. She just slept again and didn't wake up until eleven-thirty, when she really woke up, having had one of those deep naps that can refresh someone in her thirties for days.

She looked for Mickey and felt abandoned when she couldn't find him. His bathroom door was closed and she knocked on it, hoping he was inside. The first knock caused the door to open, and she saw he wasn't there. She walked through the entire apartment and got upset once again over the trash he called kitsch and the unpacked boxes. She yelled his name over and over again and was surprised that he wasn't there. After her stockinged feet kicked away three dustballs, she decided to go downstairs. She carried her shoes, bag and coat, and was reminded of unpleasant times when she left men's apartments in the middle of the night because it had taken her until the middle of the night to realize that she didn't like them or they didn't like her. Sometimes it was snoring or unclean sleeping conditions that drove her away, but mostly it was realizations.

Unfortunately she met one of the sixteen tenants' rights lawyers in the elevator. He was on his way out to walk a dog too large for anything but a ranch. A year ago they wouldn't have spoken to each other, but now that they had fought on the same side and won, they felt an obligation to inquire about each other's well-being. "How's your apartment working out?" he asked, which was, of course, one of the strangest questions ever asked. Her apartment had been her apartment for several years before the conversion, and she had never thought of it as working or not working. Dishwashers sometimes caved in. Apartments were homes. They couldn't exactly break down.

"It's working out great," said Shelly, watching the numbers overhead. "How about you? You glad you bought?" They were only at the ninth floor. He had time to answer.

"I hear the co-op market is going soft. *New York Magazine* says it's going to drop thirty percent this year, and the real estate experts at the firm are predicting it will even go lower. Who knew it would go this soft so fast?"

Shelly was angry at this loud man with his big dog. There he was, smiling as he told her her only piece of real estate was going into the toilet. She wondered what had made him so sadistic at such a late hour. Fortunately the third floor was coming up fast.

Not fast enough. Before she could get through the swiftly closing door, he managed to yell at her back, "Your boyfriend bought one too, didn't he?" She never got a chance even to gesture because the elevator protected him. She hoped the dog would do the right thing and pee on his owner's shoes.

She stood at her apartment door before going in. She promised herself that she wouldn't propose. She was wide awake and it was always dangerous when she wasn't sleepy after the eleven o'clock news. Some of her worst conversations got started because she couldn't fall asleep.

She fished into her purse for her keys. She had wanted an uncluttered bag, but she always ended up with one that had more garbage in it than any of her wastebaskets. When she didn't land her keys on the first two tries, she considered that her failure was due to the unfairness of chances. Her keys were, after all, small, while her garbage content was large. She had already hit three used, balled-up tissues. She shook the bag for key sounds and, not hearing any, panicked. Not only had she bought a co-op for more than its market value, she was locked out of it.

She hit the doorbell. It was unlikely that Lucinda had slept over since she stayed only when Shelly begged her to, but it was worth trying. Her nails were too long for doorbells, so she used a knuckle to ring. Her ring was answered, and there stood Mickey, totally naked, dripping water on her Oriental with his toothbrush in his hand. She had an immediate question: "How did you get in?" The second question—"How did you know it was me?"—never got asked. Not everything she learned in college was forgotten: during four years at Michigan, she had gotten used to nakedness.

"Your keys were in your pocketbook," he answered. She felt invaded. Here was a man with whom she was willing to be naked, have a child and marry. She didn't want him in her pocketbook, not only because there was old tissue around, but because a man didn't belong there. He had raped her closest possession. He was also getting too much water on the Oriental.

As he dried off, Mickey explained that he figured she was asleep for the night and that he would stay at her place. Now that she was alive, well and turning on the television, he could go back upstairs. It was her job not to let him go. She knew she was hours away from sleep and probably ovulating. Since he wasn't making any romantic moves, she would have to do the seducing. She didn't feel romantic—Ted Koppel was talking to some Russian about underground testing—but Shelly had a job to do. Since there was a man to arouse and a baby to get, she turned off Ted, turned on a movie with subtitles, got the lighting down, herself showered, the wine opened, the bayberry candle lit, the pillows off the bed and the sex going. It was one of those nights when she had to be the aggressor, which was not her most comfortable role. In high school her job was to keep from having a rotten reputation. You could pet to climax with no more than three boys, and in your senior year sleep with one over the summer vacation before college if you really loved him, but you always had to be the one who was pursued. If you had to put your hands on him first, it meant only one thing: You weren't pretty enough.

On this night the laying on of hands was up to Shelly. Mickey behaved as if he didn't know what was happening and he continued to watch *El Norte* even with an erection. Since this was an important erection to her, as it contained her future family, Shelly let him continue to watch. The pursuit was more tiring than the cocktail party had been, but what the hell, he had something she needed and she was willing to work for it.

He wasn't totally disinterested; it was more like a seventy-five, twenty-five split that kept her hanging in there. She knew the position that they would have intercourse in would be solely up to her, and she generously tried to think of something that wouldn't block his view of the television. He was pretending not to watch, but she knew he was into the movie. This wasn't the first time they had made love with the television on. Sometimes it just happened to be on and they just happened to be making love. It only interfered one night when she laughed at something on *Letterman*, ruining any chances of a climax. She realized this time that she had made a very bad decision with *El Norte*. She learned that the one thing you shouldn't leave on is a movie with subtitles. Position was much more important than lust. Since she couldn't think of one that would be considerate for both of them, she chose something traditional, not knowing that Mickey knew enough Spanish to follow along.

The sex was quiet. On this night he wasn't going to have to take a shower when they were through. Shelly made all the important moves. The most important was trying to roll him on top of her. He resisted. She tried again and this time the resistance was even stronger. "Didn't you forget something?" he asked. In all fairness to Mickey Burke, it must be said that he tried to have a romantic tone in his voice. Actually, he whispered the question directly into her ear, making every effort not to break the spell they might be having.

Shelly was not exactly lost in the arms of passion. Still, she was puzzled by the question. She interpreted it as having forgotten to do something to him. The erection was still there. What could she have possibly forgotten? There weren't exactly rule books for these moments. She ran over the list. She had remembered to touch, kiss and lick. As far as she knew, everything regarding foreplay had been taken care of. "I can't think of anything," she said. Her whisper was as seductive as his. They were both committed to hanging on to the mood.

"Your diaphragm." He kissed her on the neck, letting her know that she hadn't made a serious mistake. She feigned surprise and looked down as if she could see her diaphragm from there.

"Oh my God. You're right. I'll be right back." One of the things Shelly hated most was getting out of bed naked and walking across the room. She never missed her clothes while she was lying down. It was the naked parade that made her feel uneasy. Even in college, when naked was the statement to make, Shelly had held on to as much modesty as she could. She always tended to hang around the bedspreads.

If she grabbed a pillow for protection, she would lose the image of the free woman she had worked to create. Therefore she chose to back out of bed, preferring to give him that view over the rear one. She told him three times that she would be right back. Mickey didn't think that he was losing his woman to the bathroom, but he said "good" three times just to let her know that he would be happy to see her again.

As she smeared jelly on that small rubber circle that was keeping her from tricking the comedy writer in her bed, she cursed contraception. Up to now she had blessed it. "Thank God I can be in control of my body," she had said more than once, especially at times when she felt in control of nothing else. Now she wanted the freedom of not stopping sperm. It was more than ever her own, private body, and she wanted it to manufacture the family she craved. She knew, of course, that the jig was up with Mickey. Unless she could convince him that she was safe at certain times, she would always have to come to bed prepared not to conceive.

She hurried back into bed, pretending to be frisky rather than modest. The sex couldn't be great that night. He was preoccupied and she was sad. The best thing for both of them was to get it over quickly, but not to let each other know that was the objective. They pulled it off by rushing through the sex portion and clinging to each other afterward.

She watched him watch the end of the movie and then she watched him get ready for bed. He had this little ritual that he performed before going to sleep, none of it attractive. He blew his nose whether he needed to or not. He punched his pillows, testing their firmness, as if the pillows were capable of tightening up overnight and on their own. Next he looked at his feet, inspecting the bottoms and the toenails. He was relieved every night to find his feet in acceptable condition. Before he turned out the light, he tested the mattress as if he were buying it. Satisfied, he turned out the light and got into bed. He never had trouble falling asleep.

Shelly always did. She was jealous if the man in her bed was resting peacefully. She knew it was dangerous to talk in the dark. Some of her most hostile conversations happened with the lights out, maybe because she felt unattached to her voice in a darkened room. "Good night," he said, expecting to sleep. There was no way that he could see how wide Shelly's eyes were open in the dark.

"Can I ask you something?" she asked. Mickey had learned not to be happy with those five words. They had led to long, disturbing hours with sentences that began with, "I feel what I really need is . . ." They had already gone through the hint conversation, the commitment conversation more than once, the proposals and the "Do-you-really-love-me-because-if-you-did-you-wouldn't-ignore-me-like-you-do" nights.

"What do you want to know?" he asked, feeling this wasn't going to be a conversation about San Salvador, although their bed would feel wartorn.

"I want to know about us," she said. He knew "knowing about us" would be at least a couple of hours. The illuminated dial told him it was a quarter to one. By three they might be calm again.

"What about us?" He earnestly wanted to know. To him all was well.

"I don't know . . . I just feel . . . I guess I need to feel safe."

"What'll it take?" asked Mickey, opening negotiations. She knew it would take marriage. The trick was getting him there. It was a simple case of his being happy with the way things were and her needing rings on her fingers. She wished his question hadn't been so direct and that he hadn't yawned after asking it.

"Marriage," she said, proposing again. She knew now more than ever that she had a real habit. Since she had mingled something about marriage in among her good-byes before the cocktail party, this time she had gone just a little short of ten hours. The disease was spreading in her.

"The idea of marriage gives me hives," he said, with all good intentions. It was a line that he had used before, and it happened to be absolutely true. The day after his first and only marriage, he got a serious rash. Everybody but Mickey and his mother thought it was funny. He scratched during his honeymoon. His selfish wife tried to make him feel better by pointing out that "at least we took the pictures for the album before you broke out."

When the hives were still there a week after the wedding, it occurred to Mickey that he might be allergic to his wife and marriage. The doctor he went to in Hawaii, a Jewish man in his forties who had given up his wife, his children and New Jersey for the pleasures of Maui, wanted to do a battery of tests on Mickey.

Since he had always thought that he might be allergic to tomatoes and this seemed like a good time to find out, he didn't mind spending time at the clinic. He wasn't a beach person and he wasn't a good relaxer. He never could stand the idea of sipping sweet drinks with umbrellas in them.

As it turned out he wasn't allergic to anything but animal feathers. He was instructed to check out the contents of any pillow he might come in contact with and dismissed from the doctor's care. The timing was great. Dr. Finestein decided to go scuba diving for a couple of weeks and was closing up shop.

The hives disappeared, fading away slowly as he got used to sharing a sink with the woman he had pledged to love forever. Since he had told Shelly the story once before, on another proposal night, there was no need to repeat it.

"I know the top allergist in the city," Shelly said, trying to keep things light. They both knew the tears were inevitable, but they didn't have to start yet. He hadn't yet said a definite no.

"What will it take besides marriage?"

"I don't know. I'm scared."

"I'm scared too. The whole world is scared. That's why they escape by watching television and I have an opportunity to work." She didn't care to hear about the world, television or work. It amazed her to hear Mickey say he was scared. She liked it. She also wanted to nurture him into a place where he would never be scared again.

"You're not scared." She recognized the intonation in her voice. It was her father's. She was six years old and had just seen a monster outside her bedroom window for the hundredth time. Rather than comfort her, her father had told her she wasn't scared, exactly as she had just told Mickey.

"Sure I am."

"Not about me." Men had loved her. She had never made one shaky.

"Yes. About you. What if you go to a party some night and fall for some guy and the next thing I know we're having one of those talks about how we could be friends for the rest of our lives."

"It doesn't make sense. If you don't feel a hundred-percent secure and here we are supposedly in love, we should just get married." There it was. The record for the two quickest proposals yet.

"Marriage wouldn't make me feel one-hundred-percent secure. I was married. She walked out on me and we never had to divide the wedding presents because we threw them at each other."

"Why do I have to pay for her rotten attitude?"

"Because when I think of marriage, I think of ducking."

"So I don't get it. What are we to each other?"

"We're together." She would never learn that a man felt if he showed up, that meant everything.

"I know we're together. So how do I introduce you—as the man I'm together with?"

"Is that the problem, fear of introduction? Introduce me as your beloved." He squeezed the hand of hers that he held. It was his job to make her feel as secure as possible without having to get a rash.

"Come on, Mickey." This conversation was not new to their relationship. They had gone over the same questions and answers before. Mickey minded the loss of sleep. Shelly minded not getting what she wanted.

"Come on, what?" She never knew what. She was looking for labels and he wasn't giving her any.

"Would you say we have a commitment to each other?" Since they had done the script before, they both knew that the 'c' word was going to be part of this conversation.

"Yes." He wanted to qualify it with the words "for now" but he didn't want the light to come through the window before this discussion was over.

"What would you say that commitment was?" Her tone was not unlike the ones the panelists used on *What's My Line?* The show of the eighties could be *What's My Commitment?* Would you sign in, please, Mr. Burke. In case you don't know our rules, our panel here is allowed to ask you questions. They can keep asking as they get yeses. Should they get a no they lose their turn and, well, you know the rest. Should you rack up enough yeses, Mr. Burke, there's a good chance that you might find yourself married.

"What should I say that commitment was?" He repeated her question in order to buy time. This commitment talk was tricky. You had, at the exact same instant, to say words that didn't hurt the opposition and yet didn't have you renting a tuxedo. "The commitment is to each other. I'm not going anywhere. I'm not seeing anyone else." This came out sounding rehearsed. In a way, it was. He had said it many times before, as often as the question had been asked. He still wanted to add "for now" but didn't dare, fearing the hysteria it might cause.

"Yeah, but what about the future?" The thing about these questions that most impressed Mickey was how they built in intensity. Each one needed a deeper breath than the one before.

"Who can read the future? If I knew what was going to happen, I'd give up television and get into the stock market." The trick here was for her to get to the specific at the same time he was trying to deal with the general.

"I'm not talking about television and stocks. I'm talking about us. I guess what I'm really asking is, do we have a commitment for the future?" This, of course, was just another way of asking him to marry her. She realized that by now she was chain-proposing.

"We have a commitment for as far as I can see," said Mickey, thinking he was doing a good job of dancing around the answers and being poetic at the same time.

Shelly put on the light on her side of the bed because she wanted Mickey to see how distressed she was. They were still at the early enough stages of the relationship when distressed looks helped. He might eventually grow tired of them. Probably, he would grow tired of them. He might someday even hate her tears if they came often enough. Now, he still kissed them away. The light would definitely help. "If you can't see us breaking up and I can't see us breaking up, what difference does it make if we make it legal?"

"What difference does it make if we don't?" There in the light, she could see he was getting weary.

"Well, for one thing, what about kids?"

"We don't have any."

"You know what I mean, future unborn ones." They had talked about children before, but it had been as responsible citizens who were grown-up enough to talk about having children. Their feelings about it were close to the ones expressed in "Tea for Two." Although they were too modern for a girl for you, a boy for me, they had decided they wanted one of each.

"I thought that was happening later." To Mickey, children were something you created for television shows when you needed them. He had never spent time with a real kid.

"It could." She didn't want to use the biological argument. It always made her feel old, like her insides were about to dry up. "But it could happen now. I have all these normal reactions to you. I really trust them, Mickey. I spent too many years trying to believe that there was another way to live. For years, all I cared about was leaving my options open. Now I don't care about options. I care about marriage licenses and babies, and if you told me that I would have to move to Baltimore, I would move to Baltimore."

"I swear I'll never make you move across water."

"You better swear you'll never tell anybody what I'm really like. I'm not real proud of it."

"I like what you're like." He kissed her finger to prove his words.

"Yeah, well, I don't. I was supposed to be strong and independent and stand on my own two feet. The man in my life was supposed to be the frosting on a cake, not a loaf of bread that I can't live without. I never thought I would be begging anybody to marry me." Here's where the tears flowed. Not the delicate ones that make movie stars look good, but large tears that make real people look puffy.

"Don't worry about it." He knew the words were weak compared to her crying. His instinct was to tell her that he would do anything she wanted so that she could feel safe. His past life wouldn't let the words escape.

"I'm just so weak," she sobbed. "We, all my friends and I, were so happy when we realized that we had become like the men we wanted to marry, and now look, I'm willing to move south and have a garbage disposal."

"Maybe you're just tired."

"You're damn right I'm tired. I'm tired of my whole life being catering. I'm tired of canapés and hostesses pretending they stuffed the Cornish game hens themselves. I'm tired of my friends making fun of getting married. You know why? They do it anyway. They laugh at how dumb it is to be a bride and they go out and buy the longest, whitest dresses they can find. I'm really tired of feeling other women's stomachs for their fetuses' kicks. I don't want to be a good sport anymore. I don't want to be just political anymore." With this she fell into his arms. The gesture said, "Take care of me." And he did, for the moment. He held her.

Since he didn't know what to say, his arms spoke for him. He felt if he held her long enough, he wouldn't need words. He didn't for the next minute and a half, which is a very long time when two people with different points of view are talking in bed.

"I can get somebody to hate me," said Shelly softly. Her voice was tired, not only from this night but from every other conversation that she had like this.

"No," said Mickey, sure that was what she wanted him to say, and just to make sure she heard him, he added a second no.

"Yes. I've done this before. I can't shut up. Have I reminded you recently about herpes?"

"Three conversations ago."

"Well, it's true, you know. People who are married don't get it. I don't care what *Time* says. It's really hard, or maybe impossible, to get from toilet seats. All I'm saying is that, in this day and age, it's safer to be married." And then she rushed to throw in. "Not to mention AIDS. It's really dangerous out there, Mickey. I'm not saying that's the only reason to get married, but if you don't there's a hell of a chance that you could die."

"What about if you just commit to another person, and you just sleep with that one person? Are you still subject to those terrible diseases?"

"Okay, so no, but it's a known fact that married men live longer. I swear I either read that or saw it on *Donahue*, probably both. It's becoming a well-known fact."

"What if they have a miserable marriage?"

"That probably doesn't have anything to do with the basic statistics."

"Yeah, but who wants to live longer if you're not happy doing it?"

With this she sat up in bed, bringing the covers with her. No matter how angry she was, she wasn't about to make quick, uncovered moves while naked. "Are you trying to tell me that you wouldn't be that happy doing it?"

"I was referring to 'them,' the average man." Mickey closed his eyes. She hoped he was tired rather than exasperated.

"I don't know," she said. She was still sitting, her head resting against the fabric headboard, her arms crossed in front of her, her life not pulling together in the way she had hoped it would. Shelly would have let the argument go if she could. She probably hadn't become the head of a successful business by letting arguments go. It was against her nature to turn out the lights and go to sleep before winning. She would have liked to have been a more peaceful person, but winning had always been more natural to her than sleeping.

"I don't think this is going to work," she said, exhaling as if she had been smoking.

"What?"

"This arrangement. I really can't go on like this. Look, we're at different places in this relationship and I guess it's because deep down, where it really counts, I love you more than you love me." The tears started again about here. She was scared and she was already lonely thinking of the nights when Mickey wouldn't be there to annoy. "I mean, I know we could go on like this for another few months, with my pushing for marriage and you dancing around it, but what's the point? We might as well just end it now. I don't want to be with someone who doesn't want me as much as I want him. Eventually, we'll be so frustrated with each other we won't be able to live in the same building, and I don't know about you, but I don't want to sell my co-op in a soft real estate market." She was terrified. Although she had known the ultimatum would eventually come, she hadn't planned on it happening so soon.

Women don't realize the reason ultimatums never work. Women miss the men they've been with right away. The emptiness is immediate. Men, who have had to get used to going to war for centuries, don't miss their women until they need them again.

# 14
## The Down Side
## of Ultimatums

SHELLY'S entire body cried. She sat on her bed with pretzels and tissues and mourned everything bad that had ever happened to her. Nothing was as bad as losing Mickey. He had been a gentleman. He understood that she couldn't see him anymore. He didn't want to cause her any pain, he said. He told her they shouldn't worry about bumping into each other. His feelings hadn't changed, he said. She knew where to find him. I'm sorry and good-bye. He said all of this while wearily dressing to go back to 14D. He sat at the edge of the bed and talked with his back toward her. He did eventually turn around, and he zipped his fly while saying good-bye. She felt that zip was the end of an era.

She let him go and then, less than ten minutes later, she followed him upstairs, banged on his door and begged for forgiveness. She knew her pride had left her, but she didn't care. She wanted him back. Please. Please. Please. Each please took a long time to say because it was drawn out to its full meaning. No. He felt her original instincts were best. They should give it a rest.

No. She didn't want to. She wanted things the way they were before she started all the trouble. She knew that someday she would be humiliated by this scene (she almost got on her knees once), but right now she wanted Mickey back. No. They should just both go to sleep. Go to sleep? Was he crazy, how could a person sleep when she had just lost a whole person? If he would just come downstairs, she would promise to be quiet. She needed him tonight. No. She could stay up there if she wanted, but he had to get to sleep. He had to work in a few hours. Work? Didn't he understand that something had died? How could he work in the midst of such mourning?

He told her to go to sleep. She was right. Things would not have worked out between them. Eventually, she would have hated him for not giving her what she wanted. "I hate you now!" she screamed, and immediately afterward kissed his hands, saying she could never hate him and to please, please come downstairs. No. And he got into his selfish little single bed, leaving her the choice of his couch or going home. She slept on his floor, thinking that he would rescue her. He told her not to, offering his bed, which she wouldn't take, and the couch, which she said was too far away. She said she felt like a dog and she might as well rest like one.

She cried harder, and he was so worn out he couldn't help going to sleep. His last words to her were, "You're a great girl. Some guy would be lucky to marry you." And her last words to him were, "I hope you have to get up and go to the bathroom in the middle of the night and trip over me. Then at least we will be on the floor together." She didn't tell him that she hoped he would break his leg because a man in a cast would be easier to deal with. While she nursed him back to health, he would fall in love with her again.

"I love you," she mumbled into the rug that Mrs. Schimmel had left behind.

Shelly didn't sleep that night. She prayed for something she could never have. She asked God to turn the clocks back to before the ultimatum. There had to be something wrong with her. How could she have said such brave sentences and then grovel on the floor?

"Do you think I haven't degraded myself?" asked Greta. She had come to comfort. Greta had come flying. She actually did, once again, resemble a large bird as she came through the door in a bright blue cape and a blue and lavender feather combination in her hair. Greta announced spring like no calendar could.

"Not you." Misery did love company. It was twelve hours since the ultimatum, and Shelly was a little cheered by the thought of Greta's degradation.

"Of course I have. I've done all the disgusting gestures. I think I kissed a guy's feet. Funny, I do remember kissing his feet, but I can't remember now whose feet they were. That is so weird. I mean, you have to admit it's a pretty big, disgusting thing to do. I remember what the feet look like as if it were yesterday, but I have no idea who stood above those ankles."

"I slept on his floor like a dog."

"That's a minor one. I've slept on floors. You think they're going to lift you up to the bed, but they don't. They were all Boy Scouts, and this floor business is no big deal to them."

"I begged," said Shelly, "with my hands at prayer like a little Catholic girl."

"Begging is small stuff. So is threatening suicide. You know what's big?" Thank God for Greta, she could turn anything into a quiz show.

"What?"

"I have humiliated myself in front of an Arab."

"I don't believe you."

"Ask my mother. She still refers to it as my trashiest hour. Whenever I get mad at her for doing something and we're really going at it, she reminds me of the time that the Arab was on his way back to Kuwait and I got in a cab and followed his limo out to the airport. He had a limo and an eighteen-karat gold Patek Philippe watch and well-dressed men with gorgeous attaché cases around him. Where the hell were my politics?" Greta stopped here. She hadn't expected to feel any old pain or anger. Her only intention had been to cheer up her friend. But there they were, old emotions, this time in her stomach rather than her heart. "Goddamn him," Greta couldn't help saying. "I was twenty-five. He was forty-two. He was the first man to take me to really expensive restaurants. I had thought I was above being seduced by money, but I didn't know then that I was really a middle-class kid from Riverdale. He was also the first man to tell me he loved me. Remember ten, twelve years ago how everybody used to love the universe, but we had trouble loving one person? I mean I could tell a whole park of people that I loved them, but I didn't dare just tell one guy. The deal was to make love and move on. If you didn't, you just weren't hip enough, and I wanted to be the hippest kid on the block. The Arab told me he loved me, maybe a thousand times in four months. I know that if they say it too much, it's not worth anything. Don't ever trust a guy who tells you he loves you more than every other day." Greta was getting ready to smoke. She collected her smoking gear, the gold case that she had bought at auction at Parke-Bernet, the gold lighter from a grateful lover. (Shelly couldn't remember having a grateful lover.) She got the Gauloise from her purse and then reached into the bottom drawer of Shelly's end table, knowing that was where the ashtray was kept. She had started smoking to look sophisticated and had made it into an art form. She knew the story she was telling was juicy and wanted to tell it under the most flattering conditions. That meant smoking Gauloises back to back.

Even in her pain, Shelly enjoyed this moment. During her intense time with Mickey, she had had to give up time with Greta. Girlfriends understood these separations and they were used to traveling in and out of each other's lives. There were times, when relationships were beginning, that patient girlfriends had to step aside and be content with late-night phone calls that were one-sided. The woman in love had time only to recount the good things that were happening to her and to express her fears that it all might end. During the last few months, Greta had realized that Shelly's second job was Mickey. Shelly had done the same for her when she graciously put her personal life aside to hear about the exterminator. Although she hated losing Mickey, it was great being with Greta. She wanted her to stop smoking and start talking about Arabs again.

"I managed to get through his bodyguards while they were checking in the luggage."

"He had bodyguards?"

"Yeah. Sure. I mean they were called associates, but they probably had orders to kill."

"How did you meet him?" They both knew the details were unimportant and they both knew that time heals. If Shelly could buy some healing time by asking questions, her good friend Greta was willing to cooperate.

"I was working as an assistant buyer at Bergdorf's in small leather goods, and he came in to buy wallets for all of Kuwait. He paid in cash with thousand-dollar bills. All that flashy stuff. As he was waiting for everything to be packaged, he asked me out. He was dark and handsome, not tall, and I tried to pretend that he wasn't an Arab. I was only twenty-five, so after the first time we slept together, I started to fantasize about how our getting together would help the entire Middle East situation."

"Was he good in bed?"

"Yeah. Once we did it on a table, and he said I cleansed his palate. That and the telling me he loved me impressed me. My mother was impressed with the restaurants he took me to. But I told her he was a Baptist. She was on the phone every day telling me that she was trying to be liberal, but my boyfriend's religion was gnawing at her and she wasn't going to tell my father because it would kill him. She let me know that he would have to convert before I brought him home for her noodle pudding. The funny thing is, I tried to get him to convert. I really believed we could be a nice couple with a duplex on Fifth Avenue and it would be easier on my parents if he was Jewish."

"And he wouldn't?"

"He laughed at me. I remember him pouring scotch in his suite at the Pierre and laughing whenever I mentioned anything real. I could be talking about Jewish law, or the clothes I hoped to design or Vietnam, and he would throw his head back and laugh. While it was back there, he downed the scotch. I didn't realize for a long time after he went back to Kuwait that we probably had a language barrier. I think he laughed every time he didn't understand what I was saying."

"So you followed him to the airport." Considering her own circumstances, Shelly was really anxious to get to the really humiliating part.

"Yeah, but he kept waving me off. He really didn't want to know from me, and the men around him kept closing in. They walked in this fast, tight group, and I kept running after them. I swear I don't know how those heroines in movies run in their tight skirts and their high heels because I was doing a lousy job of it. I found him on the steps going up to the lounge, and I just kept yelling, 'Please,' I'm not even sure please what. Probably I just needed to have some good-bye scene since the bum just told me not to come up to his suite that day because he was on his way back to his country." Here Greta simulated her bum's accent. Shelly smiled. The story was worth a laugh; Greta was working hard, but since Shelly was suffering, it didn't get one.

"You were probably just saying, 'Please don't leave me.' " Shelly had said those exact words to Mickey's door when she pounded on it and didn't get an answer.

"Yeah. Exactly, but I got down on my knees to say it. I needed the drama. I was looking for my *Casablanca* scene, but I was doing it with zero class. End of story."

"Did he ever get married?"

"Are you kidding? He probably has a hefty harem by now." Greta sat down and rested. She smiled and Shelly smiled back. Her story deserved applause. It was an excellent fairy tale.

"Was that true?"

"Yes. Except that he wasn't royalty, he was an Arab schlepper working in the shoe department. There was no limo, and the steps were nowhere near the VIP lounge. I knelt on the steps leading up to his apartment on West Twentieth."

"Were you going to let me believe the other version?"

"Well, to tell you the truth, I've used this story on heartbroken friends before. The real version is so degrading that it's hard to let out right away. To answer your question, yes, I definitely would have told you the truth within the next twenty-four hours. I ease into it with the more princely version for my own sake."

Now Shelly felt a need to cheer up Greta, who was remembering too much. She flipped through her past relationships as if they were on index cards in her mind. She pulled a good one. "I once fought over a bisexual . . . with a man."

"No."

"Yes. We both wanted him. When he saw I wasn't going to fold, he cried. And when he cried, I cried, which was totally crazy because the guy we were crying over was this really bad sculptor, and I think he was enjoying being fought over. Neither one of us backed down, even though my opponent promised to introduce me to a dozen straight men in exchange for giving up our mutual lover. He kept insisting that it would be easier for me to find true love than he, because he was a homosexual who only liked men who could also love women." She saw that Greta was liking this. "Is that humiliating enough?"

"Oh. Yes. Definitely. Fighting for bisexuals is always good stuff. What happened?"

"The guy that we were fighting over got disgusted with both of us and threw us both out. We got into the same elevator. In Hollywood, they would have had us go out for coffee and start a family."

"Humiliation is my middle name," said Greta. "I was once willing to give up all my human rights for a stockbroker with old-world values, and I was a member of the S.D.S." Both women took the time to remember the forgotten promises they had made to themselves. Greta recovered first. "How much you want to bet I end up wrapping myself around the exterminator's legs and begging him to stay?"

"Not you."

"Yes, me. I'll do the same thing you did, without the proposing. One day I'll get tired of being scared to take him to parties. Did I tell you somebody else recognized him? Sylvie Lamon actually put in a complaint in front of me. She told Hank that the ants he annihilated were back. There she is, the snot, blaming my boyfriend for her dirty housekeeping. And he says that he'll take care of it first thing Monday morning. I don't have to tell you that I have ants in my kitchen that he doesn't have time for. Anyway, the day will come when I'll tell him to get lost, probably because my ants have gotten together to spell out SCHMUCK, and then I'll go crawling to New Jersey, begging him to come back."

"And I'll be there to help you through."

"I know you will. That's the deal, isn't it? We get to hold each other's heads while we vomit out old boyfriends."

"I wish I could throw him up. It would be great flushing him down the toilet." With these words, Shelly lifted the receiver and dialed. Had someone who had never seen a phone before watched this procedure, he would have thought the instrument was very heavy. "He's not there," she said after the eleventh ring. Some psychic had once told her that her master number was eleven, so that's the number she went for in troubled times.

"Maybe he's at the office."

"I tried the office. I tried Jerry's. I tried the hotel. I tried his mother in Miami. That was an embarrassing call. She said she had heard so much about me. So now she knows her son doesn't love me because if he did, I would know where he was."

At this point Greta reached for her jacket and Shelly panicked.

Greta had at least calmed her. Once she left, the hyperventilating might start again. And Shelly was out of control, with a Sara Lee banana cake in the refrigerator.

"Why are you leaving?" Shelly asked, like a frightened child whose mother was leaving her with a strange babysitter.

"I've got a million things to do." Shelly became frightened. She too had a million things to do but was totally incapable of doing them.

"I thought I could make us dinner." Shelly knew that wasn't going to seduce Greta into staying. Dinner worked only with a hungry man.

"Thanks anyway." Greta was wrapping a twelve-foot scarf around her neck. It was amazing how she could get it to do what she wanted it to. She worked not unlike a snake charmer.

"How did we get so desperate?" Shelly said, to stop her friend from leaving.

"I don't know."

"My material side is much more happy with life than my radical side. I tried to stay on top of things, but I'm not even sure about what's going on in San Salvador."

"I'm never going to another fund-raiser because I'm scared I'm going to give money to the wrong side."

"I really was going to save the world, and now I throw a lot of food out."

"I was going to live with a black man, but I never even went out with one."

"Maybe we should get the transcripts from *Nightline*. I would actually be embarrassed to meet Ted Koppel. I'd have to go all the way back and talk about my college scars. Participating in the lockout was the last relevant thing I did."

"As soon as we get our husbands and children, we'll have the time to be enlightened again. We'll make a better world when we're relaxed enough to do it."

"And I'll cater it."

"Right. You can't fight city hall and want to get married in it at the same time."

Shelly would have paid Greta to stay if she could have. She thought there should be some service for grieving women. All it would take was being a good listener and an ability to top the bereaved with horror stories of one's own. If you worked up half a dozen good ones, you could use them over and over. One well-placed ad in *New York Magazine* would do it.

After Greta left, Shelly managed to find the strength to get at the banana cake. When she was younger she used to trick herself into thinking that she wasn't going to eat the whole thing. At thirty-seven she didn't have the energy to trick herself. The whole cake came to bed with her. She lay there with it on her stomach, knowing that she was minutes away from devouring it. She minded the calories and hated the self-destruction, but there was no stopping the flow.

When she had finished scraping the icing from the box, she used her sticky finger to call Mickey again and again. He wasn't home or, if he was home, he was hiding out. Since Greta wasn't home and there was no other friend or relative she wanted to hear her shaky voice, she called Bloomingdale's. The entire time she dialed, she prayed that Paula would be there.

"I'll see if she's still here," the uninterested woman on the line said. Shelly supposed these women worked on commission and hoped the phone was for them. Time spent looking for another salesgirl was time spent away from their own customers. She hung on, sure that her life would never pull together again if Paula wasn't there. She made the mistake of making it into a superstition. She told herself that if Paula was there, that everything would be all right between her and Mickey. It was just a matter of her trying to get an immediate answer to the question of her destiny.

"Hello, Paula here." Thank God.

"Hi. It's Shelly Silver."

"What can I do for you, dear?" The "dear" was said coldly. Paula had never been a friendly woman and never led Shelly to believe that she cared about her in any way. Paula was the voice of New York.

"Are the Donna Karan body suits to size?"

"Yes. Pretty much."

"I thought they might run a little large. Isn't Karan a large woman?"

"I don't know her exact size. It's reported that she's big-boned, yes." Paula's attitude was protective of the designer rather than her faithful customer.

"I'd like one in charcoal gray . . ." Shelly had been about to say "in a medium" when she saw the Sara Lee carton. She thought the medium might hurt and she told Paula that she wanted the large because it would give her plenty of room.

"You want to hang on while I see if I have one?"

"No. No. That's okay. If you have it, just send it out." Shelly didn't want to lose Paula for the length of time it would take to look.

"You want the wraparound skirt that she did with them?" Shelly understood that the "she" was Donna Karan.

"Sure."

"I'll see if I have your size when I check on the body suit."

At this point Shelly figured she had bought a little time from Paula. She felt entitled to some conversation. "Let me ask you something," she began. She imagined the impatience going on at the other end of the line. Paula was the type of woman who rolled her eyes toward heaven. "What's happening this season?"

Paula didn't have to think about it. She knew what was happening in the same way that Shelly knew that Thai was out and Tex-Mex was in. "You substitute day for night." Since there were customers waiting, she wasn't about to go into a lengthy explanation, but she did add, "Don't be afraid to wear your velvets during the day and your tweeds at night. Silver accessories."

Shelly wasn't going to let her go that easily. The average woman would have spent some time trying on the clothes she had just ordered. This new information was important and confusing. Life was difficult enough with Mickey leaving and not returning her calls. She didn't need anyone dropping bombs about her velvet. "I don't understand," she pleaded.

Paula's speech was slow and slightly disgusted. She was going to spell it out for the idiot who relied on her for fashion trends. "Look, dear, it's very simple. You wear your glitz during the day. Take out your pearls, long chains, your big earrings. Don't be scared of rhinestones on denim. Think cocktail party. Put your lace under leather, if you know what I mean. Then at night you can't lose in a simple jersey whatever. Unless it's black tie, and then you pull out all the stops. Don't forget a silver shoe."

"Day for night?" Shelly asked.

"Exactly, dear. Nice talking to you."

Well, it's been horrible talking to you, Paula. You have cost me money and confused me. I like my velvet at night.

Shelly tried Mickey's number, ate an entire bag of beer pretzels, made brownies, ate three of them before they were ready, looked for something salty, ate peanut butter on rye toast, cried in the bathtub, called Mickey, tried to watch *Nightline* but found it annoying that Ms. Kirkpatrick's head was projected on a screen, making it appear one and a half times the size of Mr. Koppel's, and that it looked ridiculous that these two very different-sized heads were talking to each other, called Mickey and wrote Mickey a letter.

Dear Mickey,

You're the writer so I feel strange expressing myself with words, but here goes. I'll try to be brave about this. (I mean, not about our separation, but about writing my thoughts down.) I am so sorry about what happened the other night. Even though I had napped, I was very tired, and to say the least, I was stressed out. I had had a bad experience at work, and I'm not feeling that good. Nothing serious. I think I'm retaining water and, when I get bloated, I tend to get irritable. I promise that if we can please get together that this "problem" will never happen again. I know now not to push anything.

Mickey, I love you and I think you love me. It's really silly to ruin everything just because I got crazy one night. Please at least call so we can talk about it.

Forever yours,<br>Shelly

She never sent the letter. She crossed out the "bloat" section because it was unflattering and she decided she didn't want to look desperate. For almost an hour she gained strength and became the woman she wanted to be. She told herself things like, "If he doesn't want me, then I don't want him," and, "I'm never going to love somebody more than he loves me again." She remembered a few of the lyrics of "I'm Gonna Wash That Man Right outa My Hair." She fantasized about marching somebody just like Mickey, the same sense of humor, the same everything, maybe a little taller, right past him in the lobby. Revenge and ten milligrams of Valium made her sleepy.

When she woke up at seven the following morning, her first thought was that she had lost the man she loved. It hurt. She wished he would disappear behind the Iron Curtain. "I don't want him dead, I just want him in North Korea," she told Greta on the phone.

A note miraculously appeared under her door. Had Thomas Hardy written their story, the note would have gone under the door and subsequently under the Oriental. Since they were just two kids from today's world, the letter landed where it was supposed to. Shelly was shocked to see it there, as if it had come from heaven rather than from the floor. She picked up the envelope, saw her name written on it and got scared that it was one of those "Let's be friends" conversations in another form. If she didn't open it, she might feel safer. On the other hand, it could say that Shelly was right, they should get married. No. Nobody slipped good news into your life. Good news was said loudly, shouted clearly from rooftops and spoken right into people's faces. Good news didn't have to be written on good stationery.

Shelly carried the letter with her to the bedroom because she felt safer reading it there. If the words were as terrible as she feared they would be, she would be close to her pillows and Valium. The phone would be nearby in case she had to make an emergency call. To whom? What if Greta wasn't home? Could a person dial 911 if she had a heartache? In a city like New York there should be at least one telephone line devoted to traumas caused by unsafe relationships.

She shook out her perm before opening the envelope. This gesture had become one that would improve her hairstyle and at the same time make her look defiant. Sitting on the edge of the bed, far enough back so that her feet didn't touch the floor, Shelly looked too small for the life she had created. Even the strongest women look fragile with letters in their hands. Her toes curled up and her mouth went down.

Of course she got a paper cut opening the letter. She held Mickey's words in one hand while sucking blood from the other. She thought it appropriate to actually bleed. It was nice, under the circumstances, to see the visible side of pain. She read slowly because depression slowed her down.

Dear Shelly,

My feelings for you haven't changed. I would still be happy to share your bed. I thought we were having a great time.

I know you want to get married and I'm sorry that the thought of "tying the knot" makes me sick, scared and shaky. I hate to give you up, but I also hate to prevent you from doing what you have to do. I'm sure there are a thousand guys who would marry you in a minute, and you should go for it.

I will hurt, but I will understand. Years from now when you have thirty-four kids and I am lonely, I'm sure I'll regret turning you down. I regret it now.

I think it's best if I lay low for a while. It'll give us time to miss each other. (I wish I had asked you where Lucinda takes my dry cleaning. Already, my clothes have spots.)

I will call you soon.

Love,
Mickey

He had signed it "love," but where was the actual love, the substantial love? Shelly read the letter twice and then, as usual, wanted Mickey.

He didn't have a regular schedule, so it was hard to bump into him. He came home anywhere from four-thirty, if he had an early meeting, to nine, if he had a late inspiration. The first few days of their separation, she didn't want to be seen. There was redness and puffiness that she didn't have the confidence to reveal. It was one thing to let a man see you cry. That was appealing, but if you were smart, you didn't let a man see you swollen. Although the pain continued, the tears diminished. They were replaced by plans to recapture her man. The first one was simple. She would pull herself together, good makeup, good jeans (if they fit after the Sara Lee), and pretend to be picking up her mail. She would be the woman he fell for: fun, smiley, cookies in the oven. She would try not to talk about their relationship for as long as she could.

She was dressed by three-thirty and in the elevator by four. By five after four she was back in her apartment and running for her mink coat, although it was too warm for fur. She thought it was a nice touch to look as if she were coming in from the cold. She spent the next hour and a half fooling around in the lobby, pretending. She pretended to look for the mail, pretended to read it, pretended to be interested in the doorman Joe's writing career. (He wrote poetry that was displayed on the annual Christmas card.) She pretended to talk to a few neighbors, all of whom were panicked about the soft real estate market. She pretended to go for a short walk and would have continued pretending if Joe hadn't kept opening the door. She got embarrassed and went back upstairs.

Her old boyfriend, Robert, had disappeared on her too. She had left a message for him at least once an hour when they broke up, but they went unanswered. In the first group of messages she apologized, in the second she said she just wanted to talk, the third told him to fuck off and the fourth said she was sorry about the third. She wondered how these men could disappear so completely. She had never been able to hide anywhere, nor had any of her friends. One had to assume that men could camouflage themselves in ways that women never could.

By eight o'clock that night, after banging on his door, Shelly tried to convince the super to let her into his apartment. She had gone into her Jewish-mother phase and worried that Mickey had hurt himself. "What if he fell down in the shower?" she asked Mr. Schmidt, who was trying to do the right thing. He debated with himself and Shelly at the same time. The skeleton key went from his left hand to his right. When it was in his left, he was ready to open the door, but when it traveled back to his right he felt Mr. Burke had a right to his privacy. "Please, Mr. Schmidt. If you do me this one little favor, maybe I can do you a favor someday." Shelly knew as she said the words that they were dangerous ones. Mr. Schmidt was in his fifties, had one pair of pants and very dirty fingernails. There she was, standing in the dark basement with him and offering him a favor. No one she knew would approve.

"Well, you could do one thing, if you don't mind, miss." Mr. Schmidt was scratching the back of his head with one hand. He was creating more dandruff. The thought of this man asking to be near her was equally unbearable. Why the fuck did she have to ask him if he wanted anything? She should have slapped five dollars in his hand instead.

"Sure. Anything, Mr. Schmidt." She noticed each of his eyes was a different color. She wanted to step back but was scared of insulting him before her mission was done.

"I was wondering if you would introduce me to that nice young lady who comes to visit you all the time, the one that always wears them high shoes. I sure do love the way those shoes sound in my lobby. I don't want to do nothing but meet her and say hello." The human mind is considered a wonderful instrument. The mind of an insecure single woman is the most wonderful of all. Seconds ago, Shelly feared being touched by this foul-smelling man. Now, she was a little jealous of the way he felt about Greta.

"Yeah. Sure. She'll be happy to meet you. Sure." Greta was a good kid. Shelly was sure she'd give a dirty, middle-aged man a hello.

They went up to Mickey's apartment. Mr. Schmidt respectfully stood in the doorway while Shelly inspected the place. One could tell that Mickey wasn't there the minute the door to his apartment was opened, but she looked around the three and a half rooms, as if Mickey was hiding behind some chair or doorway. The place was as messy as usual, and there was no way of telling whether he was gone for the night or forever. His answering machine was off and his toilet seat was up. Shelly considered these clues, but never found what they led to.

# 15

# A Beautiful Woman
# Is Lost to Us

I T was Astra Rainbow who pulled everybody's life together. She didn't mean to, but her action was valiant just the same. Mickey called Shelly from Florida five days after she kicked him out of her life and then begged him to come back. He had used Sprint for the call and she heard an echo of everything he said, but she didn't complain for fear of losing him again. She would rather hear his voice doubled than not at all. He said he had needed time to think. Miami seemed like a good idea. He owed his mother and aunt a party. She pretended to understand and told him she missed him. When he didn't say he missed her, she made the mistake of asking him if did, and he said, "I've only been gone a few days." That hurt. She had missed him immediately, she said, and then couldn't help asking if it were possible, just possible, that they could get back together. He said, "Anything is possible," giving her hope and destroying it at the same time.

Mickey said good-bye and that he would call again soon, but Shelly couldn't let go. It was as if she had to remind him of every part of her so he wouldn't forget that they were once happy. She worked hard. She told him the Mr. Schmidt story, and he laughed when she said she was jealous when it was obvious that he preferred Greta. She told him about the Murray Kane bar mitzvah that was coming up and how Susan Kane wanted the napkins to coordinate with a painting of Moses. Each time he hinted at hanging up, she remembered something important that she had to tell him. She knew she might be sounding desperate, but she didn't want the conversation broken.

Finally, finally, Mickey was able to get a definite good-bye.

"Will you call again?" she asked.

"Of course. We're friends, aren't we?" She felt the pain. She hadn't signed up to be his friend.

"When?"

"When I get a chance."

"When will you be back?"

"It's hard to say, I'll finish *Afterlife* down here . . . a couple of weeks."

"That's so long." The pain came along with a wave of depression.

"It'll be good. We'll be happy to see each other again." With those words, the depression went out to sea again. It was amazing how easily she was played with.

"I'd be happy to see you now," she said, and then added the big, dangerous one. "Mickey, I love you."

"That's good," he said, not returning the words she wanted to hear.

"Mickey, come back. I promise I'll never talk about marriage again. I'd rather be single with you than married to anybody in the world."

"We'll talk when I get home." Thank God he said home. She was home.

Shelly called Greta and repeated the entire conversation. Because of analysis and additions, the retelling took almost exactly twice as long as the original. They came to the conclusion that all was not lost and that Shelly could think of it as her boyfriend having to go away to work. It was a soothing notion. Too bad it didn't help calm Shelly down. She renewed her Valium prescription.

Mickey had left Astra Rainbow in charge of copying scripts, straightening out his files and getting his baby films transferred to videotape. She felt lonely without Mr. Burke, but with the boss gone, Kurt, the office boy from a company on the tenth floor, stopped by a lot. He was twenty-one, had to shave only once a month, and sat on the edge of Rainbow's desk. He always loosened his tie and talked about the millions he could make if only he could get a job on Wall Street. Rainbow told him that she just wanted to be friends, and he said that was okay with him since he had a pain-in-the-neck girlfriend that he was going to drop as soon as he had enough money to go back to college. He tried to kiss her once, but when she pulled back, he was nice enough to apologize. "You're an asshole for not letting him," said Mary, and Rainbow almost agreed. She didn't mind this sweet boy's closeness as much as she thought she would. Sometimes she cleared off a corner of her desk, hoping he would wander down and sit near her. He was the first boy she wasn't afraid of.

Rainbow's nights were the same as they had always been. There were the tiny dinners she shared with her aunt and the small talks she had with Mary. She did the laundry and was happy to clean her clothes. Tucked into the couch at night, she thought of Mr. Burke. Shelly wasn't the only one who wanted him back. When he was there her days had a better rhythm to them. She liked the boy from upstairs, but Mr. Burke was solid. He took up so much more space and so many more hours.

The young woman's life was so simple that most people would have found it boring. She found it comforting to know exactly what was happening day to day. People talked about traveling. She passed travel agencies that urged her to go south, but she didn't feel like going. "All that moving around when I was a little girl has kept me in place," she wrote to her granny one night. While other young women of her age sought excitement, she sought sanity. The pleasure of her life was its status quo. It was as if she had decided to become a nun whether Christ wanted her or not.

On a Tuesday night Aunt Emma told her where all her important papers were. She was a poor woman with papers that weren't that important, but she took the time to explain everything, including the small life-insurance policy she had taken out in 1953. All this was done as a presentation of facts and with no fear of death. Aunt Emma had never spent a day in the hospital and didn't intend to. She died a week and a day after imparting her information, in her sleep and, as far as anyone could tell, without pain.

Astra Rainbow was surprised to see that her aunt wasn't in the kitchen that morning. She was just as surprised to see her still in bed. She called her name three times, and that's all it took. She knew that her great-aunt was dead. Rainbow kissed the woman's wrinkled hand and then slid to her knees and wept. They had spoken very few words to each other, but they had shared their lives, separated only by the generations they were born into. They had never said they loved each other, but they showed it by making each other's beds, toasting each other's bread and watching each other's television shows. Astra Rainbow cried for her aunt most of the morning. Nobody looked for either woman. Aunt Emma didn't leave the apartment every day and her trips to the local supermarket didn't happen until the afternoon. Rainbow wasn't missed either.

When she felt she could leave her aunt's side, she went into the living room and found Mr. Burke's number in Florida. Mickey answered on the second ring with a cheerful hello. The contrast of the two individuals on the phone was astonishing. He was happy and bathed in sunshine. She was devastated and in the dark.

"I'm sorry I won't be coming to work today, Mr. Burke. My aunt died."

"Your aunt died?" Mickey had heard her. He just needed confirmation.

"Yes. I'm sorry." She wasn't apologizing for not coming to work. She was stating the obvious. She was sorry.

"Oh God. How terrible. I'll be up there as soon as I can get a flight."

"You don't have to . . . I can take care . . . She showed me instructions."

"You need a friend."

"I'm in Brooklyn."

"I'll be there."

Rainbow's movements were slow, but they were efficient. By the time Mickey arrived, the body had been taken to the mortuary and the funeral arrangements had been made. Aunt Emma had left very clear instructions, and Granny wired the money and was on her way. Once everything had been taken care of, Astra Rainbow got dressed in an outfit she would have worn to church, although she wasn't going. She sat in her living room waiting for her boss.

After the mortuary carried Aunt Emma away, word spread through the building that the woman had died and neighbors came to say they were sorry. These people were America's latest immigrants, and they didn't know how to use their second language to express their grief. Mrs. Gonzales said, "It is so sad. She was a woman who was all over us." Aunt Emma had made a large meat loaf the night before, and Astra Rainbow gave these fine people slices.

One of the condolence callers was Mary. She came bursting into the apartment and pounded her heart before she could speak. She was more angry than sad. "Goddamn it. Goddamn it to hell. Your aunt. She was a nice lady, always offering me tea. 'You want a cup of tea, Mary? You want some cookies with that tea, Mary?' A beautiful woman is lost to us. That lady was a saint." Astra Rainbow almost smiled.

"She was a very nice person, and I loved her dearly. Aren't you suppposed to be in school?"

"Yeah. Sure," said Mary, not offering any further explanation.

"Don't you have to go back?" Rainbow knew she did, but hoped Mary was once again going to defy authority. She brought a brand of craziness to any situation, and that helped.

"Nah. They're gonna report me, but so what? I'll just make up some lie, and if they don't believe me, that's their problem." And then her mood changed as she turned to the bedroom where the old lady slept. "This is so crappy," said Mary, angry at God.

"At least she died peacefully." The roles were reversed, with Astra Rainbow consoling the young girl.

Mary looked around the apartment as if she had never seen it before. She picked up a small figure of a young schoolboy tying his shoelaces for maybe the first time. She put that down and picked up a shell. It was large and looked like one that could have been picked up on the beach rather than bought. It was impossible to know when it had first entered Aunt Emma's life, possibly when she was young and able to gather things. She probably hadn't gone walking on the beach for a very long time.

In her travels around the room, Mary turned on a lamp, then turned it off. It was as if she were touching and examining things that she wouldn't dare touch while Aunt Emma was alive. In truth, the elderly woman wasn't attached to material things; she just kept them clean. She would have been happy to let the child finger her seashells and turn on her lamps. But Mary had always thought that while the white lady didn't mind her saying hello, her pretty things were too valuable for a black girl to get near.

"I'm not going to leave you alone. I'll come up here and stay with you as long as you need me," said Mary. She was being surprisingly mature and caring. Usually, she dumped her body in chairs and used their arms for her legs. Today she sat straight, her posture a sign of respect for Aunt Emma. "She was sweet. It hurts my heart," she said after only a few seconds of silence.

Astra Rainbow cried again, dignified tears. She was one of the few people who could cry for someone else. Not one of her tears was for her own loss. They were all shed for a great-aunt who was no longer able to sit and enjoy *The Price Is Right*.

The day was a quiet one. Mary and Astra Rainbow sat on their chairs and nodded at neighbors who came to say they were sorry. Neither one of them noticed when it was the end of the day and the room turned dark. Mickey and Mr. Lansing, who worked for the building's landlord, arrived at the same time. Astra Rainbow was confused. At first she thought the two men were friends, but Mr. Burke hugged her, told her how deeply sorry he was and never introduced the man in the doorway behind him. Rainbow then assumed he was one of the mourners and offered him a chair. When he said he was there on business, Mary recognized him, whispered, "Jesus Christ," and headed toward the darkest corner of the room.

"I'm really sorry to bother you, miss, in your moment of grief, but I saw your aunt leaving us today." Now he looked down. He had put on a cheap, gray suit for the occasion. The shoes he looked down on nobody had ever bothered to take care of. They were not the shoes of a wealthy man.

Mickey took over. "Were you a friend of . . ." He didn't know Astra Rainbow's aunt's name so he made several vague gestures before he said, ". . . the deceased?"

"I didn't know the lady, but she was reported to be a fine person.

A fine person. I myself don't feel so fine about having to come here today on a business matter." He looked at Mickey and sized him up as a man whose temper could rise. The man in the gray suit rushed to add, "I think it would be entirely better if I came back another day." His intention was to back out of the room and return when this small, volatile man was no longer there.

Mickey followed him out into the hall. Astra Rainbow wanted to come too, but she was told by Mickey to stay put, he would take care of it. Both girls didn't move from their chairs. It was nice to have a man whispering in the hall on their behalf. Since Mary had never seen her father and Astra Rainbow's was unknown, they both needed the fathering Mickey Burke was willing to give them.

The man had come to discuss the lease. Although he was larger than Mickey, Mickey shoved him against the wall and told the son of a bitch that he had lousy timing. "I have a boss," the sleaze said.

"So what's the situation?" Mickey was in his gangster mood and willing to talk business.

"The apartment. The old lady had it for a long time. And the lease was in her name, you know." He was choosing his words carefully because he knew he could be slammed against the wall again. He would have to fight back this time. He couldn't allow this twerp to touch him more than once. Maybe if he said exactly the right thing, they wouldn't have to get into the rough stuff. "So I was just sent here to straighten out the paperwork."

Mickey wasn't buying this guy's story yet. "And?"

"And. Well, you know, sir, the usual. According to law, the rent has to go up."

"According to law?"

"Well, may I say, sir, that the law allows us to rent the apartment to a tenant of our choice, and this is a very respectable building with a new furnace. You don't hear of our tenants complaining for lack of heat." Mickey couldn't place the accent. Probably, this man's parents immigrated here and he inherited their speech patterns while assimilating.

"Just what the fuck are we talking about?" The word "talking" was spit out with maximum sarcasm.

"Well, the boss has people he owes favors to, and he's sort of promised some cousins of his that they would have the next place available. We wouldn't want to take advantage of no one at a time like this, but we have a long line of people dying to get in here, you'll excuse the expression."

"You bastards." Mickey had moved in close to scream these words into this man's face. The girls looked at each other and shrugged, since these were the first words that drifted into the apartment. Astra Rainbow felt well taken care of.

"Well, sir; perhaps we can discuss this at a more opportunity time." He had meant to say "opportune," but Mickey felt "opportunity" was the right word.

"Get this straight. This place will be rented to the young woman in there—should she decide to stay here." Mickey was finished with the conversation and was headed back into the apartment. His opponent's arm stopped him from entering.

"I'm afraid that's impossible. You see the old lady's name was on the lease, and with her unfortunate untimely passing, I'm afraid the lease is invalid." He was no longer looking at his shoes. Now his look was smug. The half-smile and raised eyebrows deserved to be smashed, but Mickey could never be the man for that job.

"Listen, you piece of shit, you tell your boss that he'll be hearing from my lawyer. And my lawyer loves to go to court. You tell him that he's in for a big pile of legal fees." Mickey was remembering his Brooklyn rhythm. You threatened with your fist, but you followed through with your lawyer. The thought of legal bills often ended arguments.

"I would hate to have to evict your daughter," said the man, right before walking toward the elevator.

This was the double punch. The eviction got him on the chin, but the thought of being considered Astra Rainbow's father caught him in the gut. He yelled, "Asshole," at the back of the man's shiny black head.

"He wants me out, doesn't he?" Astra Rainbow asked as soon as Mickey returned. She was understandably frightened. She looked at the couch where she had slept since she had come to New York and wondered where home would be.

"Don't worry about it. Jerry will take care of it. They're not allowed to make arbitrary rent increases or throw you out." Mickey wasn't sure of the facts, but it was his job to convince her that she still had a home.

"Yes, but if they don't want me here . . . I don't want to stay where I'm not wanted." She looked around the room as if she had already lost it.

"They can make it pretty tough," said Mary. "There was this lady on the sixth floor who they didn't want and they put garbage in front of her door and let these rats loose. It was something else." As usual, Mary was being overly dramatic. She crossed her arms across her stomach and rocked in her chair.

Mickey had expected to help Astra Rainbow with the funeral arrangements and offer his chest as someplace for his secretary to weep on. He didn't expect to have to deal with homelessness. There she was, sitting on the couch, her back straight, both feet on the floor. She stared straight ahead, and yet she was looking toward Mickey for her next move.

The strong man was a role that Mickey liked to play, and taking charge was natural to him. What frustrated him most about his television writing career was that he had to report to others. Since Astra Rainbow was in distress, he knew he would have to save her. It was hard to be a New York hero. They didn't have horses and they didn't have sunsets to ride into. They were always having to hail cabs, and the sun disappeared behind buildings rather than into the horizon.

"Get some things. You're coming with me."

"That's a hell of an idea," said Mary, making a romance out of the situation.

"Mary too?" Astra Rainbow asked. She was too shaky from her aunt's death to be without her girlfriend.

"Sure, why not? Mary too."

"Now you're talking." Mary, who didn't have as big an emotional investment in Aunt Emma as Astra Rainbow did, was able to get in a party mood. "I'm gonna get me some of my things and write a note for my mama. Mr. Burke, you're gonna have to give me all that info about where we're going when we head out of this dump."

Mickey hadn't meant to rescue Astra Rainbow and change Mary's life in the same hour, but it looked as if that was what he was about to do. He knew he couldn't leave Rainbow in an apartment where her aunt had just died, especially since the landlord might be back. If Mary had to come with the package, he could live with that. He would take the two girls back to his apartment, then head over to Jerry's. New York courts favored tenants, so there was a good chance that things would work out.

Mickey insisted on going to Mary's apartment to make sure she told a responsible adult where she was going. It was an unnecessary trip. Her mother sat in the dark living room surrounded by several large ashtrays that she was helping to fill by her constant smoking, watching *People's Court*. Mickey explained very carefully that he would not be in his apartment while the girls were there and that he would make Mary promise that she would continue to go to school. The mother nodded. She was slightly more interested in whether the plantiff would get the money for her damaged couch than she was in her daughter's whereabouts. The only indication that Mary had told her mother she was leaving was when the tired woman retrieved a cardboard suitcase from the back of one of the closets during a commercial. Mickey inched out of the apartment and told Mary he would meet her upstairs.

Who would have thought Mr. Schmidt would run into the mailroom and tell Shelly that Mickey was back?

"Are you sure?" She knew she loved him. Her heart didn't pound like this at any other news.

"Oh, I'm sure. He came in with those two young girls earlier this afternoon. I was in the lobby fixing those darn tiles that keep coming up. They should put in a new floor before someone falls down, breaks his back and sues."

"What two girls?" She was sure now that Mickey wasn't back. He couldn't have two girls with him.

"One was a blonde and one was black. They were both carrying suitcases and that's all I know." He left to do his work, and Shelly wondered if he realized that he had just dropped a bomb. She thought she should keep her promise to introduce him to Greta before he found ways to ruin her life. Mickey, back with girls and suitcases? The joke wasn't funny.

There were two messages for Shelly on her answering machine, both from Mickey. The first said he was back, and in a warm voice, he said he couldn't wait to see her, and the second said that it was seven o'clock and that he would be back in an hour, he was taking the girls out to dinner. The girls? Mr. Schmidt was right. Girls with suitcases were disturbing her life.

Since it was already seven-fifteen, she had the choice of calling Greta or washing her hair. She decided to call Greta but, while she was still dialing, she changed her mind and sent herself to the shower. There would be time to analyze this later. Now she had to feel reassured that her permanent would form the ringlets that they were supposed to.

The doorbell rang at five to eight, and she was in a trick outfit. Her hair was still wet, always a good look; she wore a thick white terrycloth robe—cute, but not asking for it; and she had been able to sneak on mascara, blush and lip gloss without looking as if she had makeup on. The après-shower look was one of her best.

They hugged immediately, a good long hug that told each other they cared. She had a lot of questions, but, "What's the weather like in Miami?" was the first, only because it was the most neutral. It was going to take all her energy to keep from mentioning the girls with suitcases, marriage, weddings or where their relationship was going.

"Hot. Sticky. Your shoes stick to the sidewalk, but there's a restaurant down there that has free Danish on the table. Instead of pickles, they have Danish. I took my mother, Aunt Minn and seventeen of their friends there. The Danish disappeared."

"When did you get back?" She led him to the couch as if he had never been there before and didn't know where to sit.

"Just a couple of hours ago."

"Will you stay here tonight?" She knew she was going too fast. They were just a couple of sentences away from Danish.

"I better not."

She had meant to make this a perfect reunion: happy, comfortable, just like the old days when the stakes were low and they laughed with each other. But upon hearing that Mickey wasn't going to be in her bed, her eyes filled with tears. Now, he would not only know how desperate she was, but also that she had snuck on mascara. She tried to casually brush the tears with the sleeve of her robe and made a valiant attempt to put on a happy face.

"How come?" In her attempt to sound casual, her voice came out in a slightly English accent. This probably happened because she imagined the English to be as cool and matter-of-fact as she wanted to be.

"I think it's better if I go back to the Wyndham again," Mickey said, leaning back like he used to, letting her love him again.

"Why go back?" The question encompassed their life as well as Mickey's location.

"Astra Rainbow's aunt died, and there are some complications about her staying in her apartment. I have her and her friend upstairs, and Jerry is already working on her not losing the place."

Shelly's maternal side fought with her relief. She wanted to express her sympathy for the girl, but at the same time she couldn't help smiling because she felt the girls in Mickey's apartment weren't a threat. "Is she all right?" she asked with a stupid grin.

"She is a dignified mourner. Her tears are contained." Mickey got so sad when he explained Astra Rainbow's grief that he turned away from Shelly. He had just praised Rainbow for being dignified. He was ashamed for falling apart. Shelly, always the mother, consoled him with her arms. She gave him the hug he needed and let him know that it was all right for Jews to be emotional.

"That poor child."

"I think she'll be all right. She handles tragedy well." It was Mickey's turn to wipe away his tears with a sleeve.

"You don't have to go to the Wyndham."

"Yeah I do, but that's as far as I'm going. I'm crazy about you, kid."

"You want a chocolate éclair?" She was offering him the best thing she had to give.

They impressed each other for the entire night. He impressd her with his kindness. She impressed him with the same éclairs that he had taken for granted before. They impressed each other in bed, using more energy, stroking the same old places with more passion. She had to prove they were right for each other. She didn't bring up marriage.

# 16

# Uptown Mary

IT turned out that you could take Mary out of the slums, but getting the slums out of Mary was a job that Astra Rainbow wasn't prepared for. Basically, her heart was in the right place. She was sorry that Aunt Emma's death was the thing that landed her in this cushy apartment with the doorman and the neighbors who were too polite to pile their garbage in the hall. She was sincerely sad at the funeral: "I seen a lot of people die, you know, but this here was a good lady and no one who knew her should be happy for a very long time."

"You've seen a lot of people die?" the writer in Mickey asked.

"Oh yeah, ever since I was a little kid. Once I was standing there in the subway, you know, I was real little so I was just standing there holding on my mama's hand. So anyway, this gang of boys comes running through and they pushed another kid on the track. I don't remember exactly, but I can tell you for sure that he was from another gang. And my mama just yanked my hand to get me on the train, like it was really going someplace now that it killed somebody. She kept saying to me, 'Don't look. Don't look,' but I looked anyway. It just looked like clothes lying there. We all had to get off the train. And then I had a brother, you know, when he was about two he came down with the most terrible fever and all the ladies in the building, they stayed up all night just putting washcloths on his forehead. The doctor came to the house and took Jimmy to the hospital, but he never came home. It left a hole in my heart, Mr. Mickey, but I pretended everything was the same. It never was again. Since that time, I tell you, I've had this here rain all over me, if you know what I mean. I still light candles for him, though nobody knows I do. That's when I was eight, but that rain never goes away. People is always getting themselves killed, they do all kinds of drugs and do it to themselves. They knife each other and the cops come round shooting. Sometimes I think the ladies in Brooklyn spend all their time with this funeral stuff and remembering. Miss Emma, though, I'm gonna miss her. She had things organized, if you know what I mean. Most of the ladies I know, they just let things happen to them, but Miss Emma, she made lists."

Mary kept her promise to Mickey by going to school every day. She traveled by subway to Brooklyn and got back to Central Park West as quickly as she could. About a week after the funeral and a couple of days after Granny went back to Lorain, Mary decided that she and Astra Rainbow should have some friends over. "I don't think it would be disrespectful," she said. "I mean we done all the crying we can. You don't think Miss Emma wants us to have this big place and no one to put in it, do you?"

"We can't have a party here. It wouldn't be right." Now that Granny had left, Astra Rainbow had decided to get Mr. Burke's place in order. She asked his permission to unpack his boxes, and he had smiled, put his hands on her shoulders and told her to move anything she wanted. That gave her a mission. By the time she got her apartment back, she would have his home together. To anybody who didn't know the circumstances, she would have appeared to be a young bride putting the house in order. She was planning to unpack, put up drapes, make the bathroom really cute, get a bedspread and rearrange the kitchen.

"You still stuck on him, or something?" Mary had asked when she saw all the work being done.

"I just want to do something for him."

"If you really wanted to do something for him, you could leave the mess and next time he comes home, spread those legs."

"You're crazy."

"Crazy or not, I wouldn't mind that man marrying me and giving me this park to look at every day of my life." Mary looked out of the window and marveled at what many New Yorkers have taken for granted. She had fallen in love with Central Park and didn't hide her affection.

"He's not going to marry me. He's in love with Miss Silver."

"That piece of frizz downstairs?"

"I think she's very pretty."

"Honey, you're very pretty. You put you and her up on that stage in Atlantic City, and which one of you is going to be the new Miss America?"

"She has great style."

"Yeah, who can't if you can buy all those pretty things from them magazines? Give me some cash and you'll see style coming out of my ass. You're the one with the real looks."

"Mr. Burke loves her, I think." Astra Rainbow opened a box and found a pile of blue towels. They had been packed to preserve a radio, but she was thrilled with the treasure she had found. She would take some money out of the bank and buy a blue bathroom rug and toilet-seat cover. Maybe she could even find a shower curtain.

"And what about you? You love him, or what?" Mary looked back into the park. It was getting dark and the trees were disappearing into a large, black square.

"I love him," said Astra Rainbow, folding towels. "But it's not the kind of love you're talking about."

"I'm thinking about the kind where there's a big bulge in someone's pants." Mary hugged herself and wiggled. The dance was missed by Rainbow, who was happy to be folding.

"He makes me feel safe, but . . ."

"But nothing. You want to be in Brooklyn, smelling stink, or you want to be up here in heaven saying hello to all them poodles in the elevator?" Mary had no idea she was acting like a Jewish mother.

"You know Kurt . . ."

"Kurt, the guy who works in your building? The one you said comes down and sits on your face?"

"He sits on my desk." Astra Rainbow refused to let Mary see that she was exasperated.

"Yeah, I know the guy." Mary returned to the room. The trees had left her for the night.

"Never mind." She would rather do the laundry than have Mary tell her to open her legs again.

"You noticed his bulge? Come on. We're more than friends now. We're roommates, so you have to tell me because this is the final test. When he sits on your desk, right there in front of you, do you find that your eyeballs are looking at his bulge whether you want them to or not?" Mary bent down to find out Astra Rainbow's answer. She acted as if knowing was the most important thing in the world to her.

Astra Rainbow smiled. "Sometimes I get embarrassed looking at any part of him."

"And he makes you feel hot?"

"Warm, but that's because when there are more people in a relatively small space, the temperature tends to go up."

"And do you kind of throb down there?"

"No."

"You will. You gotta have it in you and then you throb when you know what it feels like, unless he just shoved it in."

"This is silly. He's just a nice boy."

"He don't live in no big apartment."

"He's going to night school."

"For what?"

"To be a bank clerk, I think."

"Yeah, well. I don't know much about bank clerking, but I know it doesn't buy this. Couldn't you train yourself to love Mr. Mickey?"

"I do love him. Look what he's doing for us.

"Yeah. Yeah. You're just into the wrong bulge."

Astra Rainbow hugged all six towels to her chest. It was her protection against Mary and the things she was saying. "I'm not into anybody's bulge, and that's the way it's going to be for the rest of my life."

"You sure don't have to prove to me that you're crazy. How you ever going to convince anyone you're sane?"

"Look, Mary, if I don't get to be a nun, I'm going to be like my Aunt Emma. She never got together with any man."

"Yeah, I know. One day I had nothing to do so, you know, I'm headed for nothing but trouble, and I say to Miss Emma that there's really a nice guy, Mr. Magalini from 6B. He's seventy-four, but you gotta admit she was a young eighty-eight. At first she doesn't get what I'm getting at. She just nods, you know, agreeing with me about the nice things I'm saying about this Magalini guy, and I gotta tell you I don't know him all that well so I'm making up some facts like he's a real gentleman and he goes to church every day. When I get her really nodding, I start pushing for the two of them to get together, and she looks at me with those bluish eyes of hers, you got her eyes for sure, and she says, 'What for?' So I say, 'What for? He's a guy and you're a woman and maybe the two of you could get together.' Here's where she looks at me like I'm totally crazy, so I tell her that maybe they could get together and go to church, and she says, 'Why do I have to go to church with Mr. Magalini?' So do you see what I'm getting at?"

"Aunt Emma was eighty-eight years old."

"It don't matter. Some of them old ladies are at least eighty-eight and they're still smelling out guys. What I'm telling you is that you're just like your aunt. The two of you don't know what men are for."

Mary was a determined girl. She tried every night to convince Astra Rainbow that they should throw a party in this unbelievable place. As Rainbow shook her had no, Mary figured which of her friends to invite, how much beer they should buy, how many radios they would need and how they would throw their shirts over the lamps in order to get an atmosphere going. Each time Rainbow said no, absolutely not, she wasn't going to take a chance on ruining Mr. Burke's apartment and his beautiful things, Mary tried harder. She described in detail the dancing and the rubbing of bodies that would follow. She was using the wrong bait.

Mary, finally exasperated, pared her fantasy down. "How about if we just have two guys over? I'll have Frank bring a friend and we could sort of just hang around."

"No."

"Jesus. You got to be the person who wants the least fun in the world." Astra Rainbow thought the girl might be right. She wasn't looking for fun. She was hoping for peace.

Finally Mary tried for her own fun. She had pulled a chair up to the window since she spent so much time there. The tree never failed to fascinate her. Astra Rainbow was putting shelving paper in the kitchen, so the following conversation was shouted.

"How about since you don't care about nothing for you that you let me have Frank over. Just Frank. One person. You think if Frank came up here on his own that he's going to want to waste his time on messing up the place?"

"I just don't think we should have visitors. It's not our apartment."

"Mr. Mickey said, 'Have a good time.' You didn't hear him say that? You were standing right there, looking right into his face. So far I don't know anything wrong with your hearing." Since Mary was relentless, they both got exasperated.

"I heard him say that," said Astra Rainbow. She was more worried about the bubbles the contact paper was threatening to make than she was about having company over.

"So how you gonna have fun with no boys around? When they happen to talk to you nice or something, now that's fun, and what's so bad about bringing Frank up here? You want to tell me the crime? I won't let him bring crack. I'll bet if you ask that boss of yours if Frank could come up, he would say it was perfectly fine."

Mary finally wore her down. Rainbow was alphabetizing Mr. Burke's books, and Mary spoke to her back. "How 'bout if I just bring Frank up here just for a couple of hours or so. *Please*, Astra Rainbow. *Please*. I just want him to see where we's been lucky enough to be. He'll shit in his pants when he gets a look at this place. I don't mean that exactly. I means he's not going to really shit, so don't worry about the place being messed up. It's just a way of telling you how excited he'd be. And you know maybe he'd even like me better and more. Just a little while. What harm's it going to do? Please. Please."

"Okay." Astra Rainbow wondered whether to take the torn jacket off *The Mosquito Coast*. She decided not to. She had permission to unpack, but she didn't want to alter anything of Mr. Burke's.

"Okay? Did you say okay? So it's okay if I bring Frank here. You're

the best. The best, best, best. You won't be sorry. We won't use anything. I won't even let him use the toilet."

When she was trying to convince Astra Rainbow to let Frank come,
all Mary had done was beg. Now that he was coming on Friday night,
all she did was worry. "What if he doesn't come?" she asked.

"We can go to a movie."

"Who's gonna want to go to a movie if he doesn't show? If he doesn't
show, I'm gonna want to kill myself. I'll take Mr. Mickey's gun and
shoot myself in the head, like about ten times."

"Mr. Burke doesn't have a gun."

"Sure he does. That's how people like him protect themselves from
trash like Frank."

Astra Rainbow expected the evening would be the three of them
sitting around having very little to say to each other. She had never
met Frank, but she figured that he was like the hundreds of rough
boys that she had to walk past in Brooklyn. Some of them bothered
her and some of them didn't. They all threatened her just by being
there. She had seen girls like Mary with them and wondered how
hard they had to work to get what they wanted from each other.

On the night Frank was due to arrive, Astra Rainbow stopped by
a small delicatessen around the corner on Columbus Avenue and
bought a bag of pretzels and a bag of potato chips. Having made these
purchases, she considered herself a very generous hostess. When she
got home, Mary was already ready. She had squeezed her stomach
into her shortest jean skirt and her big bust into her tightest sweater
and had too much makeup on her face. As usual she looked dusty.
Astra Rainbow felt obliged to tell her to take off some of the red from
her cheeks and blue from her eyelids, but as she put the pretzels and
potato chips in bowls, Mary applied more makeup. She stood in the
bathroom with her mascara wand, making sure that every lash was
covered until it was stiff.

When she had finished applying the layer of unnecessary makeup,
she ran to the window to see if she could see him coming. She had
spent so much time at that window that she knew by now that there
was no way you could identify a person in the street. No matter how
close she got to the glass, she couldn't see anyone on the sidewalk
directly below. The best she could hope for was that Frank would
come through the park and that she could spot the brown sweater
he always wore. As she stood there waiting for him, she remembered
that she hated him. In her fantasy of having somebody over, she had
forgotten that he had never really said anything nice to her and that
all he ever wanted to do was press her against the wall, lift her skirt
and have sex. She felt hurt now for all those times. There was Astra
Rainbow arranging chairs so that they could sit and talk. Frank never

talked. Once he had even taken Angela Romata to a movie the day after banging Mary against the wall. Yet, when the house phone rang, she ran to the closest mirror to make sure she was her prettiest.

Since this was their first visitor, neither of them knew exactly what the procedure was regarding guests. Astra Rainbow picked up the phone and was told that a Frank was here to see a Miss Mary. Should he be let up? Rainbow said he was expected. The doorman was still hesitant. He was new, young and not quite sure that he should let this boy, who looked perfectly capable of robbing the building, inside. Frank had the appearance of a kid who was anxious to mug someone. "You sure you're expecting someone, miss?" he asked through the static on the phone. Rainbow said she was positive they were expecting a Frank and that it was perfectly fine to send him up. The doorman didn't think it was perfectly fine, but he let Frank up anyway. The boy gave him a salute as he entered the building, and Mrs. Hartung from 6B, who was on her way out to walk her beloved miniature schnauzer Misty, rushed past the punk in the lobby.

By the time Frank rang the doorbell, Mary had overcome her reservations and felt more excited than hurt. Instead of opening the door, she jumped a few times, grabbed on to Astra Rainbow and yelled in a whisper, "He's here. He's here."

"Go put on your shoes. I'll get the door," said Astra Rainbow, behaving like any mother whose daughter had a date.

"I don't have any shoes that match, and you figure since he's coming in and I'm not going out, I don't really need any. Someday I'm going to get a pair of those short black boots."

But that was someday and the boy was here now. When he rang the doorbell the second time Mary jumped even higher. It was up to Astra Rainbow to let him in. Mary stood behind her as she opened the door. "Is this where Mary is?" he asked. Maybe he was nervous in this uptown atmosphere and hiding behind a cocky manner that he had learned by the time he was eight.

Astra Rainbow stepped aside to reveal Mary, still partly behind her and partly behind the door. Without a word Frank strolled into the living room. He took in the surroundings, ignoring the girls for now. He looked around but did nothing to let them know he was impressed. Mary became the perfect hostess and in a rush of words let him know all about the place. "This here's the living room and you gotta come over here and look out. Since we're so high up you can look out and see the whole park. You see the guy down there in the red shorts with the dog? He runs around the park every day. And if you walk over here"—Mary took five giant steps forward—"you're in the dining area. Really, that's what they call it, right?" Astra Rainbow confirmed this by nodding. Since Frank had been nodding since he got there, Mary went on talking, surrounded by these silent people who shook their heads for too long. "And there's the kitchen." She swung the door open. "The refrigerator and stove match, and there's more buttons on everything than you've ever seen in your life." While Mary held the door open Frank stuck his head into the kitchen. He had his act down so well there was still no way of knowing whether he was impressed or bored. Mary took him by the hand toward the bedroom. "And here is the bedroom," she explained. "And the greatest thing about it is that you can sit up in bed and see the trees, not as good as if you actually get up and walk over to the window, but I swear you can see them from here. You want to try it?" Astra Rainbow, the chaperone, didn't like the idea of this boy trying anything, but she didn't quite know how to intrude, so she let Mary push him down on the bed and then make him sit up and look out the window, proving that you could see trees from there.

"You see them?" Mary asked anxiously.

"Yeah. I see them."

"Isn't it great, the way you can have a park right from your bed?"

"Yeah." Mary turned to Astra Rainbow with a look that said, "I told you he would be impressed." There was no way of knowing how Mary had read anything in this boy's blank face.

There wasn't much left to show, so the rest of the tour was explained in a sentence. "There's a bathroom in here and there's also a bathroom in the hall so that makes two bathrooms for one person."

"He must have a big ass," said Frank. Mary laughed. Rainbow was happy the children were having fun.

Astra Rainbow went into the kitchen to open cans of Coke, and she heard Mr. Burke's bedroom door close. Without looking, she knew that Mary and Frank had found their privacy. They had never had it in Brooklyn, where their lovemaking had been confined to dark corners. Now, for the first time, they were alone in a bedroom without a mother or a priest around. Rainbow looked at the door, hoping it would open again, knowing it wouldn't.

She sat on the couch waiting for them to reappear, but ten minutes went by and they didn't. She thought of hanging the kitchen rods or finishing the books, but the closed door disturbed her. There was no noise coming from the bedroom. The silence said everything. They were having sex on the other side of the door. Now she remembered the naked bodies of her youth, the things she shouldn't have seen, the time the door swung open and she thought that large man with the strip of hair down his back was hurting her mother. She had been about four years old and had tried to pull her mother out from under him. "No, no, baby," her mother had said. "You go play." How could she play while this man pounded the only adult who had ever taken care of her? It looked to her as if he would kill her with his weight. She tried once more to pull her mother from the bed, a mattress with no sheets. "It's all right, baby. Go. Go." Astra Rainbow went because staying was too hard. She shut the door behind her and expected never to see her mother again. She was surprised when her mother and the very large man came out of the room partially dressed, arm in arm. He had tried to kill her and now, here she was, being friendly to him. They even had mint tea together and her mother didn't look hurt. After that, when her mother was behind closed doors, she didn't try to rescue her. Sometimes Helen came out smiling and sometimes she just came out, but at least she was alive.

Astra Rainbow became so uncomfortable she fled the apartment. She had too many memories from an unfortunate childhood in which she'd been exposed to nakedness long before she should have been. They had called it free love, but Astra Rainbow had paid for it dearly.

Upset, she sat in the lobby in the large wine-colored chair that nobody ever really used for that purpose. Packages had been placed there. Babies had been placed there to have their snowsuits zipped up. But no one before now had really used the chair for anything but a transitory resting place. The girl wanted to cry. She had been angry at her mother and now she was angry at Mary. How dare the world make her witness to its intimate moments?

The young doorman on duty asked her if she was all right. She managed to tell him she was fine. She was just waiting for someone.

Less than half an hour after John spoke to her, Shelly came home. She had planned to go to the mailroom, but seeing Astra Rainbow in the chair, she rushed over to ask what was wrong. The girl told her that her friend was up in Mr. Burke's bedroom with a boy. She expected Miss Silver to have the same disgusted reaction that she did, but Shelly smiled and told her to come up to her place. Astra Rainbow did, following behind, helping with packages.

When they were in Shelly's apartment, Rainbow explained what happened, how Frank had come to visit, how they had closed the door, how she had bought both potato chips and pretzels that had gone untouched. Still Shelly was smiling. There she was, putting away groceries, moving boxes of rice around so that there would be room for the Fruit 'n Fibre cereal that Mickey liked, not condemning Mary. "I had a roommate in college once who was engaged four times. Correction. She was engaged four times while she was living with me. I can't tell you how often I had to sleep in someone else's room." She laughed, remembering.

"I guess I just thought it was wrong." Shelly saw her pain for the first time and was immediately compassionate. She turned from the groceries and her hands went to Rainbow's shoulders. Although the hands were still cold from putting the Dove Bars in the freezer, the girl felt Shelly's warmth.

"Oh, honey, sex isn't new to Mary, you know that."

"I guess I know that. It's just that . . . It's just that . . ." She was too embarrassed to continue. Shelly worked hard for close to an hour getting Astra Rainbow to finish her sentence. It took several hugs, hot chocolate and warm smiles before she could start to reveal why she was so upset. Finally, the mothering paid off. "When I was a little girl, I tried to pull my mother from bed. She was with this large man," Astra Rainbow began. Her story didn't pour out. It came out slowly and with difficulty and with very little perception of what actually had happened. She had no idea that her early life had been disturbing or that it was appreciably different from anyone else's formative years. At the time, all she had known were other children with naked parents making love behind closed and opened doors.

"Where were you?" asked Shelly. She assumed, at this point, that the incident was a one-time occurrence.

"All over," said Astra Rainbow. She was too little and the country was too big for her to have remembered the specifics. A place either had buildings on it or it didn't. You could see the sky or you couldn't. You could always smell the pot and hear the songs. She was small and always had to stretch to see the faces of the people who were taking care of her. For the most part, they took care of themselves.

"You mean it happened more than once?"

"It happened all the time. I only tried to stop her once. I really thought he was hurting her." Astra Rainbow said this apologetically, not wanting Miss Silver to get the idea that she would purposely ruin her mother's good times.

It wasn't until Shelly put both arms around Rainbow that more of the story came out. Her voice was as steady as her tears as she told what she remembered of her early years. The story wasn't all bad. There was love. There was food. Her mother's hand was there for her most of the time. Still, it sickened Shelly. She felt children were supposed to be protected by love and structure. Her own babies would be in safe cribs and safe nursery schools. They would be surrounded by the softness and innocence that babies deserve. She pulled back to look at Rainbow and, in her flawless face, saw the neglected child. She drew Rainbow back to her again. Shelly couldn't protect her from her early years, but she could make her feel safe now.

Shelly Silver was an exceptionally good mother that night. She lent Rainbow pajamas and turned down the bed in the second bedroom. In their robes, giggling, they slipped a note under the door of Mickey's apartment telling Mary where they were. They snuck back downstairs, hoping not to be seen. Shelly brought her child for the night a glass of warm milk. Astra Rainbow was glad she told this nice woman why she had been upset over Mary. She wondered if Miss Silver would let her stay if she knew what happened to the boy on the cliff.

We are all relatives to each other. Astra Rainbow had no trouble becoming Shelly's daughter. In return, Rainbow became her wife. Since there isn't a living soul who doesn't need a wife, the trade-off was welcome. The morning after Frank and Mary closed the door, the girl made her hostess breakfast and brought it to her. In the following days, she picked up Shelly's laundry, ran to get toilet paper and had her watch fixed. She took care of sending a package out to Shelly's mother and rented and returned tapes at the local video store. She even returned things to Bloomingdale's. Shelly protested, not wanting to take advantage of her child, but Astra Rainbow insisted.

As a result of Astra Rainbow's devotion, Shelly's life was never so orderly. As a result of Shelly's caring, Astra Rainbow had never felt so safe. Shelly assured her that she could always stay downstairs when Frank was over, and the girl looked forward to staying in the guest bedroom. For much of her life she had slept on other people's beds and couches, but this was a place that really suited her. The pale pastels of the room seemed designed for her blondness. The old prints of flowers on the wall made her happy. The lamp next to the bed was pink and pretty. She decided it would be the lamp she would buy if she ever had a room while waiting for Christ's proposal. (Although they never discussed it, this was the biggest thing that Astra Rainbow and Shelly had in common. They were both waiting for proposals from men who didn't take to marriage.)

"I really, really hope I'm not putting you out of your place," Mary said while waiting for Frank one night. She still looked for him out the window although she knew she couldn't spot him from there.

"No. No. It's okay. Shelly—she said I should call her Shelly and not Miss Silver—said I could stay there anytime. She's letting me clean out her closets."

"You did real good straightening out this place. It looks really pretty, like a home or something."

"I was thinking that when we go back to Brooklyn, maybe we could fix that place up. I could save up . . ."

"I hate to think about going back down there." Mary stared intently at the park, as if she was going to have to store the image for the rest of her life.

"We'll fix it up. I'll buy a pink lamp." Astra Rainbow felt sad, too. She might duplicate the room at Shelly's apartment, but she'd leave part of the safe feeling behind.

"You can fix it up all you want. It still ain't here. How can they do this to us, give it to us and take it away? I mean if I never had this place, then how was I gonna miss it?"

"It's not over yet. Mr. Burke's friend may take another two whole months to get the lease right."

"Yeah. A whole month." Mary's sarcasm was delivered to the windows.

"We knew we were going to have to leave sometime." Up to now, Astra Rainbow had been good at leaving. The travels with her mother had taught her no place was home.

"But it just ain't fair. It's pretty here and it's clean and the whole building doesn't stink like someone just pissed in it. You don't think you're going to run into some dead body or that your body is gonna get killed. And I'll tell you the best part. I ain't never made sex in a bed before. It's really different. It's like you wanna be there instead of you have to be there. I swear, it changed everything between me and Frank. I'm like his real girlfriend now. Like he respects me or something ever since we've been able to lie down. There's other things too. It doesn't hurt. When I used to be standing up against that wall or something, my back used to get all out of shape. The best part, though, is Frank talks nicer to me. I swear it's like he's my real boyfriend now, with respect and everything."

"He should respect you wherever you are."

"Yeah. sure. I'm telling you what I know for sure. They like you better if you got a doorman down there."

# 17

## Coming Home

THE day he found out that the lease was settled, Mickey didn't go back to the Wyndham. Nobody expected him, and he found all the women in the middle of getting on with their lives. Mary and Frank were enjoying each other in 14D, but Mickey never saw them. He went straight to Shelly's and found her and Astra Rainbow, both in pajamas, working together in Shelly's kitchen, making pretzels. He had used his key to get in, thinking, as any man would, that he would be a great surprise to them. He was right. They were thrilled to see him—Shelly, because it had been too many weeks since he had been there, and Rainbow, because it was like seeing the teacher out of school. She knew Mr. Raphelson wouldn't aprove of her being in her nightclothes, but she didn't think of Mr. Raphelson much anymore.

Shelly and Astra Rainbow danced around him squealing, admiring him, admonishing him for surprising them. He couldn't believe his luck. There they were, the blonde *and* the brunette. Betty and Veronica. Mickey's girls were happy he was home, and he had an arm of each.

Shelly opened the wine and Rainbow found the pretzels. They were content to listen to his boring account of how he'd decided to leave the hotel in a hurry.

"Don't worry, Mary and I can pack fast." Astra Rainbow was wondering if they should leave that night or wait until morning.

"Hey, no. You don't have to. You can't. Jerry's office isn't quite finished with the paperwork. It'll be another week or so."

"Great." This time it was Shelly's turn to hug them both.

It was far from bedtime, but Astra Rainbow worried about where she would sleep. Everyone was paired off. She wasn't jealous, just scared of closed doors that could swing open. It would be impossible for her to be in the same apartment as Frank and Mary. They were young and inconsiderate. Their noises found their way over, under and through obstacles in 14D. It wouldn't be as bad to be nestled in the beautiful bedroom in 3C. Shelly and Mr. Burke would be in the bedroom next door but, like a child, she could pretend that the adults weren't doing anything. Things in her life had happened so out of sync. Now that she was an adult, she could hang on to the childish notion that nothing was happening.

Rainbow headed for the fourteenth floor, but Shelly, her protector, stopped her. In a whispered conversation at the door, Shelly assured her that it was fine for her to stay. The girl kissed her on the cheek and declined. "I'll just tell Frank to go home," she whispered back.

"Good girl." Shelly gave her one of those light punches that said she was proud of Astra Rainbow's strength.

"I love you, but I can't marry you," Mickey said, giving Shelly a chance to kick him out.

"Maybe we should just have a baby," she said, taking the pillows off the bed.

Jerry finally cleared up the lease and the move back to Brooklyn was as depressing as Mary had predicted. "It's going to look like shit," she said, more than once.

They moved on a Saturday, and although it was the middle of the afternoon, the darkness of Aunt Emma's closed in on them. They had been gone only for seven weeks, but that had been long enough for Mary to learn that there was a prettier, safer way to live and long enough for Astra Rainbow to know what it was like to feel pampered.

They had decided to room together. They even tried to convince each other that they were going to have a good time. Painting the bedroom the same pinkish beige as Shelly's guest room was Astra Rainbow's idea of fun. By Saturday night they had packed up all of Aunt Emma's things. Mary handed them to Rainbow, who wrapped them in tissue paper and lay them in cartons. They seemed like dead things being buried. On Monday she would carry them to the Salvation Army and hope that all these fragile things would make other great-aunts happy. It seemed appropriate that the clutter should be broken up. Rainbow wanted to spread Aunt Emma over the neighborhood that she had learned to live peacefully in.

Little by little, with paintbrushes, bargain sheets and sewing skills learned at the 4-H and from Granny, Astra Rainbow turned her home into a poorer version of Shelly's apartment. She borrowed the colors she had learned to feel good with. Mary bitched about the work, but when the place was finished, she marched at least twenty friends through, while bragging how they had learned this uptown. "I seen stuff like this on TV," one of the friends said admiringly, and Mary had an appropriate answer. "Yeah, but when it's on TV you never think anybody has it for real."

At first Astra Rainbow hadn't wanted Frank staying there at all, but Mary convinced her that the only way that Frank would continue to have the high level of respect that he had learned in Mr. Burke's place was if they could do it in a bed once a week. "Please, Rainbow," the girl begged. "We'll do it other places the rest of the time, but I'm gonna need the bed at least once a week to keep him treating me so good."

"Every week?" She wasn't sure she could take even one night a week.

"Well, you figure we do it—what—let's say roughly twelve times a week, so considering the math, I don't think it's too much to ask for one night in a bed. I'm telling you, I really need those pillows. I banged my head real good on a wall the other night. You don't want me to have to stay out of school, do you, especially now when I'm almost getting Cs?"

"One night?"

"One night a week is all I'm asking for." She tried looking angelic at this point. She chose that particular attitude because it usually worked with Astra Rainbow. One would think the child was asking to be allowed to have ice cream once a week.

"I don't know. I hate being in the same place where people are . . ."

"We'll be very quiet. Very. I'll tell Frank no yelling."

"He yells?"

"Just sometimes. Not really a yell. Just sometimes when he comes he lets it all out. He yelps. Yeah, that's it, just a yelp, nothing to wet your pants over."

"I don't know. I don't want him walking around here naked."

"I'll tell him. So if we need something out here, like a tomato, I'll come running out and get it."

"A tomato?"

"I said tomato on account of this is really important and you're making me nervous. I said tomato as an example for something else. I need that bed."

"I don't want him using the bathroom."

"What's he supposed to do, hold it in until he can taste it?"

"We just painted it."

"He's not going to pee on the walls, for Christ sake." Mary realized she was screaming. Her arms moved to the pitch of her voice. She knew she had to calm down to win this argument, so she stopped and threw herself into a chair. Astra Rainbow saw the slipcover move and didn't like it. "Look," Mary said, if he accidentally makes a mistake and doesn't hit the bowl, I'll paint the bathroom over."

Mary always won arguments like this. Astra Rainbow straightened the slipover and gave in. She would try it. She warned Mary that if she was uncomfortable, even for one minute, that Frank would have to go. Mary agreed, and Frank sauntered in on Saturday night. Rainbow could never quite tell whether he bounced and nodded, or merely bounced, thus producing the nod. He was a selfish speaker, uttering mainly sounds instead of words. He and Astra Rainbow had never had a conversation, and she imagined that he never had one with Mary.

He arrived at seven-thirty, wearing the uniform of the neighborhood: black T-shirt, battered jeans and jean jacket. Astra Rainbow opened the door and said hello. Frank grunted and bounced right past her. He played with his one silver earring as he grunted at Mary. He took her and led her toward the bedroom, knowing instinctively where it was. With a few head movements, Mary tried to indicate that it wouldn't be nice to run off immediately to the bedroom, leaving Astra Rainbow alone. Frank didn't understand what Mary was trying to tell him because he had no understanding of politeness. He took the time to nod toward Astra Rainbow and then tried to pull Mary into the bedroom again.

"Fraaaank," Mary said, making his name last for an entire sentence. The boy continued to bounce. "Fraaaank, we should watch televison first." The girl had no idea that she was making up her own code of ethics. In her young mind, watching television first was the proper thing to do.

The three of them sat on the couch and silently watched *Golden Girls*. Frank sat between them and continued to bob even when seated, making them all nervous. At nine o'clock Astra Rainbow, in a surprise announcement, said she was tired. Mary had expected to have to sneak off, but here was her escape being offered to her.

"So we'll see you later," said Mary.

"No," Astra Rainbow warned.

"It was just an expression. We won't see you later. Don't worry." With this, the bedroom door closed.

Astra Rainbow tried not to worry, but uninvited panic moved in quickly. It started with memories of her mother being hurt by the hairy man. It seeped out of her mind onto her forehead and into her throat. Her head was wet and her mouth was dry. She didn't know she was crying until she tasted the salt. She was hot and threw the blanket off only to find she was freezing. She pulled the blanket back on. This time it didn't warm her. She shivered, her teeth making loud noises as they chattered against each other.

No sound came from behind the door, but she pictured them: first Mary and Frank pounding against each other, then her mother and the hairy man. It didn't stop there. Mary was under the hairy man and being suffocated by him. The pictures were vivid and not erasable. She dressed as quickly as she could, but the pounding in her head slowed her down. She crawled down into the street and fortunately hailed a cab right away. She went to Mr. Burke's office and immediately fell asleep on his couch. In the morning she felt well. The following week, she went to the office even before Frank arrived.

Relationships repeat themselves. The first week that Mickey was back, Shelly and Mickey seduced each other as they had in the beginning. He had flowers and time for her. She let him put his feet on her coffee table. She read his pilot and was totally supportive of it. He ate her miniature quiches and said how much he had missed them. They agreed to go to movies that the other one wanted to see without saying things like, "Hey, wait a minute. I'm a person too." They touched some part of each other's bodies even while watching television. She wore his clothes and he wore the cotton sweater she had given him, even though he considered cotton and sweater a contradiction in terms. When he was in the apartment, she didn't stay on the phone with Greta more than ten minutes, and he didn't use the remote control from the television for his own pleasure. She didn't mention marriage, and he told her he loved her.

The first week lasted a week and half. Then, almost simultaneously, Shelly started a hint phase where she walked Mickey past wedding gowns and Mickey started staring at Astra Rainbow's back. There was very little to do in the office these days, since he still hadn't gotten the notes on the second draft from the network.

The great thing about Astra Rainbow during times like this was that she continued to do secretarial work as if she were working in the offices of a large advertising firm. She always had something to type, file or Xerox. Mickey loved to watch her sit down. Her long hair always got caught in the back of her chair and she had to free it with both of her hands. He could watch her for a very long time and got slightly jealous when that tall boy from the tenth floor came by. She wouldn't let the boy stay because her boss was around, but she seemed to like him. He could tell from her body language, even though he had only a rear view.

"I'm marrying the exterminator," Greta said, too sadly for a woman who was supposed to be making a good move.

"That's great," Shelly screeched. She went to embrace Greta, who refused to be hugged. They were in Greta's SoHo loft about four in the afternoon, a time when only people who work for themselves can get together.

"I want you to cater it." Greta was being very businesslike. She went over to the large white table that she used as a desk and checked her date book. "I think April thirtieth sounds good. We'll have it here." Shelly was confused. She had been involved in enough wedding plans to know that Greta was making decisions that should have been made by her and her future husband.

"I'll be happy to cater it. It'll be my present and I'll do the best job I've ever done. How come you're not jumping up and down?"

Greta sat at the desk now. It provided the protective barrier that she would need while explaining her feelings. She wore a beautiful, soft, pale green dress that she had designed. Her hair was shiny from the overhead light. The gray outlined her waves. A photographer would have been pleased with this theatrical picture. "I'm not thrilled about this marriage because I'm shallow. For the rest of my life people are going to ask me what my husband does, and I am going to bend my head and, without meeting their eyes, say, 'He's an exterminator,' and they'll say, 'That's nice,' to me but they'll go home and wonder if his hands smell. There'll be a hundred thousand uncomfortable moments in my life. The children, if I'm lucky enough to have them, will be asked what their father does. The other fathers will be doctors, lawyers, teachers, salesmen, bus drivers. They may never run into another kid whose father chased down rats. On their college applications under 'Father's Occupation' they'll have to write, 'pest controller.' If my children inherit any of their mother's shallow genes, they'll be embarrassed by that. Do I get my engagement announcement in *The New York Times?* What does it say, 'Greta Weinstein, up-and-coming SoHo designer, to marry a . . . rat man?' We're not going to make it into magazines as the Couple of the Month. I know it's silly, but I always wanted to be the Couple of the Month and now that's not going to happen." Here Greta stood and hugged herself as if she were cold. She even rubbed her arms. Shelly was about to come up with reasons why Greta shouldn't care about the rest of the world when her friend went on. "When we get invited to dinner or to parties, it will aways be because of me. Our friends will be my friends, the ones who tolerate him. He's a wonderful man but, Shelly, he's not even a smart exterminator. He's a good man from New Jersey who doesn't even know who is Secretary of State." She sighed and threw herself on her bed, not facedown in the mournful position of sixteen-year-old girls but flat on her back, arms outstretched, ankles crossed, ready to be nailed to the cross.

Shelly stood over Greta and said the two words she had been thinking since Greta had told her about the wedding. "I'm jealous," she said.

Greta looked at her as if they weren't born in the same century. "Don't you get it? I'm settling. Probably because I was a fat kid. Don't ask me to prove it. I burned all the pictures from the time I was eleven to the time I was twenty-three."

"You love him, don't you?"

"Yes. I'm not crazy enough to marry an exterminator I don't love. You marry a bank president that you don't love."

"Just look at it this way. You'll never have to tell another man your life story."

"Why do you think I'm getting married? I don't have the energy to tell anyone new that I was art director of my high school yearbook."

"I'm jealous. I'd like to be planning your wedding *and* my wedding."

"At least you're in love with a writer. If I were marrying a writer, we could be the Couple of the Month." With this Greta sat up and laughed. Her bracelets made music as they hit each other. There was an armful of them, each one as gold as the next.

"At least you're getting married. You'll have kids."

"I always wanted to be a young mother. It's too late for that now."

"Don't you remember we had to succeed in a man's world before we could become women?"

"Is that what they told us?"

"I think that's what we heard. We were so scared of having 2.2 children that we didn't have any." They should have been happier; Greta was getting married.

The wedding was Greta's. Hank showed up. He let the rabbi marry them and then sat quietly on the side, watching Greta and her friends as if they were a movie. He might have been watching *The Great Gatsby*, since that was as foreign to him as his new wife's world.

Since Shelly was the caterer and also a guest, she increased her staff, and one of the people she hired for the night was Astra Rainbow. The wedding was on a Saturday night, Frank's night, and Rainbow was happy not to be home. When Rainbow had been living at Mickey's, she helped Shelly in the kitchen. She had a great ability to do everything precisely. Shelly knew that if she ever needed to be replaced in the kitchen, Rainbow would follow her orders exactly.

Greta had invited a large crowd, all her girlfriends, some of her ex-boyfriends (it seemed in good form to have them), her mother and her three brothers. She designed her dress, white with streamers of pastel ribbons hanging from the waist. She joked that the white was for the virginity she should have had and that the ribbons symbolized her checkered past. The groom laughed along with everybody else. Hank invited his brother, but the poor man seemed as isolated as Hank was. One would think they would have the need to talk to each other, but they sat in different corners smiling at the action. They looked like brothers, but it was easy to tell which one was moving out of New Jersey. Greta had gotten Hank to the right hairstylist and his tuxedo was Armani's latest. They were a good lesson in before and after.

"Go talk to Hank," Shelly whispered to Mickey. They were supposed to be the best friends of the newly married couple, although they hadn't really succeeded as a foursome.

The white loft was decorated with enormous baskets of spring flowers and balloons and ribbons that matched the colors on Greta's dress. Unfortunately, Hank, in his attempt to befriend Mickey, knocked over a basket, causing the two men to get on the floor and try to repair things. Greta was standing close enough to Shelly to say, "Don't they look silly?" They looked very silly, tuxedoed and crawling. They looked like some sort of domestic animal that one could easily control.

"Isn't it amazing that we can't live without those two jerks?" Shelly said this kindly. She was not the type of woman who would call a groom a jerk to his new wife.

"Why have we cried over them?" By now, the men were comically struggling with balloons.

"Why would we ever let them fool around with our hearts? They can't even deal with balloons."

"That is the man I am going to spend the rest or my life with." Greta grabbed a glass of champagne from the tray that swept by her. All the waiters were in tails and had been instructed to keep the champagne flowing.

Greta signaled for everyone's attention. First, she just yelled, "Everybody," but all that did was silence a few and get the piano player to stop playing. He was in white tails and looked ready to tap-dance. Finally, the people closest to Greta told those around them to keep quiet, the piano player played a few attention-getting chords and Greta had center stage and the attention she had demanded.

She held her champagne glass high and struck a dramatic pose. "Everybody, I would like to make a toast to my husband." All turned toward the husband, who had recently stood up and was brushing the dirt from the basket from his sleeves. He was immediately embarrassed by the attention. "To my husband," the toast began, "I want him to know on this, our wedding day, that I love him and that I will never leave him. I have spent the last five years of my life looking for a kind man and I have finally found one." There were wistful sighs of the type that one hears only at weddings and when babies are looked at in carriages. Greta should never have gone on. But she did. "He is kind. Very kind. He must take out all his hostility on the rats because he's sure nice to me when he comes home." People laughed. Hank didn't. He nodded, taking sort of an embarrassment bow, the way a schoolboy might after his teacher had praised him. Greta hadn't meant to hurt her brand-new husband. She was, however, starting a pattern in her marriage. She would make the joke before anyone else could.

Greta made her way across the loft to Hank. People parted so that she could travel the shortest distance between two points. Shelly and everyone else noticed that her steps were slightly unsteady from too much champagne, the latest glass drunk right after the toast. She landed in Hank's arms and he demonstrated that he could catch her. That seemed to be enough for the crowd. They were happy that for the rest of her married life she would be caught. Unfortunately Hank felt that he had to make a reciprocal toast. A quick waiter handed him a glass of champagne. He, too, held it high. Greta tried to drink it, but he wouldn't let her, behaving as her protector. "I'd like to toast Greta," he said uncomfortably. It was no surprise that he would muffle his words. "I don't really know what to say except that I'm happy we got married and that I'm surprised she married me." This time there was no laughter. Greta did manage to get the glass out of his hand and down the champagne. She threw off her shoes and tried to get the energy of the party going again, but people were ready to leave. They kissed her at the door and, since Hank was off again, into another far corner, they told her to thank him too. No, they weren't going on a honeymoon, she had a new line to supervise. Overachievers didn't go on honeymoons.They got married on a free weekend.

When most of the guests had gone and Greta sat down next to the piano player to sing, Shelly went into the kitchen expecting to have to supervise the cleanup. Surprisingly, it was already done. Astra Rainbow had started it and the others had kept up with her rhythm. The rented dishes were stacked back in their boxes; so were the silver and stemware. The items had been counted. Missing were three spoons, a pink napkin and five glasses. Four had been broken, but no one could account for the fifth. The leftover food was wrapped and stored in the refrigerator. Shelly was relieved. Seth, who was second in command and had only to report to Shelly, admitted, "Before I knew it, she had things under control."

Astra Rainbow was at the sink washing her hands. Before she had a chance to finish, Shelly turned her around. Some of her hair had escaped the black ribbon she used to tie it back. "Thanks," Shelly said.

"I should be thanking you. It was so beautiful here tonight. I never saw a prettier wedding. It was like a beautiful garden from another time." No matter how many times she was thanked, Rainbow insisted it was one of the most wonderful nights of her life. She looked very tall and thin in the black uniform that Shelly had provided. It was easy to see her Swedish blood under these circumstances.

Shelly, Mickey and Rainbow were the last to leave. Greta and Hank saw them to the door, and for the first time that night the bride and groom held each other. Now that the group was down to the most familiar faces, it was easy for Greta to show her love. Her marriage would always be a private triumph and a public disaster. "You're next," Hank told Mickey when he walked them to the elevator.

There was Mickey, between the brunette and the blonde, almost ready to agree that he was next. He smiled, and that gave Shelly great hope. She would have expected him to say, "No. Not me. Never." That might have led to a fight in the street. Instead, they put Astra Rainbow in a cab and got one for themselves. They didn't notice that she was headed uptown to the office, instead of home to Brooklyn.

# 18

# The Last Proposal

IT took Shelly seven days after Greta's wedding to propose. Well, why not? Haven't men for centuries done the same thing? They would see a friend get married and want the same for themselves. It was Saturday night that Shelly got out of control. She had forgotten that Greta's life wasn't perfect and remembered how the newlyweds held on to each other at the door. Whatever the problems, Greta's search was over. She would never again have to say to a man, "Thank you, I had a very nice time."

At least half a dozen times that week Shelly controlled herself. One proposal after another came to mind, but like an addict avoiding his addiction, she went through the steps of talking herself out of it, changing the activity and taking things one day at a time. When she really felt a proposal coming on, she called Paula, her Bloomingdale's shopper. Her addiction cost her a Krizia sweater.

By mid–Saturday night she broke. Bloomingdale's was closed, Greta wasn't available and there was Mickey lying there with all the necessary equipment to become a husband. All his parts were in working order. She made the mistake of forgetting what had happened during her last set of proposals. He was watching *The Purple Rose of Cairo* on cable. She was pretending to watch. Actually, she was watching him. She worded and reworded proposals in her mind, but managed to talk herself into not using them. Mickey played with the belt on his one-size-fits-all kimono-style terry robe. It wasn't the robe she would have picked for him, but even if they stayed together forever, she wasn't going to get to dress him the way Greta got to dress Hank. He flipped the belt back and forth, probably unaware he was doing it. Shelly's proposal matched the rhythm of the flipping terry cloth. "Why don't we get married?" The words got louder and louder though they remained inside her head. Mickey looked at her and smiled, unaware of the song in her mind. She returned his smile, not letting him tune in to her music.

She moved closer and laid her head on his chest. From this angle she could see that some of his hairs were gray. This man was old enough to get married. In other eras he would have been considered strange at this age and would still have been living at home with his mother. One proposal wasn't going to hurt. Just one. If he said no, she promised herself she wouldn't ask again. She should be standing in front of a group of women like herself at Proposers Anonymous. "Hi, my name is Shelly and I keep asking a man to marry me." The women on the folding chairs would yell back, "Hi, Shelly," and she would have to go on. "I started proposing just a few months ago. To tell you the truth, I didn't realize that I was doing it until I was doing it several times a day. Finally, I hit bottom. I gave him an ultimatum and then begged him to come back. I had humiliated myself and lost everything. Then I came here. I haven't proposed for days." Admiration and applause from the audience. "I'm really scared right now. My best friend got married a week ago and proposing has been on my mind. I've been hinting. Just the other night I pointed out that I came with my own engagement ring. Sometimes when my boyfriend and I are relaxing and watching television I'm petrified that I'm going to propose during a commercial." Shouts of "Don't do it," come from the group.

Shelly was sure she could handle just one proposal. She convinced herself, that if Mickey said no she could take it and not go for another one. She was sure she had enough control not to go for the ultimatum. It shouldn't have, but the gray hair on Mickey's chest gave her confidence. This was no longer a vital young man she was asking to marry her. This was an aging soul lucky to spend his twilight years with her. She curled a clump of his chest hairs around her little finger and popped the question. The actual wording was so straightforward and traditional that it surprised both of them. "Will you marry me?" she asked, as if she were in a waistcoat and on bended knee.

"Oh, Shelly." The two words said, "Why are we getting into that again? Why, when everything has been so peaceful, are you putting dynamite in our bed?"

"I want to know, Mickey, will you marry me?" She now sat up and waited for his answer. Her yellow nightgown had not quite been able to keep up with her movements and was off center, ready to expose one pretty good breast. Shelly had no idea that her gown had so comically left her behind. When Mickey sat up to face her, there was no way that he could consider her the enemy even though she was asking him to give up the tranquillity he had recently found.

"Why are you doing this?" he asked, as if she were shooting heroin into both their arms.

"You're not answering my question." She was a strong woman, this Shelly Silver.

"I'm not answering because I want everything to stay the same."

As he sat up to face her, his robe opened both above and below the belt. He looked very undignified with everything hanging out. She wanted him. "So, if you want everything the same, then your real answer is no."

Mickey was not above being scared. He didn't want a definite no hanging between them. "How about if we take one thing at a time?" he offered. "Why don't we see if we can just hang around together for the next fifty-six years?"

"You're stalling. I want to feel safe. I want kids. I'm tired of holding my stomach in."

"What?"

"Since we're not married, I keep thinking that I have to hold my stomach in." Obviously, Mickey didn't have the same concerns. His open robe allowed her to see his stomach, and it was out.

"You don't have to strain your muscles for me." He went to hug her, but a hug wasn't going to do it for her. She needed the whole package, the big one that began with a rabbi and led to buying stereos in common.

"I'm not good at this," she said wearily.

"Not good at what?"

"Not good at loving someone more than he loves you."

"Who says?" Mickey was trying desperately to lighten things up. He kissed her cheek and crawled back to his sitting position. He might have just been wearing a terry-cloth belt for all his robe covered. "Who says you love me more than I love you? It isn't possible." He smiled like a clown whose job it was to cheer another person up.

"It feels that way. The truth is I want to marry you and you don't want to marry me." Mickey sat there like a thin, small Buddha. He couldn't begin to argue with the truth.

This time the ultimatum came not with a bang, but with a whimper. "Look, Mickey. I'm willing to marry you. If you're not willing to marry me, then it's over." She said this as a very tired woman.

"You don't want to start again."

"No, I don't. What I want is a wedding, with bridesmaids and a photographer. I don't expect the pictures to end up in his window, but I want him there. And I want my mother to kiss you and your mother to kiss me. I want to want everybody to leave so we can be alone and a honeymoon in some romantic country that doesn't have terrorists. I want the super in this building to know what you think of me. I don't want to change my last name. I'm too proud to, but I want to know I could if I wanted to." With that she let her pillow support her. She had already been leaning back. Now she sank into her bed just by letting everything go.

"So . . . what do you want me to do?" He was as paralyzed as she was exhausted.

"I want you to marry me or leave."

Mickey headed away from Shelly's bed, stringing words into sentences that wouldn't help. He said they could talk about all of this in the morning, that they could compromise on something. She closed her eyes and knew that compromise was impossible. What could she suggest, getting married for half the week?

Mickey snuck out and Shelly was miserable. She was so alone she knew that, once again, she would have to crawl on her hands and knees and beg Mickey to come back. She threw on a coat without even checking out her hair and went up to the fourteenth floor. She found a note on Mickey's door as if he had expected her to come crawling. It said, "Don't ring or knock it. I went out for a while. Mickey." Of course he had meant "Don't ring or knock," but inserting the word "it" seemed appropriate. Don't knock my inability to marry you.

Since the note was obviously meant for her and said Mickey would be out for a while, not forever, Shelly decided to wait. It was too bad that on the night that she had been her strongest, she also had to be her weakest. She sat in the hall, leaning against his door, her legs outstretched before her. She hated being desperate, but she was and it would take too much energy to hide it. She couldn't help worrying about him. Mickey didn't go to bars or for walks. No sane person went for walks at one in the morning. She hoped he would hurry home and that they could have a swift reconciliation. Her jeans were too tight to last through days of Sara Lee banana cake.

Mickey went down to his office. He was too chicken to walk the streets, and he didn't feel like telling the story to Jerry. He figured he could sit in the dark and think this out. Instead he found Astra Rainbow.

When she heard the key in the door, she thought that someone was coming to kill her, as if there might be a contract out on her life. She didn't scream. She just sat up on the couch waiting to be killed. It was Mickey who screamed. He had turned on the light to find his typing paper, and there she was in her pink pajamas, holding a pink quilt up to her shoulders, looking like a twelve-year-old at a slumber party. "I'm sorry," she said, with so much remorse that Mickey's first job was going to be making her not feel guilty.

"Don't be sorry. Just tell me why you're here." He pulled his desk chair close to show that he would listen and wasn't angry.

"I shouldn't have stayed here, but . . ." Her head moved as if she were speaking, but no words came out.

"But what? It's okay. I don't mind that you're here. But what?" She was silent for a few more moments, and he had time to glance over at *Afterlife*. Tomorrow he would like it again. Tonight he thought it was trash. Here was the real story, a virgin in distress.

"It's just that I don't like to sleep at home on Saturday nights." Either Astra Rainbow had a terrific sense of drama or she didn't know that Jewish people needed to hear the whole story and were never satisfied with a simple answer to their questions. She flicked her hair back. Usually it was confined by a barrette. When it was free the woman in her was stronger than the girl.

"Why?" was all he could ask.

"Well, Mary has company over and they were right there in the next room, and it felt strange being there." She didn't bother to tell him that, physically, she couldn't stand being in the apartment when Frank was there. She was from strong stock and was always embarrassed by any physical frailty. She had hardly ever missed a day of school and never admitted to a headache.

"So how long have you been doing this?" He tried very hard not to sound like an investigator but rather like a curious friend. He was flooded with confusing emotions. He didn't know whether to father her, mother her, love her or just write about her.

"Just a couple of months. Is it illegal?" With this question she grabbed her quilt more tightly, as if that would save her from the law.

"Not exactly. You're not supposed to sleep in any office building. There are guards wandering around. I'm surprised they haven't found you."

"Oh, Sam did. I told him I was doing some work for you. I hated lying, but he had a gun." She couldn't have thought that he would kill her for using the couch. The gun must have referred to his authority.

Mickey looked at her wide eyes surrounded by a fresh face, and he knew he would have to take care of this girl. He would have liked to have scooped her up in his arms like a child who has fallen asleep on the couch and has to be carried to his bed. "Here's what's going to happen," he said. (He was always a take-charge kind of guy when dealing with Astra Rainbow.) "I'll wait outside at your desk. You get dressed and then you're coming uptown with me. Either you'll stay at my place and I'll stay with Shelly . . ." His words got less definite as he remembered where he left his relationship. "Or you'll stay downstairs and I'll . . ." He was definitely losing the strength he had started with, so he went back to the orders he was most comfortable with. "Get dressed," he said. "I'll be waiting."

"Are you mad at me?" She had to know before she moved.

"No. Absolutely not. I just think this is no place to spend the night." He left her to dress and ended up guarding the door, rather than just waiting. Since the building was empty, there was no reason for his stance.

Mickey's apartment was across from the elevators, and Shelly had spent the last hour watching the numbers stop before and after fourteen. Now that it was arriving on Mickey's floor, she didn't expect him. She was too used to having things go wrong to have him home. But there he was. She started to get up and was on her knees by the time Astra Rainbow emerged from the elevator. Shelly didn't continue to get up. She stayed on her knees, as if to beg for an explanation. There were only a few reasons she could think of why these two were together. All of them were rotten.

"Hi, Miss Silver." This from Astra Rainbow, who stood there clutching her small overnight bag.

"Shelly?" Mickey said, as if to verify it was her.

Shelly was the one who deserved the answers, but they were waiting for her to speak first. She could talk. She just couldn't stand up. "Your note said you would be back in a little while, so I waited." Not feeling worthy of standing, since she was, after all, a hall waiter, she sat down again. Immediately Mickey gave her a hand, the support she needed to be erect and equal.

"I say we go in and figure this all out." Mickey opened the door, and the two women looked at each other, not knowing which one should go first. Astra Rainbow was as confused as Shelly. She had no idea why this woman, whom she knew as strong, was sitting on the floor and looking desperate. Since they could get stuck going through the door together, both stepped back to leave the path free to the other. Only then did Shelly take the opportunity to go first. She was older and wearier and wishing she was the suffering wife rather than the bleeding ex-girlfriend.

The two women sat on the couch facing Mickey, who sat in a large, comfortable wing chair. There they were mother, father, daughter, a family that was destined to come together although none of them yet knew it. "Anybody want anything to drink?" he asked. In rhythm with each other, they shook their heads no. Mickey loved the symmetry of it. He liked this little head dance that was being performed for him. He would have liked to go on asking questions that they would shake to in unison.

"She was sleeping on the couch in my office." Mickey looked at

Shelly with a look that said, "What're we going to do with the kid?"

Shelly turned to Astra Rainbow and touched her arm. "Don't tell me Frank is still sleeping over." Mickey, who had been planning to reveal dramatically why he had brought Astra Rainbow home, was surprised that Shelly already knew the reason.

"Mary and Frank are sort of right for each other. The problem is I'm not right with them."

"And you don't have to be." Shelly put her arm around Astra Rainbow, and the girl was happy to put her head on Shelly's shoulder. Mickey wanted snapshots.

"Nobody should have to be uncomfortable, especially in her own home." Mickey realized that both he and Shelly were talking a bit stiffly. They sounded like the adults on *Leave It to Beaver*. They had cast themselves as perfect parents and their posture was good. Their words were comforting but slightly stilted.

"Sometimes I think that I should tell Mary that she can't have Frank over ever again, and other times I think she should be able to have him over every night. She used to cut school and do nothing but meet boys and talk about them. Now she goes to classes and does her homework. It's strange, but now that she's more settled she has more time for her own things. She actually read a book for English class. She didn't like it, but she read it. And she tells me that things are good between her and Frank now that they're sleeping together in a bed once a week. She says he respects her more. And you know something? I believe her."

"I believe her too." Shelly found it difficult to be anything but supportive of Astra Rainbow.

"So, here's my suggestion for the night," said Mickey. "I stay up here. The two of you go down to the third floor and get as much sleep as you can, and in the morning I'll take you both to brunch." Shelly liked the idea because the ultimatum hadn't stuck.

"I don't want to . . ." Astra Rainbow didn't quite know how to finish the sentence. She knew Shelly and Mr. Burke were a couple, and probably sexually involved, but she didn't know if these uptown people minded talking about it. "I don't want to, you know, interrupt anything. I could . . . stay up here."

Shelly wanted Mickey back in her bed, but she didn't want to take the chance of him saying no, so she quickly agreed that Astra Rainbow should come downstairs with her. He kissed her on the cheek at the door. They hadn't done badly on their first night as parents.

Every Saturday night after that, they inherited Astra Rainbow. Sometimes they got her in the middle of the week also, if Shelly needed her for catering or Mary needed to lie down. When she wasn't there, Mickey and Shelly talked about her. Sometimes they told each other the unbelievably innocent things she said. Soemtimes they had hopes and dreams for her future. Shelly hoped Rainbow could be with a man some day. Mickey thought that maybe she should take art lessons. He had seen a small sketch of hers, nothing more than the profile of an unknown person, but he was sure she had talent hidden everywhere.

She mellowed their lives. They took her out to dinner and smiled behind her back. They shopped for a birthday present for her together and decided on a pink sweater. She loved it and never imagined that it cost three hundred dollars. When she had the flu, Shelly made soup and Mickey had it delivered to Brooklyn. When Frank had the flu and missed a Saturday night, they pretended to be relieved. Once Greta asked Shelly if she and Mickey could join her and Hank for dinner on a Saturday, and Shelly surprised her by saying, "Can we make it Friday? Astra Rainbow stays here on Saturday nights."

"Sounds like you're involved in a ménage à trois."

"Don't be insane. We're the only family she has."

It was during this period that Mickey dove into a movie script. The lead character was a love child who had a roommate who had sex in her apartment once a week. The writing came quickly, and the pages piled up. At the end the heroine meets a boy who's been kicked out of his apartment every Saturday night. Shelly loved it. Astra Rainbow was shocked. She didn't think she was important enough to write about. Mickey bought her pearls in exchange for stealing her life. He was prepared to argue with her about keeping them. There was no argument. She ran up to the tenth floor to show Kurt what her boss had given her for no reason at all.

Shelly was comfortable about everything but the pearls. She hadn't been in on the gift, and the whole thing seemed on the fringe of being romantic. It was time to talk to Greta.

"It's not that I really mind. I want her to have the pearls. And it's not that I'm jealous. Mickey is actually more affectionate toward me when she's around. It's just that, well, it's jewelry, isn't it?"

"You're damn right it's jewelry," Greta said with her finger pointed in the warning position. Immediately, Shelly regretted having told on Rainbow. She quickly wanted to protect the child.

"They were tiny, no big deal; tiny and short. They were like pearls that you would buy a ten-year-old girl. So, how is married life? When you're married, do you actually discuss New Year's Eve or does something just present itself? My parents used to . . ."

"Keep her around."

"What?"

Greta tasted the spaghetti sauce she was making, so it took a while to answer. "Keep her around."

"I want to keep her around. She's nice. She relaxes me. She needs me."

"Good, because she's good for you." Greta offered Shelly a taste of the sauce. She cupped her hand under the spoon so that it wouldn't fall on the floor, or worse, on their shoes. Shelly tasted the sauce. It was ordinary, but Shelly put her thumb up. She was sure she couldn't design a dress.

"I don't know how good she is for me. All I know is that I like her. She's learning to be a good little caterer." Shelly grabbed a napkin for the sauce that had escaped to her chin.

"When's the last time you and Mickey had a big fight? I'm not talking about the little ones that begin with, 'You could have at least told me that you were going to be late.' I'm talking about the big ones, where you get scared before they're over."

"Things have been relatively peaceful. I think it's because Mickey's gotten some pretty good feedback on his screenplay. His agents have been calling to tell him how great it is. There's someone at Columbia who's interested. I don't know the details, but he is definitely thrilled from all the great response. He was whistling the other day. I've never heard him whistle before."

Greta again tasted the sauce. One would have thought she had grown the tomatoes from scratch. Actually she was deciding whether to add more Ragú. She had a row of spices, nothing exotic, just thyme, basil, grocery-story items. She didn't reach for any of them. They might have even been an untouched engagement gift. She just kept adding Ragú and garlic salt and thinking she was a great chef. Even though it took her almost a full minute to answer, she didn't forget where the conversation had led them. "He's whistling because he has two women. If you want to keep him around, keep her. The possibility of having her—mind you, I'm just saying the possibility, so don't get crazy—makes it easier for him to love you. Did you ever think she might be your guardian angel? In one way or another, she's always brought him back to you." She added just a pinch of garlic salt, tasted the sauce and closed her eyes as if she were tasting heaven.

"How come you know everything?" Shelly asked. She asked it so sincerely that it couldn't be misconstrued as a rhetorical question.

"I don't. I know everything about your relationships. I know nothing about my own. When you're in pain, you don't know anything."

Things happened quickly. Mickey said he had something to tell her, she should put a bottle of champagne on ice. Her mother thought Mickey was going to propose.

"He's going to pop the question," said Mrs. Silver, who was so excited she held the phone receiver with both hands. Shelly was scared that the only thing Mickey was going to pop was a Moët cork.

"I hope so, Mom."

Nettie Silver, who had to live with a daughter who didn't care about having a marriage license, couldn't help reminding Shelly of her past feelings. "I told you one day you were going to make things legal. I can't believe this is the daughter who once told me that she would never get married because marriage was an outdated institution."

"I want him to marry me, Mom."

"You aggravated me for so many years with that antilicense talk."

"Sorry, Mom."

"You think it was easy for us, seeing you move in with that poor lawyer with the untrimmed beard?"

"Sorry, Mom."

"Don't do anything crazy. If he proposes, don't go quoting Gloria Steinem. Believe me, that magazine of hers doesn't replace children."

"If he asks to marry me, I'll say yes."

"Proposals are not prison."

"You're right, Mom. I've proposed to Mickey dozens of times."

"You what?" The connection was clear. Mrs. Silver had no trouble hearing her daughter, just understanding her.

"I proposed to Mickey."

"Are you paying for the champagne?" Mrs. Silver wanted to know.

Greta thought that Mickey planned to deliver selfish news rather than initiate any discussion about marriage. "Men think that their own good news is going to make the world happy. I went out with a guy once who said he had a surprise for me. All day I was picturing the boxes I would be opening. This guy had money, so the boxes I imagined ranged in size from little, tiny jewelry ones to the huge ones fur coats come in. His big surprise for me was that he had switched from glasses to contact lenses. I'll bet the news Mickey has is about him."

Paula at Bloomingdale's thought she could get away with wearing a Zoran-like outfit at home. "It's so understated," she said. Paula suggested a simple gray cashmere pull-on pant, and Paula was right. It was so understated that it looked like an eight-hundred-dollar sweat suit. While Paula was running her charge card through the machine, Shelly had her full attention. "If a man says to put champagne in the refrigerator because he has a surprise, what would you guess that surprise is?"

Paula was a very short, small-boned woman blessed with a head of thick white hair. When she chose to speak, her hair spoke with her. Although it didn't move on its own, thanks to Spray Net, one heard

Paula's voice and saw her hair move around as if it were part of the Muppet family. Conversations on the phone with Paula were definitely more intimate than those she held in person. When Shelly asked her question, the saleswoman held up one finger with an extremely pointed nail, asking for silence until she finished her paperwork. Only then, her head was raised. This move caused her to have to push her glasses back in place. With her other hand she gave Shelly the sales slip to sign. "What were you asking?" Paula's smile was as fake as her oversized earrings.

Shelly thought of dropping her question, but she had spent eight hundred and fifty dollars and she felt that entitled her to one short opinion. Two women with clothes in their arms were waiting for Paula, but Shelly needed some attention from the thin, obnoxious woman. "I just wanted to know, if a man says put a bottle of champagne in the refrigerator because he has a surprise, what do you think the surprise could be?"

Paula gave the question no thought. "He's going to ask you to go to Hawaii." And then she coughed a smoker's cough.

Life is strange. Paula came closest to being correct. Mickey's news poured out before the champagne. He sprang into the apartment, his down jacket flapping in the breeze that he created by moving so fast. He paced in front of Shelly, using his whole body for emphasis. "Okay, where do I begin? Barry called a couple of hours ago. Columbia wants me out there as soon as possible to work on revisions." Here he stopped to get angry. "Fuckers buy something, and the first thing they want to do is change it." He stopped, sucked in all the air in Shelly's kitchen and convinced himself that he was telling a good story, not a bad one. "I'll deal with that. No problem. How big could they be? They just want me out there for a few days. They're buying my script!" Shelly stood up and applauded. She was with him all the way, the woman not behind, but surrounding, the man. Since she was his audience he felt he had a right to go on. "I figured, why wait? So I made reservations and that's what I had to ask you. Will you go with me?" Shelly leapt on him, hugging him, causing him to jump for joy with her. She forgot that they had a two-career relationship and that she had to ask things like how long they would be away. They didn't dance, but they made a small circle clinging to each other. This is what the world knew as, "Success is nothing unless you have someone to share it with."

The champagne was drunk, the love was made. Mickey fell asleep first. Shelly stayed up worrying about her business, worrying that she couldn't not propose in a tropical climate and worrying that Paula would not know what to wear in California this time of the year. It wasn't until the following morning that she had the presence of mind to ask, "When?"

"We leave on Thursday and come back the following Monday." She smiled, not telling him that she had a twenty-fifth-anniversary party to cater on the Saturday they would be gone. He knew she worked. He just didn't remember her job while his dreams were being fulfilled.

When Mickey left for his apartment in order to get dressed for another day of praise, Shelly made some adjustments. She called Seth and asked if he could handle the party without her. He could, if Astra Rainbow were there to help. Shelly was happy with his request. It was nice to know there were others who saw Rainbow's value as clearly as she did. She called Rainbow at Mickey's office and told her what Seth had said. The girl was flattered that Seth would want her. She couldn't believe that she was not only a character in a screenplay that they liked in California but also requested by Shelly's assistant, all at the same time. She had never meant to intrude on anybody's life, and there she was, assisting in everybody's triumphs. Maybe there was more than one way to serve man.

Shelly then called Nicki Fieldstein, a tough customer. She had confided in Shelly that even though they were having a twenty-fifth-anniversary party, she really didn't like her husband. This was revealed the second time they met and while Shelly was trying to convince the unhappy Mrs. Fieldstein to go the "abundance of shellfish" route. "Wait until you meet him," Nicki said. "You have never met anyone who toots his own horn so much. I don't know how much more of this I can take." Why the party, then? His family gave really great cash gifts, and she wanted to replant the terrace.

Nicki Fieldstein, like many women with enough money to give a party at home for a hundred and twenty-five, was a perfectionist. She called Shelly at eleven-thirty one night to tell her that the mirrors that they put under the flowers (a catering trick that made it look like there were twice as many blossoms) should be top-quality glass and have beveled edges. She had made Shelly promise to be there.

The lie came easily. "Due to a family tragedy, I won't be able to be there on Saturday night," she told Nicki face to face. "I have a man who has worked with me closely who knows everything I know. A young woman, who I consider a daughter, will assist him. I promise you the party will be perfect."

"How much do I get off?" Nicki asked.

"Pardon me?" Shelly had expected a fight, not a negotiation.

"I figure we're paying a pretty stiff figure for this affair and that the price is so high because you don't come cheap. So I'm sorry about your family tragedy, but how much do we get off? I'm campaigning for a sapphire ring surrounded by diamonds, not as big as the one

Princess Di has, but it'll help to know that we're saving a little here."

"How about twenty percent?" Shelly would just be breaking even, but her freedom was worth it.

"How about twenty-five?"

"Fine." She could take a loss if she was near palm trees with the man she loved.

Mickey and Shelly's relationship had never been traditional. For one thing, the only way they could live with each other was living without each other. It seemed normal to them first to have the honeymoon and then the final proposal.

California shone for them. They had expected to be cynical about it but ended up enchanted, holding hands while wearing pastels. They stayed at the Bel Air Hotel and even liked the swans that were forced to live on the fake little lake, waiting for weekend brides. They overate and pretended to play tennis and wanted what all the other successful young couples had: the feeling of knowing that they could buy anything in the world if they wanted it. The saleswomen on Rodeo made Paula look shabby.

The biggest symbol of the union was how consistently they held hands. They entwined their fingers for most of the trip. There were no fights. Shelly didn't mind that Mickey was trashing the hotel room and Mickey didn't mind that Shelly had no bed to sleep in but theirs.

The script meetings were brief. The second act needed some juice, they said, and in the bright California sun, Mickey and Shelly, whom he consulted every day, thought they might be right. Everything needed a little juice when it was eighty-nine degrees outside.

Shelly called Astra Rainbow, who told her the Fieldstein affair ran smoothly. "Mrs. Fieldstein gave me twenty dollars, and I tried to give it back to her, but she made me keep it." Shelly assured her it was all right to take the tip and told Mickey the story over dinner at Spago. They reminded each other what a good job they were doing with the kid and how great it was they had her so they could get away. She squeezed his knee when she thought Ryan O'Neal and Farrah Fawcett had walked into the restaurant.

The night before they left, their lovemaking was hotter than usual. He undressed her, which he hadn't done since they got together the first time. One of her buttons popped off a very good blouse, and she didn't even go crawling around looking for it. In retaliation, she unzipped his pants. Their clothes flew, having a life of their own once they hit the air. The garments intertwined like their owners. His pants landed on her skirt, and they blended together. Mickey and Shelly were left naked and standing. Over the months, they had become lazy about sex, and hadn't been naked and standing at the same time since . . . actually this might have been the first time. They had definitely not ever been standing naked and with the lights on. (That was not Shelly's most comfortable thing to do. When she lay on the bed naked, she imagined any excess she might have accumulated was given a chance to spread evenly.) He felt creative. Columbia just wanted minor changes. The days had been warm and friendly. He wanted this to be a night to remember. They had tried out a few different sexual positions at the beginning of their relationship when they were trying to impress each other with their skill. None of the unusual ones had really worked out, and they were basically down to four, or to be honest, three. Mostly he rolled on top of her.

He knew it was possible to do it standing up. In the good old days, when other people were getting stoned and he was writing twelve hours a day, an aspiring writer who idolized him invited herself to his apartment and then into his shower. You don't lie down in showers. Shelly was leading him toward the bed. It looked inviting, but not exciting enough. He had always felt the more creative the sex, the further one was from the mattress. He gently refused to go. She gently tried to get him there again. This gentle tug-of-war brought a puzzled expression to her face. He was going to have to make some quick, smooth moves in order to erase her confusion. He pressed against her and began foreplay. She followed his lead and there they were, kissing and touching with all the appropriate sounds. When she was foreplayed out, she tried to lead him to the bed again, but he kept her there. They were in California. They were young. They were their own bosses. They were going to do it standing up.

In later years Shelly would remember this night as the one that broke her back. That was a bit of an exaggeration: She broke only two vertebrae. In a real attempt to make this standing-up business work, Mickey had lifted Shelly's left leg. Unfortunately her right one couldn't do the work for both of them. It gave way and her body went crashing to the floor. The noise was embarrassingly loud. The pain was immediate. Still her first thought was that she would rather be naked and lying down than naked and standing. She never really screamed because the breath was knocked out of her. Her face told the story of the pain and, through the tears in her eyes, she saw Mickey lose his erection.

She was hurt, and he was guilty and worried. He bent down to be with her, asking if she was okay, knowing already that a Tylenol wasn't going to be able to take care of this. "I'm sorry," he said more than once.

Deciding it was better for the relationship to be a brave little soldier than a crybaby, she whispered, "Don't worry about it." Above all, she didn't want to spoil the vacation.

She was cold and he ran for a blanket. Then he just sat there next to her on the floor saying he was sorry and waiting for her to get up. The aspiring writer in the shower had probably been a gymnast. Shelly didn't move. Several minutes later, she found out she couldn't move. He held her hand and kissed her forehead and she thought, This is the way to get Mickey Burke to really love you. You have to let him break your back.

"You're sure you can't sit up?"

"I'm positive." The slightest shift of movement brought excruciating pain.

Mickey called the front desk, who reached the hotel manager. Shelly felt they had been caught, two single people sharing a room in too classy a hotel. The manager wanted to know if the young lady could be taken to the emergency room at UCLA. Since it was Friday night, a physician was going to be hard to get. Mickey asked Shelly if she thought she could make it to the car. She was sure she couldn't make it to the door. Mickey was guilty enough to become her protector. Still nude and not looking very authoritative, he lowered his voice and told the hotel manager that there must be some doctor available in Los Angeles who would come to their room and the manager had better find him. "She slipped in *your* room," he said, threatening years of lawsuits.

"What did he say?" It hurt to talk, but there were things she had to know.

"He said he'd find somebody. I need a cigarette." Mickey hadn't smoked in years and knew there wasn't a cigarette between them. Instead of smoking, he sat down next to Shelly again, taking one of her hands in his two. Even this small movement hurt like hell, but Shelly was very Jewish about things like this. She complained into the night about a stiff headache, but the larger pains she suffered through silently. She got this from her mother, who stayed in bed with a sore throat and danced through her hysterectomy.

"Do you want anything?" Mickey asked gently, as if words might worsen her injury.

"I better get dressed if the doctor's coming."

"He's just going to check you out anyway." Men were always too practical about being clothed.

"Mickey, please." It hurt to talk so she stopped until she regained her courage to go on. "I can't . . . it's embarrassing."

He nodded and went for the clothes that he had just taken off her. He had no idea of the impracticality of putting panty hose and a short black leather skirt on a woman who was incapable of moving. When she saw what he was going to attempt, she knew she had to talk again.

The pain was increasing so the instructions had to be short. "Under-pants, nightgown, robe," she said, wincing between each word.

He looked at the clothing in his hands as if he were making the final decision of what was going on her body. Finally, he relinquished them, dropping them over the chair. The legs of the panty hose hung down to the floor, still conforming to the shape Shelly had given them when she wore them that night. She was once again disappointed with her thighs.

Shelly had packed two nightgowns and two robes, and Mickey found the wrong combination. She didn't have the guts to protest. Let the doctor find her in a pink Natori gown with a red Sanchez robe. Let him worry why she was in this clown outfit.

She couldn't help him dress her. The slightest movement caused her to think of words that turned PG movies into Rs. Mickey moved the garments as slowly as he could around her. As he empathized with her pain, his face formed the same contortions hers did. The underpants were the hardest to handle because she couldn't lift her rear. He had to inch them up on one side and then run around to the other for another slight pull.

The whole process took about twenty minutes, and when he fin-ished he stood back to admire his handiwork. The job was not well done. The clothes definitely looked as if they had been put on after the fall. Instead of draping on both sides of her, the red robe flowed to the left, looking more like a backdrop arranged for a painting than like something being worn. The gown also favored the left. One seam that was supposed to be on the side stretched across her body, starting under the left arm and ending at the right foot. The underpants were never jacked high enough. If she were able to stand, they would have fallen off. Still, for modesty's sake, everything was in place.

"Well, all right. You look . . . pretty."

Shelly closed her eyes in lieu of nodding her head. Mickey threw on jeans and left his chest and feet bare. He pulled up a chair and looked at Shelly. Forgetting that it hurt her only to talk, not to listen, he was very quiet for a while. She imagined he was feeling very guilty. Actually, he was trying to remember just how he had executed love-making in the shower. It was a long time ago, but he was pretty sure that it involved at least one raised leg.

The doctor and hotel manager arrived at the same time, and it was impossible to tell which was which. Mickey hoped the older, wiser-looking, gray-haired man was the doctor. Of course, he was the hotel manager, extending his sympathies. The twelve-year-old doctor, not realizing what a serious situation his patient was in, had to run back to the car for his bag. It was a good thing he was wearing Nikes. He started backing out the door, but the hotel manager stopped him, assuring the young doctor that the bag could be brought to the room. "What kind of car do you have?" the manager asked while picking up the phone.

"Oh, you can't miss it. It's a sixty-six Mustang and you can't open the passenger's door. It's from an accident before I bought it, and I never did have it fixed." Shelly wondered if she wanted to put her body into the hand of a doctor who drove a dented Ford.

He turned out to be a pretty nice fellow whose only fault was offering too many options. "Do you want a shot for the pain or not?" he asked. She wanted it. "Do you want to go down to the emergency room tonight where they'll have you sitting around forever or do you want to come into the office tomorrow where we can get some good X rays?" She wanted to wait until tomorrow. "Do you want me to tape it? It will do no real medical good, but it might feel better." She wanted tape.

He poked and touched, asking where it hurt, but Shelly was so afraid of his finger that the probing didn't do much good. She hurt all over. The shot was given and, as gently as possible, the three men raised her to the bed. She worried about her weight. The young doctor ordered some Darvon to be sent over in a cab from an all-night drugstore, then gave his final instructions. "Call for an ambulance in the morning, because they're going to have to bring her in on a stretcher. He wrote down the address of his office, but Mickey was already planning on finding the best orthopedic man in L.A. in the morning.

The shot was beginning to take effect, and Shelly explained that they couldn't come to the doctor's office because they had to leave in the morning. Young Dr. Milfred thought that was pretty funny. His laugh was hearty, especially considering it was the middle of the night. Only the young could laugh that hard at such a late hour.

The manager and the doctor were in the doorway before the doctor thought to ask, "Hey, how did this happen anyway?" Shelly heard the question, but she was too out of it to answer. Her mouth wouldn't move. She was, however, awake enough to wonder what the answer would be.

"We were . . . fooling around," said Mickey, looking at his naked toe. He prayed it would be left at that.

"Yeah, but how?" It was at this point that Mickey realized that the doctor was doing his duty. He must have learned in medical school that when you find a hurt woman and a man in a room together that the woman may have been battered.

"Really, we were just . . ." In order not to be accused, Mickey was going to have to fill in some details. "We were trying to fornicate standing up and she lost her balance." He obviously chose his words carefully while talking to this medical man. The doctor, however, needed verification and went over to the bed.

"Is that true, miss?" Shelly didn't love the idea of being called "miss" under the circumstances. Why was she never mistaken for somebody's wife?

"Oh, yes, doctor," she said earnestly, using all her effort to speak. She wanted to add that she didn't lose her balance. It was important to her that this stranger know that she wasn't the klutz, that Mickey had flipped her, but she didn't have the energy to explain.

The doctor was content enough to leave. The manager went with him but not before mentioning that an accident report would have to be filled out. Mickey knew the word fornicating would appear on it. He worried that the hotel had a file of weirdos whom they would never let back in.

The following morning Mickey pulled all the strings he had and got Shelly an appointment with a Dr. Harry Nederman. Shelly was carried on a stretcher from the room, full of Darvon and holding Mickey's hand. Too bad that poor woman had to be carried right past a wedding. Passersby didn't know whether to sigh over the bride or the girl on the stretcher.

Because of the accident, Shelly and Mickey returned to New York four days late. He said he didn't mind. He was used to hotels and room service. After two days she felt guiltier than he did. Since she needed the bed for herself, the hotel sent up a cot for him. At first he was her nurse, watching even when she slept. Although she encouraged him to go out and get a tan, he stayed in the room, holding her hand, leaving on the television fourteen hours a day. Finally, Shelly convinced him to go see some of the people he knew when he lived there. She had gone from Darvon to Percodan and things were back under control.

His first day out, Mickey met someone for lunch at the hotel and was back in an hour. When he saw she was still living, his trips out became longer and his apologies shorter. She was going to live. She could get to the bathroom alone. Some bad things happened to good people. The last couple of days on the coast, Mickey traveled from the Valley to Malibu, calling into the hotel to make sure things were fine. Shelly would report her accomplishments over the phone: "I got all the way to the bathroom by myself on the crutches," she said proudly. He tipped the staff extra heavily that day.

They flew home on Friday and were greeted by Astra Rainbow, who had once again followed orders. She had gotten the Percodan and moved into the guest room. She was staying for a while just to help Shelly and Mr. Burke out. As she packed to leave Brooklyn, Frank was moving in. He bobbed past her with an armload of shirts, unpacked and unpressed.

Astra Rainbow could not have been a better daughter. She was downstairs in the lobby when the limousine arrived from the airport. She was strong enough to be a good crutch, and the two women made it upstairs with Mickey and the doorman dealing with luggage behind them. Although Mickey still had terrible waves of guilt, he couldn't help enjoying seeing his blonde and brunette entwined. They walked together as if they were in a three-legged race.

Astra Rainbow helped Shelly get to bed, knowing where her things were, picking the right nightgown, assuring her that Seth had the business running smoothly. There were flowers on the end table. Shelly had once mentioned she loved white tea roses, and there they were. They should have been from Mickey, but they were from Astra Rainbow, who didn't want credit for her thoughtfulness.

There was a strange dance going on between the three of them. Mickey left the room when Astra Rainbow came in. He had clearly handed over the care of Shelly to the girl. He stood in the hallway watching as Astra Rainbow helped Shelly get into bed. The pain pills had worked, and they laughed over how awkwardly they were performing even the simplest movements. The last two things Astra Rainbow did were to plump the pillows and hand Shelly a hairbrush. Mickey would never have thought of those details. He thought women were wonderful. Men, he realized, could take care of the broad strokes of life, but the women provided the details. And the details were what made one life so different from the next. Maybe if he stayed close to these women he could learn to fill in the broad strokes.

When Astra Rainbow had taken care of everything, she left and gently urged Mickey in. Since they had returned from Lorain, Astra Rainbow hadn't touched her boss, and now she mimed her urging with a swing of the arms. Mickey went in to find Shelly sitting up in bed, one hand on a closed copy of *Vogue*, the other raised in a queenly greeting. This was a better meeting than they had had in days. He no longer had to worry about her care, and she no longer had to feel she was robbing him of time.

"Is a hug a possibility?" Mickey asked politely. He didn't even approach the bed. There was something polite and English about his attitude.

"How about a light hand squeeze? We could pretend we're aliens with all our erogenous zones in our thumbs."

Mickey rushed to the bed but stopped abruptly before sitting down. There had been too many accidental bumps since the accident. He held her hand, but kept his body back. He had no idea that the mental bumps he had given her were far worse than the broken back.

"You can sit down," she said. She patted the bed where she wanted him, and obediently he went to the exact spot she indicated. He sat like a young boy would sit on a chair that he knows is to fancy for him.

"You're feeling all right?" He wanted her to say yes so badly that he nodded, hoping she would join him. She did.

"I'm feeling fine." It may have been the medication or his sweet look that made her sentimental. Shelly cried. "I'm lucky," she said. "I'm lucky to have you."

He felt unworthy. He had hurt her. The bandages were his fault. Because of him she was going to have to be alone in bed too long for someone her age. "I don't make you happy enough," he said. "I mean, there I am on the fourteenth floor and . . ." He couldn't finish. There was nothing more to say. There he was on the fourteenth floor. That was the whole story.

"I like you on the fourteenth floor," she said. "It's all right. It's better, Mickey. Our hearts are living together. That doesn't mean we have to share closets. Maybe we just got too old and too successful to share closets."

"I don't know how you can be so happy with a broken back."

"I guess I'm in love."

"I love you too, kid."

She felt the proposal coming from deep within. It was like a sneeze that couldn't be stifled. Soon she would be proposing whether she wanted to or not. She tried holding it in, but there it was, traveling from her brain to her lips. "If we love each other . . ." It was too late to stop it. ". . . you can still live upstairs. Why can't we get married?" she asked.

His sigh could have been heard throughout the entire Upper West Side. It was the sigh of a generation of men who had been caught for the second time, those boys who couldn't remember wanting to get married once and now here they were standing before rabbis again and again. They wanted to play, but they chose serious women to play with. The sigh signaled to Shelly that she was going to be turned down again. She had skipped over the hint and was too tired to go to the ultimatum. So there the sigh sat until Mickey said, "All right. Let's do it." Once having said it, he relaxed his face into a very bright smile. He had no proof that he could be married and happy at the same time, but at least he would try it.

They couldn't hug and he was too scared to move the bed and his life out of balance by doing anything other than try to look happy.

She looked happy back. There really was nothing more to say. They had made their deal and now, they hoped, for the rest of their lives they could live with it.

Shelly was tired from the trip, the medication and the victory. She would have expected to celebrate, but instead she fell asleep. This is the way her single life ended: not with a bang, but peacefully. Mickey watched her sleep for a short while. His conclusion was that he got a good woman.

The wedding was reflective of the decades Shelly had survived. It was at the Tavern on the Green, a symbol of the early sixties, a time when where the wedding took place was as important as the groom. The bride and groom wrote their own vows. Although they weren't barefoot in a field, their ceremony was reminiscent of all the brides and grooms of the seventies who, in their antique clothing, vowed to bake bread together during the Age of Aquarius. They introduced the eighties by sharing the cost right down the middle. And the nineties by having a prenuptial agreement. There was even a little fifties thrown in. They never made love off the bed again.

# 19

# Propagating
# the Race

H E'S beautiful," said Shelly, looking at the tiny boy lying in the crib for the privileged newly born. When she looked at the baby she was happy for Greta, but when she walked away her emptiness returned. Shelly had been trying for eighteen months to conceive. She and Mickey had had the tests, saved the sperm, followed the infertility specialist's advice and remained barren. Although they couldn't be positive, they were, let's say, ninety-nine-percent sure that the fault lay within Shelly. She had to admit that she had taken a lot of chances and had never conceived. "But what about all those miracles you see on television?" she asked doctor after doctor. Test-tube babies were no longer rare. They froze embryos for years. Where was the miracle for her? There was none. There was a laser operation in Tennessee where they opened your tubes, but there was no guarantee. She had the operation and dealt with more percentages. "There's a twenty-percent chance you could get lucky," she was told. She and Mickey tried to get lucky. They had sex on all the right days. (They didn't call it making love anymore. This was business.) Shelly got upset every month when she saw it hadn't happened for her. There were a couple of hopeful times and a couple of pregnancy tests. The nurses sounded sad when she called for the results.

Her mother told her to relax, as if a woman who got sick at the sight of every Aprica carriage in the street could relax. Greta became pregnant and hardly mentioned it, knowing Shelly was in pain. She herself had had a hard time conceiving and knew the pain of feeling empty. "I can't get myself pregnant," she had said, as if there was no husband. When Mickey and Shelly visited her in the hospital, mother and baby were doing fine and Hank was in the corner. When they congratulated him, he said, "Nah," as if he had nothing to do with it. Now that the baby was home, he was moved into Greta's bedroom and Hank was moved out.

"You're so lucky," Shelly told Greta, who already knew she was. These were women who had always known that babies are wonderful.

"I looked at him and thought, Who put the eyebrows in the right place?" Greta, who had always looked motherly, now more than ever had the hips and breasts for the job. Her whole body had spread as a welcome mat for this baby.

"It's the best thing I've ever done," said Greta, still taking full credit.

"And Hank is sleeping in the other room?"

"Yeah. Look at us. You and I couldn't wait until we got married, and in a way we're more alone than we've ever been." Shelly couldn't deny it. Mickey was still on the fourteenth floor, and although her mother thought that was inviting trouble, Shelly liked him there. Greta kissed the top of her sleeping baby's head and was happy her husband was in another bedroom.

Mickey said it didn't matter that they didn't have kids. And that hurt more. Here she was letting surgeons into her body, and he could live without a child. "I just don't think we should get ourselves all crazy about this." Mickey said. But she did get crazy. Craziness was called for when you couldn't have the baby you wanted. It angered her when he refused to cry over not having an heir. She dragged him to specialist after specialist in the hopes that the percentage would change. They did, but they were never high enough. One doctor suggested getting a surrogate mother, but Shelly imagined her baby housed in a woman who wouldn't play music for or read to the embryo. On their second anniversary, when she refused to make love because they would be wasting sperm, Mickey begged Shelly to give up the pursuit of a baby. Had he forgotten what a persistent person she could be?

Most of the time Shelly dealt well with her inability to become pregnant, but there were times when she allowed the depression that hung over her to enter her body. Sometimes she cried into the hairs on Mickey's chest. Once she let a tear fall on Greta's baby. Greta didn't see it happen, and fortunately her tear mingled with the baby's. More than once she cried while she and Astra Rainbow were in the kitchen pulling together upcoming parties. The first time she blamed it on the onions that were surrounding the brisket. The next time they were filling miniature cream puffs, and she got caught.

"What's the matter?" Astra Rainbow's hand went to her heart and a minor gasp escaped.

"Nothing . . . I was just thinking." The tears flowed and she couldn't find the faucet to turn them off.

"Well, it must be something. Come on."

Rainbow was so distressed that Shelly knew she would have to say something. Tears the size of hers had to be explained. "I just sometimes know that I'm never going to have a baby."

"That can't be true."

"It's true. I asked Dr. Welch the other day to give it to me straight, and he did. In his medical opinion it would never happen." In contrast to her depressed mood, Shelly licked the whipped cream from her fingers as though she had accepted the worst and knew it was time to have something sweet again.

"Is there no way?"

"No. And they tell you not to feel inadequate, but you do. If Mickey had married somebody else, he'd have all these creative kids reaching his knees by now."

They sat on stools, holding hands, staring into the window that became a black hole at night, feeling sad with each other. "Maybe . . ." Astra Rainbow was finally able to say, but there were no words to finish the sentence. Whenever they worked in the kitchen, she wore a large muslin apron that reminded Shelly of a past century. The apron was never needed. It always went home as clean as it had come.

"There are no maybes anymore. Welch even suggested a surrogate to carry the baby, but I couldn't do that. I'd want to be there all day, every day, making sure she was drinking milk and not lying on her stomach." Shelly got up and went back to work. The cream puffs waited in rows to be filled, and she was just the woman to fill them. Astra Rainbow followed behind, putting her completed pastries on the round silver trays for serving. Together they were such a well-coordinated team that their movement could have used a musical accompaniment.

Mickey had called the family meeting. He liked to write dramatic moments in life as well as on the page. His blonde was to his left, looking chic in the brown suede skirt that Shelly had picked out for her birthday. She never would have thought to want it, but now it had become her uniform. She looked ready for life even though those closest to her knew that she wasn't. His brunette was to the right of him, dressed for running. She reminded him of the girls across the lake at camp. They were always in shorts and never sat still. Shelly was stealing some attention from Mickey by doing stretching exercises.

Mickey stood in front of the fireplace. If the decorator hadn't removed the mantel for a sleek look, he would be leaning on it. Mickey Burke had settled into a country-gentleman look since his marriage. He refused to wear anything stiff or scratchy and hung on to his old corduroys as if they were maturing bonds. His feet often had leather slippers on them as he shuffled between the fourteenth and third floors. If his shirt slipped out of his pants he never knew it, and every weekend he managed to have a three-day growth. Now he cleared his throat, more to get their attention than because he needed to. "As you know, it isn't really my movie anymore." They knew because they had been around to hear him express his fury. Two different sets of writers had rewritten it. The director had changed it daily, and Diane Keaton was playing Astra Rainbow. Surprisingly, Mickey had never even tried to put his head through a wall. He cursed them with his fist in the air, no less a revolutionary than he used to be, but he had learned to preserve his head. Quietly he was writing his first novel. He hoped in the book world he would be a king. "Now ladies," he continued formally, "since it's not my movie there is no way that I want to go to the opening." Here he brought out Exhibit A, the invitation to the movie. It was an ordinary ecru card with black lettering. The women looked at the card and then at each other. Shelly shrugged, letting Astra Rainbow know that she had no idea what Mickey was up to. "I would like the two of you to go in my place and report everything that happens."

Shelly stood up now and took the invitation from Mickey. It was for a Wednesday night. She couldn't prevent outfits from appearing in her head. "You really want us to go?" Shelly was actually excited about the show business event. Greta envied her because she had married a man in an exciting field. Shelly had assured her that his field never entered their lives. Mickey ran from his business whenever he could. "You want to go?" Shelly asked Astra Rainbow. She tugged her skirt down before answering. Modesty seemed to be an important part of her answer.

"Well, if Mr. Burke wants us to." Astra Rainbow had done some adjusting to the world the last couple of years, but she still didn't like traveling on new ground and preferred being only where she felt safe. She felt no excitement about the evening. She hoped to spend her nights simply.

"Mr. Burke wants you to," said Mickey. He teased her because she still refused to call him Mickey. She couldn't give up the formality.

Mickey sat down on the hassock between them. He liked this Saturday and hoped this minute could last. It coudn't. He expected Shelly to run off first. One of her sneakered feet kept moving. Instead it was Astra Rainbow who stood, again tugging down her skirt. It was meant to reach only above her knees, but she didn't like it there. It was never going to obey, but she wasn't ready to give it up.

She went to the fireplace but didn't have the courage to stand where Mickey had. She hugged the edge of it and studied the carpet. She held her own hand and had her arms outstretched like a second grader in her school play. "I've decided something," she said. By now she was sorry she had made such a bold move. She wanted to pull down her skirt, sit down and take back her sentence. She couldn't. There they were, wondering what she had decided to do. The last decision she had made was to move to New York. Both of them smiled in encouragement, so the only thing that kept her from continuing was her own insecurity.

"So what? Tell us," Mickey said in his old-man, Brooklyn voice. Shelly sometimes allowed herself to be taken care of by Rainbow, but by now Mickey was consistently Rainbow's father.

Astra Rainbow, really not wanting to go on, started from the beginning. Adding further to her scared schoolgirl look, her knees and toes were now turned toward each other. "I have decided to do something." And then with some courage she raced on, breathing in deeply first as if she were starting a sports event. "I decided to become a surrogate mother." Spontaneously both Shelly and Mickey made moves toward her. But now that her secret was out, she had an orchestra leader's authority. With both hands, she gestured them back into their seats. "I went to the clinic at Doctors Hospital, and over the last two weeks I saw four of their doctors and three counselors. They gave me pamphlets." She reached for her purse, also a gift from Mickey and Shelly. Her move was miscalculated. She had just bent forward and couldn't quite reach the bag. Mickey made up the difference by handing it to her. She whispered a thank-you that wasn't part of her speech. Astra Rainbow always had an orderly purse, and the pamphlets were easily retrieved. There were three of them. She handed them first to Mickey, intending that he pass them on to Shelly. She took a moment to catch her breath and, since her speech had been rehearsed, she closed her eyes to find her place. Once she did, she barreled on. "I also visited Dr. Welch on East Sixty-second Street and showed him the findings of the clinic. He said I was an excellent candidate. At the hospital they were happy I had come. They asked a couple of questions like, 'Are you sure you want to do this?' and one woman warned me that it wasn't easy to give up a baby. I assured her that I really wanted to do this and they believed me right away. I guess because they wanted to. Dr. Welch really tried to talk me out of it. But he didn't talk for too long because there were about ten patients waiting. He said that I was qualified, but if I were his daughter he would do everything in the world to try to stop me." Here she turned mostly toward Mickey. "But I'm not his daughter and he doesn't know me. I'm stronger than he thinks I am. I'm stronger than I thought I was." Now she turned toward Shelly. "I thought I would faint going to a gynecologist." She stood tall. "But I didn't. I called Granny one day on my lunch hour—don't worry Mr. Burke, I charged the call to my own phone—and I told her what I was going to do, and she was perfectly willing to understand why I want to do this. I have to do it. And I want to do it for the two of you. I need you to let me." Her assurance was now replaced by emotion. "I have to do it because of my past. You know, Mr. Burke, that I owe the world a baby and once that score is settled, maybe . . ." She wasn't quite sure where that maybe would lead her. A good psychiatrist could have helped her fill in the blank. "Maybe I can start living life," would have been a good ending—as well as a beginning. Astra Rainbow nodded at her audience of two, letting them know she was finished.

Both Shelly and Mickey ran to hug her and she hugged them back, but not one at a time. All three formed a hugging ball. It seemed more right than two people embracing. It had taken three of them to make a marriage. Perhaps it was right that they should have a baby together.

After one last squeeze the circle was broken, and for a satisfying moment they were all too emotional to talk. Mickey was the first one to speak. "It's a lovely thought, but you can't possibly do it," he said.

"I have to do it."

"Did you tell the doctor that you're a virgin?" Shelly asked.

"I'm not." Mickey and Shelly looked at each other. Could they be wrong about their little girl?

Shelly knew what to ask next. "You're not because you're technically not? I mean you grew up on a farm. You have ridden horses. Or you're not because you've been with a man?"

Astra Rainbow had anticipated this question. She knew these people who had taken care of her weren't going to let her be artificially inseminated without ever having intercourse. She knew lying was a sin, but she was about to tell a lie for a greater good. She had to return a baby to the world, and through the miracle of modern science she could have a Virgin Birth. Christ, it was clear, didn't want her. That was one of the reasons she accepted the suede miniskirt. She could be better than a nun. Mr. Burke was somewhere between God and man. He hadn't created earth but he had, in *Afterlife*, created heaven. If she manipulated everything exactly right she could be a virgin mother, maybe even the first in close to a thousand years. "I've been with a man," lied Astra Rainbow.

"I knew it. I knew it," shouted Mickey. "It was with that kid sitting on your desk. I knew it."

"What's he talking about?" Shelly asked Rainbow.

"I've seen Kurt every once in a while these last couple of years." That part was true. They had shared apple pie and many cups of coffee.

"You like him?" Shelly loved that Rainbow had someone.

"Of course I like him. He understands why I want to have your baby."

"We couldn't . . ." There was an end to that sentence that Shelly couldn't get out. The complete thought was, We couldn't use you that way.

"If you don't want me as your surrogate mother, I'll do it for somebody else." She had a determination they had never seen.

"What about your ambition to become a nun?" asked Mickey.

"You know something, Mr. Burke, I'm tired of waiting." She looked toward heaven, giving Chirst His ultimatum.

Shelly was the first to move away from the circle because she was the most confused. Not knowing much about Astra Rainbow's childhood, she couldn't see the real motivation for this. She walked around a chair while searching for the right speech. "I agree with Mickey. You shouldn't do this. I mean, it's too self-sacrificial. Your entire body would be involved."

"I need to make a sacrifice." Astra Rainbow looked toward Mickey with a conspiratorial glance. Shelly caught it.

"Is there something the two of you know that I don't?" Shelly sat down to listen because she knew there was.

"Promise you won't hate me."

"Oh, honey, I couldn't . . . I couldn't."

Astra Rainbow told the story of what had happened when she was five. She used as few words as possible. It was a story she didn't want to tell and didn't want to remember. Once it was out she wished she could spray the air with fragrance and have it gone, the way you get rid of bad smells. She looked away from both of them, so she didn't see Shelly come to her. She was surprised by her touch, but happy to be brought into her arms. There they stayed, the two of them. Shelly rocked her gently to the rhythm of, "It's not your fault. It's not your fault."

It was Astra Rainbow who pulled away first. "I think I know it's not my fault, but I feel something here." She touched her heart. "And when I think of giving a baby back to the world, I feel good. Maybe other people feel good all the time, but I never had until I thought of this."

"I couldn't let you do it for us . . . It's too big a gift." Shelly looked to Mickey for support.

"I'd like you to feel good without having to do that," Mickey said.

He had pulled a pipe out of his pocket, which only added to his fatherliness.

"Don't you think I've tried to?" Astra Rainbow asked, telling them how deep her pain was.

The two women giggled as they dressed for Mickey's opening. He had never enjoyed his blonde and brunette more. Shelly, who hadn't found the need to speak to Paula since she'd been married, was supervising both of their outfits. The dresses had both come from Greta's showroom. Wholesale. Mickey, who had no idea what women's clothing cost, coughed when he wrote out the check. Shelly wore a creamy knee-length satin cocktail dress and had chosen a sophisticated antique black beaded dress for Astra Rainbow. Their hair went up, their lip gloss went on and they squirted Joy, the most expensive perfume in the world, at each other. Mickey felt as if he had the privilege of sneaking into a girl's dorm. There was some whispering and some urging, and they both came out and modeled the dresses, Shelly pulling Astra Rainbow. Shelly had acquired flair and did her turns well. Astra Rainbow had youth and just had to stand there. Because of Greta's generosity, they each had a fur from her closet. She had insisted that Shelly wear the light fox and Astra Rainbow the dark mink. The effect was striking since they were each other's negatives.

Mickey repeated his instructions at the door. They were to mingle before and after the film. They were to try to remember everything that was said about him. They were not to applaud when his name appeared. They were to eavesdrop. He didn't want them back until at least midnight. If they returned earlier, he knew they weren't doing their job. He'd be upstairs waiting.

"What if we meet two cute guys?" Shelly asked as she waltzed out, ruining her exit by checking her keys.

"Oh, we won't, Mr. Burke. She's just kidding," said Astra Rainbow. She needed this marriage.

Mickey had arranged for a limousine to take them to Radio City. Shelly tried to be sophisticated, although every time she got into a limo the little girl inside her reminded her she was doing something that the Vanderbilts did. Astra Rainbow sat straight and obedient, although she would have loved to touch some of the buttons that would provide music. There was a bar that neither of them considered at first, but they got into some thick traffic around the theater. "I think we deserve champagne," Shelly said, opening the tiny refrigerator. Astra Rainbow shook her head no, but accepted the glass when Shelly gave it to her. She had accepted glasses of champagne before, but she took only sips, and Mickey and Shelly always ended up draining her glass. Neither one of them came from backgrounds that allowed them to throw out anything that cost more than ten dollars a bottle. For the first time ever, Rainbow drank it all. After subsequent glasses during the evening, Shelly would learn that the young woman became even more sober as she drank.

The movie got an overdose of reaction all the way through. The laughs were too loud, the applause at the end too long. Clearly, it was a not a good movie. It had been meant to be a simple piece about Astra Rainbow, but none of her or Mickey remained. Shelly couldn't understand the overwhelming applause and the pats on the back this crowd was giving itself. Didn't they know their movie made very little sense? These were the filmmakers and their friends. She could understand it if they were just being polite, but these people were reacting as if they had a hit on their hands.

The party was in the movie theater lobby. It was elaborate even from a caterer's point of view, with tables of fresh shellfish and caviar. Shelly grabbed two glasses of champagne and whispered to Astra Rainbow, "Did you like it?"

"No," she said. "Everybody was just joking around all the time. I mean, nobody jokes around every minute of every day." Her perception of it was not unlike that of *The New York Times*. The paper accused all the characters of behaving like stand-up comedians.

"What're we going to tell him?" Astra Rainbow asked. The only sign that she had had several glasses of champagne was that her eyes were wider. They were also clearer than ever before.

"He wants the movie to be no good because they took it away from him. I think he'll be happy that it is."

When it was time to go, they easily found their driver, who was considerate enough to wait right outside the building. Most of the other drivers were in groups of threes and fours, passing the time talking about their cars. They were always talking about what great books their lives would make.

On the way home they shared a split of champagne. Astra Rainbow leaned back, making herself comfortable for the first time in a world she didn't know. She still pulled her dress down, but she had acquired the sophisticated look that beautiful girls get after they're in New York for a couple of years. In Greta's clothes she managed to look like a woman. Some of her fine hair had escaped its pins but her makeup was still in place. Shelly's had already been absorbed into her skin.

Rainbow's hand gracefully brought the champagne to her lips and, after what would have to be defined as more than a sip, she turned to Shelly. "I have an appointment with Dr. Welch tomorrow. It's my

time of the month to conceive and I'm going in for artificial insemination."

"You've decided to . . ."

"I told you I was going to."

Astra Rainbow had never been calculating, but Shelly felt she was
trying to manipulate a situation here. "I still think you shouldn't. It's
such a big move."

"I know you think I shouldn't, and that's why I wasn't even going
to tell you. I was just going to let you see me get bigger and bigger
and then I wouldn't even have to tell you and there would be nothing
that any of us could do about it except watch this life grow."

"Why did you tell me?"

"Because I want you to let me do this for you and Mr. Burke. Dr.
Welch is really a sweet man. He said I could cancel even a minute
before. We could wait a month." This was her most passionate plea
so far.

"You may want to keep the baby. You'll be close to it for all that
time."

"I don't want a baby. I don't. I'd be scared of hurting it." She said
this as if Shelly should have known this already. Why would Shelly
think she'd ever want a baby? Her purpose was to give one up.

They were silent the rest of the way home. They sat on opposite
sides of the back seats, but their close hands reached out for each
other. The driver had been tipped, so they could run from the car to
the building. One gust of wind caught them both and they had to
work hard to keep their clothes close to their bodies.

They were tired and close enough not to have to say anything. They
both leaned against the back wall of the elevator. The long night had
gotten to both of them.

Mickey, however, was wide awake. He was at the door seconds
after Shelly rang the bell.

"So?" he asked, even before inviting them into his apartment.

"The movie wasn't good, but everybody there thought it was."

He smiled, big, broad and long. He even let out a big Texan "yahoo"
and let them in. "I knew they couldn't do it without me. I knew it."
Both hands were raised and making fists of victory. He skipped around
the room like a boxer after a fight. The moves were right. The business
he was in had fighters and winners.

His brunette and his blonde were caught up in his happiness. Soon
they were all celebrating the flop. "Did it end in Brooklyn?" he asked.

"It ended at this big wedding," said Astra Rainbow.

"A wedding? I knew they would take it too far." He threw back his
head and laughed much too loud for this time of night. "They really
fucked it up. Great. I can't wait to see the lousy reviews." He smiled,

gave the victory sign and continued his dance around the room. "What about the song? Was it any good?"

"I don't remember it."

"Great." His head went back once more to laugh that laugh again. "The performances?"

"They were okay."

"Yeah, but not good enough to override the lousiness of the entire production. I am a happy man, and I thank you for going." He had an arm and a kiss for each of them.

"I just have to show Mickey something in the other room," Shelly said after the squeeze. It was a feeble excuse, but the first one she thought of. Astra Rainbow, always the obedient child, sat stiffly on the couch. She was very careful to straighten out the dress before she sat down.

Shelly closed the bedroom door and faced her husband. At first he thought he was going to be seduced, but that was confusing because there was Astra Rainbow on his old leather couch. "She is scheduled to have artificial insemination tomorrow," Shelly said.

"What? No! She said she needed the day off to go to the doctor."

Mickey looked at the door, knowing Astra Rainbow was on the other side of it. He realized he had made a silly move, facing a door that wasn't going to help the confusion. "Well, we have to stop her."

"I tried to talk her out of it. I couldn't. She really believes that carrying someone else's baby is going to give her peace. And maybe it will." Shelly sat on the edge of Mickey's bed. She knew she was formulating a proposal. She wanted to make sure before she spoke that her argument would be convincing. "I think she should have our baby, Mickey. That's what she really wants. And in a way, that's what I want too. And yes it's scary. I mean, what if the two of you got close and left me out of things? What if you started to love the mother of your child? It's a hell of a chance, but it seems right."

"I don't know. I'm not the one that's campaigning for this kid."

"Yeah, but you have a habit of learning to love things." With that she pulled him next to her on the bed. They sat side by side and looked very much like two people with a problem.

"She's really going to do it?"

"She really is. I think she knows that when it's all over she can forgive herself."

"She has nothing to forgive."

"I know that. You know that. She has lived with guilt all her life. She never got punished for it so she's punishing herself."

"I don't know. What do I have to do?"

"Go with her to Dr. Welch in the morning. Tell her thank you and thank whoever you have to for sending her to us."

# Epilogue

MAYBE there is a God. Something bigger than ordinary life had looked over these three. Astra Rainbow conceived Mickey and Shelly's baby. When they found out, Mickey hugged Shelly first but quickly brought Astra Rainbow into their now familiar circle. Both Mr. Burke (Rainbow could never break her old habit) and Shelly insisted that the mother-to-be move in with Shelly for the duration of her pregnancy. That made Mary, who was on her third Frank, very happy. She got Aunt Emma's apartment, and the latest Frank, who was twenty and a mechanic at a Shell station in Queens, was able to pay the rent. "Maybe I'm gonna marry this one," she said, and cautiously added, "but not until I'm sure that he's never gonna hit me."

Astra Rainbow thrived in Shelly's guest room. Since this wasn't her baby, she wasn't thinking about becoming a mother. Instead she was allowed to be a child. Shelly insisted that she drink her milk and took care of her the way Rainbow should have been taken care of the first six years of life. Mickey took up the habit of patting her on the head, even though he had to reach up to do it. She was the center of their lives for those months, which turned out be to very good for her soul. She has never been the center of her own universe before. Nor had she ever been given the unconditional love she was getting now.

On November tenth, Dr. Welch had told Astra Rainbow and Shelly, who accompanied her on all the visits, that he would probably see them in the hospital before the week was out. They ran to Saks to get more tiny clothes for the baby. "Your baby is going to have the biggest wardrobe in town," Rainbow said while Shelly paid the saleswoman. Like all the other saleswomen they had bought baby clothes from, this one was confused. The baby was born on November fourteenth. Thankfully it wasn't a dramatic birth.

When Rainbow went into labor, both Mickey and Shelly were there with her. "Are you scared?" Shelly asked her on the way to the hospital.

"Only about where I'm going to sleep from now on," said Astra Rainbow. She was sitting between them in the back seat of the cab. Shelly and Mickey had identical questioning looks on their faces. Still she didn't explain further.

"Where you're going to sleep?" Shelly asked her for the both of them.

"Well, my room is going to be the nursery." According to modern-day Jewish tradition, everything for the baby was ordered and waiting in the expensive stores where they were purchased. One call from Shelly and it all would be delivered.

Both Shelly and Mickey raced to comfort Rainbow. Shelly got there first. "Your room will be the nursery, but the baby will be sleeping in my room at first. You'll still be with us." Mickey reached over and kissed the top of Astra Rainbow's head.

A contraction stopped the flow of conversation. Shelly did the breathing with her. Mickey wrote down the time. She squeezed both their hands. The pain lasted a few seconds, and Astra Rainbow continued the conversation. "Yes, but I can't stay with you forever. The baby will be there." They had made her their child. Now they faced sibling rivalry.

"You can stay with us as long as you want," said Mickey, with Shelly agreeing. Shelly kissed one cheek while Mickey kissed an eighth of a lip near the other.

"Then I'm not scared anymore."

They should have guessed Mickey's genes would be hard to suppress. There was no mistaking that their little girl looked a lot like him. Her hair and eyes were dark, her nose was a miniature of his. They laughed about plastic surgery before leaving the hospital.

Astra Rainbow was slightly scared of her offspring. She was proud that she had been so strong in delivery, but she really didn't want to handle the baby. The nurse would come in and try to hand the baby to her, but she always redirected the infant to Shelly. Shelly had moved into the hospital and was happy with her motherhood. Once, while she was feeding Alison, Astra Rainbow looked at them and said, "I'm afraid of hurting her."

"You wouldn't."

"I might," she said, and she picked up a copy of *Glamour*. Unfortunately she had picked up a clothes habit from Shelly.

"Maybe Mickey and I could give you a present in exchange for this beautiful baby." Astra Rainbow was interested. She had turned to a page with a bright red coat that she could see herself in. She held up the page and turned it toward Shelly. It was just at the time that Shelly started burping Alison but, being the perfect mother, she gave both of them her attention. The baby got her fairly confident hands while Astra Rainbow's magazine picture got her eyes.

"Yes. That's wonderful for you. We'll have to order it. And I think the rest of the present should be some sessions with a really nice psychiatrist."

The baby burped just as Astra Rainbow said, "Granny doesn't believe in psychiatrists. She said they make you crazy. She had a good friend once who was put into a mental institution, and when Ida went in she was just a little crazy and she got more and more nuts while she was there. And I'll tell you something, she never led a normal life again." When Astra Rainbow told stories of back home, she always sounded like a Midwesterner.

"You're not going to be put in any institution. You could just go and talk to someone about your problems and fears. I went to a psychiatrist for a year and a half once, just to help me sort some things out." The baby burped again. She had sat her up and rubbed her stomach like the nurse told her to, but Shelly had never expected it actually to work.

"You went to a psychiatrist? You did?" The magazine was on her lap now. "No."

"Yes. I did. I was young, twenty-five, my sister had just gotten married and moved to Houston. I felt lonely." She picked Alison up and kissed her on the cheek. Knowing the baby was going back to the nursery soon made Shelly appreciate her even more.

"Wow," said Astra Rainbow. "Sign me up."

Life wasn't going to be the same. Alison overflowed her room, destroying the look of the whole apartment. When she was old enough for a playpen, it was put in the living room. If Snoopy could have a place in Shelly's apartment, so could her husband. His clutter was just going to complete the family. Shelly begged Mickey to move in with the same persistence she had begged for the marriage and the baby. They needed to be a normal family, she said. She wanted him in her bed every night. She swore she didn't care about his hair in her sink. She promised he could put his deco desk anywhere he wanted.

Slowly he moved downstairs. When he wasn't home, Shelly and Astra Rainbow snuck upstairs and like thieves brought armloads of his sweaters, ties and shoes to 3C.

As Mickey moved down, Astra Rainbow moved up to the four-hundred-thousand-dollar apartment that Mickey vacated. "My shrink said it would be good for me," she announced.

PARENT
A SIGN OF THE EIGHTIES